George Henry Lewes

The story of Goethe's life

George Henry Lewes

The story of Goethe's life

ISBN/EAN: 9783742830432

Manufactured in Europe, USA, Canada, Australia, Japa

Cover: Foto ©Andreas Hilbeck / pixelio.de

Manufactured and distributed by brebook publishing software
(www.brebook.com)

George Henry Lewes

The story of Goethe's life

THE

STORY OF GOETHE'S LIFE.

BY

GEORGE HENRY LEWES.

(Abridged from his "Life and Works of Goethe.")

Eleventh Edition.

BOSTON:
HOUGHTON, MIFFLIN AND COMPANY.
New York: 11 East Seventeenth Street.
The Riverside Press, Cambridge.
1890.

PREFACE.

———◦◦◦———

IT has been represented to me, by my friend the publisher, that there are many readers who may feel considerable interest in the story of a great poet's life and aims, though they are not greatly attracted by criticisms and details in relation to works written in a foreign language and but partially accessible through translations. In compliance with this suggestion, I have detached from my *Life of Goethe* a continuous narrative, which will present the outward events of an ever-memorable career, and indicate the leading characteristics of an immortal genius.

The present volume is in no sense intended to replace the original Biography, which will probably continue to have the greater interest for readers whose tastes and acquirements lie in the direction of German literature.

THE PRIORY, November, 1872.

CONTENTS.

BOOK THE FOURTH.

1775 to 1779.

BOOK THE FIFTH.

1779 to 1793.

BOOK THE SIXTH.

1794 to 1805.

BOOK THE SEVENTH.

1805 to 1832.

THE STORY OF GOETHE'S LIFE.

BOOK THE FIRST.

1749 TO 1765.

CHAPTER I.

PARENTAGE.

QUINTUS CURTIUS tells us that, in certain seasons, Bactria was darkened by whirlwinds of dust, which completely covered and concealed the roads. Left thus without their usual landmarks, the wanderers awaited the rising of the stars, —

> " To light them on their dim and perilous way."

May we not say the same of Literature? From time to time its pathways are so obscured beneath the rubbish of the age, that many a footsore pilgrim seeks in vain the hidden route. In such times it may be well to imitate the Bactrians : ceasing to look upon the confusions of the day, and turning our gaze upon the great Immortals who have gone before, we may seek guidance from their light. In all ages the biographies of great men have been fruitful in lessons ; in all ages they have been powerful stimulants to a noble ambition ; in all ages they have been regarded as armories wherein are gathered the weapons with which great battles have been won.

There may be some among my readers who will dispute Goethe's claim to greatness. They will admit that he was a great poet, but deny that he was a great man. In denying it, they will set forth the qualities which constitute their ideal of greatness, and finding him deficient in some of these qualities, will dispute his claim. But in awarding him that title, I do not mean to imply that he was an ideal man; I do not present him as the exemplar of all greatness. No man can be such an exemplar. Humanity reveals itself in fragments. One man is the embodiment of one kind of excellence, another of another. Achilles wins the victory, and Homer immortalizes it: we bestow the laurel crown on both. In virtue of a genius such as modern times have only seen equalled once or twice, Goethe deserves the epithet of great. Nor is it in virtue of genius alone that he deserves the title. Merck said of him that what he lived was more beautiful than what he wrote; and his life, amid all its weaknesses and all its errors, presents a picture of a certain grandeur of soul, which cannot be contemplated unmoved. I shall make no attempt to conceal his faults. Let them be dealt with as harshly as severest justice may dictate, they will not eclipse the central light that shines throughout his life. And without wishing to excuse or to conceal faults which he assuredly had, we must always bear in mind that the faults of a celebrated man are apt to carry an undue emphasis: they are thrown into stronger relief by the very splendor of his fame. Had Goethe never written *Faust*, no one would have heard that he was an inconstant lover, and a tepid politician. His glory immortalizes his shame.

In the middle of the seventeenth century the little town of Artern, in the Grafschaft of Mansfeld, in Thuringia, numbered among its scanty inhabitants a farrier, by name Hans Christian Goethe. His son Frederick, being probably of a more meditative turn, selected a more meditative employment than that of shoeing horses : he became a tailor. Having passed an apprenticeship, he commenced his wanderings, in the course of which he reached Frankfurt. Here he soon found employment, and being, as we learn, "a ladies' man," he soon also found a wife. The master tailor, Sebastian Lutz, gave him his daughter on his admission to the citizenship of Frankfurt and to the guild of tailors. This was in 1687. Several children were born, and vanished ; in 1700 his wife, too, vanished, to be replaced, five years afterwards, by Frau Cornelia Schellhorn, the daughter of another tailor, Georg Walter ; she was then a widow, blooming with six-and-thirty summers, and possessing the solid attractions of a good property, namely, the hotel "Zum Weidenhof," where her new husband laid down the scissors, and donned the landlord's apron. He had two sons by her, and died in 1730, aged seventy-three.

Of these two sons, the younger, Johann Caspar, was the father of our poet. Thus we see that Goethe, like Schiller, sprang from the people. He makes no mention of the lucky tailor, nor of the Thuringian farrier, in his autobiography. This silence may be variously interpreted. At first, I imagined it was aristocratic prudery on the part of *von* Goethe, minister and nobleman ; but it is never well to put ungenerous constructions, when others, equally plausible and more honorable, are ready ; let us rather follow the advice of Sir Arthur Helps. and " employ our *imagination* in the service of charity." We can easily imagine that Goethe was silent about the tailor, because, having never known him, there was none of that affectionate remembrance which encircles the objects of early life, to make this grandfather figure in the autobiography beside the grandfather Textor, who *was* known and loved. Probably, also, the tailor was seldom talked of in the parental circle. There is a peculiar and indelible ridicule attached to the idea of a tailor in Germany, which often prevents people of much humbler pretensions than Goethe from whispering their connection with such a trade.   Goethe does mention this grandfather in the Second Book of his *Autobiography*, and tells us how he was teased by the taunts of boys respecting his humble parentage ; these taunts even went so far as to imply that he might possibly have had several grandfathers ; and he began to speculate on the possibility of some latent aristocracy in his descent.   This made him examine with some curiosity the portraits of noblemen, to try and detect a likeness.

Johann Caspar Goethe received a good education, travelled into Italy, became an imperial councillor in Frankfurt, and married, in 1748, Katharina Elizabeth, daughter of Johann Wolfgang Textor, the chief magistrate (*Schultheiss*).*

Goethe's father was a cold, stern, formal, somewhat pedantic, but truth-loving, upright-minded man.   He hungered for knowledge ; and, although in general of a laconic turn, freely imparted all he learned.   In his domestic circle his word was law.   Not only imperious, but in some respects capricious, he was, nevertheless, greatly respected, if little loved, by wife, children, and friends.   He is characterized by Krause as *ein geradliniger Frankfurter Reichsbürger,* — " a formal Frankfurt citizen," whose habits were as measured as his gait.†   From

---

* The family of Textor and Weber exist to this day, and under both names, in the Hohenlohe territory.   Karl Julius Weber, the humorous author of *Democritus* and of the *Briefe eines in Deutschland reisenden Deutschen*, was a member of it.   In the description of the *Jubilæum* of the Nürnberg University of Altorf, in 1723, mention is made of one Joannes Guolfgangus Textor as a bygone ornament of the faculty of law ; and Mr. Demmler, to whom I am indebted for these particulars, suggests the probability of this being the same John Wolfgang who died as Oberbürgermeister in Frankfurt, 1701.

† Perhaps *geradliniger* might be translated as "an old square-toes."

him the poet inherited the well-built frame, the erect carriage, and the measured movement which in old age became stiffness, and was construed as diplomacy or haughtiness; from him also came that orderliness and stoicism which have so much distressed those who cannot conceive genius otherwise than as vagabond in its habits. The craving for knowledge, the delight in communicating it, the almost pedantic attention to details, which are noticeable in the poet, are all traceable in the father.

The mother was more like what we conceive as the proper parent for a poet. She is one of the pleasantest figures in German literature, and one standing out with greater vividness than almost any other. Her simple, hearty, joyous, and affectionate nature endeared her to all. She was the delight of children, the favorite of poets and princes. To the last retaining her enthusiasm and simplicity, mingled with great shrewdness and knowledge of character, *Frau Aja*, as they christened her, was at once grave and hearty, dignified and simple. She had read most of the best German and Italian authors, had picked up considerable desultory information, and had that "mother wit" which so often in women and poets seems to render culture superfluous, their rapid intuitions anticipating the tardy conclusions of experience. Her letters are full of spirit: not always strictly grammatical; not irreproachable in spelling; but vigorous and vivacious. After a lengthened interview with her, an enthusiast exclaimed, "Now do I understand how Goethe has become the man he is!"* Wieland, Merck, Bürger, Madame de Staël, Karl Au-

having reference to the antiquated cut of the old man's clothes. The fathers of the present generation dubbed the stiff coat of their grandfathers, with its square skirts and collars, by the name of *magister matheseos*, the name by which the Pythagorean proposition is known in Germany.

* *Ephemeriden der Literatur*, quoted in *Nicolovius über Goethe.*

gust, and other great people sought her acquaintance. The Duchess Amalia corresponded with her as with an intimate friend ; and her letters were welcomed eagerly at the Weimar Court. She was married at seventeen to a man for whom she had no love, and was only eighteen when the poet was born.* This, instead of making her prematurely old, seems to have perpetuated her girlhood. " I and my Wolfgang," she said, "have always held fast to each other, because we were both young together." To him she transmitted her love of story-telling, her animal spirits, her love of everything which bore the stamp of distinctive individuality, and her love of seeing happy faces around her. " Order and quiet," she says in one of her charming letters to Freiherr von Stein, " are my principal characteristics. Hence I despatch at once whatever I have to do, the most disagreeable always first, and I gulp down the devil without looking at him. When all has returned to its proper state, then I defy any one to surpass me in good-humor." Her heartiness and tolerance are the causes, she thinks, why every one likes her. " I am fond of people, and *that* every one feels directly, young and old. I pass without pretension through the world, and that gratifies men. I never *bemoralize* any one, — *always seek out the good that is in them, and leave what is bad to him who made mankind, and knows how to round off the angles.* In this way I make myself happy and comfortable." Who does not recognize the son in those accents? One of the kindliest of men inherited his loving happy nature from one of the heartiest of women.

He also inherited from her his dislike of unnecessary emotion : that deliberate avoidance of all things capable of disturbing his peace of mind, which has been construed as

---

* Lovers of parallels may be reminded that Napoleon's mother was only eighteen when he was born.

coldness. Her sunny nature shrank from storms. She stipulated with her servants that they were not to trouble her with afflicting news, except upon some positive necessity for the communication. In 1805, when her son was dangerously ill at Weimar, no one ventured to speak to her on the subject. Not until he had completely recovered did she voluntarily enter on it. "I knew it all," she remarked, "but said nothing. Now we can talk about him without my feeling a stab every time his name is mentioned."

In this voluntary insulation from disastrous intelligence there is something so antagonistic to the notorious craving for excitement felt by the Teutonic races, something so unlike the morbid love of intellectual drams, — the fierce alcohol of emotion with which we intoxicate ourselves, — that it is no wonder if Goethe has on this account been accused of insensibility. Yet, in truth, a very superficial knowledge of his nature suffices to show that it was not from coldness he avoided indulgence in the "luxury of woe." It was excess of sensibility, not want of sympathy. His delicate nature shrank from the wear and tear of excitement. That which to coarser natures would have been only a stimulus, was to him a disturbance. It is doubtless the instinct of an emotional nature to seek such stimulants ; but his reason was strong enough to keep this instinct under control. Falk relates that when Goethe heard he had looked upon Wieland in death, "and thereby procured myself a miserable evening, and worse night, he vehemently reproved me for it. 'Why,' said he, 'should I suffer the delightful impression of the features of my friend to be obliterated by the sight of a disfigured mask ? I carefully avoided seeing Schiller, Herder, or the Duchess Amalia in the coffin. I, for my part, desire to retain in my memory a picture of my departed friends more full of soul than the mere mask can furnish me.'"

B

This subjection of the instinct of curiosity to the dictates of reason is not coldness.   There is danger, indeed, of carrying it too far, and of *coddling* the mind ; but into this extreme neither Goethe nor his mother can be said to have fallen. At any rate, let the reader pronounce what judgment he thinks fit, it is right that he should at the outset distinctly understand it to be a characteristic of the man.   The self-mastery it implies forms the keystone of his character.   In him the emotive was subjected to the intellectual.   He was " king over himself."   He, as he tells us, found men eager enough to lord it over others, while indifferent whether they could rule themselves —

> " Das wollen alle Herren seyn,
> Und keiner ist Herr von sich ! "

He made it his study to subdue into harmonious unity the rebellious impulses which incessantly threatened the supremacy of reason.   Here, on the threshold of his career, let attention be called to this cardinal characteristic : his footsteps were not guided by a light tremulous in every gust, liable to fall to the ground amid the hurrying agitation of vulgar instincts, but a torch grasped by an iron will, and lifted high above the currents of those lower gusts, shedding a continuous steady gleam across the path.   I do not say he never stumbled.   At times the clamorous agitation of rebellious passions misled him as it misleads others ; but viewing his life as it disposes itself into the broad masses necessary for a characteristic appreciation, I say that in him, more than in almost any other man of his time, naked vigor of resolution, moving in alliance with steady clearness of intellect, produced a self-mastery of the very highest kind.*

* " All I have had to do I have done in kingly fashion," he said ; " I let tongues wag as they pleased.   What I saw to be the right thing, that I did."

This he owed partly to his father and partly to his mother. It was from the latter he derived those characteristics which determined the movement and orbit of his artistic nature; her joyous, healthy temperament, humor, fancy, and susceptibility were, in him, creative, owing to the marvellous insight which gathered up the scattered and vanishing elements of experience into new and living combinations.

———◆———

CHAPTER II.

THE PRECOCIOUS CHILD.

JOHANN WOLFGANG GOETHE was born on the 28th August, 1749, as the clock sounded the hour of noon, in the busy town of Frankfurt-on-the-Maine. The busy town, as may be supposed, was quite heedless of what was then passing in the corner of that low, heavy-beamed room in the *Grosse Hirsch-graben*, where an infant, black, and almost lifeless, was watched with agonizing anxiety, — an anxiety dissolving into tears of joy, as the aged grandmother exclaimed to the pale mother, " *Räthin er lebt!* he lives ! "

It is not the biographer's province to write a history of an epoch while telling the story of a life ; but some historical indication is necessary, in order that the time and place should be vividly before the reader's mind ; and perhaps the readiest way to call up such a picture in a paragraph will be to mention some of the " notables " of that period, and at what points in their career they had arrived. In that very month of August, Madame du Chatelet, the learned translator of Newton, the loving but hot-tempered *Uranie* of Voltaire, died in childbed, leaving him without a companion, and without a counsellor to prevent his going to the court of Frederick the Great.   In that year Rousseau was seen in the brilliant circle of Madame d'Epinay, disputing with the Encyclopedists, declaiming eloquently on the sacredness of maternity, and going home to cast his new-born infant into the basket of the Foundling Hospital.   In that year Samuel Johnson was toiling manfully over his English dictionary; Gibbon was at Westminster, trying with unsuccessful diligence to master the Greek and Latin rudiments; Goldsmith was delighting the Tony Lumpkins of his district, and the "wandering bear-leaders of genteeler sort," with his talents, and enjoying that "careless idleness of fireside and easy-chair," and that " tavern excitement of the game of cards to which he looked back so wistfully from his first hard London struggles."   In that year Buffon, whose scientific greatness Goethe was one of the first to perceive, produced the first volume of his *Histoire Naturelle.*   Haller was at Göttingen performing those experiments on Sensibility and Irritability which were to immortalize him.   John Hunter, who had recently left Scotland, joined Cheselden at the Chelsea Hospital.   Mirabeau and Alfieri were tyrants in their nurseries; and Marat was an innocent boy of five years old, toddling about in the Val de Travers, unmolested as yet by the wickedness of " les aristocrats."

If these names have helped to call up the period, we must seek in Goethe's own pages for a picture of the place.   He has painted the city of Frankfurt as one who loved it.   No city in Germany was better fitted for the birthplace of this cosmopolitan poet.   It was rich in speaking memorials of the past, remnants of old German life, lingering echoes of the voices which sounded through the Middle Ages: such as a town within a town, the fortress within a fortress, the walled cloisters, the various symbolical ceremonies still preserved from feudal times, and the Jews' quarter, so picturesque, filthy, and strikingly significant. But if Frankfurt was representative of the past, it was equally representative of the present. The travellers brought there by the Rhine-stream, and by the great northern roads, made it a representative of Europe, and an emporium of Commerce. It was thus a centre for that distinctively modern idea, Industrialism, which began, and must complete, the destruction of Feudalism. This twofold character Frankfurt retains to the present day : the storks, perched upon its ancient gables, look down upon the varied bustle of Fairs held by modern Commerce in the ancient streets.

The feeling for antiquity, and especially for old German life, which his native city would thus picturesquely cultivate, was rivalled by a feeling for Italy and its splendors, which was cultivated under the paternal roof. His father had lived in Italy, and had retained an inextinguishable delight in all its beauties. His walls were hung with architectural drawings and views of Rome ; and the poet was thus familiar from infancy with the Piazza del Popolo, St. Peter's, the Coliseum, and other centres of grand associations. Typical of his own nature and strivings is this conjunction of the Classic and the German, — the one lying nearest to him, in homely intimacy, the other lying outside, as a mere *scene* he was to contemplate.

Thus much on time and place, the two cardinal conditions of life. Before quitting such generalities for the details of biography, it may be well to call attention to one hitherto unnoticed, namely, the moderate elevation of his social status. Placed midway between the two perilous extremes of affluence and want, his whole career received a modifying impulse from this position. He never knew adversity. This alone must necessarily have deprived him of one powerful chord

which vibrates through Literature.   Adversity, the sternest
of teachers, had nothing to teach him.   He never knew the
gaunt companionship of Want, whispering terrible suggestions.   He never knew the necessity to conquer for himself
breathing-room in the world ; and thus all the feelings of bitterness, opposition, and defiance, which accompany and per-
plex the struggle of life, were to him almost unknown ; and
he was taught nothing of the aggressive and practical energy
which these feelings develop in impetuous natures.   How
much of his serenity, how much of his dislike to politics, may
be traced to this origin ?

That he was the loveliest baby ever seen, exciting admiration wherever nurse or mother carried him, and exhibiting, in
swaddling-clothes, the most wonderful intelligence, we need
no biographer to tell us.   Is it not said of every baby?   But
that he was in truth a wonderful child we have undeniable
evidence, and of a kind less questionable than the statement
of mothers and relatives.   At three years old he could seldom
be brought to play with little children, and only on the condition of their being pretty.   One day, in a neighbor's house,
he suddenly began to cry and exclaim, "That black child
must go away ! I can't bear him !"   And he howled till he
was carried home, where he was slowly pacified ; the whole
cause of his grief being the ugliness of the child.

A quick, merry little girl grew up by the boy's side.   Four
other children also came, but soon vanished.   Cornelia was
the only companion who survived, and for her his affection
dated from her cradle.   He brought his toys to her, wanted
to feed her and attend on her, and was very jealous of all
who approached her.   "When she was taken from the cradle,
over which he watched, his anger was scarcely to be quieted.
He was altogether much more easily moved to anger than to
tears."

In old German towns, Frankfurt among them, the ground-floor consists of a great hall where the vehicles are housed. This floor opens in folding trap-doors, for the passage of wine-casks into the cellars below. In one corner of the hall there is a sort of lattice, opening by an iron or wooden grating upon the street. This is called the *Geräms*. Here the crockery in daily use was kept; here the servants peeled their potatoes, and cut their carrots and turnips, preparatory to cooking; here also the housewife would sit with her sewing, or her knitting, giving an eye to what passed in the street (when anything did pass there) and an ear to a little neighborly gossip. Such a place was of course a favorite with the children.

One fine afternoon, when the house was quiet, Master Wolfgang, with his cup in his hand and nothing to do, finds himself in this *Geräms*, looking out into the silent street, and telegraphing to the young Ochsensteins who dwelt opposite. By way of doing something he begins to fling the crockery into the street, delighted at the smashing music which it makes, and stimulated by the approbation of the brothers Ochsenstein, who chuckle at him from over the way. The plates and dishes are flying in this way, when his mother returns: she sees the mischief with a housewifely horror, melting into girlish sympathy, as she hears how heartily the little fellow laughs at his escapade, and how the neighbors laugh at him.

This genial, indulgent mother employed her faculty for story-telling to his and her own delight. "Air, fire, earth, and water I represented under the forms of princesses; and to all natural phenomena I gave a meaning, in which I almost believed more fervently than my little hearers. As we thought of paths which led from star to star, and that we should one day inhabit the stars, and thought of the great

spirits we should meet there, I was as eager for the hours of
story-telling as the children themselves; I was quite curious
about the future course of my own improvisation, and any
invitation which interrupted these evenings was disagreeable.
There I sat, and there Wolfgang held me with his large black
eyes; and when the fate of one of his favorites was not
according to his fancy, I saw the angry veins swell on his
temples, I saw him repress his tears. He often burst in with,
'But, mother, the princess won't marry the nasty tailor, even
if he does kill the giant.' And when I made a pause for the
night, promising to continue it on the morrow, I was certain
that he would in the mean while think it out for himself, and
so he often stimulated my imagination. When I turned the
story according to his plan, and told him that he had found
out the *dénouement*, then was he all fire and flame, and one
could see his little heart beating underneath his dress! His
grandmother, who made a great pet of him, was the confidante
of all his ideas as to how the story would turn out; and as
she repeated these to me, and I turned the story according
to these hints, there was a little diplomatic secrecy between
us, which we never disclosed. I had the pleasure of continuing my story to the delight and astonishment of my hearers,
and Wolfgang saw with glowing eyes the fulfilment of his own
conceptions, and listened with enthusiastic applause." What
a charming glimpse of mother and son!

The grandmother here spoken of lived in the same house,
and when lessons were finished, away the children hurried to
her room, to play. The dear old lady, proud as a grandmother, "spoiled" them of course, and gave them many an
eatable, which they would get only in her room. But of all
her gifts nothing was comparable to the puppet-show with
which she surprised them on the Christmas eve of 1753, and
which Goethe says "created a new world in the house."

The reader of *Wilhelm Meister* will remember with what solemn importance the significance of such a puppet-show is treated, and may guess how it would exercise the boy's imagination.

There was also the grandfather Textor, whose house the children gladly visited, and whose grave personality produced an impression on the boy, all the deeper because a certain mysterious awe surrounded the monosyllabic dream-interpreting old gentleman. His portrait presents him in a *perruque à huit étages*, with the heavy golden chain round his neck, suspending a medal given him by the Empress Maria Theresa ; but Goethe remembered him more vividly in his dressing-gown and slippers, moving amid the flowers of his garden, weeding, training, watering ; or seated at the dinner-table where on Sundays he received his guests.

The mother's admirable method of cultivating the inventive activity of the boy, finds its pendant in the father's method of cultivating his receptive faculties. He speaks with less approbation than it deserved of his father's idea of education : probably because late in life he felt keenly his deficiencies in systematic training. But the principle upon which the father proceeded was an excellent one, namely, that of exercising the intellect rather than the memory. An anecdote was dictated, generally something from every-day life, or perhaps a trait from the life of Frederick the Great ; on this the boy wrote dialogues and moral reflections in Latin and German. Some of these have been preserved and published ; a glance at them shows what a mastery over Latin was achieved in his eighth year. We can never be *quite* certain that the hand of the master is not mingled with that of the child ; but the very method of independence which the master throughout pursued is contrary to a supposition of his improving the exercises, although the style is certainly above what even advanced pupils usually achieve. Dr. Wisemann of Frankfurt, to whom we are indebted for these exercises and compositions, written during Goethe's sixth, seventh, and eighth years, thinks there can be no doubt of their being the unassisted productions of the boy. In one of the dialogues there is a pun which proves that the dialogue was written in Latin first, and then translated into German. It is this : the child is making wax figures, his father asks him why he does not relinquish such trivialities. The word used is *nuces*, which, meaning trivialities in a metaphorical sense, is by the boy wilfully interpreted in its ordinary sense, as *nuts* — " *cera nunc ludo non nucibus*," — " I play with wax, not with nuts." The German word *nüsse* means nuts simply, and has no metaphorical meaning.

His progress in Greek was remarkable, as may be seen from his published exercises. Italian he learned by listening to his father teaching Cornelia. He pretended to be occupied with his own lesson, and caught up all that was said. French, too, he learned, as the exercises testify ; and thus before he is eight, we find him writing German, French, Italian, Latin, and Greek.

He was, in fact, a precocious child. This will probably startle many readers, especially if they have adopted the current notion that precocity is a sign of disease, and that marvellous children are necessarily evanescent fruits which never ripen, early blossoms which wither early. *Observatum fere est celerius occidere festinatam maturitatem*, says Quintilian, in the mournful passage which records the loss of his darling son ; and many a proud parent has seen his hopes frustrated by early death, or by matured mediocrity following the brilliant promise. It may help to do away with some confusion on this subject, if we bear in mind that men distinguish themselves by *receptive* capacity and by *productive* capacity ;

they learn, and they invent. In men of the highest class
these two qualities are united. Shakespeare and Goethe are
not less remarkable for the variety of their knowledge, than
for the activity of their invention. But as we call the child
clever who learns his lessons rapidly, and the child clever
who shows wit, sagacity, and invention, this ambiguity of
phrase has led to surprise when the child who was "so
clever" at school, turns out a mediocre man ; or, conversely,
when the child who was a dunce at school turns out a man
of genius. Goethe's precocity was nothing abnormal. It
was the activity of a mind at once greatly receptive and
greatly productive.

Other boys, besides Goethe, heard the Lisbon earthquake
eagerly discussed ; but they had not their religious doubts
awakened by it, as his were awakened in his sixth year.
This catastrophe, which, in 1755, spread consternation over
Europe, he has described as having greatly perturbed him.
The narratives he heard of a magnificent capital suddenly
smitten — churches, houses, towers falling with a crash,
the bursting land vomiting flames and smoke, and sixty
thousand souls perishing in an instant — shook his faith
in the beneficence of Providence. " God, the creator and
preserver of heaven and earth," he says, " whom the first
article of our creed declared to be so wise and benignant,
had not displayed paternal care in thus consigning both
the just and the unjust to the same destruction. In vain
my young mind strove to resist these impressions. It was
impossible ; the more so as the wise and religious themselves could not agree upon the view to be taken of the
event."

We are not, however, to suppose that the child rushed hastily to such a conclusion. He debated it in his own mind as
he heard it debated around him. Bettina records that on

2

his coming one day from church, where he had listened to a
sermon on the subject, in which God's goodness was justified, his father asked him what impression the sermon had
made.   "Why," said he, "it may after all be a much simpler
matter than the clergyman thinks ; God knows very well
that an immortal soul can receive no injury from a mortal
accident."

Doubts once raised would of course recur, and the child
began to settle into a serious disbelief in the benignity of
Providence, learning to consider God as the wrathful Deity depicted by the Hebrews. This was strengthened by the foolish
conduct of those around him, who, on the occasion of a terrible thunder-storm which shattered the windows, dragged
him and his sister into a dark passage, "where the whole
household, distracted with fear, tried to conciliate the angry
Deity by frightful groans and prayers."

The doubts which troubled Wolfgang gradually subsided.
In his family circle he was the silent reflective listener to
constant theological debates. The various sects separating
from the established church all seemed to be animated by
the one desire of approaching the Deity, especially through
Christ, more nearly than seemed possible through the ancient
forms.   It occurred to him that he, also, might make such an
approach, and in a more direct way. Unable to ascribe a
form to the Deity, he "resolved to seek him in his works,
and in the good old Bible fashion, to build an altar to him."
For this purpose he selected some types, such as ores and
other natural productions, and arranged them in symbolical
order on the elevations of a music-stand ; on the apex was
to be a flame typical of the soul's aspiration, and for this a
pastille did duty.   Sunrise was awaited with impatience.
The glittering of the house-tops gave signal ; he applied
a burning-glass to the pastille, and thus was the worship con-

summated by a priest of seven years old, alone in his bed-room ! *

Lest the trait just cited should make us forget that we are tracing the career of a child, it may be well to recall the anecdote related by Bettina, who had it from his mother; it will serve to set us right as to the childishness. One day his mother, seeing him from her window cross the street with his comrades, was amused with the gravity of his carriage, and asked laughingly, if he meant thereby to distinguish himself from his companions. The little fellow replied, "I *begin* with this. Later on in life I shall distinguish myself in far other ways."

On another occasion, he plagued her with questions as to whether the stars would perform all they had promised at his birth. "Why," said she, "must you have the assistance of the stars, when other people get on very well without?" "I am not to be satisfied with what does for other people!" said the juvenile Jupiter.

He had just attained his seventh year when the Seven Years' War broke out. His grandfather espoused the cause of Austria, his father that of Frederick. This difference of opinion brought with it contentions, and finally separation between the families. The exploits of the Prussian army were enthusiastically cited on the one side and depreciated on the other. It was an all-absorbing topic, awakening passionate partisanship. Men looked with strange feelings on the struggle which the greatest captain of his age was maintaining against Russia, Austria, and France. The ruler of not more than five millions of men was fighting unaided against the rulers of more than a hundred millions ; and, in spite of his alleged violation of honor, it was difficult to hear

---

* A similar anecdote is related of himself by that strange romancist, once the idol of his day, and now almost entirely forgotten, Restif de la Bretonne. See *Les Illuminés*, par GÉRARD DE NERVAL.

without enthusiasm of his brilliant exploits.   Courage and
genius in desperate circumstances always awaken sympathy;
and men paused not to ask what justification there was for
the seizure of Silesia, nor why the Saxon standards drooped
heavily in the churches of Berlin.   The roar of victorious
cannon stunned the judgment; the intrepid general was
blindly worshipped.   The Seven Years' War soon became a
German epos.   Archenholtz wrote its history (1791); and
this work — noisy with guard-room bragging and folly, the
rant of a *miles gloriosus* turned *philosophe* — was nevertheless
received with enthusiasm, was translated into Latin, and read
in schools in company with Tacitus and Cæsar.

This Seven Years' War was a circumstance from which, as
it is thought, Goethe ought to have received some epic inspiration.   He received from it precisely that which was food
to his character.   He caught the grand enthusiasm, but, as
he says, it was the *personality* of the hero, rather than the
greatness of his cause, which made him rejoice in every victory, copy the songs of triumph, and the lampoons directed
against Austria.   He learned now the effects of party spirit.
At the table of his grandfather he had to hear galling sarcasms, and vehement declamations showered on his hero.
He heard Frederick "shamefully slandered."   "And as in my
sixth year, after the Lisbon earthquake, I doubted the beneficence of Providence, so now, on account of Frederick, I
began to doubt the justice of the world."

Over the doorway of the house in which he was born were
a lyre and a star, announcing, as every interpreter will certify,
that a poet was to make that house illustrious.   The poetic
faculty early manifested itself.   We have seen him inventing
conclusions for his mother's stories; and as he grew older,
he began to invent stories for the amusement of his play-
fellows, after he had filled his mind with images, —

"Lone sitting on the shores of old Romance."

He had read the *Orbis Pictus*, Ovid's *Metamorphoses*, Homer's *Iliad* in prose, *Virgil* in the original, *Telemachus*, *Robinson Crusoe*, *Anson's Voyages*, with such books as *Fortunatus*, *The Wandering Jew*, *The Four Sons of Aymon*, etc. He also read and learned by heart most of the poets of that day : Gellert, Haller, who had really some gleams of poetry ; and Canitz, Hagedorn, Drollinger, — writers then much beloved, now slumbering upon dusty shelves, unvisited, except by an occasional historian, and by spiders of an inquiring mind.

Not only did he tell stories, he wrote them also, as we gather from a touching little anecdote preserved by Bettina. The small-pox had carried off his little brother Jacob. To the surprise of his mother, Wolfgang shed no tears, believing Jacob to be with God in heaven. "Did you not love your little brother, then," asked his mother, "that you do not grieve for his loss?" He ran to his room, and from under the bed drew a quantity of papers on which he had written stories and lessons. "All these I had written that I might teach them to him," said the child. He was then nine years old.

Shortly before the death of his brother he was startled by the sound of the warder's trumpet from the chief tower, announcing the approach of troops. This was in January, 1759. On came the troops in continuous masses, and the rolling tumult of their drums called all the women to the windows, and all the boys in admiring crowds into the streets. The troops were French. They seized the guard-house, and in a little while the city was a camp. To make matters worse, these troops were at war with Frederick, whom Wolfgang and his father worshipped. They were soon billeted through the town, and things relapsed into their usual routine, varied by a military occupation. In the

Goethe-house an important person was quartered, — Count de Thorane, the king's lieutenant, a man of taste and munificence, who assembled round him artists and celebrities, and won the affectionate admiration of Wolfgang, though he failed to overcome the hatred of the old councillor.

This occupation of Frankfurt brought with it many advantages to Goethe. It relaxed the severity of paternal book education, and began another kind of tuition, — that of life and manners. The perpetual marching through the streets, the brilliant parades, the music, the " pomp, pride, and circumstance," were not without their influence. Moreover, he now gained conversational familiarity with French,* and acquaintance with the theatre. The French nation always carries its "civilization" with it, — namely, a *café* and a theatre. In Frankfurt both were immediately opened, and Goethe was presented with a " free admission " to the theatre, a privilege he used daily, not always understanding, but always enjoying what he saw. In tragedy the measured rhythm, slow utterance, and abstract language enabled him to understand the scenes better than he understood comedy, wherein the language, besides moving amid the details of private life, was also more rapidly spoken. But, at the theatre, boys are not critical, and do not need to understand a play in order to enjoy it. A *Racine*, found upon his father's shelves, was eagerly studied, and the speeches were declaimed with more or less appreciation of their meaning.

The theatre, and acquaintance with a chattering little braggart, named Derones, gave him such familiarity with the language, that in a month he surprised his parents with his facility. This Derones was acquainted with the actors, and introduced him "behind the scenes." At ten years of age to

* He says that he had never learned French before ; but this is erroneous, as his exercises prove.

go "behind the scenes" means a great deal. We shall see hereafter how early he was introduced behind the scenes of life. For the present let it be noted that he was a frequenter of the green-room, and admitted into the dressing-room, where the actors and actresses dressed and undressed with philosophic disregard to appearances; and this, from repeated visits, he also learned to regard as quite natural.

A grotesque scene took place between these two boys. Derones excelled, as he affirmed, in "affairs of honor." He had been engaged in several, and had always managed to disarm his antagonist, and then nobly forgive him. One day he pretended that Wolfgang had insulted him: satisfaction was peremptorily demanded, and a duel was the result. Imagine Wolfgang, aged twelve, arrayed in shoes and silver buckles, fine woollen stockings, dark serge breeches, green coat with gold facings, a waistcoat of gold cloth, cut out of his father's wedding waistcoat, his hair curled and powdered, his hat under his arm, and little sword, with silk sword-knot. This little manikin stands opposite his antagonist with the-atrical formality; swords clash, thrusts come quick upon each other, the combat grows hot, when the point of Derones' rapier lodges in the bow of Wolfgang's sword-knot; here-upon the French boy, with great magnanimity, declares that he is satisfied! The two embrace, and retire to a *café* to re-fresh themselves with a glass of almond milk.*

Theatrical ambition, which stirs us all, soon prompted Wolfgang. As a child he had imitated Terence; he was now to make a more elaborate effort in the style of Piron. When the play was completed he submitted it to Derones, who, pointing out several grammatical blunders, promised to ex-amine it more critically, and talked of giving it *his* support

---

* To remove incredulity, it may be well to remind the reader that to this day German youths fight out their quarrels with swords, — not fists.

with the manager.   Wolfgang saw, in his mind's eye, the name
of his play already placarded at the corners of the street!
Unhappily, Derones in his critical capacity was merciless.
He picked the play to pieces, and stunned the poor author
with the critical jargon of that day ; proclaimed the absolute
integrity of the Three Unities, abused the English, laughed at
the Germans, and maintained the sovereignty of French taste
in so confident a style, that his listener was without a reply.
If silenced, however, he was not convinced.   It set him to
thinking on those critical canons.   He studied the treatise on
the Unities by Corneille, and the prefaces of Racine.   The result of these studies was profound contempt for that system ;
and it is, perhaps, to Derones that we owe something of the
daring defiance of all "rule," which startled Germany in *Götz
von Berlichingen.*

CHAPTER III.

VARIOUS STUDIES.

AT length, June, 1761, the French quitted Frankfurt ; and
studies were seriously resumed.   Mathematics, music, and
drawing were commenced under paternal superintendence.
For mathematics Wolfgang had no aptitude ; for music, little ;
he learned to play on the harpsichord, and subsequently on
the violoncello, but he never attained any proficiency.   Drawing continued through life a pleasant exercise.

Left now to the calm of uninterrupted studies, he made
gigantic strides.   Even the hours of recreation were filled
with some useful occupation.   He added English to his poly-
glot store ; and to keep up his several languages, he invented
a Romance, wherein six or seven brothers and sisters scat

tered over the world corresponded with each other. The eldest describes in good German all the incidents of his travels; his sister answers in womanly style with short, sharp sentences, and nothing but full stops, much as *Siegwart* was afterwards written. Another brother studies theology, and therefore writes in Latin, with postscripts in Greek. A third and a fourth, clerks at Hamburg and Marseilles, take English and French; Italian is given to a musician; while the youngest, who remains at home, writes in Jew-German. This romance led him to a more accurate study of geography. Having placed his characters in various parts of the globe, he was not satisfied till he had a distinct idea of these localities, so that the objects and events should be consonant with probability. While trying to master the strange dialect, — Jew-German, — he was led to the study of Hebrew. As the original language of the Old Testament, this seemed to him an indispensable acquisition. His father consented to give him a Hebrew master; and although he attained no scholarship in that difficult language, yet the reading, translating, and committing to memory of various parts of the Bible brought out the meaning more vividly before him; as every one will understand who compares the lasting effect produced by the laborious school-reading of Sallust and Livy with the facile reading of Robertson and Hume. The Bible made a profound impression upon him. To a boy of his constitutional reflectiveness, the severe study of this book could not fail to exercise a deep and permeating influence; nor, at the same time, in one so accustomed to think for himself, could it fail to awaken certain doubts. "The contradiction," he says, "between the actual or possible, and tradition, forcibly arrested me. I often posed my tutors with the sun standing still on Gibeon, and the moon in the valley of Ajalon; not to mention other incongruities and impossibilities. All my doubts were now awakened, as in order to master the Hebrew I studied the literal version by Schmidt, printed under the text."

One result of these Hebrew studies was a biblical poem on Joseph and his Brethren; which he dictated to a poor half-idiot who lived in his father's house, and who had a mania for copying or writing under dictation. Goethe soon found the process of dictation of great service; and through life it continued to be his favorite mode of composition. All his best thoughts and expressions, he says, came to him while walking; he could do nothing seated.

To these multifarious studies in Literature must be added multifarious studies of Life. The old Frankfurt city, with its busy crowds, its fairs, its mixed population, and its many sources of excitement, offered great temptations, and great pasture to so desultory a genius. This is perhaps a case where-in Circumstance may be seen influencing the direction of Character. A boy of less impressionable nature, of less many-sided curiosity, would have lived in such a city undisturbed; some eyes would see little of the variety, some minds would be unsolicited by the exciting objects. But Goethe's desultory, because impulsive, nature found continual excitement in fresh objects; and he was thus led to study many things, to grasp at many forms of life, instead of concentrating himself upon a few. A large continuity of thought and effort was perhaps radically uncongenial to such a temperament; yet one can-not help speculating whether under other circumstances he might not have achieved it. Had he been reared in a quiet little old German town, where he would have daily seen the same faces in the silent streets, and come in contact with the same characters, his culture might have been less various, but it might perhaps have been deeper. Had he been reared in the country, with only the changing seasons and the sweet serenities of Nature to occupy his attention when released from study, he would certainly have been a different poet. The long summer afternoons spent in lonely rambles, the deepening twilights filled with shadowy visions, the slow uniformity of his external life necessarily throwing him more and more upon the more subtile diversities of inward experience, would inevitably have influenced his genius in quite different directions, would have animated his works with a very different spirit. Yet who shall say that to him this would have been all gain? Who shall say that it would not have been a loss? For such an organization' as his the life he led was perhaps the very best. He was desultory, and the varieties of objects which solicited his attention, while they helped to encourage that tendency, also helped to nourish his mind with images and experience, such as afterwards became the richest material for his art.

The boy saw much of life, in both the lower and the upper classes. He passed from the society of the Count de Thorane, and of the artists whom the Count assembled round him (from whom the boy learned something of the technical details of painting), to the society of the Jews in the strange, old, filthy, but deeply interesting *Judengasse;* or to that of various artisans, in whose shops his curiosity found perpetual food. The Jews were doubly interesting to him : as social pariahs, over whom there hovered a mingled mystery of terror and contempt ; and as descendants of the Chosen People, who preserved the language, the opinions, and many of the customs of the old Biblical race. He was impressed by their adherence to old customs ; by their steadfastness and courageous activity ; by their strange features and accents ; by their bright cleverness and good-nature. The pretty Jewish maidens also smiled agreeably upon him. He began to mingle with them, managed to get permission to be present at some of their ceremonies, and attended their schools.

As to artisans, he was all his life curious about their handi-
crafts, and fond of being admitted into their family circles.
Scott himself was not fonder of talking to them ; nor did
Scott make better use of his manifold experience. Frederika's sister told her visitor that Goethe knew several handi-
crafts, and had even learned basket-making from a lame man
in Sesenheim.   Here in Frankfurt the boy was welcome in
many a shop.   The jeweller, Lautensack, gladly admitted
him to witness the mysteries of his art, while he made the
bouquet of jewels for the Kaiser, or a diamond snuff-box
which Rath Goethe had ordered as a present for his wife ;
the boy asking eager questions respecting precious stones,
and the engravings which the jeweller possessed. Nothnagel,
the painter, had established an oil-cloth manufactory ; and
Goethe not only learned all the processes, but lent a helping
hand.

Besides these forms of life, there were others whose influence must not be overlooked ; one of these brings before us
the Fräulein von Klettenberg, of whom we first get a glimpse
in connection with his Confirmation, which took place at this
period, 1763.   The readers of *Wilhelm Meister* are familiar
with this gentle and exquisite character, where she is represented in the "Confessions of a Beautiful Soul."*   In the
"Confessions" we see that the "piety" and retirement are
represented less as the consequences of evangelical illumina-
tion, than of moral serenity and purity shrinking from contact with a world of which it has been her fate to see the
coarsest features.   The real Fräulein von Klettenberg it is
perhaps now impossible to separate from the ideal so beauti-

---

* Or as we in England, following Carlyle, have been misled into calling it, the "Confessions of a Fair Saint."   The *schöne Seele — une belle
âme*, was one of the favorite epithets of the last century.   Goethe applies
it to Klopstock, who was neither "saint nor fair."

fully painted by Goethe. On him her influence was avowedly very great, both at this period and subsequently. It was not so much the effect of religious discussion as the experience it gave him of a deeply religious nature. She was neither bigot nor prude. Her faith was an inner light which shed mild radiance around her.* Moved by her influence, he wrote a series of *Religious Odes*, after the fashion of that day, and greatly pleased his father by presenting them copied neatly in a quarto volume. His father begged that every year he would present him with such a volume.

A very different sort of female influence has now to be touched on. His heart began to flutter with the emotions of love. He was not quite fifteen, when Gretchen, the sister of one of his companions, first set his youthful pulses throbbing to the movements of the divine passion. The story is told in a rambling way in the *Autobiography*, and may here be very briefly dismissed. He had often turned his poetical talents to *practical* purposes, namely, writing wedding and funeral verses, the produce of which went in joyous feastings. In these he was almost daily thrown with Gretchen ; but she, though kind, treated him as a child, and never permitted the slightest familiarity. A merry life they led in picnics and pleasure bouts ; and the coronation of the Kaiser Joseph II. was the occasion of increased festivity. One night, after the fatigues of a sight-seeing day, the hours rolled unheeded over these thoughtless, merry heads, and the stroke of midnight startled them. To his dismay, Wolfgang found he had forgotten the door-key with which hitherto he had been able to evade paternal knowledge of his late hours. Gretchen proposed that they should all remain together, and

---

* In VARNHAGEN VON ENSE's *Vermischte Schriften* (Vol. III. p. 33) the reader will find a few significant details respecting this remarkable person, and some of her poems.

pass the night in conversation. This was agreed on. But, as in all such cases, the effort was vain. Fatigue weighed down their eyelids ; conversation became feebler and feebler; two strangers already slumbered in corners of the room ; one friend sat in a corner with his betrothed, her head reposing on his shoulder ; another crossing his arms upon the table, rested his head upon them, and snored. The noisy room had become silent. Gretchen and her lover sat by the window talking in undertones. Fatigue at length conquered her also, and drooping her head upon his shoulder she too slept. With tender pride he supported that delicious burden, till like the rest he gave way, and slept.

It was broad day when he awoke. Gretchen was standing before a mirror, arranging her cap. She smiled on him more amiably than ever she had smiled before ; and pressed his hand tenderly as he departed. But now, while he seemed drawing nearer to her, the *dénouement* was at hand. Some of the joyous companions had been guilty of nefarious practices, such as forgeries of documents. His friend and Gretchen ere involved in the accusation, though falsely. Wolfgang had to undergo a severe investigation, which, as he was perfectly innocent, did not much afflict him ; but an affliction came out of the investigation, for Gretchen, in her deposition concerning him, said, " I will not deny that I have often seen him, and seen him with pleasure, but I treated him as a child, and my affection for him was merely that of a sister." His exasperation may be imagined.

But pride came to his aid ; pride and that volatility of youth, which compensates for extra sensitiveness by extra facility in forgetting. He threw himself into study, especially of philosophy, under guidance of a tutor, a sort of *Wagner* to the young *Faust*. This tutor, who preferred dusty quartos to all the landscapes in the world, used to banter him upon

being a true German, such as Tacitus describes, avid of the
emotions excited by solitude and scenery.   The banter was
powerless.   He was enjoying his first sorrow : the luxury of
melancholy, the romance of a forlorn existence, drove him
into solitude.   Like Bellerophon he fed upon his own heart
away from the haunts of men.   He made frequent walking
excursions.   Those mountains, which from earliest childhood
had haunted him like a passion, were now his favorite resorts.
He visited Homburg, Kronburg, Königstein, Wiesbaden,
Schwalbach, Biberich, and there filled his mind with lovely
images.

Severer studies were not neglected.   To please his father
he was diligent in application to jurisprudence ; to please
himself he was still more diligent in literature; Morhof's
Polyhistor, Gessner's *Isagoge,* and Bayle's *Dictionary* filled
him with the ambition to become an University Professor.
Herein, as, indeed, throughout his career, we see the strange
impressibility of his nature, which, like the fabled chameleon,
takes its color from every tree it lies under.

The melancholy fit did not last long.   A circle of lively
friends, among them Horn, of whom we shall hear more
anon, drew him into gayety again.   Their opinion of his
talents appears to have been enormous ; their love for him,
and interest in all he did, was of a kind which followed him
through life.   No matter what his mood, — in the wildest
student-period, in the startling genius-period, and in the diplomatic period, — whatever offence his manner created was
soon forgotten in the irresistible fascination of his nature.
The secret of that fascination was his own overflowing lovingness, and his genuine interest in every individuality, however
opposite to his own.

CHAPTER IV.

THE CHILD IS FATHER TO THE MAN.

As in the soft round lineaments of childhood we trace the features which after years will develop into more decided forms, so in the moral lineaments of the Child may be traced the characteristics of the Man.   But an apparent solution of continuity takes place in the transition period ; so that the Youth is in many respects unlike what he has been in child-hood, and what he will be in maturity.   In youth, when the passions begin to stir, the character is made to swerve from the orbit previously traced.   Passion, more than Character, rules the hour.   Thus we often see the prudent child turn out an extravagant youth ; but he crystallizes once more into prudence, as he hardens with age.

This was certainly the case with Goethe, who, if he had died young, like Shelley or Keats, would have left a name among the most *genial*, not to say extravagant, of poets ; but who, living to the age of eighty-two, had fifty years of crys-tallization to acquire a definite figure which perplexes critics. In his childhood, scanty as the datails are which enable us to reconstruct it, we see the main features of the man.   Let us glance rapidly at them.

And first, of his *manysidedness*.   Seldom has a boy exhib-ited such variety of faculty.   The multiplied activity of his life is prefigured in the varied tendencies of his childhood. We see him as an orderly, somewhat formal, inquisitive, rea-soning, deliberative child, a precocious learner, an omnivorous reader, and one who thinks for himself, — so independent, that at six years of age he doubts the beneficence of the Creator ; at seven, doubts the competence and justice of the world's judgment. He is inventive, poetical, proud, loving, volatile, with a mind open to all influences, swayed by every gust, and yet, while thus swayed as to the direction of his activity, he is master over that activity. The most diverse characters, the most antagonistic opinions, interest him. He is very studious, no bookworm more so; alternately busy with languages, mythology, antiquities, law, philosophy, poetry, and religion; yet he joins in all festive scenes, gets familiar with life in various forms, and stays out late o' nights. He is also troubled by melancholy, dreamy moods, forcing him ever and anon into solitude.

Among the dominant characteristics are seriousness, formality, rationality. He is by no means a naughty boy. He gives his parents no tremulous anxiety as to what will become of him. He seems very much master of himself. It is this which in later years perplexed his critics, who could not reconcile this appearance of self-mastery, this seeming absence of enthusiasm, with their conceptions of a poet. Assuredly he had enthusiasm, if ever man had it: at least, enthusiasm (being "full of the God") means being filled with a divine idea, and by its light working steadily. He had little of the other kind of enthusiasm, — that insurrection of the feelings carrying away upon their triumphant shoulders the Reason which has no longer power to guide them; for his intellect did not derive its whole momentum from his feelings. And hence it is that whereas the quality which first strikes us in most poets is *sensibility*, with its caprices, infirmities, and generous errors, the first quality which strikes us in Goethe — the Child and Man, but *not* the Youth — is *intellect*, with its clearness and calmness. He has also a provoking degree of immunity from error. I say provoking, for we all gladly overlook the errors of enthusiasm; partly because these errors appeal to our compassion; and partly because these errors establish a community of impulse between the sinner and ourselves, forming, as it were, broken edges which show us where to look for support, — scars which tell of wounds we have escaped.   Whereas, we are pitiless to the cold prudence which shames our weakness and asks no alms from our charity.   Why do we all preach Prudence, and secretly dislike it?   Perhaps, because we dimly feel that life without its generous errors might want its lasting enjoyments ; and thus the very mistakes which arise from an imprudent, unreflecting career are absolved by that instinct which suggests other aims for existence beyond prudential aims.   This is one reason why the erring lives of Genius command such deathless sympathy.

Having indicated so much, I may now ask those who are distressed by the calm, self-sustaining superiority of Goethe in old age, whether, on deeper reflection, they cannot reconcile it with their conceptions of the poet's nature?   We admire Rationality, but we sympathize with Sensibility.   Our dislike of the one arises from its supposed incompatibility with the other.   But if a man unites the mastery of Will and Intellect to the profoundest sensibility of Emotion, shall we not say of him that he has in living synthesis vindicated both what we preach and what we love?   That Goethe united these will be abundantly shown in this Biography.   In the chapters about to follow we shall see him wild, restless, aimless, erring, and extravagant enough to satisfy the most ardent admirer of the vagabond nature of genius : the Child and the Man will at times be scarcely traceable in the Youth.

One trait must not be passed over, namely, his *impatient susceptibility*, which, while it prevented his ever thoroughly mastering the technic of any one subject, lay at the bottom of his multiplied activity in directions so opposed to each other.   He was excessively impressible, caught the impulse from every surrounding influence, and was thus never constant to one thing, because his susceptibility was connected with an impatience which soon made him weary.   There are men who learn many languages, and never thoroughly master the grammar of one.   Of these was Goethe.   Easily excited to throw his energy in a new direction, he had not the patience which begins at the beginning, and rises gradually, slowly into assured mastery.   Like an eagle he swooped down upon his prey ; he could not watch for it with cat-like patience.   It is to this impatience we must attribute the fact of so many works being left fragments, so many composed by snatches during long intervals.   *Prometheus, Mahomet, Die Natürliche Tochter, Elpenor, Achilleis, Nausikäa,* remain fragments.   *Faust, Egmont, Tasso, Iphigenia, Meister,* were many years in hand.   Whatever could be done in a few days — while the impulse lasted — was done ; longer works were spread over a series of years.

BOOK THE SECOND.

1765 TO 1771.

—◆—

CHAPTER I.

THE LEIPSIC STUDENT.

In the month of October, 1765, Goethe, aged sixteen, arrived in Leipsic, to commence his collegiate life, and to lay, as he hoped, the solid foundation of a future professorship. He took lodgings in the Feuerkugel, between the Old and New Markets, and was by the rector of the University inscribed on the 19th as student "in the Bavarian nation." At that period, and until quite recently, the University was classed according to four "nations," namely, the *Misnian*, the *Saxon*, the *Bavarivn*, and the *Polish*. When the inscription was official, the "nations" were what in Oxford and Paris are called "tongues"; when not official, they were students' clubs, such as they exist to this day. Goethe, as a Frankfurter, was placed in the Bavarian.*

He first presented himself to Hofrath Böhme, a genuine professor, shut within the narrow circle of his speciality. To him Literature and the Fine Arts were trivialities; and when the confiding youth confessed his secret ambition of studying *belles lettres*, in lieu of the jurisprudence commanded by his father, he met with every discouragement. Yet it was not difficult to persuade this impressible student that to rival Otto and Heineccius was the true ambition of a vigorous

* OTTO JAHN, in the *Briefe an Leipziger Freunde*, p. 9.

mind. He set to work in earnest, at first, as students usually
do on arriving at seats of learning. His attendance at the
lectures on philosophy, history of law, and jurisprudence was
assiduous enough to have pleased even his father. But this
flush of eagerness quickly subsided. Logic was repugnant to him. He hungered for realities, and could not be
satisfied with definitions. To see operations of his mind,
which, from childhood upwards, had been conducted with
perfect ease and unconsciousness, suddenly pulled to pieces,
in order that he might gain the superfluous knowledge
of what they were, and what they were called, was to him
tiresome and frivolous. "I fancied I knew as much about
God and the world as the professor himself, and logic seemed
in many places to come to a dead standstill." We are here on
the threshold of that experience which has been immortalized
in the scene between Mephistopheles and the Student. Jurisprudence soon became almost equally tiresome. He already
knew as much law as the professor thought proper to com-
municate ; and what with the tedium of the lectures, and the
counter-attraction of delicious fritters, which used to come
"hot from the pan precisely at the hour of lecture" no wonder
that volatile Sixteen soon abated attendance.

Volatile he was, wild, and somewhat rough, both in appearance and in speech. He had brought with him a wild, uneasy
spirit struggling towards the light. He had also brought with
him the rough manners of Frankfurt, the strong Frankfurt
dialect and colloquialisms, rendered still more unfit for the
Leipsic *salon* by a mixture of proverbs and Biblical allu-
sions. Nay, even his costume was in unpleasant contrast
with that of the society in which he moved. He had an
ample wardrobe, but unhappily it was doubly out of fashion :
it had been manufactured at home by one of his father's
servants, and thus was not only in the Frankfurt style, but

grotesquely made in that style. To complete his discom-
fiture, he saw a favorite low comedian throw an audience
into fits of laughter by appearing on the stage dressed precisely in that costume, which he had hitherto worn as the
latest novelty! All who can remember the early humiliations
of being far behind their companions in matters of costume
will sympathize with this youth.

Dissatified with College, he sought instruction elsewhere.
At the table where he dined daily, kept by Hofrath Ludwig,
the rector, he met several medical students. He heard little
talked of but medicine and botany, and the names of Haller,
Linnæus, and Buffon were incessantly cited with respect.
His ready quickness to interest himself in all that interested
those around him threw him at once into these studies, which
hereafter he was to pursue with passionate ardor, but which
at present he only lightly touched. Another source of instruction awaited him, one which through life he ever gratefully acknowledged, namely, the society of women.

In Leipsic, he was glad to learn from Frau Böhme not only
some of the requisites for society, but also some principles
of poetic criticism. This delicate, accomplished woman was
able to draw him into society, to teach him l'ombre and
picquet, to correct some of his awkwardnesses, and lastly to
make him own that the poets he admired were a deplorable
set, and that his own imitations of them deserved no better
fate than the flames. He had got rid of his absurd wardrobe
at one fell swoop, without a murmur at the expense. He
now had also to cast away the poetic wardrobe brought
from home with so much pride. He saw that it was
poetic frippery, — saw that his own poems were lifeless;
accordingly, a holocaust was made of all his writings, prose
and verse, and the kitchen fire wafted them into space.

Schlosser, afterwards his brother-in-law, came to Leipsic,

and by his preaching and example once more roused the productive activity which showed itself in German, French, English, and Italian verses. Schlosser, who was ten years his senior, not only awakened emulation by his own superior knowledge and facility, but further aided him by introducing him to a set of literary friends with whom poetic discussions formed the staple of conversation. This circle met at the house of one Schönkopf, a *Weinhändler* and *Hauswirth*, living in the Brühl, No. 79.* To translate these words into English equivalents would only mislead the reader. Schönkopf kept neither a hotel, nor a public house, but what in Germany is a substitute for both. He sold wine, and kept a *table-d'hôte;* occasionally also let bedrooms to travellers. His wife, a lively, cultivated woman, belonging to a good family in Frankfurt, drew Frankfurt visitors to the house ; and with her Goethe soon became on terms of intimacy which would seem surprising to the English reader who only heard of her as an innkeeper's wife. He became one of the family, and fell in love with the daughter. I must further beg the reader to understand that in Germany, to this day, there is a wide difference between the dining customs and our own. The English student, clerk, or bachelor, who dines at an eating-house, chop-house, or hotel, goes there simply to get his dinner, and perhaps look at *The Times.* Of the other diners he knows nothing, cares little. It is rare that a word is interchanged between him and his neighbor. Quite otherwise in Germany. There the same society is generally to be found at the same table. The *table-d'hôte* is composed of a circle of *habitués*, varied by occasional visitors, who in time become, perhaps, members of the circle. Even with strangers conversation is freely interchanged ; and in a little while

---

* The house still stands there, but has been almost entirely re-modelled.

friendships are formed over these dinner-tables, according as natural tastes and likings assimilate, which, extending beyond the mere hour of dinner, are carried into the current of life. Germans do not rise so hastily from the table as we; for time with them is not so precious; life is not so crowded; time can be found for quiet after-dinner talk. The cigars and coffee, which appear before the cloth is removed, keep the company together; and in that state of suffused comfort which quiet digestion creates, they hear without anger the opinions of antagonists. In such a society must we imagine Goethe in the Schönkopf establishment, among students and men of letters, all eager in advancing their own opinions, and combating the false taste which was not their own.

To complete this picture, and to separate it still more from our English customs, you must imagine host and hostess dining at the table, while their charming daughter, who had cooked or helped to cook the dinner, brought them the wine. This daughter was the Anna Katharina, by intimates called Kathchen, and by Goethe, in the *Autobiography*, designated as Annchen and Annette. Her portrait, still extant, is very pleasing. She was then nineteen, lively and loving; how could she be insensible to the love of this glorious youth, in all the fervor of genius, and with all the attractions of beauty? They saw each other daily, not only at dinner but in the evenings, when he accompanied the piano of her brother by a feeble performance on the flute. They also got up private theatricals, in which Goethe and Kathchen played the lovers. *Minna von Barnhelm*, then a novelty, was among the pieces performed. That these performances were of a strictly amateur order may be gathered from the fact that in one of them the part of a nightingale, which is important, was represented by a handkerchief, rolled up into such ornithological resemblance as art could reach.

Imagine this somewhat fantastic youth assured that his passion is returned, and then imagine him indulging in the boyish caprice of tormenting his beloved. There is nothing more cruel than youth ; and youthful lovers, once assured of victory, are singularly prone to indulge in the most frivolous pretexts for ingeniously tormenting. " Man loves to conquer, likes not to feel secure," Goethe says, in the piece wherein he dramatized this early experience : —

> " Erringen will der Mensch ; er will nicht sicher seyn."

Had Kathchen coquetted with him, keeping him in the exquisite pain of suspense, she would have been happier ; but as he said in his little poem, *Der Wahre Genuss,* " she is perfect, and her only fault is — that she loves me " : —

> " Sie ist vollkommen, und sie fehlet
> Darin allein dass sie mich liebt."

He teased her with trifles and idle suspicions ; was jealous without cause, convinced without reason ; plagued her with fantastic quarrels, till at last her endurance was exhausted, and her love was washed away in tears. No sooner was he aware of this than he repented, and tried to recover the jewel which like a prodigal he had cast away. In vain. He was in despair, and tried in dissipation to forget his grief. A better issue was poetry. Several of his lyrics bore the burden of this experience ; and one entire play, or pastoral, is devoted to a poetical representation of these lovers' quarrels : this is *Die Laune des Verliebten,* which is very curious as the earliest extant work of the great poet, and as the earliest specimen of his tendency to turn experience into song. In the opera of *Erwin und Elmire* he subsequently treated a similar subject in a very different manner. The first effort is the more curious of the two. The style of composition is an imitation of those pastoral dramas which, originated by

Tasso and Guarini in the soft and almost luscious *Aminta* and *Pastor Fido*, had by the French been made popular all over Europe.

Young, curious, and excitable as he was, nothing is more natural than that he should somewhat shock the respectabilities by his pranks and extravagances.   The friends were displeased to see young Goethe falling thus away from good society into such a disreputable course ; but just as Lessing before him had neglected the elegant Leipsic world for actors and authors of more wit than money, and preferred Mylius, with his shoes down at heel, to all that the best drest society could offer ; so did young Goethe neglect *salon* and lecture-hall for the many-colored scene of life in less elegant circles.   Enlightened by the result, we foresee that the poet will receive little injury from these sources ; he is gaining experience, and experience even of the worst sides of human nature will be sublimated into noble uses, as carrion by the wise farmer is turned into excellent manure.   In this great drama of life every Theatre has its Green-room ; and unless the poet knows how it is behind the scenes, he will never understand how actors speak and move.

Goethe had often been "behind the scenes," looking at the skeleton which stands in almost every house.   His adventure with Gretchen, and its consequences, early opened his eyes to the strange gulfs which lie under the crust of society.   "Religion, morals, law, rank, habits," he says, "rule over the *surface* of social life.   Streets of magnificent houses are kept clean ; every one outwardly conducts himself with propriety ; but the disorder within is often only the more desolate ; and a polished exterior covers many a wall which totters, and falls with a crash during the night, all the more terrible because it falls during a calm.   How many families had I not more or less distinctly known in which bankruptcy, divorce, seduction, murder, and robbery had wrought destruction ! Young as I was, I had often, in such cases, lent my succor; for as my frankness awakened confidence, and my discretion was known, and as my activity did not shun any sacrifice, — indeed, rather preferred the most perilous occasions, — I had frequently to mediate, console, and try to avert the storm ; in the course of which I could not help learning many sad and humiliating facts."

It was natural that such sad experience should at first lead him to view the whole social fabric with contempt. To relieve himself he — being then greatly captivated with Molière's works — sketched the plans of several dramas, but their plots were so uniformly unpleasant, and the catastrophes so tragic, that he did not work out these plans. *The Fellow-Sinners* (*Die Mitschuldigen*) is the sole piece which was completed, and it now occupies a place among his writings. Few, in England at least, ever read it ; yet it is worth a rapid glance, and is especially remarkable as the work of a youth not yet eighteen.

———◆———

CHAPTER II.

ART STUDIES.

FRAU BÖHME died. In her he lost a monitress and friend, who had kept some check on his waywardness, and drawn him into society. The Professor had long since cooled towards him, after giving up all hopes of making him another Heineccius. It was pitiful ! A youth with such remarkable dispositions, who would *not* be assiduous in attendance at lecture, and whose amusement during lecture was to sketch caricatures of various law dignitaries in his note-book ; another ornament to jurisprudence irrecoverably lost! Indeed, the collegiate aspect of this Leipsic residence was not one promising to professors ; but we — instructed by the result — know how much better he was employed than if he had filled a hundred volumes of note-books by diligent attendance at lecture. He studied much, in a desultory manner : he studied Molière and Corneille ; he began to translate *Le Menteur.* The theatre was a perpetual attraction ; and even the uneasy, u satisfied condition of his affections was instructing him in directions whither no professor could lead him. But greater than all was the influence of Shakespeare, whom he first learned a little of through Dodd's *Beauties of Shakespeare*, a work not much prized in England, where the plays form part of our traditional education, but which must have been a revelation to the Germans something analogous to what Charles Lamb's *Specimens of the Old English Drama* was to us. The marvellous strength and beauty of language, the bold and natural imagery of these *Beauties*, startled the young poets of that day, like the discovery of huge fossil remains of some antediluvian fauna ; and to gratify the curiosity thus awakened, he says there came Wieland's prose translation of several plays, which he studied with enthusiasm.*

There are no materials to fill up the gaps of his narrative here, so that I am forced to leave much indistinct. For instance, he has told us that Kathchen and he were no longer lovers ; but we find him writing to her in a friendly and even lover-like tone from Frankfurt, and we know that friendly intercourse still subsisted between them. Of this, however, not a word occurs in the *Autobigraphy.* Nor are we accu-

---

* It is possible that Wieland's translation only then fell into Goethe's hands, but the publication was commenced before his arrival in Leipsic, namely, in 1761.

rately informed how he made the acquaintance of the Breitkopf family. Breitkopf was a bookseller in Leipsic, in whose
house Literature and Music were highly prized. Bernhard,
the eldest son, was an excellent performer, and composed
music to Goethe's songs, which were published in 1769,
under this title, *Neue Lieder in Melodieen gesetzt von Bernhard Theodor Breitkopf.* The poet is not named. This
Liederbuch contains twenty songs, the majority of which were
subsequently reprinted in the poet's works. They are love-
songs, and contain a love-philosophy more like what is to be
found in Catullus, Horace, and Wieland, than what one
would expect from a boy, did we not remember how the
braggadocio of youth delights in expressing *roué* sentiments,
as if to give itself airs of profound experience. This youth
sings with gusto of inconstancy : —

> " Da fühl ich die Freuden der wechselnden Lust."

He gayly declares that if one mistress leaves you another
will love you, and the second is sweeter to kiss than the
first : —

> " Es küsst sich so süsse der Busen der Zweiten,
>   Als kaum sich der Busen der Ersten geküsst."

Another acquaintance, and one more directly influential,
was that of Oeser, the director of the Drawing Academy.
He had been the friend and teacher of Winckelmann, and
his name stood high among connoisseurs. Goethe, who at
home had learned a little drawing, joined Oeser's class,
where, among other fellow-students, was the Hardenberg who
afterwards made such a noise in the Prussian political world.
He joined the class, and did his best to acquire by labor the
skill which only a talent can acquire. That he made little
progress in drawing we learn from his subsequent confession
no less than from his failure ; but tuition had this effect at
least, — it taught him to use his eyes.

Instruction in the theory of Art he gained from Oeser, from Winckelmann, and from *Laokoon*, the incomparable little book which Lessing at this period carelessly flung upon the world.   Its effect upon Goethe can only be appreciated by those who early in life have met with this work, and risen from it with minds widened, strengthened, and inspired.* It opened a pathway amid confusion, throwing light upon many of the obscurest problems which torment the artist. It awakened in Goethe an intense yearning to see the works of ancient masters ; and these beckoned from Dresden.   To Dresden he went.   But here, in spite of Oeser, Winckelmann, and Lessing, in spite of grand phrases about Art, the invincible tendency of his nature asserted itself, and instead of falling into raptures with the great Italian pictures, he confesses that he took their merits upon trust, and was really charmed by none but the landscape and Dutch painters, whose subjects appealed directly to his experience.   He did nor feel the greatness of Italian Art ; and what he did not feel he would not feign.

It is worth noticing that this trip to Dresden was taken in absolute secrecy.   As, many years later, he stole away to Italy without letting his friends even suspect his project, so now he left Leipsic for Dresden without a word of intimation.   Probably the same motive actuated him in both instances.   He went to see, to enjoy, to learn, and did not want to be disturbed by personal influence, — by other people's opinions.   .

On his return he was active enough with drawing.   He made the acquaintance of an engraver named Stock,† and

---

* Lord Macaulay told me that the reading of this little book formed an epoch in his mental history, and that he learned more about Art from it than he had ever learned elsewhere.

† This Stock had two amiable daughters, one of whom married (1785) Körner, the correspondent of Schiller, and father of the poet.

with his usual propensity to try his hand at whatever his
friends were doing, he forthwith began to learn engraving.
In the *Morgenblatt* for 1828 there is a detailed account of
two of his engravings, both representing landscapes with
small cascades shut in by rocks and grottoes ; at the foot of
each are these words : *peint par A. Theile, gravé par Goethe.*
One plate is dedicated *à Monseieur Goethe Conseiller actuel de
S. M. Impériale, par son fils très obéissant.* In the room
which they show to strangers in his house in Frankfurt, there
is also a specimen of his engraving, — very amateurish ; but
Madame von Goethe showed me one in her possession which
really has merit.

Melancholy, wayward, and capricious, he allowed Lessing
to pass through Leipsic without making any attempt to see
the man he so much admired : a caprice he afterwards repented, for the opportunity never recurred. Something of
his hypochondria was due to mental, but more to physical
causes. Dissipation, bad diet (especially the beer and coffee),
and absurd endeavors to carry out Rousseau's preaching
about returning to a state of nature, had seriously affected
his health. The crisis came at last. One summer night
(1768) he was seized with violent hemorrhage. He had
only strength enough to call to his aid the fellow-student who
slept in the next room. Medical assistance promptly came.
He was saved ; but his convalescence was embittered by the
discovery of a tumor on his neck, which lasted some time.
His recovery was slow, but it seemed as if it relieved him
from all the peccant humors which had made him hypochondriacal, leaving behind an inward lightness and joyousness
to which he had long been a stranger. One thing greatly
touched him, — the sympathy expressed for him by several
eminent men ; a sympathy he felt to be quite undeserved,
for there was not one among them whom he had not vexed

or affronted by his caprices, extravagances, morbid opposition, and stubborn persistence.

One of these friends, Langer, not only made an exchange
of books with him, giving a set of classic authors for a set of
German, but also, in devout yet not dogmatic conversation,
led his young friend to regard the Bible in another light than
that of a merely human composition. " I loved the Bible
and valued it, for it was almost the only book to which I
owed my moral culture. Its events, dogmas, and symbols
were deeply impressed on my mind." He therefore felt little
sympathy with the Deists, who were at this time agitating
Europe ; and although his tendency was strongly against the
Mystics, he was afraid lest the poetical spirit should be swept
away along with the prophetical. In one word, he was in a
state of religious doubt, — "destitute of faith, yet terrified at
scepticism."

This unrest and this bodily weakness he carried with him,
September, 1768, from Leipsic to Frankfurt, whither we will
follow him.

CHAPTER III.

RETURN HOME.

HE returned home a boy in years, in experience a man.
Broken in health, unhappy in mind, with no strong impulses
in any one direction, uncertain of himself and of his aims,
he felt, as he approached his native city, much like a repent-
ant prodigal who has no vision of the fatted calf awaiting
him. His father, unable to perceive the real progress he
had made, was very much alive to the slender prospect of his
becoming a distinguished jurist. The fathers of poets are

seldom gratified with the progress in education visible to them ; and the reason is that they do not know their sons to be poets, nor understand that the poet's orbit is not the same as their own.   They tread the common highway on which the milestones accurately mark distances ; and seeing that their sons have trudged but little way according to this measurement, their minds are filled with misgivings.   Of that silent progress, which consists less in travelling on the broad highway than in development of the limbs which will make a sturdy traveller, parents cannot judge.

Mother and sister, however, touched by the worn face, and, woman-like, more interested in the man than in what he had achieved, received him with an affection which compensated for his father's coldness.   There is quite a pathetic glimpse given of this domestic interior in the *Autobiography*, where he alludes to his father's impatience at his illness, and anxiety for his speedy recovery.

We find him in cold, unpleasant relations with his father, who had almost excited the hatred of his other child, Cornelia, by the stern, pedantic, pedagogic way in which he treated her.   The old man continued to busy himself with writing his travels in Italy, and with instructing his daughter. She, who was of a restless, excitable, almost morbid disposition, secretly rebelled against his tyranny, and made her brother the confidant of all her griefs.   The poor mother had a terrible time of it, trying to pacify the children, and to stand between them and their father.

Very noticeable is one detail recorded by him.   He had fallen ill again ; this time with a stomach disorder, which no therapeutic treatment in the power of Frankfurt medicine seemed to mitigate.   The family physician was one of those duped dupers who still clung to the great promises of Alchemy.   It was whispered that he had in his possession a

marvellous panacea, which was only to be employed in times
of greatest need, and of which, indeed, no one dared openly
speak. Frau Aja, trembling for her son, besought him to
employ this mysterious salt. He consented. The patient
recovered, and belief in the physician's skill became more
complete. Not only was the poet thus restored once more to
health, he was also thereby led to the study of Alchemy, and,
as he narrates, employed himself in researches after the
" virgin earth." In the little study of that house in the
Hirsch-graben, he collected his glasses and retorts, and following the directions of authorities, sought, for a time, to
penetrate the mystery which then seemed so penetrable. It
is characteristic of his ardent curiosity and volatility that he
should have now devoted the long hours of study to works
such as Welling's *Opus Mago-cabbalisticum et Theosophicum*,
and the unintelligible mystifications and diatribes of Paracel-
sus. He also tried Van Helmont (an interesting though fantastic writer), Basil Valentine, and other Alchemists. These,
however, must quickly have been laid aside. They were
replaced by the *Compendium* and the *Aphorisms* of Boerhaave,
who at that period filled Europe with the sound of his name.*
Goethe's studies of these writings were valuable as preparations for *Faust;* and were not without influence on his subsequent career in science.

Renewed intercourse with Fräulein von Klettenberg, together with much theological and philosophical reading,
brought Religion into prominence in his thoughts. Paoli,
the Corsican Patriot, passed through Frankfurt at this time,

---

* So little can contemporary verdicts settle an author's position, that
Boerhaave, whose *Institutions* were thought worthy of a Commentary in
seven quartos by the great Haller, and whose *Aphorisms* were expanded
into five quartos by the illustrious Van Swieten, is now nothing but a
name.

and Goethe saw him in the house of Bethmann, the rich merchant; but, with this exception, Frankfurt presented nothing remarkable to him, and he was impatient to escape from it. His health was sufficiently restored for his father to hope that now jurisprudence could be studied with some success; and Strasburg was the university selected for that purpose.

CHAPTER IV.

STRASBURG.

HE reached Strasburg on the 2d April, 1770. He was now turned twenty, and a more magnificent youth never, perhaps, entered the Strasburg gates. Long before celebrity had fixed all eyes upon him he was likened to an Apollo; and once, when he entered a dining-room, people laid down their knives and forks to stare at the beautiful youth. Pictures and busts, even when most resembling, give but a feeble indication of that which was most striking in his appearance; they give the form of features, but not the play of features; nor are they very accurate as to the form. His features were large and liberally cut, with the fine sweeping lines of Greek art. The brow was lofty and massive, and from beneath it shone large lustrous brown eyes of marvellous beauty, their pupils seeming of almost unexampled size. The slightly aquiline nose was large and well cut. The mouth was full, with a short, arched upper lip, very sensitive and expressive. The chin and jaw were boldly proportioned; and the head rested on a handsome and muscular neck.

In stature he was rather above the middle size; but although not really tall, he had the aspect of a tall man, and is

usually so described, because his presence was very imposing.* His frame was strong, muscular, yet sensitive. While
excelling in all active sports, he was almost a barometer in
sensitiveness to atmospheric influences.

Such, externally, was the youth who descended at the
Hotel zum Geist, in Strasburg, this 2d April, and who, rid-
ding himself of the dust and *ennui* of a long imprisonment
in the diligence, sallied forth to gaze at the famous cathedral,
which made a wonderful impression on him as he came up to
it through the narrow streets. The Strasburg Cathedral not
inaptly serves as the symbol of his early German tendencies ;
and its glorious tower is always connected, in my mind, with
the brief but ardent endeavors of his Hellenic nature to
throw itself into the old German world. German his spirit
was not, but we shall see him, under the shadow of this
tower, for a moment inspired with true German enthusiasm.

His lodgings secured, — No. 80, on the south side of the
Fish Market (now called *le quai de batelier*), — he delivered
his letters of introduction, and arranged to dine at a *table-
d'hôte* kept by two maiden ladies, named Lauth, in the
Krämergasse, No. 13. The guests here were about ten in
number, mostly medical. Their president was Dr. Salzmann,
a clean old bachelor of eight-and-forty, scrupulous in his
stockings, immaculate as to his shoes and buckles, with hat
under his arm, and scarcely ever on his head, — a neat, dap-
per old gentleman, well instructed, and greatly liked by the
poet, to whom he gave excellent advice, and for whom he
found a valuable *repetent*. † In spite of the services of this

---

* Rauch, the sculptor, who made the well-known statuette of Goethe,
explained this to me as owing to his large bust and erect carriage.

† The medical student will best understand what a repetent is, if the
word be translated a *grinder ;* the university student, if the word be
translated a *coach*. The repetent prepares students by an examination,

excellent repetent, jurisprudence wearied him considerably, according to his account ; at first, however, he seems to have taken to it with some pleasure, as we learn by a letter, in which he tells Fräulein von Klettenberg a different story : "Jurisprudence begins to please me very much. Thus it is with all things as with Merseburg beer : the first time we shudder at it, and having drunk it for a week, we cannot do without it." The study of jurisprudence, at any rate, did not absorb him. Schöll has published a note-book kept during this period, which reveals an astonishing activity in desultory research.* When we remember that the society at his *table-d'hôte* was principally of medical students, we are prepared to find him eagerly throwing himself into the study of anatomy and chemistry. He attended Lobstein's lectures on anatomy, Ehrmann's clinical lectures, with those of his son on midwifery, and Spielman's on chemistry. Electricity occupied him, Franklin's great discovery having brought that subject into prominence. No less than nine works on electricity are set down in the note-book to be studied. We also see from this note-book that chromatic subjects begin to attract him, — the future antagonist of Newton was preluding in the science. Alchemy still fascinated him ; and he wrote to Fräulein von Klettenberg, assuring her that these mystical studies were his secret mistresses. With such a direction of his thoughts, and the influence of this pure, pious woman still operating upon him, we can imagine the disgust which followed his study of the *Système de la Nature*, then making so great a noise in the world. This dead and dull exposition of an atheism as superficial as it was dull, must have been every way revolting to him : irritating to his piety, and

and also by repeating and explaining in private what the professor has taught in the lecture-hall.

* *Briefe und Aufsätze von Goethe.* Herausgegeben von ADOLF SCHÖLL.

unsatisfying to his reason. Voltaire's wit and Rousseau's sarcasms he could copy into his note-book, especially when they pointed in the direction of tolerance ; but he who could read Bayle, Voltaire, and Rousseau with delight, turned from the *Système de la Nature* with scorn ; especially at a time when we find him taking the sacrament, and trying to keep up an acquaintance with the pious families to which Fräulein von Klettenberg had introduced him.   I say *trying*, because even his good-will could not long withstand their dulness and narrowness ; he was forced to give them up, and confessed so much to his friend.

In a letter of this date, he intimates that he is " so improved in knowledge of Greek, as almost to read Homer without a translation.   I am a week older ; *that*, you know, says a great deal with me, not because I do much, but many things." Among these many things, we must note his ardent search through mystical metaphysical writings for the material on which his insatiable appetite could feed.   Strange revelations in this direction are afforded by his note-book.   On one page there is a passage from Thomas à Kempis, followed by a list of mystical works to be read ; on another page, sarcastic sentences from Rousseau and Voltaire ; on a third a reference to Tauler.   The book contains an analysis of the *Phædon* of Moses Mendelssohn, contrasted with that of Plato ; and a defence of Giordano Bruno against the criticism of Bayle.

Time was not all consumed by these studies, multifarious as they were.   Lively Strasburg had its amusements, and Goethe joined his friend Salzmann in many a pleasant party. The various pleasure-grounds and public gardens were always crowded with promenaders, and there the mixture of the old national costume with modern fashions gave charming variety to the scene, and made the pretty women still more attractive.

He found himself in the presence of two sharply defined

nationalities. Alsatia, and especially Strasburg, although belonging to France, still preserved its old German character.
Eight hundred years of national life were not to be set aside
at once, when it pleased the powers, at the peace of Westphalia, to say that Alsatia should be French.   Until the middle of the eighteenth century the old German speech, costume,
and manners were so dominant, that a Frankfurter, or a
Mainzer, found himself at once at home there.   But just before the outbreak of the French Revolution the gradual influx
of officials brought about a sort of fashion in French costume.
Milliners, friseurs, and dancing-masters had done their best,
or their worst, to "polish" society.   But the surface was
rough, and did not take kindly to this polishing.   Side by side
with the French *employé*, there was the old German professor,
who obstinately declined to acquire more of the foreigners'
language than sufficed for daily needs and household matters ;
for the rest he kept sturdily Teutonic.   Even in costume the
imitation was mainly confined to the upper classes.*   Goethe
describes the maidens of the bourgeoisie still wearing their
hair in one long plait, falling behind, and their petticoats of
picturesque but perilous brevity.

Salzmann introduced him to several families, and thus more
than by all his advice helped to soften down the exuberant
expression of animal spirits which very often sinned against
quiet conventionalities; for by inducing him to frequent
society, it forced him to learn that demeanor which society
imperatively demands.   In *Wilhelm Meister* great stress is
laid upon the culture necessary to fit a man of genius for
society ; and one of the great motives advanced for the pur-
suance of a theatrical career is the facility it affords a man
of gaining address.

* STOEBER, *Der Aktuar Salzmann*, 1855, p. 7.

F

An excitable, impetuous youth, ambitious of shining in society, yet painfully conscious of the unsuitableness of his previous training for the attainment of that quietness deemed so necessary, would require to attend to every trifle which might affect his deportment.   Thus, although he had magnificent hair, he allowed the hairdresser to tie it up in a bag, and affix a false queue.   This obliged him to remain propped up powdered, from an early hour of the morning, and also to keep from overheating himself, and from violent gestures, lest he should betray the false ornament.   " This restraint contributed much towards making me for a time more gentle and polite in my bearing ; and I got accustomed to shoes and stockings, and to carrying my hat under my arm ; I did not, however, neglect wearing fine under-stockings as a protection against the Rhine gnats."   To these qualifications as a cavalier, he added those of an excellent swordsman and rider.   With his fellow-students, he had abundant exercise in the use of the rapier ; and prompted, I presume, by his restless desire to do all that his friends did, he began to learn the violoncello !

His circle of friends widened ; and even that of his fellow-boarders in the Krämergasse increased.   Among the latter, two deserve special mention, — Jung Stilling and Franz Lerse.   Stilling has preserved an account of their first meeting.*   About twenty were assembled at dinner, when a young man entered the room in high spirits, whose large, clear eyes, splendid brow, and beautifully proportioned figure irresistibly drew the attention of Troost and Stilling.   The former remarked, " That must be an extraordinary man ! "   Stilling assented ; but feared lest they might be somewhat annoyed by him, he looked such a wild, rollicking fellow.   Meanwhile they learned that this student, whose unconstrained freedom and

* STILLING's *Wanderschaft*, p. 158.

àplomb made them draw under their shells, was named Herr Goethe. Dinner proceeded. Goethe, who sat opposite Stilling, had completely the lead in conversation, without once seeking it. At length one of the company began quizzing the wig of poor Stilling; and the fun was relished by all except Troost, Salzmann, and one who, indignantly reproving them for making game of so inoffensive a person, silenced the ridicule immediately; this was none other than the large-eyed student whose appearance had excited Stilling's uneasiness. The friendship thus begun was continued by the sympathy and tender affectionateness Goethe always displayed towards the simple, earnest, and unfriended thinker, whose deep religious convictions, and trusting child-like nature, singularly interested him. Goethe was never tired of listening to the story of his life. Instinctively he sought on all sides to penetrate the mysteries of humanity, and, by probing every man's experience, to make it his own. Here was a poor charcoal-burner, who from tailoring had passed to keeping a school; that failing, he had resumed his needle; and having joined a religious sect, had, in silent communion with his own soul, gained for himself a sort of culture which raised him above the ordinary height of men: what was there in his life or opinions to captivate the riotous, sceptical, prosperous student? There was earnestness,—there was genuineness. Goethe was eminently qualified to become the friend of one who held opposite convictions to his own, for his tolerance was large and genuine, and he respected every real conviction. Sympathizing with Stilling, listening to him, and dexterously avoiding any interference with his religious faith, he was not only enabled to be his friend, but also to learn quietly and surely the inner nature of such men.

Franz Lerse attracted him by different qualities: upright manliness, scrupulous orderliness, dry humor, and a talent for reconciling antagonists. As a memorial of their friendship his name is given to the gallant fellow in *Götz von Berlichingen* who knows how to subordinate himself with dignity.

Salzmann had some years before founded a sort of club, or, as Stilling calls it, *Gesellschaft der Schönen Wissenschaften*, the object of which was to join a book-society with a debating-club. In 1763 – 64 this club had among its members no less a person than O. F. Müller, the renowned helminthologist; and now in 1770–71 it numbered, among others, Goethe, Lerse, Jung Stilling, Lenz, Weyland, and was honored by the presence of Herder, who was then writing his work on the *Origin of Language.*

Generally speaking, Goethe is so liberal in information about his friends and contemporaries, and so sparing of precise indications of his own condition, that we are left in the dark respecting much that would be welcome knowledge. There is one thing mentioned by him which is very significant : although his health was sufficiently established for ordinary purposes, he still suffered from great irritability. Loud sounds were disagreeable to him ; diseased objects aroused loathing and horror. And he was especially troubled with giddiness, which came over him whenever he looked down from a height. All these infirmities he resolved to conquer, and that somewhat violently. In the evening when they beat the tattoo, he went close to the drums, though the powerful rolling and beating of so many seemed enough to make his heart burst in his bosom. Alone he ascended the highest pinnacle of the cathedral, and sat in what is called the neck, under the crown, for a quarter of an hour before venturing to step out again into the open air. Standing on a platform scarcely an ell square, he saw before him a boundless prospect, the church and the supports of his standing-place being concealed by the ornaments. He felt exactly as if carried up in a balloon. These painful sensations he repeated until they became quite indifferent ; he subsequently derived great advantage from this conquest in mountainous excursions and geological studies. Anatomy was also of double value, as it taught him to tolerate the most repulsive sights, while satisfy-ing his thirst for knowledge. He succeeded so well, that no hideous sight could disturb his self-possession. He also sought to steel himself against the terrors of imagination. The awful and shuddering impressions of darkness in church-yards, solitary places, churches and chapels by night, he con-trived to render indifferent, — so much so, that when a desire came over him to recall in such scenes the pleasing shudder of youth, he could scarcely succeed, even by the strangest and most terrific images.

A handsome youth unable to dance was an anomaly in Strasburg. Not a Sunday evening passed without the pleas-ure-gardens being crowded with gay dancers ; galas frequently enlivened the week ; and the merry Alsatians, then as now, seldom met but they commenced spinning round in the waltz. Into these gardens, amidst these waltzers, Goethe constantly went, — yet could not waltz. He resolved at length to learn. A friend recommended him to a dancing-master of repute, who soon pronounced himself gratified with the progress made.

This master, a dry, precise, but amiable Frenchman, had two daughters, who assisted him at his lessons, acting both as partners and correctors. Two pretty girls, both under twenty, charming with French vivacity and coquetry, could not fail to interest the young poet ; nor could the graceful, handsome youth fail to create an impression on two girls whose lives were somewhat lonesome. Symptoms of this interest very soon showed themselves. The misfortune was that the state of their feelings made what dramatists call a "situation."

Goethe's heart inclined towards Emilia, who loved another; while that of Lucinda, the elder sister, was bestowed upon him. Emilia was afraid to trust herself too much with him; but Lucinda was always at hand, ready to waltz with him, to protract his lesson, or to show him little attentions. There were not many pupils; so that he often remained after his lesson to chat away the time, or to read aloud to them a romance: dangerous moments!

He saw how things stood, yet puzzled himself about the reserve of the younger sister. The cause of it came out at last. One evening, after the dance was over, Lucinda detained him in the dancing-room, telling him that her sister was in the sitting-room with a fortune-teller, who was disclosing the condition of a lover to whom the girl's heart was given. "Mine," said Lucinda, "is free, and I must get used to its being slighted."

He tried to parry this thrust by divers little compliments; and, indiscreetly enough, advised her to try her own fate with the fortune-teller, offering to do the same himself. Lucinda did not like that tampering with fate, declaring that the disclosures of the oracle were too true to be made a matter of sport. Probably this piqued him into a little more earnestness than he had shown, for ultimately he persuaded her to go into the sitting-room with him. They found Emilia much pleased with the information that she had received from tne pythoness, who was highly flattered at the new devotee to her shrine. A handsome reward was promised her if she should disclose the truth. With the customary ceremonial she began to tell the fortune of the elder sister. She hesitated. "O, I see," said Emilia, "that you have something unpleasant to tell." Lucinda turned pale, but said, "Speak out; it will not cost me my life." The fortune-teller heaved a deep sigh, and proceeded with her disclosures. Lucinda,

she said, was in love; but her love was not returned, —
another person standing in the way. And she went on with
more in the same style. It is not difficult to imagine that
the sibyl should readily enough interpret the little drama
which was then acting by the youth and two girls before
her eyes. Lucinda showed evidence of distress, and the old
woman endeavored to give a better turn to the affair by throwing out hopes of letters and money. "Letters," said Lucinda,
"I do not expect, and money I do not want. If I love as
you say, I have a right to be loved in return." The fortune-
teller shuffled the cards again, but that only made matters
worse; the girl now appeared in the oracular vision in greater
trouble, her lover at a greater distance. A third shuffle of the
cards was still worse : Lucinda burst into a passionate flood
of tears, and rushed from the room. "Follow her," said
Emilia, "and comfort her." But he hesitated, not seeing
what comfort he could well give, as he could not assure her
of some return for her affection. "Let us go together,"
he replied. Emilia doubted whether her presence would do
good; but she consented. Lucinda had locked herself
in ; and paying the old woman for her work, Goethe left the
house.

He had scarcely courage to revisit the sisters ; but on the
third day Emilia sent for him, and he received his lesson as
usual. Lucinda, however, was absent, and when he asked
for her, Emilia told him that she was in bed, declaring that
she should die. She had thrown out great reproaches against
him for his ungrateful behavior. "And yet I do not know,"
said he, "that I am guilty of having expressed any sort of
affection for her. I know somebody who can bear me witness
of that." Emilia smiled. "I comprehend," she said ; "but
if we are not careful we shall all find ourselves in a disastrous position. Forgive me if I say that you must not go on

with your lessons. My father says that he is ashamed to
take your money any longer, unless you mean to pursue the
art of dancing, since you know already what is needed by a
young man in the world." "Do you tell me to avoid the
house, Emilia?" he asked. "Yes," she said, "but not on
my own account. When you had gone the other day, I had
the cards cut for you, and the same answer was given thrice.
You were surrounded by friends, and all sorts of good fortune, but the ladies kept aloof from you: my poor sister
stood farthest of all. One other constantly came near to
you, but never close, for a third person, a man, always came
between. I will confess that I thought I was myself this
second lady, and now you will understand my advice. I
have promised myself to another, and until now I loved him
more than any one. Yet your presence might become more
dangerous to me than it has been, and then what a position
would be yours between two sisters, one of whom you would
have made miserable by your affection, and the other by your
coldness." She held out her hand and bade him farewell ;
she then led him to the door, and in token that it was to be
their last meeting, she threw herself upon his bosom and
kissed him tenderly. Just as she had put his arms round her,
a side door flew open, and her sister, in a light but decorous
dressing-gown, rushed in, crying, "You shall not be the only
one to take leave of him!" Emilia released him. Lucinda
took him in her arms, pressed her black locks against his
cheeks, remained thus for some time, and then drawing back
looked him earnestly in the face. He took her hand and
tried to muster some kind expressions to soothe her, but she
turned away, walked passionately up and down the room, and
then threw herself in great agitation into a corner of the
sofa. Emilia went up to her, but was violently repulsed, and
a scene ensued which had in it, says the principal performer,

nothing really theatrical, although it could only be represented on the stage by an actor of sensibility. Lucinda poured forth reproaches against her sister. "This," said she, "is not the first heart-beating for me that you have wheedled away. Was it not so with the one now betrothed to you, while I looked on and bore it? I, only, know the tears it cost me; and now you would rob me of this one. How many would you manage to keep at once? I am frank and easy-tempered, and all think they understand me at once, and may slight me. You are secret and quiet, and make people wonder at what may be concealed behind; there is nothing there but a cold, selfish heart, sacrificing everything to itself." Emilia seated herself by her sister, and remained silent; while Lucinda, growing more excited, began to betray matters not quite proper for him to hear. Emilia made a sign to him to withdraw; but Lucinda caught the sound, sprang towards him, and then remained lost in thought. "I know that I have lost you," she said: "I claim you no more; but neither shall you have him." So saying, she grasped him wildly by the head, with her hands thrust among his hair, pressed her face to his, and kissed him repeatedly on the mouth. "Now fear my curse! Woe upon woe, for ever and ever, to her who for the first time after me kisses these lips! Dare to sport with him now! Heaven hears my curse! And you, begone, begone while you may!"

He hurried from the house, never to return.

CHAPTER V.

HERDER AND FREDERIKA.

ONE thing very noticeable in this Strasburg period is the thoroughly German culture it gave him. In those days culture was mostly classical and French. Classical studies had never exercised much influence over him; and, indeed, throughout his career, he approached antiquity more through Art than through Literature. To the French, on the other hand, he owed a great deal, both of direction and material. A revival of the old German nationality was, however, actively agitated at this epoch. Klopstock, Lessing, Herder, Shakespeare, and Ossian were the rivals opposed to France. A feeling of national pride gave its momentum to this change in taste. Gothic art began to be considered the true art of modern times.

At the *table-d'hôte* our friends, all German, not only banished the French language, but made a point of being in every way unlike the French. French literature was ridiculed as affected, insincere, unnatural. The truth, homely strength, and simplicity of the German character were set against this literature of courtiers. Goethe had been dabbling in mediæval studies, had been awe-struck by the cathedral, had been inspired by Shakespeare, and had seen Lessing's iconoclastic wit scattering the pretensions of French poetry. Moreover, he had read the biography of *Götz von Berlichingen*, and the picture of that Titan in an age of anarchy had so impressed itself upon him, that the conception of a dramatic reproduction of it had grown up in his mind. *Faust* also lay there as a germ. The legend of that wonder-worker especially attracted him, now that he was in the condition into which youths so readily fall after a brief and unsatisfactory attempt to penetrate the mysteries of science. "Like him, too, I had swept the circle of science, and had early learned its vanity; like him, I had trodden various paths, always returning unsatisfied." The studies of alchemy, medicine, jurisprudence, philosophy, and theology, which had so long engaged him, made him feel a personal interest in the old Faust legend.

In such a mood the acquaintance with Herder was of great importance. Herder was five years his senior, and had already created a name for himself. He came to Strasburg with an eye-disease, which obliged him to remain there the whole winter, during the cure. Goethe, charmed with this new vigorous intellect, attended on him during the operation, and sat with him morning and evening during his convalescence, listening to the wisdom which fell from his lips, as a pupil listens to a much-loved master. Great was the contrast between the two men, yet the difference did not separate them. Herder was decided, clear, pedagogic; knowing his own aims, and fond of communicating his ideas. Goethe was sceptical and inquiring, Herder rude, sarcastic, and bitter; Goethe amiable and infinitely tolerant. The bitterness which repelled so many friends from Herder could not repel Goethe: it was a peculiarity of his to be at all times able to learn from antagonistic natures; meeting them on the common ground of sympathy, he avoided those subjects on which inevitably they must clash. It is somewhat curious that although Herder took a great liking to his young friend, and was grateful for his kind attentions, he seems to have had little suspicion of his genius. The only fragment we have of that period, which gives us a hint of his opinion, is in a letter to his bride, dated February, 1772: "Goethe is really a good fellow, only somewhat light and sparrow-like,* for which I

* *Nur etwas leicht und Spatzenmässig:* I translate the phrase, leaving

incessantly reproach him. He was almost the only one who visited me during my illness in Strasburg whom I saw with pleasure ; and I believe I influenced him in more ways than one to his advantage." His vanity may have stood between Goethe and himself; or he may have been too conscious of his young friend's defects to think much of his genius. " Herder, Herder," Goethe writes to him from Strasburg, " be to me what you are. If I am destined to be your planet, so will I be, and willingly and truly, a friendly moon to your earth. But you must feel that I would rather be Mercury, the last, the smallest of the seven, to revolve with you about the sun, than the first of the five which turn around Saturn." *   In his *Autobiography*, he says, that he withheld from Herder his intention of writing "Götz" ; but there is a passage in Herder's work on German Art, addressed to Goethe, which very plainly alludes to this intention. † Such oversights are inevitable in retracing the minor details of the past.

There was contrast enough between the two, in age, character, intellect, and knowledge, to have prevented any very close sympathy. Herder loved the abstract and ideal in men and things, and was forever criticising and complaining of the individual, because it did not realize the ideal standard. What Gervinus says of Herder's relation to Lessing, namely, that he loved him when he considered him as a whole, but could never cease plaguing him about details, holds good also of

---

the reader to interpret it, for twenty Germans have given twenty different meanings to the word "sparrow-like," some referring to the chattering of sparrows, others to the boldness of sparrows, others to the curiosity of sparrows, and others to the libertine character of sparrows. Whether Herder meant gay, volatile, forward, careless, or amorous, I cannot decide.

* *Aus Herder's Nachlass*, I. p. 28.
† HERDER, *Von deutschen Art und Kunst*, p. 112.

his relation to Goethe through life. Goethe had little of that love of mankind in the abstract, which to Herder and so many others seems the substitute for individual love, — which animates philanthropists who are sincere in their philanthropy, even when they are bad husbands, bad fathers, bad brothers, and bad friends. He had, instead of this, keen sympathy with individual men. His concrete and affectionate nature was more attracted to men than to abstractions. It is because his antagonists do not recognize this that they declaim against his "indifference" to political wants, to history, and to many of the great questions which affect humanity.

Herder's influence on Goethe was manifold, but mainly in the direction of poetry. He taught him to look at the Bible as a magnificent illustration of the truth that poetry is the product of a national spirit, not the privilege of a cultivated few. From the poetry of the Hebrew people he led him to other illustrations of national song, Homer and Ossian at their head. It was at this time that Ossian made the tour of Europe, and everywhere met believers. Goethe was so delighted with the wild northern singer, that he translated the song of "Selma," and afterwards incorporated it in *Werther*. Besides Shakespeare and Ossian, he also learned through Herder to appreciate the *Vicar of Wakefield;* and the exquisite picture there painted, he was now to see living in the parsonage of Frederika's father.

Upon the broad and lofty gallery of the Strasburg Cathedral he and his companions often met " to salute the setting sun with brimming goblets of Rhine wine." The calm wide landscape stretched itself for miles before them, and they pointed out the several spots which memory endeared to each. One spot, above all others, has interest for us, — Sesenheim, the home of Frederika. Of all the women who enjoyed the distinction of Goethe's love, none have been made so fascinating as Frederika.   Her idyllic presence is familiar to every lover of Geman literature, through the charming episode of the *Autobiography*, over which the poet lingered with peculiar delight.   The secretary to whom this episode was dictated, told me how much affected Goethe seemed to be as these scenes revisited memory; walking up and down the room, with his hands behind him, he often stopped in his walk, and paused in the dictation : then after a long silence, followed by a deep sigh, he continued the narrative in a lower tone.

Weyland, a fellow-boarder, had often spoke of a clergyman who, with his wife and two amiable daughters, lived near Drusenheim, a village about sixteen miles from Strasburg. Early in October, 1770, Weyland proposed to his friend to accompany him on a visit to the worthy pastor.   It was agreed between them that Weyland should introduce him under the guise of a shabby theological student.   His love of incognito often prompted him to such disguises.   In the present instance he borrowed some old clothes, and combed his hair in such a way that when Weyland saw him he burst out into a fit of laughter.   They set forth in high glee.   At Drusenheim they stopped, Weyland to make himself spruce, Goethe to rehearse his part.   Riding across the meadows to Sesenheim, they left their horses at the inn, and walked leisurely towards the parsonage, — an old and somewhat dilapidated farm-house, but very picturesque, and very still.   They found Pastor Brion at home, and were welcomed by him in a friendly manner.   The rest of the family were in the fields.   Weyland went after them, leaving Goethe to discuss parish interests with the pastor, who soon grew confidential.   Presently the wife appeared ; and she was followed by the eldest daughter bouncing into the room, inquiring after Frederika, and hurrying away again to seek her.

Refreshments were brought, and old acquaintances were talked over with Weyland, — Goethe listening.   Then the daughter returned, uneasy at not having found Frederika.   This little domestic fuss about Frederika prepared the poet for her appearance.   At length she came in.   Both girls wore the national costume, with its short, white, full skirt and fur-below, not concealing the neatest of ankles, a tight bodice and black taffeta apron.   Frederika's straw hat hung on her arm ; and the beautiful braids of her fair hair drooped on a delicate white neck.   Merry blue eyes, and a piquant little *nez retroussé* completed her attractions.   In gazing on this bright young creature, then only sixteen, Goethe felt ashamed of the disguise.   It hurt his *amour-propre* to appear thus before her like a bookish student, shorn of all personal advantages.   Meanwhile conversation rattled on between Weyland and the family.   Endless was the list of uncles, aunts, nieces, cousins, gossips, and guests they had something to say about, leaving him completely excluded from the conversation.   Frederika, seeing this, seated herself by him, and with charming frankness began to talk to him.   Music was lying on the harpsichord ; she asked him if he played, and on his modestly qualified affirmative, begged him "to favor them."   Her father, however, suggested that *she* ought to begin, by a song.   She sat down to the harpsichord, which was somewhat out of tune, and, in a provincial style, performed several pieces, such as then were thought enchanting. After this she began to sing.   The song was tender and melancholy, but she was apparently not in the mood, for, acknowledging her failure, she rose and said, "If I sing badly it is not the fault of my harpsichord nor of my teacher : let us go into the open air, and then you shall hear my Alsatian and Swiss songs."   Into the air they went, and soon her merry voice carolled forth : —

> "I come from a forest as dark as the night,
>   And believe me, I love thee, my only delight.
>   Ei ja, ei ja, ei, ei, ei, ei, ja, ja, ja!"*

He was already a captive.

His tendency to see pictures and poetry in the actual scenes of life here made him see realized the Wakefield family. If Pastor Brion did not accurately represent Mr. Primrose, yet he might stand for him; the elder daughter for Olivia, the younger for Sophia; and when at supper a youth came into the room, Goethe involuntarily exclaimed, "What, Moses, too!" A very merry supper they had; so merry that Weyland, fearing lest wine and Frederika should make his friend betray himself, proposed a walk in the moonlight. Weyland offered his arm to Salome, the elder daughter (always named *Olivia* in the *Autobiography*), Frederika took Goethe's arm. Youth and moonlight, — need one say more? Already he began to scrutinize her tone in speaking of cousins and neighbors, jealous lest it should betray an affection. But her blithe spirit was as yet untroubled, and he listened in delicious silence to her unembarrassed loquacity.

On retiring for the night the friends had much to talk over. Weyland assured him the incognito had not been betrayed; on the contrary, the family had inquired after the young Goethe, of whose joviality and eccentricities they had often heard. And now came the tremulous question: was Frederika engaged? No. That was a relief! Had she ever been in love? No. Still better! Thus chatting, they sat till deep in the night, as friends chat on such occasions, with hearts too full and brains too heated for repose. At dawn Goethe was awake, impatient to see Frederika with the dew of morning on her cheek. While dressing he looked at his

---

* The entire song is to be found in the *Sesenheimer Liederbuch*, and in VIEHOFF, *Goethe Erläutert*, Vol. I. p. 110.

costume in disgust, and tried in vain to remedy it.   His hair could be managed ; but when his arms were thrust into his threadbare coat, the sleeves of which were ludicrously short, he looked pitiable ; Weyland, peeping at him from under the coverlet, giggled.   In his despair he resolved to ride back to Strasburg, and return in his own costume.   On the way another plan suggested itself.   He exchanged clothes with the son of the landlord at the Drusenheim inn, a youth of his own size ; corked his eyebrows, imitated the son's gait and speech, and returned to the parsonage the bearer of a cake. This second disguise also succeeded, so long as he kept at a distance ; but Frederika running up to him and saying, " George, what do you here ? " he was forced to reveal himself.   " Not George, but one who asks forgiveness."   " You shocking creature ! " she exclaimed, " how you frightened me ! "   The jest was soon explained and forgiven, not only by Frederika, but by the family, who laughed heartily at it.

Gayly passed the day ; the two hourly falling deeper and deeper in love.   Passion does not chronicle by time : moments are hours, hours years, when two hearts are rushing into one.   It matters little, therefore, that the *Autobiography* speaks of only two days passed in this happy circle, whereas a letter of his says distinctly he was there "some days — *einige Tage*" (*less* than three cannot be understood by *einige*). He was there long enough to fall in love, and to captivate the whole family by his gayety, obligingness, and poetic gifts. He had given them a taste of his quality as a romancist, by telling the story of *The New Melusina* (subsequently published in the *Wanderjahre*).   He had also interested himself in the pastor's plans for the rebuilding of the parsonage, and proposed to take away the sketches with him to Strasburg.

The pain of separation was lightened by the promise of

speedy reunion. He returned to Strasburg with new life in
his heart. He had not long before written to a friend that
for the first time he knew what it was to be happy without
his heart being engaged. Pleasant people and manifold
studies left him no time for *feeling.* " Enough, my present
l fe is like a sledge journey, splendid and sounding, but with
just as little for the heart as it has much for eyes and ears."
Another tone runs through his letters now, to judge from the
only one which has been recovered.* It is addressed to
Frederika, dated the 15th October : —

" DEAR NEW FRIEND, — I *dare* to call you so ; for if I can
trust the language of eyes, then did mine in the first glance
read the hope of this new friendship in yours ; and for our
hearts I will answer. You, good and gentle as I know you,
will you not show some favor to one who loves you so ?

" Dear, dear friend : —

" That I have something to say to you there can be no
question ; but it is quite another matter whether I exactly
know wherefore I now write, and *what* I may write. Thus
much I am conscious of by a certain inward unrest, — that I
would gladly be by your side ; and a scrap of paper is as
true a consolation and as winged a steed for me here, in
noisy Strasburg, as it can be to you in your quiet, if you truly
feel the separation from your friend.

" The circumstances of our journey home you can easily
imagine, if you marked my pain at parting, and how I longed
to remain behind. Weyland's thoughts went forwards, mine
backwards ; so you can understand how our conversation
was neither interesting nor copious.

---

* SCHÖLL, *Briefe und Aufsätze*, p. 51. The letters in Pfeiffer's book
are manifest forgeries.

" At the end of the Wanzenau we thought to shorten our route, and found ourselves in the midst of a morass. Night came on ; and we only needed the storm which threatened to overtake us, to have had every reason for being fully convinced of the love and constancy of our princesses.*

" Meanwhile, the scroll which I held constantly in my hand — fearful of losing it — was a talisman, which charmed away all the perils of the journey. And now ? — O, I dare not utter it, — either you can guess it, or you will not believe it.

" At last we arrived, and our first thought, which had been our joy on the road, was the project soon to see you again.

" How delicious a sensation is the hope of seeing again those we love ! And we, when our coddled heart is a little sorrowful, at once bring it medicine and say : Dear little heart, be quiet, you will not long be away from her you love ; be quiet, dear little heart ! Meanwhile we give it a chimera to play with, and then is it good and still as a child to whom the mother gives a doll instead of the apple which it must not eat.

" Enough, we are *not* here, and so you see you were wrong. You would not believe that the noisy gayety of Strasburg would be disagreeable to me after the sweet country pleasures enjoyed with you. Never, Mamsell, did Strasburg seem so empty to me as now. I hope, indeed, it will be better when the remembrance of those charming hours is a little dimmed, — when I no longer feel so vividly how good, how amiable my friend is. Yet ought I to forget that, or to wish it ? No ; I will rather retain a little sorrow and write to you frequently.

" And now, many, many thanks and many sincere remem-

---

* An allusion doubtless intelligible to the person addressed, but I can make nothing of it.

brances to your dear parents. .To your dear sister many
hundred . . . . what I would so willingly give you again !"

A few days after his return, Herder underwent the operation previously alluded to.   Goethe was constantly with him ;
but as he carefully concealed all his mystical studies, fearing
to have them ridiculed, so one may suppose he concealed
also the new passion which deliciously tormented him.   In
silence he occupied himself with Frederika, and carefully
sketched plans for the new parsonage.   He sent her books,
and received from her a letter, which of course seemed
priceless.

In November he was again at Sesenheim.   Night had
already set in when he arrived ; his impatience would not
suffer him to wait till morning, the more so as the landlord
assured him the young ladies had only just gone home, where
" they expected some one."   He felt jealous of this expected
friend, and he hastened to the parsonage.   Great was his surprise to find them *not* surprised ; greater still to hear Frederika whisper, "Did I not say so ?   Here he is !"   Her
loving heart had prophesied his coming, and had named the
very day.

The next day was Sunday, and many guests were expected.
Early in the morning Frederika proposed a walk with him,
leaving her mother and sister to look after domestic preparations.   In that walk the youthful pair abandoned themselves
without concealment to all the delightful nothings of newly
awakened love.   They talked over the expected pleasures of
the day, and arranged how to be always together.   She
taught him several games ; he taught her others ; and underneath these innocent arrangements, Love serenely smiled.
The church bell called them from their walk.   To church they
went, and listened — not very attentively — to the worthy pas-

tor.   Another kind of devotion made their hearts devout. He meditated on her charming qualities, and as his glance rested on her ruddy lips, he recalled the last time woman's lips had been pressed to his own ; recalled the curse which the excited French girl had uttered, a curse which hitherto had acted like a spell.

This superstition not a little troubled him in games of forfeits, where kisses always form a large proportion ; and his presence of mind was often tried in the attempts to evade them ; the more so as many of the guests, suspecting the tender relation between him and Frederika, sportively took every occasion to make them kiss.   She, with natural instinct, aided him in his evasions.   The time came, however, when, carried away by the excitement of the dance and games, he felt the burning pressure of her lips crush the superstition in a

> "Kiss, a long, long kiss
> Of youth and beauty gathered into one."

He returned to Strasburg, if not a formally betrothed, yet an accepted lover.   As such the family and friends seem to have regarded him.   Probably no betrothal took place, on account of his youth, and the necessity of obtaining his father's consent.   His muse, lately silent, now found voice again, and several of the poems Frederika inspired are to be read in his published works.*

He had been sent to Strasburg to gain a doctor's degree. His Dissertation had been commenced just before this Sesenheim episode.   But Shakespeare, Ossian, *Faust*, *Götz*, and, above all, Frederika, scattered his plans, and he followed the advice of friends, to choose, instead of a Dissertation, a number of Theses, upon which to hold a disputation.   His father

---

* The whole have been reprinted in the *Sesenheimer Liederbuch* ; and in VIEHOFF's *Goethe Erläutert.*

would not hear of such a thing, but demanded a regular Dissertation. He chose, therefore, this theme, "*That it is the duty of every law-maker to establish a certain religious worship binding upon clergy and laity.*" A theme he supported by historical and philosophical arguments. The Dissertation was written in Latin, and sent to his father, who received it with pleasure. But the dean of the faculty would not receive it, — either because its contents were paradoxical, or because it was not sufficiently erudite. In lieu thereof he was permitted to choose Theses for disputation. The Disputation was held on the 6th of August, 1771, his opponent being Franz Lerse, who pressed him hard. A jovial *Schmaus*, a real students' banquet, crowned this promotion of Dr. Goethe.*

He could find no time for visits to Sesenheim during this active preparation for his doctorate ; but he was not entirely separated from Frederika : her mother had come with both daughters to Strasburg, on a visit to a rich relative. He had been for some time acquainted with this family, and had many opportunities of meeting his beloved. The girls, who came in their Alsatian costume, found their cousins and friends dressed like Frenchwomen ; a contrast which greatly vexed Olivia, who felt "like a maid-servant" among these fashionable friends. Her restless manners evidently made Goethe somewhat ashamed of her. Frederika, on the other hand, though equally out of her element in this society, was more self-possessed, and perfectly contented so long as he was by her side. There is in the *Autobiography* a significant phrase : this visit of the family is called a "peculiar test of his love." And test it was, as every one must see who considers the relations in which the lovers stood. He was the son of an im-

---

* There is some obscurity on this point. From a letter to Salzmann, it seems he only got a licentiate degree at this time. The doctorate he certainly had ; but *when* his diploma was prepared is not known.

portant Frankfurt citizen, and held almost the position of a
nobleman in relation to the poor pastor's daughter. Indeed,
the social disparity was so great, that many explain his not
marrying Frederika on the ground of such a match being
impossible, — "his father," it is said, "would not have listened to such a thing for a moment." Love in nowise troubles
itself about station, never asks, "What will the world say?"
but there is quite a different solicitude felt by Love when approaching Marriage.   In the first eagerness of passion a
prince may blindly pursue a peasant, but when his love is
gratified by return, when reflection reasserts its duties, then
the prince will consider what will be the estimation of his
mistress in other minds.   Men are very sensitive to the opinions of others on their mistresses and wives, and Goethe's
love must indeed have been put to the test, on seeing Frederika and her sister thus in glaring contrast with the society in
which he moved.   In the groves of Sesenheim she was a
wood-nymph, but in Strasburg *salons* the wood-nymph seemed
a peasant.   Who is there that has not experienced a similar
destruction of illusion, in seeing an admired person lose almost all charm in the change of environment?

Frederika laid her sweet commands on him one evening,
and bade him entertain the company by reading *Hamlet* aloud.
He did so, to the great enjoyment of all, especially Frederika,
"who from time to time sighed deeply, and a passing color
tinged her cheeks." Was she thinking of poor Ophelia, —
placing herself in that forlorn position?

> "For Hamlet and the trifling of his favor,
> Hold it a fashion and a toy in blood!"

She may have had some presentiment of her fate. The applause, however, which her lover gained was proudly accepted
by her, "and in her graceful manner she did not deny herself
the little pride of having shone through him."

The mention of *Hamlet* leads us naturally into the society where he sought oblivion, when Frederika quitted Strasburg. Her departure, he confesses, was a *relief* to him. She herself felt on leaving that the end of their romance was approaching. He plunged into gayety to drown tormenting thoughts. " If you could but see me," he wrote to Salzmann, after describing a dance which had made him forget his fever : " my whole being was sunk in dancing. And yet could I but say, I am happy ; that would be better than all. 'Who is't can say I am at the worst?' says Edgar (in *Lear*). That is some comfort, dear friend. My heart is like a weathercock when a storm is rising, and the gusts are changeable." Some days later he wrote : " All is not clear in my soul. I am too curiously awake not to feel that I grasp at shadows. And yet . . . . To-morrow at seven my horse is saddled, and then adieu ! "

Besides striving to drown in gayety these tormenting thoughts, he also strove to divert them into channels of nobler activity; stimulated thereto by the Shakespearian fanaticism of his new friend Lenz.

Reinhold Lenz, irrevocably forgotten as a poet, whom a vain effort on the part of Gruppe has tried to bring once more into public favor,* is not without interest to the student of German literature during the *Sturm und Drang* period. He came to Strasburg in 1770, accompanying two young noblemen as their tutor, and mingling with them in the best society of the place; and, by means of Salzmann, was introduced to the Club. Although he had begun by translating Pope's *Essay on Criticism*, he was, in the strictest sense of the word, one of the Shakespeare bigots, who held to the severest orthodoxy on Shakespeare as a first article of their creed, and who not only maintained the Shakespeare clowns to be incom-

* Gruppe, *Reinhold Lenz, Leben und Werke,* 1861.

parable, but strove to imitate them in their language.   Many
an extravagant jest and many an earnest discussion served to
vary the hours.   It is not easy for us to imagine the effect
which the revelation of such a mind as Shakespeare's must
have produced on the young Germans.   His profundity of
thought, originality and audacity of language, his beauty,
pathos, sublimity, his wit and overflowing humor, and the
accuracy of his observation as well as depth of insight into
the mysteries of passion and character, were qualities which
no false criticism, and, above all, no national taste, prevented
Germans from appreciating.   It was very different in France.
There an established form of art, with which national pride
was identified, and an established set of critical rules, upon
which Taste securely rested, necessarily made Shakespeare
appear like a Cyclops of Genius, — a monster, though of
superhuman proportions.   Frenchmen could not help being
shocked at many things in Shakespeare ; yet even those who
were most outraged, were also most amazed at the pearls to
be found upon the dunghill.   In Germany the pearls alone
were seen.   French taste had been pitilessly ridiculed by
Lessing.   The French Tragedy had been contrasted with
Shakespeare, and pronounced unworthy of comparison.   To
the Germans, therefore, Shakespeare was a standard borne by
all who combated against France, and his greatness was
recognized with something of wilful preference.   The state
of German literature also rendered his influence the more
prodigious.   Had Shakespeare been first revealed to *us* when
Mr. Hayley was the great laureate of the age, we should have
felt something of the eagerness with which the young and
ardent minds of Germany received this greatest poet of all
ages.

Three forms rise up from out the many influences of Strasburg into distinct and memorable importance, — Frederika, —

Herder, the Cathedral. A charming woman, a noble thinker, and a splendid monument, were his guides into the regions of Passion, Poetry, and Art. The influence of the cathedral was great enough to make him write the little tractate on German architecture, *D. M. Erwini à Steinbach ;* the enthusiasm of which was so incomprehensible to him in after years, that he was with difficulty persuaded to reprint the tractate among his works. Do we not see here — as in so many other traits — how different the youth is from the child and man ?

Inasmuch as in England many professed admirers of architecture appear imperfectly acquainted with the revival of the taste for Gothic art, it may not be superfluous to call attention to the fact that Goethe was among the very first to recognize the peculiar beauty of that style, at a period when classical, or pseudo-classical taste was everywhere dominant. It appears that he was in friendly correspondence with Sulpiz Boisserée, the artist who made the restored design of the Cologne Cathedral ; from whom he doubtless learned much. And we see by the *Wahlverwandtschaften* that he had a portfolio of designs illustrative of the principle of the pointed style. This was in 1809, when scarcely any one thought of the Gothic ; long before Victor Hugo had written his *Notre Dame de Paris ;* long before Pugin and Ruskin had thrown their impassioned energy into this revival ; at a time when the church in Langham Place was thought beautiful, and the Temple Church was considered an eyesore.

And now he was to leave Strasburg, — to leave Frederika. Much as her presence had troubled him of late, in her absence he only thought of her fascinations. He had not ceased to love her, though he already felt she never would be his. He went to say adieu. "Those were painful days, of which I remember nothing. When I held out my hand to her from my horse, the tears were in her eyes, and I felt sad at heart. As I rode along the footpath to Drusenheim a strange fantasy took hold of me. I saw in my mind's eye my own figure riding towards me, attired in a dress I had never worn, — pike-gray with gold lace. I shook off this fantasy, but eight years afterwards I found myself on the very road, going to visit Frederika, and that too in the very dress which I had seen myself in, in this phantasm, although my wearing it was quite accidental." The reader will probably be somewhat sceptical respecting the dress, and will suppose that this prophetic detail was afterwards transferred to the vision by the imagination of later years.*

---

* The correspondence with the Fräu von Stein contains a letter written by him a day or two after this visit, but, singularly enough, *no* mention of this coincidence.

BOOK THE THIRD.

1771 TO 1775.

———◆———

CHAPTER I.

DR. GOETHE'S RETURN.

ON the 25th or 28th of August, 1771, he quitted Strasburg. His way led through Mannheim; and there he was
first thrilled by the beauty of ancient masterpieces, some of
which he saw in plaster-cast. Whatever might be his predi-
lection for Gothic Art, he could not view these casts without
feeling himself in presence of an Art in its way also divine;
and his previous study of Lessing lent a peculiar interest to
the Laokoön group, now before his eyes.

Passing on to Mainz he fell in with a young wandering
harpist, and invited the ragged minstrel to Frankfurt, promising him a lodging in his father's house. It was lucky that
he thought of acquainting his mother with this invitation.
Alarmed at its imprudence, she secured a lodging in the
town, and so the boy wanted neither shelter nor patronage.

Rath Goethe was not a little proud of the young Doctor.
He was also not a little disturbed by the young Doctor's manners; and often shook his ancient respectable head at opinions which exploded like bombshells in the midst of quiet
circles. Doctoral gravity was but slightly attended to by this
young hero of the *Sturm und Drang.* The revolutionary
movement known by the title of the *Storm and Stress* was
then about to astonish Germany, and to startle all conventions, by works such as Gerstenberg's *Ugolino*, Goethe's

Götz von Berlichingen, and Klinger's *Sturm und Drang* (from whence the name). The wisdom and extravagance of that age united in one stream : the masterly criticisms of Lessing, — the enthusiasm for Shakespeare, — the mania for Ossian and the northern mythology, — the revival of ballad literature, — and imitations of Rousseau, — all worked in one rebellious current against established authority. There was one universal shout for Nature. With the young, Nature seemed to be a compound of volcanoes and moonlight ; her force explosion, her beauty sentiment. To be insurgent and sentimental, explosive and lachrymose, were the true signs of genius. Everything established was humdrum. Genius, abhorrent of humdrum, would neither spell correctly, nor write correctly, nor demean itself correctly. It would be *German,* — lawless, rude, and natural. Lawless it was, and rude it was, — but natural? Not according to Nature of any reputable type.

It is not easy, in the pages of the *Autobiography,* to detect in Goethe an early leader of the *Sturm und Drang ;* but it is easy enough to detect this in other sources. Here is a glimpse, in a letter from Mayer of Lindau (one of the Strasburg set) to Salzmann, worth chapters of the *Autobiography* on such a point. " *O Corydon, Corydon, quæ te dementia cepit !* According to the chain in which our ideas are linked together, *Corydon* and *dementia* put me in mind of the extravagant Goethe. He is still at Frankfurt, is he not ? "

That such a youth, whose wildness made friends nickname him the " bear " and the " wolf," could have been wholly pleasing to his steady, formal father, is not to be expected. Yet the worthy sire was not a little proud of his son's attainments. The verses, essays, notes, and drawings which had accumulated during the residence in Strasburg were very gratifying to him. He began to arrange them with scrupulous neatness, hoping to see them shortly published. But the poet had a virtue, perhaps of all virtues the rarest in youthful writers, — a reluctance to appear in print. Seeing, as we daily see, the feverish alacrity with which men accede to that extremely imaginary constraint, the " request of friends," and dauntlessly rush into print, — seeing the obstinacy with which they cling to all they have written, and insist on what they have written being printed, — Goethe's reluctance demands an explanation. And, if I may interpret according to my own experience, the explanation is, that his delight in composition was rather the pure delight of intellectual activity, than a delight in the result : delight, not in the *work*, but in the *working*. Thus, no sooner had he finished a poem than his interest in it began to fade ; and he passed on to another. Thus it was that he left so many works fragments, his interest having been exhausted before the whole was completed.

He had a small circle of literary friends to whom he communicated his productions, and this was publication enough for him. We shall see him hereafter, in Weimar, writing solely for a circle of friends, and troubling himself scarcely at all about a public. It was necessary for him to occupy himself with some work which should absorb him, as *Götz* did at this time, for only in work could he forget the pain, almost remorse, which followed his renunciation of Frederika. If at Strasburg he had felt that an end was approaching to this sweet romance, at Frankfurt, among family connections, and with new prospects widening before him, he felt it still more. He wrote to her. Unhappily that letter is not preserved. It would have made clear much that is now conjectural. " Frederika's answer," he says, " to the letter in which I had bidden her adieu, tore my heart. I now, for the first time, became aware of her bereavement, and saw no possibility of alleviating it. She was ever in my thoughts ;

I felt that she was wanting to me ; and, worst of all, I could not forgive myself!   Gretchen had been taken from me ; Annchen had left me ; but now, for the first time, I was guilty ; I had wounded, to its very depths, one of the most beautiful and tender of hearts.   And that period of gloomy repentance, bereft of the love which had so invigorated me, was agonizing, insupportable.   But man will live ; and hence I took a sincere interest in others, seeking to disentangle their embarrassments, and to unite those about to part, that they might not feel what I felt.   Hence I got the name of the ' Confidant,' and also, on account of my wanderings, I was named the ' Wanderer.'   Under the broad open sky, on the heights or in the valleys, in the fields and through the woods, my mind regained some of its calmness.   I almost lived on the road, wandering between the mountains and the plains.   Often I went, alone or in company, right through my native city as though I were a stranger in it, dining at one of the great inns in the High Street, and after dinner pursuing my way.   I turned more than ever to the open world and to Nature ; there alone I found comfort.   During my walks I sang to myself strange hymns and dithyrambs.   One of these, the *Wanderer's Sturmlied*, still remains.   I remember singing it aloud in an impassioned style amid a terrific storm. The burden of this rhapsody is that a man of genius must walk resolutely through the storms of life, relying solely on himself" ; a burden which seems to give expression to what he then felt respecting his relation to Frederika.

Although we have no exact knowledge of the circum- stances, from the height of which to judge his conduct, the question must be put, Why did he not marry Frederika?   It is a question often raised, and as often sophistically answered. By one party he is angrily condemned ; disingenuously ab- solved by another.   But he himself acknowledged his fault.

He himself never put forth any excuse. He does not hint at disparity of station, he does not say there were objections from his parents. He makes *no* excuse, but confesses the wrong, and blames himself without sophistication. Yet the excuses he would not suggest, partisans have been eager to suggest for him. Some have sought far and wide in the gutters of scandal for materials of defence. One gets up a story about Frederika being seduced by a Catholic priest; whence it is argued that Goethe could not be expected to marry one so frail; whence also it follows, by way of counterblast, that it was *his* desertion which caused her fall.* The basis of fact on which this lie is reared (there is usually some basis, even for the wildest lies), is that Frederika brought up the orphan child of her sister Salome.

Let me endeavor, without sophistication, to state the case, at least as far as the imperfect evidence admits of a judgment. It seems to have been forgotten by most writers who have discussed this topic, that our judgment is misled by the artistic charm which Goethe has thrown over the narrative : we fail to separate the Fact from the Fiction ; we read the poem he has made up from his early experience, and read it as if the poem were an unvarnished record of that experience. He has painted Frederika so charmingly ; he has told the story of their simple youthful love with so much grace, and quiet emotion ; he has made us believe so entirely in the Idyl, that our sympathies are rudely disturbed when we find the Idyl is not to end in a marriage.

But if we consider the case calmly, divesting it, as much as possible, of the illusive suggestions of romance, we may, perhaps, come to the conclusion, that it was, after all, only a "love affair" between a boy and a girl, a temporary fascina-

* Strangely enough, although Goethe read the MS. in which Näke repeats this story, he takes no notice of it.

tion, such as often stirs the affections of youth, without deepening into serious thought of marriage. Doubtless the reader can from his or her own history rapidly recall such an experience; certainly the experience of their friends will supply such cases. If we read the story in this light all is clear. The boy and girl are fascinated by each other; they look into each other's eyes, and are happy; they walk together, talk together, and, when separated, think of each other. But they never think of marriage; or think of it vaguely as a remote contingency. Young love's dream is enough for them. They are pained at parting; perhaps all the more so, because they dimly feel that the awakening is at hand. But there is a sort of tacit understanding that marriage is not the issue to be looked for. Had any one hinted to either Goethe or Frederika that their passion was but a "youthful stirring of the blood," and not an eternal union of souls, they would assuredly have resented it with emphatic denial. Yet so it was. Goethe soon consoled himself; and there is positive evidence that Frederika, shortly afterwards, allowed herself to be consoled by Lenz.

Such, after mature deliberation, I believe to have been the real story. When in old age Goethe, reviewing the pleasant dreams of youth, and weaving them into an artistic narrative, avowedly half fiction, came to that episode with Frederika, he thought of it as we all think of our early loves, with a mingled tenderness and pain; his imagination was kindled, and he turned his experience into a poem. But the fact thus idealized was a very ordinary fact; the story thus poetized was a very common story, and could be told by ninety out of every hundred students, who do *not* marry the idol of the last university term. That Goethe, with his affectionate, sensitive nature, was for a time in love with Frederika, is possible. It is certain that whatever the agitation of his

feelings, they were not *deeply* moved ; she had laid no firm
hold of his soul ; there were none of those ties between
them which grow stronger with advancing time.

No sooner had he made this decisively clear to himself,
than he wrote to Frederika to tell her so.   No woman can be
given up without feeling pain, and probably Frederika's affections were far more deeply engaged than his were ; nevertheless, in spite of the pain she doubtless felt, and patheti-
cally expressed in her letter to him, we find her presently
engaged in another "love affair," with the poet Lenz, which,
though it ended in a breach, certainly went so far as the
exchange of vows ; and, according to Lenz, the growth of
the passion was rapid.   "It was with us both," he writes to
his friend, "as with Cæsar : *veni, vidi, vici.* Through unconscious causes grew our confidence, — and now it is sworn,
and indissoluble."   When, in after years, Goethe visited
Frederika, she—having long given up Lenz, whose madness must have made her rejoice in her escape — told him
of Lenz having pretended to be in love with her, but omitted
to say anything about her own reciprocity ; and she omitted
this from motives which every woman will appreciate.   But
however obscure the story may be, it seems certain that at
least for a short time she believed in and returned Lenz's
passion.*

After this exposition of what I conceive to be the real
case, it will be easy to answer the outcry of the sentimentalists against Goethe's "faithlessness" and his "cruel treatment of Frederika," without recurring to the excuses sometimes put forth, that to have been faithful to her he must have
been faithless to his genius ; and that it was better one
woman's heart should be broken (which it was *not*) than that

* For full details see GRUPPE, *Reinhold Lenz, Leben und Werke,*
1861, pp. 11, *seq.*

the poet's experience should be narrowed within the small circle of domestic life. It is a mistake to speak of faithlessness at all. We may regret that he did not feel the serious affection which would have claimed her as a wife; we may upbraid him for the thoughtlessness with which he encouraged the sentimental relation; but he was perfectly right to draw back from an engagement which he felt his love was not strong enough properly to fulfil. It seems to me that he acted a more moral part in relinquishing her, than if he had swamped this lesser in a greater wrong, and escaped one breach of faith by a still greater breach of faith, — a reluctant, because unloving, marriage. The thoughtlessness of youth, and the headlong impetus of passion, frequently throw people into rash engagements; and in these cases the *formal* morality of the world, more careful of externals than of truth, declares it to be nobler for such rash engagements to be kept, even when the rashness is felt by the engaged, than that a man's honor should be stained by a withdrawal. The letter thus takes precedence of the spirit. To satisfy this prejudice a life is sacrificed. A miserable marriage rescues the honor; and no one throws the burden of that misery upon the prejudice. I am not forgetting the necessity of being stringent against the common thoughtlessness of youth in forming such relations; but I say that this thoughtlessness once having occurred, reprobate it as we may, the pain which a separation may bring had better be endured, than evaded by an unholy marriage, which cannot come to good.

Frederika herself must have felt so too, for never did a word of blame escape her; and we shall see how affectionately she welcomed him, when they met after the lapse of years. This, however, does not absolve him from the blame of having thoughtlessly incurred the responsibility of her affection. That blame he must bear. The reader will apportion it according as he estimates the excuses of temperament, and the common thoughtlessness of youth in such matters.

Although I think Goethe's conduct in this matter perfectly upright, and justifiable from a far more serious point of view than that of being faithful to his genius, I am not at all disposed to acquiesce in the assumption that marriage with Frederika would have crippled his genius by narrowing his sympathies. The cause of his relinquishing her was the want of a sufficiently powerful love ; and that also is his justification. Had he loved her enough to share a life with her, his experience of woman might have been less extensive, but it would assuredly have gained an element it wanted. It would have been deepened. He had experienced, and he could paint (no one better) the exquisite devotion of woman to man ; but he had scarcely ever felt the peculiar tenderness of man for woman, when that tenderness takes the form of vigilant protecting fondness. He knew little, and that not until late in life, of the subtle interweaving of habit with affection, which makes life saturated with love, and love itself become dignified through the serious aims of life. He knew little of the exquisite *companionship* of two souls striving in emulous spirit of loving rivalry to become better. to become wiser, teaching each other to soar. He knew little of this ; and the kiss he feared to press upon the loving lips of Frederika, and the life of sympathy he refused to share with her, are wanting to the greatness of his works.

In such a mood as that which followed the rupture with Frederika, it is not wonderful if Frankfurt and the practice of law were odious to him. Nothing but hard work could do him good : and he worked hard. From the Herder Correspondence it appears that he read Greek writers with some eagerness, his letters being studded with citations fron Plato, Homer and Pindar. *Die Griechen sind mein einzig Studium,*

he says. We find him also working at *Götz von Berlichingen.*
Gothic Art, a kindred subject, occupies him, and from thence,
by an easy transition, he passes to the Bible, to study it anew.
The results of this study are seen in two little tractates published in 1773, one called *Brief des Pastor's zu*** an den
neuen Pastor zu****; the other, *Zwo wichtige bisher unerörtete
biblische Fragen, zum erstenmal gründlich beantwortet von einem
Landgeistlichen in Schwaben.*   The influence of Fräulein von
Klettenberg is traceable in the religious sentiment of these
works ; while his own affectionate nature speaks in the tolerance preached.   Of the two Biblical questions, one goes to
prove that it was not the ten commandments which stood on
the tables of Moses, but ten laws of the Israelitish-Jehovah
covenant.   The second is an answer, by no means clear, to
the question : " What is it to speak with tongues ? " which he
explains as a " speech of the Spirit, more than pantomime,
and yet inarticulate."

The *Frankfurter Gelehrten Anzeigen* was a point of reunion,
bringing Goethe into relation with many persons of ability.
It also afforded him an opportunity of exercising himself in
criticism.   Thirty-five of the articles he wrote for this journal have been collected into his works, where the curious
student will seek them.   In these studies the time flew
swiftly. He had recommenced horse and sword exercise, and
Klopstock having made skating illustrious, it soon became an
amusement of which he was never tired ; all day long and
deep into the night he was to be seen wheeling along ; and
as the full moon rose above the clouds over the wide noc-
turnal fields of ice, and the night wind rushed at his face,
and the echo of his movements came with ghostly sound
upon his ear, he seemed to be in Ossian's world.   Indoors
there were studies and music. " Will you ask my violoncello-
master," he writes to Salzmann, " if he still has the sonatas

for two basses, which I played with him, and if so, send them to me as quickly as convenient? I practise this art somewhat more earnestly than before. As to my other occupations, you will have gathered from my drama (*Götz*) that the purposes of my soul are becoming more earnest."

It has before been hinted that *Sturm und Drang*, as it manifested itself in the mind and bearing of the young doctor, was but very moderately agreeable to the old Rath Goethe ; and whatever sympathy we may feel with the poet, yet, as we are all parents, or hope to be, let us not permit our sympathy to become injustice ; let us admit that the old Rath had considerable cause for parental uneasiness, and let us follow the son to Wetzlar without flinging any hard words at his father.

CHAPTER II.

WETZLAR.

In the spring of 1772 he arrived at Wetzlar with *Götz* in his portfolio, and in his head many wild, unruly thoughts. In Wetzlar there were two buildings interesting above all others to us, — the Imperial Court of Justice, and *Das Teutsche Haus*. The Imperial Court was a Court of Appeal for the whole empire, a sort of German Chancery. In no country does Chancery move with railway speed, and in Germany even the railways are slow. Such a chaotic accumulation of business as this Wetzlar *Kammergericht* presented, was perhaps never seen before. Twenty thousand cases lay undecided on Goethe's arrival, and there were but seventeen lawyers to dispose of them. About sixty was the utmost they could get through in a year, and every year brought more

than double that number to swell the heap. Some cases had
lingered through a century and a half, and still remained far
from a decision.   This was not a place to impress the sincere
and eminently practical mind of Goethe with a high idea of
Jurisprudence.

Das Teutsche Haus was one of the remnants of the ancient
institution of the *Teutsche Ritter*, or Teutonic Order of
Knighthood, celebrated in German mediæval history.   The
student is familiar with the black armor and white mantles
of these warrior-priests, who fought with the zeal of mission-
aries and the terrible valor of knights, conquering for themselves a large territory, and still greater influence.   But it
fared with them as with the knights of other Orders.   Their
strength lay in their zeal ; their zeal abated with success.
Years brought them increasing wealth, but the spiritual
wealth and glory of their cause departed.   They became
what all corporations inevitably become ; and at the time
now written of they were reduced to a level with the knights
of Malta.   The Order still possessed property in various
parts of Germany, and in certain towns there was a sort of
steward's house, where rents were collected and the business
of the Order transacted ; this was uniformly styled *das Teutsche Haus*.   There was such a one in Wetzlar ; and the *Amtmann*, or steward, who had superintendence over it, was a
certain Herr Buff, on whom the reader is requested to fix his
eye, not for any attractiveness of Herr Buff, intrinsically considered, but for the sake of his eldest daughter, Charlotte.
She is the heroine of this Wetzlar episode.

Nor was this house the only echo of the ancient Ritter-
thum in Wetzlar.   Goethe, on his arrival, found there another
and more consciously burlesque parody, in the shape of a
Round Table and its Knights, bearing such names as St.
Amand the Opinionative, Eustace the Prudent, Lubormirsky

the Combative, and so forth. It was founded by August
Friedrich von Goué, secretary to the Brunswick Embassy, of
whom we shall hear more : a wild and whimsical fellow, not
without a streak of genius, who drank himself to death.   He
bore the title of Ritter Coucy, and christened Goethe "*Götz
von Berlichingen der Redliche,* — Götz the Honest."

Of this Round Table and its buffooneries, Goethe has
merely told us that he entered heartily into the fun at first,
but soon wearying of it, relapsed into his melancholy fits.   A
description of him, written by Kestner at this period, is very
interesting, as it gives us faithfully the impression he produced on his acquaintances before celebrity had thrown its
halo round his head, and dazzled the perceptions of his admirers : —

" In the spring there came here a certain Goethe, by trade *
a *Doctor Juris,* twenty-three years old, only son of a very
rich father ; in order — this was his father's intention — that
he might get some experience in *praxi,* but according to his
own intention, that he might study Homer, Pindar, etc., and
whatever else his genius, his manner of thinking, and his
heart might suggest to him.

"At the very first the *beaux esprits* here announced him to
the public as a colleague, and as a collaborator in the new
Frankfurt *Gelehrte Zeitung,* parenthetically also as a philosopher, and gave themselves trouble to become intimate with
him.   As I do not belong to this class of people, or rather
am not so much in general society, I did not know Goethe
until later, and quite by accident.   One of the most distinguished of our *beaux esprits,* the Secretary of Legation
Gotter, persuaded me one day to go with him to the village
of Garbenheim, — a common walk.   There I found him on

---

* *Seiner Handthierung nack.* The word is old German, and now fallen
out of use, although the verb *handthieren* is still occasionally used.

the grass, under a tree, lying on his back, while he talked to
some persons standing around him, — an epicurean philosopher (von Goué, a great genius), a stoic philosopher (von
Kielmansegge), and a hybrid between the two (Dr. König) —
and thoroughly enjoyed himself. He was afterwards glad that
I had made his acquaintance under such circumstances.
Many things were talked of, — some of them very interesting.
This time, however, I formed no other judgment concerning
him than that he was no ordinary man. You know that I do
not judge hastily. I found at once that he had genius, and a
lively imagination ; but this was not enough to make me estimate him highly.

"Before I proceed further, I must attempt a description of
him, as I have since learned to know him better. He has a
great deal of talent, is a true genius, and a man of character ;
possesses an extraordinarily vivid imagination, and hence generally expresses himself in images and similes. He often
says, himself, that he always speaks figuratively, and can
never express himself literally ; but that when he is older he
hopes to think and say the thought itself as it really is. He
is ardent in all his affections, and yet has often great power
over himself. His manner of thinking is noble : he is so free
from prejudices that he acts as it seems good to him, without
troubling himself whether it will please others, whether it is
the fashion, whether conventionalism allows it. All constraint is odious to him.

"He is fond of children, and can occupy himself with
them very much. He is *bizarre*, and there are several things
in his manners and outward bearing which might make him
disagreeable. But with children, women, and many others,
he is nevertheless a favorite. He has a great respect for the
female sex. In *principiis* he is not yet fixed, and is still
striving after a sure system. To say something of this, he

5 *

has a high opinion of Rousseau, but is not a blind worshipper of him.   He is not what is called orthodox.   Still
this is not out of pride or caprice, or for the sake of
making himself a *rôle*.   On certain important subjects he
opens himself to few, and does not willingly disturb the contentment of others in their own ideas.   It is true he hates
scepticism, strives after truth and after conviction on certain main points, and even believes that he is already convinced as to the weightiest ; but, as far as I have observed,
he is not yet so.   He does not go to church or to the sacrament, and prays seldom.   For, says he, I am not hypocrite
enough for that.   Sometimes he seems in repose with regard
to certain subjects, sometimes just the contrary.   He vener-
ates the Christian religion, but not in the form in which it is
presented by our theologians.   He believes in a future life,
in a better state of existence.   He strives after truth, yet
values the feeling of truth more than the demonstration.   He
has already done much, and has many acquirements, much
reading ; but he has thought and reasoned still more.   He
has occupied himself chiefly with the *belles lettres* and the fine
arts, or rather with all sorts of knowledge, except that which
wins bread."

On the margin of this rough draught, Kestner adds : " I
wished to describe him, but it would be too long a business,
for there is much to be said about him.   In one word, *he is a
very remarkable man.*"

In conjunction with Gotter the young poet translated
Goldsmith's *Deserted Village*, though he speaks slightingly
of his share in it.   Through Gotter's representations he
was also persuaded to publish some little poems in Boie's
Annual.

It was a period of deep unrest in Europe, — the travail of
the French Revolution.   In Germany the spirit of the Revolu-

tion issued from the study and the lecture-hall; it was a
literary and philosophic insurrection, with Lessing, Klopstock, Kant, Herder, and Goethe for leaders.   Authority
was everywhere attacked, because everywhere it had shown
itself feeble or tyrannous.   The majestic peruke of Louis
XIV. was lifted by an audacious hand, which thus revealed
the baldness so long concealed.   No one then believed in
that Grand Monarque; least of all Goethe, who had *Götz
von Berlichingen* in his portfolio, and to whom Homer and
Shakespeare were idols.   " Send me no more books," writes
Werther, " I will no longer be led, incited, spurred by them.
There is storm enough in this breast.   I want a cradle-mel-
ody, and that I have in all its fulness in Homer.   How
often do I lull with it my raging blood to rest!"   The Kestner correspondence proves, what before was known, that
Werther is full of biography, and that Goethe was then
troubled with fits of depression following upon days of the
wildest animal spirits.   He was fond of solitude; and the
lonely hours passed in reading, or making sketches of the
landscape in his rough imperfect style.

The image which was to supplant that of Frederika was
none other than of the Charlotte Buff, before mentioned.
Two years before his arrival, her mother had died.   The
care of the house and children devolved upon her; she was
only sixteen, yet good sense, housewifely aptitude, and
patient courage carried her successfully through this task.
She had for two years been betrothed to Kestner, secretary
to the Hanoverian Legation, then aged four-and-twenty: a
quiet, orderly, formal, rational, cultivated man, possessing
great magnanimity, as the correspondence proves, and a
dignity which is in nowise represented in the Albert of *Werther*, from whom we must be careful to distinguish him, in spite
of the obvious identity of position.   How Goethe came to know

Kestner has already been seen ; how he came to know Lotte may now be told.* The reader with *Werther* in hand may compare the narrative there given with this extract from Kestner's letter to a friend, " It happened that Goethe was at a ball in the country where my maiden and I also were. I could only come late, and was forced to ride after them. My maiden, therefore, drove there in other society. In the carriage was Dr. Goethe, who here first saw Lottchen. He has great knowledge, and has made Nature in her physical and moral aspects his principal study, and has sought the true beauty of both. No woman here had pleased him. Lottchen at once fixed his attention. She is young, and although not regularly beautiful, has a very attractive face. Her glance is as bright as a spring morning, and especially it was so that day, for she loves dancing. She was gay, and in quite a simple dress. He noticed her feeling for the beauty of Nature, and her unforced wit, — rather humor than wit. He did not know she was betrothed. I came a few hours later ; and it is not our custom in public to testify anything beyond friendship to each other. He was excessively gay (this he often is, though at other times melancholy) ; Lottchen quite fascinated him, the more so because she took no trouble about it, but gave herself wholly to the pleasure of the moment. The next day, of course, Goethe called to inquire after her. He had seen her as a lively girl, fond of dancing and pleasure ; he now saw her under another and a better aspect, — in her domestic quality."

To judge from her portrait, Lotte must, in her way, have been a charming creature : not intellectually cultivated, not poetical, — above all, not the sentimental girl described by *Werther ;* but a serene, calm, joyous, open-hearted German

* Lotte and Lottchen, it is perhaps not altogether superfluous to add, are the favorite diminutives of Charlotte.

maiden, an excellent housewife, and a priceless manager. Goethe at once fell in love with her. An extract from Kestner's account will tell us more. After describing his engagement to Lotte, he adds : "She is not strictly a brilliant beauty, according to the common opinion ; to me she is one : she is, notwithstanding, the fascinating maiden who might have hosts of admirers, old and young, grave and gay, clever and stupid, etc. But she knows how to convince them quickly that their only safety must be sought in flight or in friendship. One of these, as the most remarkable, I will mention, because he retains an influence over us. A youth in years (twenty-three), but in knowledge, and in the development of his mental powers and character, already a man, an extraordinary genius, and a man of character, was here, — as his family believed, for the sake of studying the law, but in fact to track the footsteps of Nature and Truth, and to study Homer and Pindar. He had no need to study for the sake of a maintenance. Quite by chance, after he had been here some time, he became acquainted with Lottchen, and saw in her his ideal : he saw her in her joyous aspect, but was soon aware that this was not her best side ; he learned to know her also in her domestic position, and, in a word, became her adorer. It could not long remain unknown to him that she could give him nothing but friendship ; and her conduct towards him was admirable. Our coincidence of taste, and a closer acquaintance with each other, formed between him and me the closest bond of friendship. Meanwhile, although he was forced to renounce all hope in relation to Lottchen, and *did* renounce it, yet he could not, with all his philosophy and natural pride, so far master himself as completely to repress his inclination. And he has qualities which might make him dangerous to a woman, especially to one of susceptibility and taste. But Lottchen knew how to

treat him so as not to encourage vain hope, and yet make
him admire her manner towards him. His peace of mind
suffered : there were many remarkable scenes, in which
Lottchen's behavior heightened my regard for her ; and he
also became more precious to me as a friend ; but I was
often inwardly astonished that love can make such strange
creatures even of the strongest and otherwise the most self-
sustained men. I pitied him, and had many inward struggles ; for, on the one hand, I thought that I might not be in
a position to make Lottchen so happy as he would make her ;
but, on the other hand, I could not endure the thought of
losing her. The latter feeling conquered, and in Lottchen I
have never once been able to perceive a shadow of the same
conflict."

Another extract will place this conflict in its true light :
" I am under no further engagement to Lottchen than that
under which an honorable man stands when he gives a young
woman the preference above all others, makes known that he
desires the like feeling from her, and when she gives it, receives from her not only this, but a complete acquiescence.
This I consider quite enough to bind an honorable man,
especially when such a relation lasts several years. But in
my case there is this in addition, that Lottchen and I have
expressly declared ourselves, and still do so with pleasure,
without any oaths and asseverations." This absence of any
legal tie between them must have made Kestner's position
far more trying. It gives a higher idea both of his generous
forbearance and of the fascination exercised by Goethe : for
what a position ! and how much nobility on all sides was
necessary to prevent petty jealousies ending in a violent rupture ! Certain it is that the greatest intimacy and the most
affectionate feelings were kept up *without* disturbance. Confident in the honor of his friend and the truth of his mistress,

Kestner never spoiled the relation by a hint of jealousy. Goethe was constantly in Lotte's house, where his arrival was a jubilee to the children, who seized hold of him, as children always take loving possession of those who are indulgent to them, and forced him to tell them stories. It is a pleasant sight to see Goethe with children ; he always shows such hearty fondness for them ; and these brothers and sisters of Lotte were doubly endeared to him because they belonged to her.

One other figure in this Wetzlar set arrests our attention : it is that of a handsome blond youth, with soft blue eyes and a settled melancholy expression. His name is Jerusalem, and he is the son of the venerable Abbot of Riddagshausen.* He is here attached as secretary to the Brunswick Legation, a colleague, therefore, of von Goué. He is deeply read in English literature, and has had the honor of Lessing's friendship ; a friendship subsequently expressed in the following terms, when Lessing, acting as his editor, wrote the preface to his Philosophical Essays : "When he came to Wolfenbüttel he gave me his friendship. I did not enjoy it long, but I cannot easily name one who in so short a space of time excited in me more affection. It is true I only learned to know one side of his nature, but it was the side which explains all the rest. It was the desire for clear knowledge ; the talent to follow truth to its last consequences ; the spirit of cold observation ; but an ardent spirit not to be intimidated by truth. . . . . How sensitive, how warm, how active this young inquirer was, how true a man among men, is better known to more intimate friends."

The melancholy of his disposition led him to think much

---

* No Catholic, as this title might seem to imply, but a Protestant ; his abbey, secularized two centuries before, yielded him only a title and revenues.

of suicide, which he defended on speculative grounds.   And
this melancholy, and these meditations, were deepened by an
unhappy passion for the wife of one of his friends.   The
issue of that passion we shall have to narrate in a future
chapter.   For the present it is enough to indicate the presence of this youth among the circle of Goethe's acquaintances.   They saw but little of each other, owing to the
retiring sensitiveness of Jerusalem ; probably the same cause
had kept them asunder years before in Leipsic, where they
were fellow-students ; but their acquaintance furnished Goethe
with material which he was afterwards to use in his novel.

Jerusalem's unhappy passion and Goethe's unhappy passion, one would think, must have been a bond of union
between them ; but in truth Goethe's passion can scarcely
have been called " unhappy," — it was rather a delicious uneasiness.   Love, in the profound, absorbing sense, it was not.
It was an *imaginative passion*, in which the poet was more
implicated than the man.   Lotte excited his imagination ;
her beauty, her serene gayety, her affectionate manners,
charmed him ; the romance of his position heightened the
charm, by giving an *unconscious security* to his feelings.   I am
persuaded that if Lotte had been free, he would have fled
from her as he fled from Frederika.   In saying this, however,
I do not mean that the impossibility of obtaining her gave
him any comfort.   He was restless, impatient, and, in a certain sense, unhappy.   He believed himself to be desperately
in love with her, when in truth he was only in love with the
indulgence of the emotions she excited ; a paradox which
will be no mystery to those acquainted with the poetic temperament.

The following extracts from Kestner's *Diary* will remind
the reader of Goethe's departure from Leipsic without saying
adieu to Käthchen.   His dislike of " scenes " made him

shrink from those emotions of leave-taking usually so eagerly sought by lovers : —

" *Sept.* 10*th*, 1772. To-day Dr. Goethe dined with me in the garden; I did not know that it was the last time. In the evening Dr. Goethe came to the *Teutsche Haus.* He, Lottchen, and I had a remarkable conversation about the future state ; about going away and returning, etc., which was not begun by him, but by Lottchen. We agreed that the one who died first should, if he could, give information to the living, about the conditions of the other life. Goethe was quite cast down, for he knew that the next morning he was to go."

" *Sept.* 11*th*, 1772. This morning at seven o'clock Goethe set off without taking leave. He sent me a note with some books. He had long said that about this time he would make a journey to Coblentz, where the paymaster of the forces, Merck, awaited him, and that he would say no good byes, but set off suddenly. So I had expected it. But that I was, notwithstanding, unprepared for it, I have felt, — felt deep in my soul. In the morning I came home. ' Herr Dr. Goethe sent this at ten o'clock.' I saw the books and the note, and thought what this said to me, — ' He is gone ! ' — and was quite dejected. Soon after, Hans * came to ask me if he were really gone. The *Geheime Räthin* Langen had sent to say by a maid-servant : ' It was very ill-mannered of Dr. Goethe to set off in this way, without taking leave.' Lottchen sent word in reply : ' Why had she not taught her nephew better? ' Lottchen, in order to be certain, sent a box which she had of Goethe's, to his house. He was no longer there. In the middle of the day the *Geheime Räthin* Langen sent word again : ' She would, however, let Dr. Goethe's mother know how he had conducted himself.'

* One of Lotte's brothers.

Every one of the children in the *Teutsche Haus* was saying:
'*Doctor Goethe is gone!*'   In the middle of the day I talked
with Herr von Born, who had accompanied him, on horseback, as far as Brunnfells.   Goethe had told him of our
evening's conversation.   Goethe had set out in very low
spirits.   In the afternoon I took Goethe's note to Lottchen.
She was sorry about his departure ; the tears came into her
eyes while reading.   Yet it was a satisfaction to her that he
was gone, since she could not give him the affection he
desired.   We spoke only of him ; indeed, I could think of
nothing else, and defended the manner of his leaving, which
was blamed by a silly person ; I did it with much warmth.
Afterwards I wrote him word what had happened since his
departure."

How graphically do these simple touches set the whole
situation before us : the sorrow of the two lovers at the
departure of their friend, and the consternation of the children on hearing that Dr. Goethe is gone !   One needs such
a picture to reassure us that the episode, with all its strange
romance, and with all its danger, was not really a fit of morbid sentimentalism.   Indeed, had Goethe been the sentimental Werther he has represented, he would never have had
the strength of will to tear himself from such a position.   He
would have blown his brains out, as Werther did.   On the
other hand, note what a worthy figure is this of Kestner,
compared with the cold Albert of the novel.   A less generous nature would have rejoiced in the absence of a rival, and
forgotten, in its joy, the loss of a friend.   But Kestner, who
knew that his friend was his rival, — and such a rival, that
doubts crossed him whether this magnificent youth were not
really more capable of rendering Lotte happy than he himself was, — grieved for the absence of his friend !

Here is Goethe's letter, referred to in the passage just
quoted from the *Diary:* —

" He is gone, Kestner ; when you get this note, he is gone ! Give Lottchen the enclosed. I was quite composed, but your conversation has torn me to pieces. At this moment I can say nothing to you but farewell. If I had remained a moment longer with you I could not have restrained myself. Now I am alone, and to-morrow I go. O my poor head ! "

This was the enclosure, addressed to Lotte : —

" I certainly hope to come again, but God knows when ! Lotte, what did my heart feel while you were talking, know-ing, as I did, that it was the last time I should see you? Not the last time, and yet to-morrow I go away. He is gone ! What spirit led you to that conversation ? When I was expected to say all I felt, alas ! what I cared about was here below, was your hand, which I kissed for the last time. The room, which I shall not enter again, and the dear father who saw me to the door for the last time. I am now alone, and may weep ; I leave you happy, and shall remain in your heart. And shall see you again ; *but not to-morrow is never !* Tell my boys, He is gone. I can say no more."

----·----

CHAPTER III.

PREPARATIONS FOR WERTHER.

HAVING sent his luggage to the house of Frau von Laroche, where he was to meet Merck, he made the journey down the Lahn, on foot. A delicious sadness subdued his thoughts as he wandered dreamily along the river banks ; and the lovely scenes which met his eye solicited his pencil, awakening once more the ineffectual desire (which from time to time haunted him) of becoming a painter. He had really no faculty in

this direction, yet the desire, often suppressed, now rose up
in such a serious shape, that he resolved to settle forever
whether he should devote himself to the art or not. The
test was curious. The river glided beneath, now flashing in
the sunlight, now partially concealed by willows. Taking a
knife from his pocket he flung it with his left hand into the
river, having previously resolved that if he saw it fall he was
to become an artist; but if the sinking knife were concealed
by the willows he was to abandon the idea. No ancient
oracle was ever more ambiguous than the answer now given
him. The willows concealed the sinking knife, but the
water splashed up like a fountain, and was distinctly visible.
So indefinite an answer left him in doubt.*

He wandered pleasantly on the banks till he reached Ems,
and then journeyed down the river in a boat. The old Rhine
opened upon him; and he mentions with peculiar delight the
magnificent situation of Oberlahnstein, and, above all, the
majesty of the castle of Ehrenbreitstein. On arriving at the
house of Laroche, where he had been announced by Merck,
he was most kindly received by this excellent family. His
literary tendencies bound him to the mother; his joyousness
and strong sense, to the father; his youth and poetry, to the
daughters. The Frau von Laroche, Wieland's earliest love,
had written a novel in the Richardson style, *Die Geschichte
des Fräuleins von Sternheim;* and Schäfer remarks that she

* This mode of interrogating fate recalls that strange passage in
ROUSSEAU's *Confessions* (Livre VI.), where he throws a stone at a tree:
if he hits, it is a sign of salvation; if he misses, of damnation ! Fortunately he hits : " Ce qui, véritablement, n'était pas difficile, car j'avais
eu le soin de le choisir fort gros et fort près ; depuis lors je n'ai plus
douté de mon salut." Had Goethe read this passage ? The *Confessions*
appeared in 1768, that is, four years before this journey down the Lahn.
Yet from a passage in one of his letters to the Frau von Stein, it seems
as if he then, 1782, first read the *Confessions*.

probably gathered Merck, Goethe, and others into her house with a view to favorable criticisms of this novel. If this were her design, she succeeded with Goethe, who reviewed her book in the *Frankfurter Gelehrten Anzeigen.* Whether this compliance was extorted by herself, or by the charms of her daughter Maximiliane, history saith not ; certain it is that the dark eyes of the daughter made an impression on the heart of the young reviewer. She is the Mdlle. B. introduced in *Werther;* but she is even still more interesting to us as the future mother of Bettina. They seem to have looked into each other's eyes, flirted and sentimentalized, as if no Lotte had been left in Wetzlar. Nor will this surprise those who have considered the mobile nature of our poet. He is miserable at moments, but the fulness of abounding life, the strength of victorious will, and the sensibility to new impressions, keep his ever-active nature from the despondency which killed Werther. He is not always drooping because Charlotte is another's. He is open to every new impression, serious or gay. Thus, among other indications, we find him throwing off in *Pater Brey* and *Satyros,* sarcasm and humor which are curious as products of the Werther period, although of no absolute worth ; and we follow him up the Rhine, in company with Merck and his family, leisurely enjoying Rheinfels, St. Goar, Bacharach, Bingen, Elfeld, and Biberich, sketching as if life were a leisure summer day.

He returned to Frankfurt, and busied himself with law, literature, and painting. Wandering Italians, then rare, brought casts of antique statues to Frankfurt ; and with delighted eagerness he purchased a complete set, thus to revive as much as possible the grand impression he received at Mannheim. Among his art-studies must be noted the attention bestowed on the Dutch painters. He began to copy some still-life pictures ; one of these he mentions with pride, and what, think you, this one was?—a copy of a tortoise-shell knife-handle in-laid with silver! He has *Götz von Berlichingen* in his port-folio, and delights in copying a knife-handle!

To law he devoted himself with greater assiduity than ever. His father, delighted at going through the papers with him, was peculiarly gratified at this honorable diligence, and in his delight was willing to overlook the other occupations of "this singular creature," as he rightly named him. Goethe's literary plans were numerous, and the *Frankfurt Journal* gave him constant opportunities for expressing himself on poetry, theology, and even politics.

When *Götz* appeared the effect on the public was instanta-neous, startling. Its bold expression of the spirit of Freedom, its defiance of French criticism, and the originality, no less than the power of the writing, carried it triumphant over Ger-many. It was pronounced a masterpiece in all the *salons* and in all the beer-houses of that uneasy time. Imitations fol-lowed with amazing rapidity; the stage was noisy with the clang of chivalry, and the bookshelves creaked beneath the weight of resuscitated Feudal Times.

An amusing example of "the trade" is mentioned by Goethe. A bookseller paid him a visit, and with the air of a man well satisfied with his proposal, offered to give an *order* for a dozen plays in the style of *Götz*, for which a handsome *honorarium* should be paid. His offer was the more gener-ous, because such was the state of literature at this period, that, in spite of the success *Götz* achieved, it brought no money to its author,—pirated editions circulating everywhere, and robbing him of his reward. Moreover, what the book-seller proposed was what the public expected. When once a writer has achieved success in any direction, he must continue in that direction, or peril his reputation. An opinion has been formed of him,—he has been *classed;* and the public will not have its classification disturbed. Nevertheless, if he repeat himself, this unreasoning public declaims against his "poverty." No man ever repeated himself less than Goethe. He did not model a statue, and then amuse himself with taking casts of it in different materials. He lived, thought, and suffered ; and because he had lived, thought, and suf. fered, he wrote. When he had once expressed his experi-ence in a work, he never recurred to it. The true artist, like the snake, casts his skin, but never resumes it. He works ac-cording to the impulse from within, not according to the de-mand from without. And Goethe was a genuine artist, never exhausting a lucky discovery, never working an impoverished vein. Every poem came fresh from life, coined from the mint of his experience.

Götz is the greatest product of the *Sturm und Drang* movement. As we before hinted, this period is not simply one of vague wild hopes and retrospections of old German life, it is also one of unhealthy sentimentalism. Goethe, the great representative poet of his day — the secretary of his age — gives us masterpieces which characterize both these tendencies. Beside the insurgent Götz stands the dreamy Werther. And yet, accurately as these two works represent two active tendencies of that time, they are both far removed above the perishing extravagances of that time ; they are both *ideal* expressions of the age, and as free from the disease which corrupted it as Goethe himself was free from the weakness of his contemporaries. Wilkes used to say that he had never been a Wilkite. Goethe was never a Werther. To appreciate the distance which separated him and his works from his sentimental contemporaries and their works, we must study the characters of such men as Jacobi, Klinger, Wagner, and Lenz, or we must read such works as *Woldemar.* It will then be plain why Goethe turned with aversion from

such works, his own included, when a few years had cleared
his insight, and settled his aims.   Then also will be seen the
difference between genius which idealizes the spirit of the
age, and talent which panders to it.*

It was, indeed, a strange epoch ; the unrest was the unrest
of disease, and its extravagances were morbid symptoms.
In the letters, memoirs, and novels, which still remain to
testify to the follies of the age, may be read a self-questioning and sentimental introspection, enough to create in healthy
minds a distaste both for sentiment and self-questioning.   A
factitious air is carried even by the most respectable sentiments ; and many *not* respectable array themselves in rose-
pink.   Nature is seldom spoken of but in hysterical enthusiasm,   Tears and caresses are prodigally scattered, and
upon the slightest provocations.   In Coburg an *Order of
Mercy and Expiation* is instituted by sensitive noodles.
Leuchsenring, whom Goethe satirized in *Pater Brey* as a
professional sentimentalist, gets up a secret society, and calls
it the *Order of Sentiment*, to which tender souls think it a
privilege to belong.   Friendship is fantastically deified ;
brotherly love draws trembling souls together, not on the
solid grounds of affection and mutual service, but on entirely
imaginary grounds of " spiritual communion "; whence arose,
as Jean Paul wittily says, " an universal love for all men and
beasts, — except reviewers."   It was a sceptical epoch, in
which everything established came into question.   Marriage,
of course, came badly off among a set of men who made the
first commandment of genius to consist in loving your neighbor *and* your neighbor's wife.

These were symptoms of disease ; the social organization

---

* As Karl Grün epigrammatically says of Goethe and his contemporaries, "he was at once patient and physician, they were patients and
nothing else."

was out of order ; a crisis, evidently imminent, was heralded by extravagances in literature, as elsewhere. The cause of the disease was want of faith. In religion, in philosophy, in politics, in morals, this eighteenth century was ostentatious of its disquiet and disbelief. The old faith, which for so long had made European life an organic unity, and which in its tottering weakness had received a mortal blow from Luther, was no longer universal, living, active, dominant ; its place of universal directing power was vacant, — a new faith had not arisen. The French Revolution was another crisis of that organic disturbance which had previously shown itself in another order of ideas, — in the Reformation. Beside this awful crisis, other minor crises are noticeable. Everywhere the same Protestant spirit breaks through traditions in morals, in literature, and in education. Whatever is established, whatever rests on tradition, is questioned. The classics are no longer believed in ; men begin to maintain the doctrine of progress, and proclaim the superiority of the moderns. Art is pronounced to be in its nature progressive. Education is no longer permitted to pursue its broad traditional path ; the methods which were excellent for the past, no longer suffice for the present ; everywhere new methods rise up to ameliorate the old. The divine right of institutions ceases to gain credence. The individual claimed and proclaimed his freedom, — freedom of thought and freedom of act. Freedom is the watchword of the eighteenth century.

Enough has been said to indicate the temper of those times, and to show why *Werther* was the expression of that temper. Turning to the novel itself, we find it so bound up with the life of its author, that the history of his life at this epoch is the record of the materials from which it was created ; we must, therefore, retrace our steps again to the point where Goethe left Wetzlar, and, by the aid of his let-

6

ters to Kestner, follow the development of this strange romance.

Götz was published in the summer of 1773. It was in the autumn of 1772 that Goethe left Wetzlar, and returned home. His letters to Kestner and Charlotte are full of passionate avowals and tender reminiscences. The capricious orthography and grammar to be noticed in them belong to a period when it was thought unworthy of a genius to conform to details so fastidious as correct spelling and good grammar; but the affectionate nature which warms these letters, the abundant love the writer felt and inspired, these belong to him, and not to his age. If a proof were wanted of Goethe's loving disposition, we might refer to these letters, especially those addressed to the young brother of Charlotte. The reader of this Biography, however, will need no such proof, and we may therefore confine ourselves to the relation of Goethe to the Kestners. " God bless you, dear Kestner," runs one of the early letters, " and tell Lotte that I often believe I can forget her ; but then I have a relapse, and it is worse with me than ever." He longs once more to be sitting at her feet, letting the children clamber over him. He writes in a strain of melancholy, which is as much poetry as sorrow : when a thought of suicide arises, it is only one among the many thoughts which hurry through his mind. There is a very significant passage in the *Autobiography*, which aptly describes his real state of mind : " I had a large collection of weapons, and among them a very handsome dagger. This I placed by my bedside every night, and before extinguishing my candle I made various attempts to pierce the sharp point a couple of inches into my breast ; but, not being able to do it, I laughed myself out of the notion, threw aside all hypochondriacal fancies, and resolved to live." He played with suicidal thoughts, because he was restless, and suicide was a fashionable speculation of the day ; but whoever supposes these thoughts of suicide were serious, has greatly misunderstood him. He had them not, even at this period ; and when he wrote *Werther* he had long thrown off even the faint temptation of poetic longings for death. In October, 1772, the report reaches him that his Wetzlar friend, Goué, has shot himself : " Write to me at once about Goué," he says to Kestner ; " *I honor such an act, and pity mankind,* and let all the Philisters make their tobacco-smoke comments on it and say : There, you see ! Nevertheless, I hope never to make my friends unhappy by such an act myself." He was too full of life to do more than coquette with the idea of death. Here is a confession : " I went to Homburg, and there gained new love of life, seeing how much pleasure the appearance of a miserable thing like me can give such excellent people." On the 7th of November he suddenly appeared in Wetzlar with Schlosser, and stayed there till the 10th, in a feverish, but delicious, enthusiasm. He writes to Kestner on reaching home : " It was assuredly high time for me to go. Yesterday evening I had thoroughly criminal thoughts as I lay on the sofa. . . . . And when I think how above all my hopes your greeting of me was, I am very calm. I confess I came with some anxiety. I came with a pure, warm, full heart, dear Kestner, and it is a hell-pain when one is not received in the same spirit as one brings. But so — God give you a whole life such as those two days were to me ! "

The report of Goué's suicide, before alluded to, turned out to be false ; but the suicide of Jerusalem was a melancholy fact. Goethe immediately writes to Kestner : —

" Unhappy Jerusalem ! The news was shocking, and unexpected ; it was horrible to have this news as an accompaniment to the pleasantest gift of love. The unfortunate man ! But the devil, that is, the infamous men who enjoy nothing but the chaff of vanity, and have the lust of idolatry in their hearts, and preach idolatry, and cramp healthy nature, and overstrain and ruin the faculties, are guilty of this misery, of our misery.   If the cursed parson is not guilty, God forgive me that I wish he may break his neck like Eli.   The poor young man !   When I came back from a walk, and he met me in the moonlight, I said to myself, he is in love.   Lotte must still remember that I laughed about it.   God knows, loneliness undermined his heart, and for seven years * his form has been familiar to me.   I have talked little with him. When I came away I brought with me a book of his ; I will keep that and the remembrance of him as long as I live."

Among the many inaccuracies of the *Autobiography*, there is one of consequence on the subject of *Werther*, namely, the assertion that it was the news of Jerusalem's suicide which suddenly set him to work.   The news reached him in October, 1772, and in November, Kestner sent him the narrative of Jerusalem's last days.   Not until the middle and end of 1773 did he write *Werther*.   In fact, the state of his mind at this period is by no means such as the *Autobiography* describes.   Read this letter, written in December : "That is wonderful !   I was about to ask if Lenchen † had arrived, and you write to tell me she is.   If I were only there I would nullify your discourse, and astonish all the tailors ; I think I should be fonder of her than of Lotte.   From the portrait she must be an amiable girl, much better than Lotte, if not precisely the . . . . *And I am free and thirsting for love.*   I must try and come ; yet that would not help me.   Here am I once more in Frankfurt, and carry plans and fancies about with me, which I should not do if I had but a maiden."   In January he seems to have found a maiden, for he writes : " Tell

---

* This "seven years" refers to the first sight of Jerusalem at Leipsic.
† A sister of Charlotte's.

Lotte there is a certain maiden here whom I love heartily, and whom I would choose before all others if I had any thought of marriage, and she also was born on the 11th January.* It would be pretty: such a pair! Who knows what God's will is?" I agree with Viehoff against Düntzer, that this alludes to Anna Antoinette Gerock, a relation of Schlosser's, who is known to have loved him passionately, and to have furnished some traits for Mignon. Clear it is that he is not very melancholy. "Yesterday I skated from sunrise to sunset. And I have other sources of joy which I can't relate. Be comforted that I am almost as happy as people who love, like you two, that I am as full of hope, and that I have lately *felt* some poems. My sister greets you, my maiden also greets you, my gods greet you." Thus we see, that, although Lotte's picture hangs by his bedside, although her image hovers constantly before him, and the *Teutsche Haus* is the centre of many yearning thoughts, he is not pining despondently for Charlotte. He has rewritten *Götz*, and allowed Merck to carry it to the printer's. He is living in a very merry circle, one figure in which is Antoinette Gerock, as we gather from a letter written in February, 1773, a month after that in which he refers to his "maiden." Here is the passage : " At Easter I will send you a quite adventurous novelty. My maiden greets Lotte. In character she has much of Lenchen, and my sister says resembles her portrait. If we were but as much in love as you two — meanwhile I will call her my 'dear little wife,' for recently she fell to me in a lottery as my wife."

And now the day approaches when Lotte is to be married and leave Wetzlar. He writes to her brother Hans, begging him, when Lotte departs, to write at least once a week, that the connection with the *Teutsche Haus* may not be broken, although its jewel is carried away. He writes to Kestner to be

---

* Lotte's birthday.   † *Götz.*

allowed to get the wedding ring. "I am wholly yours, but from henceforth care not to see you nor Lotte. Her portrait too shall away from my bedroom the day of her marriage, and shall not be restored till I hear she is a mother ; and from that moment a new epoch begins, in which I shall not love her but her children, a little indeed on her account, but that's nothing to do with it ; and if you ask me to be godfather, my spirit shall rest upon the boy, and he shall make a fool of himself for a maiden like his mother." Enclosed was this note to Lotte : "May my memory with this ring forever remain with you in your happiness. Dear Lotte, some time hence we shall see each other again, you with this ring on your finger, and I as always thine. I know no name or by-name to sign this with. You know me." When the marriage takes place he writes to Kestner : "God bless you ; you have surprised me. I had meant to make a holy sepulchre on Good Friday, and bury Lotte's portrait. But it hangs still by my bed, and shall remain there till I die. Be happy. Greet for me your angel, and Lenchen ; she shall be the second Lotte, and it shall be as well with her. I wander in the desert where no water is, my hair is my shade, and my blood my spring." The bridesmaid brings him the bridal bouquet, a flower of which he sticks in his hat, as he walks to Darmstadt, in a melancholy mood ; but to show that his passion for Charlotte was after all only a poetic passion, here is a passage in the letter he sent to Kestner immediately after the marriage : "O Kestner, when have I envied you Lotte in the human sense? for not to envy you her in the spiritual sense I must be an angel without lungs and liver. Nevertheless I must disclose a secret to you. That you may know and behold. When I attached myself to Lotte, and you know that I was attached to her from my heart, Born talked to me about it, *as people are wont to talk.* 'If I were K., I should not like it.   How can it end?   You quite cut him out!' and the like.   Then I said to him in these very words, in his room, it was in the morning : 'The fact is, I am fool enough to think the girl something remarkable ; if she deceived me, and turned out to be as girls usually are, and used K. as capital in order to make the most of her charms, the first moment which discovered that to me, the first moment which brought her nearer to me, would be the last of our acquaintance,' and this I protested and swore.   And between ourselves, without boasting, I understand the maiden somewhat, and you know how I have felt for her and for everything she has seen and touched, and wherever she has been, and shall continue to feel to the end of the world.   And now see how far I am envious, and must be so.   For either I am a fool, which it is difficult to believe, or she is the subtlest deceiver, or then, Lotte, the very Lotte of whom we are speaking."   A few days afterwards he writes : " My poor existence is petrified to barren rock.   This summer I lose all.   Merck goes.   My sister too.   And I am alone."

The marriage of Cornelia, his much-loved sister, was to him a very serious matter, and her loss was not easily supplied.   It came, too, at a time when other losses pained him.   Lotte was married, Merck was away, and a dear friend had just died.   Nevertheless, he seems to have been active in plans.   Among them was most probably that of a drama on *Mahomet*, which he erroneously places at a later period, after the journeys with Lavater and Basedow, but which Schäfer, very properly, restores to the year 1773, as Boie's *Annual* for 1774 contains the *Mahomet's Song*.   Goethe has narrated in full the conception of this piece, which is very grand.   He tells us the idea arose within him of illustrating the sad fact, noticeable in the biographies of genius, that every man who attempts to realize a great idea comes in contact with the low-

er world, and must place himself on its level in order to influence it, and thus compromises his higher aims, and finally forfeits them.   He chose Mahomet as the illustration, never
having regarded him as an impostor.   He had carefully
studied the Koran and Mahomet's life, in preparation.   "The
piece," he says, " opened with a hymn sung by Mahomet
alone under the open sky.   He first adores the innumerable
stars as so many gods ; but as the star-god (Jupiter) rises, he
offers to him, as the king of the stars, exclusive adoration.
Soon after, the moon ascends the horizon, and claims the eye
and heart of the worshipper, who, refreshed and strengthened
by the dawning sun, is afterwards stimulated to new praises.
But these changes, however delightful, are still unsatisfactory,
and the mind feels that it must rise still higher, and mounts
therefore to God, the One Eternal, Infinite, to whom all these
splendid but finite creatures owe their existence.   I composed this hymn with great delight ; it is now lost, but might
easily be restored as a cantata, and is adapted for music by
the variety of its expression.   It would, however, be necessary to imagine it sung according to the original plan, by
the leader of a caravan with his family and tribe ; and thus
the alternation of the voices and the strength of the chorus
would be secured.

"Mahomet converted, imparts these feelings and sentiments to his friends : his wife and Ali become unconditional
disciples.   In the second act, he attempts to propagate this
faith in the tribe ; Ali still more zealously.   Assent and opposition display themselves according to the variety of character.   The contest begins, the strife becomes violent, and
Mahomet flies.   In the third act, he defeats his enemies,
makes his religion the public one, and purifies the Kaaba
from idols ; but this being impracticable by force, he is
obliged to resort to cunning.   *What in his character is earthly*

increases and develops itself; the divine retires and is obscured. In the fourth act, Mahomet pursues his conquests, his doctrine becomes a *means* rather than an *end*, all kinds of practices are employed, nor are horrors wanting. A woman, whose husband has been condemned by Mahomet, poisons him. In the fifth act, he feels that he is poisoned. His great calmness, the return to himself and to his better nature, make him worthy of admiration. He purifies his doctrine, establishes his kingdom, and dies.

" This sketch long occupied my mind ; for, according to my custom, I was obliged to let the conception perfect itself before I commenced the execution. All that genius, through character and intellect, can exercise over mankind, was therein to be represented, and what it gains and loses in the process. Several of the songs to be introduced in the drama were rapidly composed ; the only one remaining of them, however, is the *Mahomet's Gesang.* This was to be sung by Ali, in honor of his master, at the apex of his success, just before the change resulting from the poison." Of all his unrealized schemes, this causes me the greatest regret. In grandeur, depth, and in the opportunities for subtle psychological unravelment of the mysteries of our nature, it was a scheme peculiarly suited to his genius. How many *Clavigos* and *Stellas* would one not have given for such a poem ?

The satirical farce, *Götter, Helden und Wieland,* is alluded to in this passage of a letter to Kestner, May, 1774, and must therefore have been written some time before : " My rough joke against Wieland makes more noise than I thought. He behaves very well in the matter, as I hear, so that I am in the wrong." The origin of this farce was a strong feeling in the circle of Goethe's friends, that Wieland had modernized, misrepresented, and traduced the Grecian gods and heroes. One Sunday afternoon "the rage for dramatizing everything"

6*

seized him, and with a bottle of Burgundy by his side he wrote off the piece just as it stands. The friends were in raptures with it. He sent it to Lenz, then at Strasburg, who insisted on its at once being printed. After some demurring, consent was given, and at Strasburg the work saw the light. In reading it, the public, unacquainted with the circumstances and the mood to which it owed its origin, unacquainted also with the fact of its never having been designed for publication, felt somewhat scandalized at its fierceness of sarcasm. But in truth there was no malice in it. Flushed with the insolence and pride of wit, he attacked a poet whom, on the whole, he greatly loved. Wieland took no offence at it, but reviewed it in the *Teutsche Mercur*, recommending it to all lovers of pasquinade, *persiflage*, and sarcastic wit This reminds one of Socrates standing up in the theatre, when he was lampooned by Aristophanes, that the spectators might behold the original of the sophist they were hooting on the stage. *Götter, Helden und Wieland* is really amusing, and under the mask of its buffoonery contains some sound and acute criticism.* The peculiarity of it, however, consists in its attacking Wieland for treating heroes unheroically, at a time when, from various parts of Germany, loud voices were raised against Wieland as an immoral, an unchristian, nay, even an atheistical writer. Lavater called upon Christians to pray for this sinner ; theologians forbade their followers to read his works ; pulpits were loud against him. In 1773 the whole Klopstock school rose against him † in moral indignation, and burned his works on Klopstock's birthday. Very different was Goethe's ire. He saw that the gods and heroes were represented in peruques and satin breeches, that their

* It called forth a retort, *Thiere, Menschen und Goethe ;* which has not fallen in my way. Critics speak of it as personal, but worthless.

† *Gervinus,* IV. p. 285.

cheeks were rouged, their thews and sinews shrunk to those of a petit-maître ; and against such a conception of the old Pagan life he raised his voice.

On the 11th February, Knebel paid him a visit, and informed him that the two princes, Karl August and Constantine, were desirous of seeing him. He went, and was received with flattering kindness, especially by Karl August, who had just read *Götz.* He dined with his royal hosts in a quiet way, and left them, having received and produced an agreeable impression. They were going to Mainz, whither he promised to follow them. His father, like a sturdy old burgher who held aloof from princes, shook his sceptical head at the idea of this visit. To Mainz, however, the poet went a day or two afterwards, and spent several days with the young princes, as their guest. This was his first contact with men of high rank.

In the following May he hears with joy that Lotte is a mother, and that her boy is to be called Wolfgang, after him ; and on the 16th of June he writes to Lotte : " I will soon send you a friend who has much resemblance to me, and hope you will receive him well ; he is named Werther, and is and was — but that he must himself explain."

Whoever has followed the history thus far, moving on the secure ground of contemporary documents, will see how vague and inaccurate is the account of the composition of *Werther* given by its author, in his retrospective narrative. It was not originated by growing despair at the loss of Charlotte. It was not originated by tormenting thoughts of self-destruction. It was not to free himself from suicide that he wrote this story of suicide. All these several threads were indeed woven into its woof ; but the rigor of dates forces us to the conviction that *Werther*, although taken from his experience, was not written while that experience was being undergone.   Indeed, the true philosophy of art would, *a priori*, lead us to the conviction that, although he cleared his " bosom of the perilous stuff" by moulding this perilous stuff into a work of art, he must have essentially outlived the storm before he painted it, — conquered his passion, and subdued the rebellious thoughts, before he made them plastic to his purpose.   The poet cannot see to write when his eyes are full of tears ; cannot sing when his breast is swollen with sighs, and sobs choke utterance.   He must rise superior to his grief before he can sublimate his grief in song.   The artist is a master, not a slave ; he *wields* his passion, he is not hurried along by it ; he possesses, and is not possessed. Art enshrines the great sadness of the world, but is itself not sad.   The storm of passion weeps itself away, and the heavy clouds roll off in quiet masses, to make room for the sun, which, in shining through, touches them to beauty with its rays.   While pain is in its newness, it is pain, and nothing else ; it is not Art, but Feeling.   Goethe could not write *Werther* before he had outlived Wertherism.   It may have been, as he says, a "general confession," and a confession which brought him certain relief ; but we do not confess until we have repented, and we do not repent until we have outlived the error.

Werther was written rapidly.   " I completely isolated my-self," he says ; "nay, prohibited the visits of my friends, and put aside everything that did not immediately belong to the subject.   Under such circumstances, and under so many preparations in secret, I wrote it in four weeks, without any scheme of the whole, or treatment of any part being pre-viously put on paper."   It is of this seclusion Merck writes : " Le grand succès que son drame a eu lui tourne un peu la tête.   Il se détache de tous ses amis, et n'existe que dans les compositions qu'il prépare pour le public."

It is a matter of some interest to ascertain the exact truth respecting the date of the composition of *Werther*. As before stated, his own account is manifestly inaccurate; and the only thing which renders it difficult to assign the dates with tolerable precision, is his statement that it was written in four weeks, without any scheme of the whole or treatment of any part having been previously put on paper. If we consent to believe that his memory in this case deceived him, the correspondence of the period furnishes hints from which we may conclude that in 1772, on the arrival of the news about Jerusalem's suicide, he made a general sketch, either in his mind or on paper; and that during the following year he worked at it from time to time.   In June, 1773, he writes to Kestner: " And thus I dream and ramble through life, writing plays and *novels*, and the like."   In July he writes: " I am working my own situation into art for the consolation of gods and men.   I know what Lotte will say when she sees it, and I know what I shall answer her."   The word in the original is *Schauspiel*, — play, drama; Viehoff suggests that he does not mean drama, but a work which will bring his situation *zur Schau*, — before the public eye.   In September of the same year he writes: "You are always by me when I write.   At present I am working at a novel, but it gets on slowly."   In November, Frau Jacobi writes to him, acknowledging the receipt of a novel, in manuscript, no doubt, which delights her. In February, 1774, Merck writes of him : " Je prévois qu'un roman, qui paraîtra de lui à pâques, sera aussi bien reçu que son drame."   As we have nowhere a hint of any other novel besides *Werther* at this epoch, it is difficult to resist the evidence of these dates; and we must, therefore, conclude that the assertion in the *Autobiography* is wholly inexact.

In September, 1774, he wrote to Lotte, sending her a copy of *Werther:* " Lotte, how dear this little book is to me thou

wilt feel in reading it, and this copy is as dear to me as if it
were the only one in the world.   Thou must have it, Lotte ;
I have kissed it a hundred times ; have kept it locked up
that no one might touch it.   O, Lotte !   And I beg thee let
no one except Meyers see it yet ; it will be published at the
Leipsic fair.   I wish each to read it alone, — thou alone,
Kestner alone, — and each to write me a little word about it.
Lotte, adieu, Lotte ! "

While the public was reading the tragic story of *Werther*
through fast-flowing tears, a painful sense of indignation rose
in the breasts of Kestner and Charlotte at seeing themselves
thus dragged into publicity, their story falsified.   The narrative was in many respects too close to reality not to be very
offensive in its *deviations* from reality.   The figures were unmistakable ; and yet they were not the real figures.   The
eager public soon found out who were the principal person-
ages, and that a real history was at the bottom of the romance ; but as the whole truth could not be known, the
Kestners found themselves in a very false light.   They were
hurt by this indiscretion of their friend ; more hurt perhaps
than they chose to confess ; and we may read, in the following fragment of the sketch of the letter sent by Kestner on
receipt of the books, the accents of an offended friend whose
pride restrains the full expression of his anger : —

" Your *Werther* might have given me great pleasure, since
it could have reminded me of many interesting scenes and
incidents.   But as it is, it has in certain respects given me
little edification.   You know I like to speak my mind.

" It is true, you have woven something new into each person, or have fused several persons into one.   So far good.
But if in this interweaving and fusing you had taken counsel
of your heart, you would not have so prostituted the real persons whose features you borrow.   You wished to draw from

Nature, that your picture might be truthful ; and yet you have combined so much that is contradictory, that you have missed the very mark at which you aimed.   The distinguished author will revolt against this judgment, but I appeal to reality and truth itself when I pronounce that the artist has failed.   The real Lotte would in many instances be grieved if she were like the Lotte you have there painted.   I know well that it is said to be a character compounded of two, but the Mrs. H. whom you have partly inwoven was also incapable of what you attribute to your heroine.   But this expenditure of fiction was not at all necessary to your end, to nature and truth, for it was without any such behavior on the part of a woman — a behavior which must ever be dishonorable even to a more than ordinary woman — that Jerusalem shot himself.

" The real Lotte, whose friend you nevertheless wish to be, is in your picture, which contains too much of her not to suggest her strongly : is, I say — but no, I will not say it, it pains me already too much only to think it.   And Lotte's husband — you called him your friend, and God knows that he was so — is with her.

"The miserable creature of an Albert !   In spite of its being an alleged fancy picture and not a portrait, it also has such traits of an original (only external traits, it is true, thank God, only external), that it is easy to guess the real person.   And if you wanted to have him act so, need you have made him such a blockhead ? that forthwith you might step forward and say, see what a fine fellow I am ! "

Kestner here touches on a point of morality in literature worth consideration.   While emphatically declaring that the artist must take his materials from reality, must employ his own experience, and draw from the characters he has really known, I must emphatically declare that he is bound as a creative artist to resist the temptation to be a mere chronicler :

he is bound to reproduce the materials under *new* forms, not only under forms sufficiently different from the reality to prevent the public reading actual histories beneath his invention, to prevent their recognizing the persons he has employed as lay figures, whenever those persons are assigned parts which they would reject, but also to present the materials under forms which, while preserving the symbolism of events, and retelling the old story, do nevertheless make the old story a new one, by the peculiarity and novelty of the conditions and characters. That is just the distinction between an artist and an historian. There is, of course, great difficulty in keeping to truth while avoiding the betrayal of actual occurrences; but it is a difficulty which is commanded by Art not less than by Morality.

Goethe was evidently astounded at the effect his book had produced on his friends : " I must at once write to you, my dear and angry friends, and free my heart. The thing is done ; the book is out ; forgive me if you can. I will hear nothing till the event has proved how exaggerated your anxiety is, and till you have more truly felt, in the book itself, the innocent mingling of fiction and truth. Thou hast, dear Kestner, exhausted everything, cut away all the ground of my excuse, and left me nothing to say ; yet I know not, my heart has still more to say, although I cannot express it. I am silent, but the sweet presentiment I must still retain, and I hope eternal Fate has that in store for me which will bind us yet closer one to the other. Yes, dear ones, I, who am so bound to you by love, must still remain debtor to you and your children for the uncomfortable hours which my — name it as you will — has given you. . . . . And now, my dear ones, when anger rises within you, think, oh think only that your old Goethe, ever and ever, and now more than ever, is your own."

Their anger fell. They saw that he had committed an indiscretion, but had done no more. They wrote forgiveness, as we gather from this letter Goethe sent on the 21st of November : —

"Here I have thy letter, Kestner! On a strange desk, in a painter's studio, for yesterday I began to paint in oil, I have thy letter, and must give thee my thanks! Thanks, dear friend! Thou art ever the same good soul! O that I could spring on thy neck, throw myself at Lotte's feet, one, one minute, and all, all that should be done away with, explained, which I could not make clear with quires of paper! O ye unbelieving ones! I could exclaim. Ye of little faith! Could you feel the thousandth part of what *Werther* is to a thousand hearts, you would not reckon the sacrifice you have made towards it! Here is a letter, read it, and send me word quickly what thou thinkest of it, what impression it makes on thee. Thou sendest me Hennings's letter; he does not condemn me: he excuses me. Dear brother Kestner! if you will wait, you shall be contented. I would not, to save my own life, call back Werther, and believe me, believe in me, thy anxieties, thy *gravamina*, will vanish like phantoms of the night if thou hast patience ; and then, between this and a year, I promise you in the most affectionate, peculiar, fervent manner, to disperse, as if it were a mere north-wind fog and mist, whatever may remain of suspicion, misinterpretation, etc., in the gossiping public, though it is a herd of swine. Werther must — must be! You do not feel *him*, you only feel *me* and *yourselves*; and that which you call *stuck on*, and in spite of you, and others, is *interwoven*. If I live, it is thee I have to thank for it; thus thou art not Albert. And thus —

"Give Lotte a warm greeting for me, and say to her : 'To know that your name is uttered by a thousand hallowed lips

with reverence, is surely an equivalent for anxieties which would
scarcely, apart from anything else, vex a person long in common life, where one is at the mercy of every tattler.'

" If you are generous and do not worry me, I will send
you letters, cries, sighs after Werther, and if you have faith,
believe that all will be well, and gossip is nothing, and weigh
well your philosopher's letter, which I have kissed.

"O then ! — hast not felt how the man embraces thee, con-
soles thee, and in thy — in Lotte's worth, finds consolation
enough under the wretchedness which has terrified you even
in the fiction ?   Lotte, farewell, — Kestner, love me and do
not worry me."

The pride of the author in his darling breaks out in this
letter, now his friends have forgiven him. We must admit that
Kestner had reason to be annoyed : the more so as his friends,
identifying him with the story, wrote sympathetically about
it.   He had to reply to Hennings on the subject, and in telling him the true story, begged him to correct the false reports.   He says : " In the first part of *Werther*, Werther is
Goethe himself.   In Lotte and Albert he has borrowed
traits from us, my wife and myself.   Many of the scenes are
quite true, and yet partly altered ; others are, at least in our
history, unreal.   For the sake of the second part, and in order to prepare for the death of Werther, he has introduced
various things into the first part which do not at all belong to
us.   For example, Lotte has never either with Goethe or
with any one else stood in the intimate relation which is there
described ; in this we have certainly great reason to be offended with him, for several accessory circumstances are too
true and too well known for people not to point to us.   He
regrets it now, but of what use is that to us ?   It is true he
has a great regard for my wife ; but he ought to have depicted
her more faithfully in this point, that she was too wise and

delicate ever to let him go so far as is represented in the first part. She behaved to him in such way as to make her far dearer to me than before, if this had been possible. Moreover, our engagement was never made public, though not, it is true, kept a secret: still she was too bashful ever to confess it to any one. And there was no engagement between us but that of hearts. It was not till shortly before my departure (when Goethe had already been a year away from Wetzlar at Frankfurt, and the disguised Werther had been dead half a year) that we were married. After the lapse of a year, since our residence here, we have become father and mother. The dear boy lives still, and gives us, thank God, much joy. For the rest, there is in Werther much of Goethe's character and manner of thinking. Lotte's portrait is completely that of my wife. Albert might have been made a little more ardent. The second part of *Werther* has nothing whatever to do with us. . . . . When Goethe had printed his book, he sent us an early copy, and thought we should fall into raptures with what he had done. But we at once saw what would be the effect, and your letter confirms our fears. I wrote very angrily to him. He then for the first time saw what he had done; but the book was printed, and he hoped our fears were idle." In another letter to the same, Kestner says: "You have no idea what a man he is. But when his great fire has somewhat burnt itself out, then we shall all have the greatest joy in him."

CHAPTER IV.

THE LITERARY LION.

GOETHE was now at the perilous juncture in an author's career, when, having just achieved a splendid success, he is in danger either of again snatching at laurels in presumptuous haste, or of suffering himself to repose upon the laurels he has won, talking of greatness instead of learning to be great. Both perils he avoided. He neither traded on his renown, nor conceived that his education was complete. Wisely refraining from completing fresh important works, he kept up the practice of his art by trifles, and the education of his genius by serious studies. Among these trifles are *Clavigo*, the *Jahrmarktsfest zu Plundersweilen*, and the *Prolog zu Bahrdt's Neuesten Offenbarungen.*

He was beginning to feel himself a man of consequence; the notable men of the day eagerly sought his acquaintance. Among these men we must note Klopstock, Lavater, Basedow, Jacobi, and the Stolbergs. Correspondence led to personal intercourse. Klopstock arrived in Frankfurt in this October, 1774, just before *Werther* appeared. Goethe saw him, read the fragments of *Faust* to him, and discussed skating with him. But the great religious poet was too far removed from the strivings of his young rival to conceive that attachment for him which he felt for men like the Stolbergs, or to inspire Goethe with any keen sympathy.

In June, Lavater also came to Frankfurt. This was a few months before Klopstock's visit. He had commenced a correspondence with Goethe on the occasion of the *Briefe des Pastors*. Those were great days of correspondence. Letters were written to be read in circles, and were shown about like the last new poem. Lavater pestered his friends for their portraits, and for ideal portraits (according to their conception) of our Saviour, all of which were destined for the work on *Physiognomy* on which he was then engaged. The artist who took Goethe's portrait sent Lavater the portrait of Bahrdt instead, to see what he would make of it; the physiognomist was not taken in; he stoutly denied the possibility of such a resemblance. Yet when he saw the actual Goethe he was not satisfied. He gazed in astonishment, exclaiming, "Art thou he?" "I am he," was the answer; and the two embraced each other. Still the physiognomist was dissatisfied. "I answered him with my native and acquired realism, that as God had willed to make me what I was, he, Lavater, must even so accept me."

The first surprise over, they began to converse on the weightiest topics. Their sympathy was much greater than appears in Goethe's narrative, written many years after the characters of both had developed themselves.

So strong was the attraction of Lavater's society that Goethe accompanied him to Ems. The journey was charming; beautiful summer weather and Lavater's cheerful gayety formed pleasant accompaniments to their religious discussions. On returning to Frankfurt, another and very different celebrity was there to distract his attention, — Basedow, the education reformer. No greater contrast to Lavater could have been picked out of the celebrities of that day. Lavater was handsome, clean, cheerful, flattering, insinuating, devout; Basedow ugly, dirty among the dirty, sarcastic, domineering, and aggressively heterodox. One tried to restore Apostolic Christianity; the other could not restrain the most insolent sarcasms on the Bible, the Trinity, and every form of Christian creed. One set up as a Prophet, the other as a Pedagogue.

Basedow (born 1723) was also early in indicating his future part.   At school the wild and dirty boy manifested rebellious energy against all system and all method ; studied in a desultory, omnivorous manner, as if to fit himself for everything ; ran away from home, and became a lackey in a nobleman's house ; caught up Rousseau's doctrine about a state of Nature, which he applied to Education ; wrote endless works, or rather incessant repetitions of one work ; shouted with such lusty lungs that men could not but hear him ; appealed to the nation for support in his philanthropic schemes ; collected "a rent " from philanthropists and dupes ; attacked established institutions, and parenthetically all Christian tenets; and proved himself a man of restless energy, and of vast and comprehensive ignorance.   He made considerable noise in the world ; and in private lived somewhat the life of a restless hog who has taken to philanthropy and free thinking.

Much as such a character was opposed to his own, Goethe, eager and inquiring, felt an attraction towards it, as towards a character to study.   Like many other studies, this had its drawbacks.   He was forced to endure the incessant smoking and incessant sarcasms of the dirty educationist.   The stench he endured with firmness ; the anti-Christian tirades he answered with paradoxes wilder than any he opposed.   " Such a splendid opportunity of exercising, if not of elevating, my mind," he says, " was not to be thrown away ; so prevailing on my father and friends to undertake my law business, I once more set off for the Rhine in Basedow's company." Basedow filled the carriage with smoke, and killed the time with discussions.   On the way they fell in with Lavater, and the three visited several châteaux, especially those of noble ladies, everywhere anxious to receive the literary Lions. Goethe, we may parenthetically note, is in error when he says that he was on this voyage greatly pestered by the women wanting to know all about the truth of *Werther*; the fact being that *Werther* did not appear until the following October; for although the exigencies of my narrative have caused a certain anticipation in chronology, this journey with Lavater and Basedow, here made to follow the publication of *Werther*, came *before* it in Goethe's life. If we are not to believe that the women crowded around him with questions about Lotte, we can readily believe that children crowded round him, begging him to tell them stories.

Wild and "genius-like" was his demeanor. " Basedow and I," he says, " seemed to be ambitious of proving who could behave the most outrageously." Very characteristic is the glimpse we catch of him quitting the ball-room, after a heating dance, and rushing up to Basedow's room. The Philanthropist did not go to bed. He threw himself in his clothes upon the bed, and there, in a room full of tobacco-smoke and bad air, dictated to his scribe. When fatigue overcame him, he slept awhile, his scribe remaining there, pen in hand, awaiting the awakening of the Philanthropist, who, on opening his eyes, at once resumed the flow of his dictation. Into such a room sprang the dance-heated youth, began a fierce discussion on some problem previously mooted between them, hurried off again to look into the eyes of some charming partner, and before the door closed, heard Basedow recommence dictating.

This union of philosophy with amusement, of restless theorizing with animal spirits, indicates the tone of his mind. " I am contented," he said to Lavater, " I am happy. That I feel; and yet the whole centre of my joy is an overflowing yearning towards something which I have not, something which my soul perceives dimly." He could reach that "something" neither through the pious preaching of Lavater, nor through the aggressive preaching of Basedow. Very graphic and ludicrous is the picture he gives of his sitting like a citizen of the world between a prophet on the right and a prophet on the left hand, —

> " Prophete rechts, Prophete links,
>   Das Welt-Kind in der Mitten," —

quietly eating a chicken while Lavater explains to a country parson the mystery of the Revelations, and Basedow astonishes a dancing-master with a scornful exposure of the inutility of baptism.*

Nor could he find this " something" in Jacobi, with whom he now came into sentimental intimacy. He could to some extent sympathize with Jacobi's sentimental cravings, and philosophic, religious aspirations, for he was bitten with the Wertherism of the epoch. He could gaze with him in uneasy ecstasy upon the moonlight quivering on the silent Rhine, and pour forth the songs which were murmuring within his breast. He could form a friendship, believing it to rest upon an eternal basis of perfect sympathy; but the inward goad which drove him onwards and onwards was not to be blunted until fresh experience had brought about fresh metamorphoses in his development. It is the Youth we have before us here, the Youth in his struggles and many-wandering aims, not the Man grown into clearness.

Jacobi thought that in Goethe he had at length found the man his heart needed, whose influence could sustain and direct him. "The more I consider it," he wrote to Wieland, " the more intensely do I feel how impossible it is for one who who has not seen and heard Goethe, to write a word about this extraordinary creation of God's. One needs be with him but an hour to see that it is utterly absurd to expect him to think and act otherwise than as he does. I do not mean that there

---

* See the poem *Diné zu Coblentz.*

is no possibility of an improvement in him ; but nothing else is possible with his nature, which develops itself as the flower does, as the seed ripens, as the tree grows into the air and crowns itself."

Goethe's wonderful *personality* seems almost everywhere to produce a similar impression.   Heinse, the author of *Arding-hello*, writes of him at this period to Gleim : "Goethe was with us, a beautiful youth of five-and-twenty, who is all genius and strength from head to foot, his heart full of feeling, his soul full of fire and eagle-winged ; I know no man in the whole History of Literature who at such an age can be compared to him in fulness and completeness of genius."   Those, and they are the mass, who think of him as the calm and stately minister, the old Jupiter throned in Weimar, will feel some difficulty perhaps in recognizing the young Apollo of this period.   But it must be remembered that not only was he young, impetuous, bursting into life, and trying his eagle wings with wanton confidence of strength ; he was, moreover, a Rhinelander, with the gay blood of that race stimulated by the light and generous wine of the Rhine.   When I contrast young Goethe with a Herder, for example, it is always as if a flask of Rhenish glittered beside a seidel of Bavarian beer.

Such answer to his aspirations as the youth could at this period receive, he found in Spinoza.   In his father's library there was a little book written against Spinoza, one of the many foolish refutations which that grand Hebrew's misunderstood system called forth.   "It made little impression on me, for I hated controversies, and always wanted to know *what* a thinker thought, and not what another conceived he *ought to have thought.*"   It made him, however, once more read the article Spinoza, in Bayle's *Dictionary*, which he found pitiable, —as indeed it is.   If a philosophy is to be judged by its fruits, the philosophy which guided so great and so virtuous a

life as that of Spinoza, could not, Goethe thought, deserve
the howls of execration which followed Spinozism.   He procured the *Opera Posthuma* and studied them ; with what
fruit let the following confession indicate : " After looking
around the world in vain for the means of developing my
strange nature, I met with the *Ethics* of that philosopher. Of
what I read *in* the work, and of what I read *into* it, I can
give no account, but I found in it a sedative for my passions,
and it seemed to unveil a clear, broad view over the material
and moral world.   But what especially riveted me to him was
the boundless disinterestedness which shone forth in every
sentence.   That wonderful sentiment, *He who truly loves God,
must not require God to love him in return,* together with all the
preliminary propositions on which it rests, and all the consequences deduced from it, filled my mind.*   To be disinter-
ested in everything, but most of all in love and friendship, was
my highest desire, my maxim, my practice, so that that saucy
speech of *Philine's,* 'If I love thee, what is that to thee?' was
spoken right out of my heart.   Moreover, it must not be forgotten here that the closest unions rest on contrasts.   The
all-equalizing calmness of Spinoza was in striking contrast
with my all-disturbing activity ; his mathematical method was
the direct opposite of my poetic style of thought and feeling,
and that very precision which was thought ill adapted to
moral subjects made me his enthusiastic disciple, his most decided worshipper.   Mind and heart, understanding and sense,
sought each other with eager affinity, binding together the
most different natures.   But now all within was fermenting
and seething in action and reaction."

Although he studied Spinoza much and reverently, he

---

* The proposition to which Goethe refers is doubtless the xix. of
Book V.: *Qui deum amat, conari non potest, ut Deus ipsum contra
amet.*

never studied him systematically. The mathematical form into which that thinker casts his granite blocks of thought, was an almost insuperable hindrance to systematic study on the part of one so impatient, so desultory, and so unmathematical as Goethe. But a study may be very fruitful which is by no means systematic ; a phrase may fructify, when falling on a proper soil.

CHAPTER V.

LILI.

"I must tell you something which makes me happy; and that is the visit of many excellent men of all grades, and from all parts, who, among unimportant and intolerable visitors, call on me often, and stay some time. We first know that we exist, when we recognize ourselves in others (*man weiss erst dass man ist, wenn man sich in Andern wiederfindet*)." It is thus he writes to the Countess Augusta von Stolberg, with whom he had formed, through correspondence, one of those romantic friendships which celebrated men, some time in their lives, are generally led to form. This correspondence is among the most characteristic evidences we have of his mental condition, and should be read by every one who wishes to correct the tone of the *Autobiography*. Above all, it is the repository of his fluctuating feelings respecting Lili, the woman whom, according to his statement to Eckermann, he loved more than any other. "She was the first, and I can also add she is the last, I truly loved ; for all the *inclinations* which have since agitated my heart were superficial and trivial in comparison."* There is no statement he has made

* *Gespräche*, III. p. 299.

respecting a matter of feeling, to which one may oppose a flatter contradiction.   Indeed we find it difficult to believe he uttered such a sentence, unless we remember how carelessly in conversation such retrospective statements are made, and how, at his very advanced age, the memory of youthful feelings must have come back upon him with peculiar tenderness. Whatever caused him to make that statement, the statement is very questionable.   It nowhere appears that he loved Lili more than Frederika ; and we shall hereafter have positive evidence that his love for the Frau von Stein, and for his wife, was of a much deeper and more enduring nature.   " My love for Lili," he said to Eckermann, " had something so peculiar and delicate that even now it has influenced my style in the narrative of that painfully happy epoch.   When you read the fourth volume of my *Autobiography,* you will see that my love was something quite different from love in novels."

Well, the fourth volume is now open to every one, and he must have peculiar powers of divination who can read any profound passion in the narrative.   A colder love-history was never written by a poet.   There is no emotion warming the narrative ; there is little of a loving recollection, gathering all details into one continuous story ; it is, indeed, with great difficulty one unravels the story at all.   He seems to seize every excuse to interrupt the narrative by general reflections, or by sketches of other people.   He speaks of himself as " the youth of whom we now write " !   He speaks of her, and her circle, in the vaguest manner ; and the feelings which agitated him we must " read between the lines."

It is very true, however, that the love there depicted is unlike the love depicted in novels.   In novels, whatever may be the amount of foolishness with which the writers adumbrate their ideal of the passion, this truth, at least, is everywhere set forth, that to love we must render up body and soul, heart and mind, all interests and all desires, all prudences and all ambitions, identifying our being with that of another, in union to become elevated. To love is for the soul to choose a companion, and travel with it along the perilous defiles and winding ways of life; mutually sustaining, when the path is terrible with dangers, mutually exhorting, when it is rugged with obstructions, and mutually rejoicing, when rich broad plains and sunny slopes make the journey a delight, showing in the quiet distance the resting-place we all seek in this world.

It was not such companionship he sought with Lili; it was not such self-devotion which made him restlessly happy in her love. This child of sixteen, in all the merciless grace of maidenhood, proudly conscious of her power, ensnared his roving heart through the lures of passionate desire, but she never touched his soul; as the story we have to tell will sufficiently prove.

Anna Elizabeth Schönemann, immortalized as Lili, was the daughter of a great banker in Frankfurt, who lived in the splendid style of merchant princes. She was sixteen when Goethe first fell in love with her. The age is significant. It was somewhat the age of Frederika, Lotte, Antoinette, and Maximiliane: an age when girlhood has charms of grace and person, of beauty and freshness, which even those will not deny who profoundly feel the superiority of a developed woman. There is poetry in this age; but there is no depth, no fulness of character. Imagine the wide-sweeping mind of the author of *Götz, Faust, Prometheus, The Wandering Jew, Mahomet,* in companionship with the mind of a girl of sixteen!

Nor was Lili an exceptional character. Young, graceful, and charming, she was confessedly a coquette. Early in their acquaintance, in one of those pleasant hours of overflowing egotism wherein lovers take pride in the confession of faults

(not without intimation also of nobler qualities), Lili told him
the story of her life; told him what a flirt she had been; told
him, moreover, that she had tried her spells on him, and was
punished by being herself ensnared. Armida found herself
spell-bound by Rinaldo; but this Rinaldo followed her into
the enchanted gardens more out of adventurous curiosity than
love.

There was considerable difference in their stations; and
the elegant society of the banker's house was every way discordant to the wild youth, whose thoughts were of Nature and
unconstrained freedom. The balls and concerts to which he
followed her were little to his taste. "If," he writes to Augusta von Stolberg, — " if you can imagine a Goethe in a braid-
ed coat, from head to foot in the gallantest costume, amid
the glare of chandeliers, fastened to the card-table by a pair
of bright eyes, surrounded by all sorts of people, driven in
endless dissipation from concert to ball, and with frivolous
interest making love to a pretty blonde, then will you have a
picture of the present Carnival-Goethe."

Lili coquetted, and her coquetry seems to have cooled his
passion for a while, though she knew how to rekindle it. She
served him as he served poor Käthchen, in Leipsic; and as
in Leipsic he dramatized his experience under the form of *Die
Laune des Verliebten*, so here he dramatizes the new experience
in an opera, *Erwin und Elmire*, wherein the coquetry of a
mistress brings a lover to despair, — a warning to Lili, which
does not seem to have been altogether without effect.

Not only had he to suffer from her thoughtlessness, but also
from the thoughtfulness of parents on both sides. It was not
a marriage acceptable to either house. The banker's daughter, it was thought, should marry into some rich or noble
family. A poet, who belonged to a well-to-do yet compara-
tively unimportant family, was not exactly the bridegroom

most desired. On the other hand, the proud, stiff old Rath did not greatly rejoice in the prospect of having a fine lady for his daughter-in-law. Cornelia, who knew her father, and knew his pedantic ways, wrote strongly against the marriage. Merck, Crespel, Horn, and other friends, were all decidedly opposed to so incompatible a match. But of course the lovers were only thrown closer together by these attempts to separate them.

A certain Demoiselle Delf managed to overcome objections, and gain the consent of both families. "How she commenced it, how she got over the difficulties, I know not, but one evening she came to us bringing the consent. 'Take each other's hands,' she cried in a half-pathetic, half-imperious manner; I advanced to Lili and held out my hand : in it she placed hers, not indeed reluctantly, yet slowly. With a deep sigh we sank into each other's arms, greatly agitated." No formal betrothal seems to have taken place. Indeed, the consent which was obtained seems in nowise to have altered the feeling of friends and relatives. The nearer marriage seemed, the more impracticable it appeared. To Goethe, after the first flush of joy had subsided, the idea of marriage was in itself enough to make him uneasy, and to sharpen his sense of the *disparity* in station. The arrival of the two Counts Stolberg, and their proposal that he should accompany them in a tour through Switzerland, gave an excuse for freeing himself from Lili, "as an experiment to try whether he could renounce her."

Before accompanying him on his journey, it is necessary to cast a retrospective glance at some biographical details, omitted while the story of Lili was narrated. The mornings were devoted to poetry, the middle of the day to jurisprudence. Poetry was the breathing-room of his heart. In it he sought to escape from the burden of intolerable doubts. "If I did

not write dramas I should be lost," he tells Augusta von
Stolberg.   Among these dramas we must place *Stella*, for
which, as we learn from a letter to Merck, the publisher
offered twenty dollars, — that is to say, three pounds sterling.
What an insight this gives into the state of literature ; the
author of two immensely popular works is offered three
pounds for a drama in five acts ! Poor Schiller, subsequently,
was glad to write histories and translate memoirs for fifteen
or eighteen shillings the sheet of sixteen pages.

Besides *Stella*, he seemed to have worked at *Faust*, and to
have written the opera of *Claudine von Villa Bella*, several
passages for Lavater's *Physiognomy*, and many smaller poems.

The Stolbergs, with whom the Swiss journey was made,
were two ardent admirers of Klopstock, and two specimens
of the defiant "genius" class which scorned convention.
They hated imaginary tyrants ; outraged sober citizens by
their reckless recurrence to a supposed state of Nature ; and
astonished sensible citizens by their exaggerated notions of
friendship.   Merck was pitiless in his sarcasms and warnings.   He could not tolerate the idea of Goethe's travelling
with these *Burschen*.   But Goethe had too much of kindred
deviltry in him, breaking out at moments, to object to the
wildness of his companions ; though he began to suspect all
was not right when, after violating every other *convenance*,
they insisted on bathing in public.   Nature having nothing
to say against naked youths in the bright sunshine, what
business had old Humdrum to cover its eyes with modest
hands, and pretend to be shocked ?   However, so little prepossessed was Humdrum in favor of the Nude, that stones
were showered upon these children of Nature, — a criticism
which effectively modified their practice, if it failed to alter
their views.

Drinking the health of Stolberg's mistress, and then dash-

ing the glasses against the wall to prevent their being dese-
crated by other lips after so solemn a consecration (a process
which looked less heroic when *item'd* in the bill next day),
and otherwise demeaning themselves like true children of
"genius," they passed a wild and merry time. This journey
need not longer detain us. Two visits alone deserve mention. One was to Karl August, who was then in Karlsruhe
arranging his marriage with the Princess Luise, and who very
pressingly invited the poet to Weimar. The other was to his
sister Cornelia, who earnestly set before him all the objections to a marriage with Lili. "I made no promises," he
says, "although forced to confess that she had convinced
me. I left her with that strange feeling in my heart with which
passion nourishes itself; for the boy Cupid clings obstinately
to the garment of Hope even when she is preparing with
long strides to depart." The image of Lili haunted him
amid the lovely scenes of Nature. It was her image which
endeared him to his native land. His father, always desirous
he should see Italy, was now doubly anxious he should go
there, as the surest means of a separation from Lili. But
"Lombardy and Italy," says the poet, "lay before me a
strange land; while the dear home of Germany lay behind,
full of sweet domesticities, and where — let me confess it —
she lived who so long had enchained me, in whom my existence was centred. A little golden heart, which in my happiest hours I had received from her, still hung round my neck.
I drew it forth and covered it with kisses."

On his return to Frankfurt he learned that Lili's friends
had taken advantage of his absence to try and bring about
a separation, arguing, not without justice, that his absence
was a proof of lukewarmness. But Lili remained firm; and
it was said that she had declared herself willing to go with
him to America. A sentence from the *Autobiography* is

7 *

worth quoting, as a specimen of that love " so unlike the love to be found in novels," which he declared had given a peculiar tone to his narrative. It is in reference to this willingness of Lili to go to America : " The very thing which should have animated my hopes depressed them. My fair paternal house, only a few hundred paces from hers, was after all more endurable and attractive than a remote, hazardous spot beyond the seas ! " A sentence which recalls Gibbon's antithesis, on his resignation of his early love : " I sighed as a lover, I obeyed as a son."

He was restless and unhappy during these months, for he was not strong enough to give up Lili, nor sufficiently in love to marry her ; jealous of those who surrounded her, hurt by her coldness, he was every now and then led captive by her tenderness. There were moments when bygone days seemed once more restored, and then instantly vanished again. His poem of *Lili's Ménagerie* expresses his surly disgust at the familiar faces which surround her. The Bear of the ménagerie is a portrait of himself.

Turning to Art for consolation, he began the tragedy of *Egmont*, which he completed many years afterwards in Italy. It was a work which demanded more repose than could be found in his present condition, and I hasten to the *dénouement* of an episode which, amid fluctuations of feeling, steadily advanced to an end that must have been foreseen. The betrothal was cancelled. He was once more free. Free, but not happy. His heart still yearned for her, rather because there lay in his nature a need of loving, than because she was the woman fitted to share his life. He lingered about the house o' nights, wrapped in his mantle, satisfied if he could catch a glimpse of her shadow on the blind as she moved about the room. One night he heard her singing at the piano. His pulses throbbed as he distinguished his own song, —

> " Wherefore so resistlessly dost draw me
> Into scenes so bright ? " —

the song he had written in the morning of their happiness !
Her voice ceased. She rose and walked up and down the
room, little dreaming that her lover was beneath her window.

To give decision to his wavering feelings, there came, most
opportunely, a visitor to Frankfurt. Karl August, with his
bride, on his way to Weimar, once more pressed him to
spend a few weeks at his court. The rapid inclination which
had sprung up between the Prince and the Poet, — the desire to see something of the great world, — the desire, moreover, to quit Frankfurt, all combined to make him eagerly
accept the invitation. His father, indeed, tried to dissuade
him ; partly because he did not like the intercourse of plain
citizens with princes ; partly because the recent experience
of Voltaire with Frederick the Great seemed to point to an
inevitable termination in disgrace, if not evaded by servility.
His consent was extorted at last, however, and Goethe quitted forever the paternal roof.

BOOK THE FOURTH.

1775 TO 1779.

———◆———

CHAPTER I.

WEIMAR IN THE EIGHTEENTH CENTURY.

ON the 7th of November, 1775, Goethe, aged twenty-six, arrived at the little city on the banks of the Ilm, where his long residence was to confer on an insignificant Duchy the immortal renown of a German Athens.

Small indeed is the space occupied on the map by the Duchy of Saxe-Weimar, yet the historian of the German Courts declares, and truly, that after Berlin there is no Court of which the nation is so proud.* Frederick the Great and Wolfgang Goethe have raised these Courts into centres of undying interest. Of Weimar it is necessary we should form a distinct idea, if we would understand the outward life of the poet.

> " Klein ist unter den Fürsten Germaniens freilich der meine,
>   Kurz und schmal ist sein Land, mässig nur was er vermag."

" Small among German princes is mine, poor and narrow his kingdom, limited his power of doing good." Thus sings Goethe in that poem, so honorable to both, wherein he acknowledges his debt to Karl August. The geographical importance of Weimar was and is small ; but we in England have proud reason to know how great a place in the world

---

* VEHSE : *Geschichte der Deutschen Höfe seit der Reformation*, Vol. XXVIII. p. 3.

can be filled by a nation whose place is trivial on the map. We know, moreover, that the Athens which it is the pride of Weimar to claim as a patronymic was but a dot upon the surface of Europe, — a dot of earth, feeding some twenty thousand freemen, who not only extended the empire of their arms from Eubœa to the Thracian Bosphorus, but who left their glories in Literature, Philosophy, and Art, as marvels and as models for the civilized world. It is interesting, therefore, to know how small this Duchy of Saxe-Weimar was, that we may appreciate the influence exercised by means so circumscribed. We must know how absurdly scant the income of its generous prince, who, as I am credibly informed, would occasionally supply the deficiencies of his purse by the princely unprinceliness of selling to the Jews a diamond ring or ancestral snuff-box, that he might hand the proceeds to some struggling artist or poet. I mention this lest it should be supposed that a sarcastic spirit has dictated the enumeration of unimposing details in the following attempt to reconstruct some image of Weimar and its Court.

Weimar is an ancient city on the Ilm, a small stream rising in the Thuringian forests, and losing itself in the Saal, at Jena; this stream, on which the sole navigation seems to be that of ducks, meanders peacefully through pleasant valleys, except during the rainy season, when mountain-torrents swell its current, and overflow its banks. The Trent, between Trentham and Stafford, — "the smug and silver Trent," as Shakespeare calls it, — will give an idea of this stream. The town is charmingly placed in the Ilm valley, and stands some eight hundred feet above the level of the sea. "Weimar," says the old topographer, Mathew Merian, "is *Weinmar*, because it was the wine market for Jena and its environs. Others say it was because some one here in ancient days began to plant the vine, who was hence called *Wein-*

mayer. But of this each reader may believe just what he pleases." *

On a first acquaintance, Weimar seems more like a village bordering a park, than a capital with a Court, having all courtly environments. It is so quiet, so simple; and although ancient in its architecture, has none of the picturesqueness which delights the eye in most old German cities. The stone-colored, light brown, and apple-green houses have high-peaked slanting roofs, but no quaint gables, no caprices of architectural fancy, none of the mingling of varied styles which, elsewhere charms the traveller. One learns to love its quiet simple streets, and pleasant paths, fit theatre for the simple actors moving across the scene; but one must live there some time to discover its charm. The aspect it presented, when Goethe arrived, was of course very different from that presented now; but by diligent inquiry we may get some rough image of the place restored. First be it noted that the city walls were still erect; gates and portcullis still spoke of days of warfare. Within these walls were six or seven hundred houses, not more, most of them very ancient. Under these roofs were about seven thousand inhabitants,—for the most part not handsome. The city gates were strictly guarded. No one could pass through them in cart or carriage without leaving his name in the sentinel's book; even Goethe, minister and favorite, could not escape this tiresome formality, as we gather from one of his letters to the Frau von Stein, directing her to go out alone, and meet him beyond the gates, lest their exit together should be known. During Sunday service a chain was thrown across the streets leading to the church, to bar out all passengers; a practice to this day partially retained: the chain is fastened, but the passengers step over it without ceremony. There was little safety at night in

* *Topographia Superioris Saxoniæ, Thuringiæ,* etc., 1650, p. 188.

those silent streets ; for if you were in no great danger from marauders, you were in constant danger of breaking a limb in some hole or other ; the idea of lighting streets not having presented itself to the Thuringian mind. In the year 1685 the streets of London were first lighted with lamps : in 1775 Germany had not yet ventured on that experiment. If in 1854 Weimar is still innocent of gas, and perplexes its inhabitants with the dim obscurity of an occasional oil-lamp slung on a cord across the streets, we can suppose that in 1775 it had not even advanced so far. And our supposition is exact.*

The palace, which now forms three sides of a quadrangle, and is truly palatial in appearance, was in ashes when Goethe arrived. The ducal pair inhabited the Fürstenhaus, which stands opposite. The park was not in existence. In its place there was the *Welsche Garten*, a garden arranged after the pattern of Versailles, with trees trimmed into set shapes, with square beds, canals, bridges, and a Babylonic spiral tower called *Die Schnecke*, in which the people assembled to hear music, and to enjoy punch and sweet cakes. To the left of this garden stood the nucleus of the present park, and a wooded mass stretching as far as Upper Weimar.

Saxe-Weimar has no trade, no manufactures, no animation of commercial, political, or even theological activity. This part of Saxony, be it remembered, was the home and shelter of Protestantism in its birth. Only a few miles from Weimar stands the Wartburg, where Luther, in the disguise of Squire George, lived in safety, translating the Bible, and hurling his inkstand

---

* In a decree made at Cassel, in 1775, this sentence is noticeable : "In every house, as soon as the alarum sounds at night, every inhabitant must hold out a lighted lantern, in order that the people may find their way in the streets." Quoted by BIEDERMANN, *Deutschland im 18ten Jahrhundert*, I. p. 370.

at the head of Satan, like a rough-handed disputant as he was. In the market-place of Weimar stand to this day two houses, from the windows of which Tetzel advertised his indulgences, and Luther afterwards in fiery indignation fulminated against them. These records of religious struggle still remain, but are no longer suggestions for the continuance of the strife. The fire is burnt out; and perhaps in no city of Europe is theology so placid, so entirely at rest. The Wartburg still rears its picturesque eminence over the lovely Thuringian valleys; and Luther's room is visited by thousands of pilgrims; but in this very palace of the Wartburg, besides the room where Luther struggled with Satan, the visitors are shown the Banqueting Hall of the Minnesingers, where poet challenged poet, and the *Sängerkrieg,* or Minstrels' Contest, was celebrated. The contrast may be carried further. It may be taken as a symbol of the intellectual condition of Saxe-Weimar, that while the *relics* of Luther are simply preserved, the Minstrel Hall is now being restored in more than its pristine splendor. Lutheran theology is crumbling away, just as the famous *inkspot* has disappeared beneath the gradual scrapings of visitors' pen-knives; but the minstrelsy of which the Germans are so proud daily receives fresh honor and adulation. Nor is this adulation a mere revival. Every year the Wartburg saw assembled the members of that numerous family (the Bachs) which, driven from Hungary in the early period of Reform, had settled in Saxony, and had given, besides the great John Sebastian Bach, many noble musicians to the world. Too numerous to gain a livelihood in one city, the Bachs agreed to meet every year at the Wartburg. This custom, which was continued till the close of the eighteenth century, not only presented the singular spectacle of one family consisting of no less than a hundred and twenty musicians, but was also the occasion of musical entertainments such as were never heard before. They begin by religious hymns, sung in chorus ; they then took for their theme some popular song, comic or licentious, varying it by the improvisation of four, five, or six parts ; these improvisations were named *Quolibets*, and are considered by many writers to have been the origin of German opera.

The theologic fire has long burnt itself out in Thuringia. In Weimar, where Luther preached, another preacher came, whom we know as Goethe. In the old church there is one portrait of Luther, painted by his friend Lucas Kranach, greatly prized, as well it may be ; but for this one portrait of Luther, there are a hundred of Goethe. It is not Luther, but Goethe, they think of here ; poetry, not theology, is the glory of Weimar. And, corresponding with this, we find the dominant characteristic of the place to be no magnificent church, no picturesque ancient buildings, no visible image of the earlier ages, but the sweet serenity of a lovely park. The park fills the foreground of the picture, and always rises first in the memory. Any one who has spent happy hours wandering through its sunny walks and winding shades, watching its beauties changing through the fulness of summer, and the striking contrasts of autumn as it deepens into winter, will easily understand how Goethe could have been content to live in so small a city, which had, besides its nest of friends, so charming a park. It was indeed mainly his own creation ; and as it filled a large space in his life, it demands more than a passing allusion here.

Southwards from the palace it begins, with no obstacle of wall or iron gate, servant or sentinel, to *seem* to shut us out, so let us enter and look round. In the dew of morning, and in the silence of moonlight, we may wander undisturbed as if in our own grounds. The land stretches for miles away without barrier ; park and yellow corn-lands forming one

K

friendly expanse.   If we pass into it from the palace gates, a winding path to the right conducts us into the Belvedere Allée, — a magnificent avenue of chestnut-trees, two miles long, stretching from the new street to the summer palace of Belvedere.   This affords a shaded promenade along the park, in summer grateful for its coolness, in autumn looking like an avenue of golden trees.   It terminates in the gardens of the Belvedere, which has its park also beautifully disposed. Here the Weimarians resort, to enjoy the fresh air after their fashion, namely, with accompaniments of bad beer, questionable coffee, and detestable tobacco.

If, instead of turning into the Belvedere Allée, we keep within the park, our walks are so numerous that choice becomes perplexing.   Let us cross the *Stern Brücke*, a bridge leading from the palace.   Turning to our right and passing along through noble trees, we reach the broad road leading to Upper Weimar.   On this road, which skirts a meadow washed by the Ilm, we shall pass Goethe's *Gartenhaus* (Garden House, to be described hereafter), and then winding round the meadow, cross another bridge, and enter a shadowy path, picturesque with well-grouped trees, — the solemn pine, the beech whose dark green patches of moss increase the brilliancy of its silver bark, the weeping birch with its airy elegance of form, the plane-tree, the elm, the chestnut, and the mountain-ash brilliant with berries hanging like clusters of coral against the deep blue of the sky.   One steep side of this path is craggy with masses of moss-covered rock ; beneath the other flows the Ilm.   A few paces from the bridge which leads us here stands the *Borkenhaus* (Bark House), a hermit's hut, erected by Goethe for a fête of the duchess, and subsequently the favorite residence of the duke. It is only twenty feet long and fourteen deep, built entirely of wood, and plastered (so to speak) with the bark of trees.

It rests against a rock amid the trees, and is surrounded by a wooden gallery, reached by rough wooden steps. Where is the prince who would live in such a hut nowadays? Where are the ministers who would attend council in such a hut? Yet here Karl August lived alone, glad to escape from the tedium of etiquette, and the palling pleasures of a little court. Here he debated affairs of state, not less momentous to him because they were trivial in European politics. Here he bathed in the Ilm running beneath. Here he could see the Garden House of his poet, and make signs to him across the park. In this single room, which was at once dining-room, council-chamber, study, and bedroom, the manly duke lived alone for months.

From the *Borkenhaus* a small flight of stone steps conducts us to a mimic Ruin, and thence a narrow winding path leads to a stone monument, interesting as a witness to the growth of a mythos. It is an antique column, four feet high, round which a serpent winds, in the act of devouring the offering cakes on the top. The inscription says, *Genio Loci.* But the Weimar *plebs*, disregarding antique symbols, and imperfectly acquainted with Virgil, has a legend to tell; a legend sprung, no one knows whence, rapid and mysterious as the growth of fungi, like most legends, to satisfy the imperious craving for *explanations;* a legend which certifies how, formerly, a huge serpent dwelt in this spot, the terror of Weimar, until a cunning baker bethought him of placing poisoned cakes within the monster's reach; and when the greedy ignorance of the serpent had relieved Weimar of the monster, a grateful people erected this monument to an energetic and inventive baker : *Et voilà comme on écrit l'histoire.*

I will not fatigue the reader by dragging him all over this much-loved park, which must be enjoyed directly, not through description;* enough for present purposes if it be added that while the summer palace of Belvedere is connected with Weimar by the chestnut avenue, the summer palace and park of Tiefurt is also connected with Wiemar by a richly wooded road, the Webicht.   This Tiefurt is a tiny little place, quite a curiosity of diminutiveness.   The park, through which runs a branch of the Ilm, is tiny but picturesque.   The upper story of the palace is a labyrinth of tiny rooms, some of them so small that, standing with your back against one wall, you can touch the opposite wall with your hand.   It was here the Duchess Amalia lived.

" I have lived here fifty years," said Goethe to Eckermann, " and where have I not been ? but I was always glad to return to Weimar."   The stranger may wonder wherein lies the charm ; but a residence at Weimar soon reveals the secret. Among the charms are the environs.   First there is Ettersburg, with its palace, woods, and park, some seven miles distant.   Then there is Bercka with its charming valley, dear to all pedestrians, within half a dozen miles ; a little farther is Jena and its enchanting valley, from whose heights we look down on the sombre city, rendered illustrious by so many sounding names.   Jena was to science what Weimar was to poetry.   Assembled there were men like Griesbach, Paulus, Baumgarten-Crusius, and Danz, to teach theology ; Schelling, Fichte, Hegel, Reinhold, and Fries, to teach philosophy ; Loder, Hufeland, Oken, Döbereiner, to teach science ; Luden, Schultz, and others, for history.   The Schlegels and the Humboldts also lent their lustre to the place.   Besides Jena, we must mention Ilmenau, Eisenach, the Thuringian forests, and the valley of the Saal: environs attractive enough for the most restless wanderer.

* If a fuller description be desired, the reader will find one in the charming pages of Stahr's *Weimar und Jena*, to which I take this occasion of acknowledging a large debt.

Having thus sketched the main features of the *place*, it will now be desirable to give some indication of the *times*, that we may understand the atmosphere in which Goethe lived. Difficult as the restoration of Weimar has been to me, and only possible through the aid of what still remains from the old time, the difficulty has been tenfold with regard to the more changing aspects of society and opinion. Curiously enough the Germans, famous for writing on all subjects, have produced no work on the state of manners and the domestic conditions of this much-bewritten period. The books on Goethe are endless; there is not one which tells us of the outward circumstances among which he moved. From far and wide I have gathered together some details which may aid in forming a picture.

Remember that we are in the middle of the eighteenth century. The French Revolution is as yet only gathering its forces together; nearly twenty years must elapse before the storm breaks. The chasm between that time and our own is vast and deep. Every detail speaks of it. To begin with Science, — everywhere the torch of civilization, — it is enough to say that Chemistry did not then exist. Abundant materials indeed existed, but that which makes a science, namely, the power of *prevision* based on *quantitative* knowledge, was still absent; and Alchemy maintained its place among the conflicting hypotheses of the day. Goethe in Frankfurt was busy with researches after the " virgin earth." The philosopher's stone had many eager seekers. In 1787, Semler sent to the Academy of Berlin his discovery that gold grew in a certain atmospheric salt, when kept moist and warm. Klaproth, in the name of the Academy, examined this salt, and found indeed gold leaf in it — which had been put there by Semler's servant to encourage his master's credulity. This age, so incredulous in religion, was credulous in science.

In spite of all the labors of the encyclopedists, in spite of all the philosophic and religious "enlightenment," in spite of Voltaire and La Mettrie, it was possible for Count St. Germain and Cagliostro to delude thousands; and Casanova found a dupe in the Marquise d'Urfé, who believed he could restore her youth, and make the moon impregnate her! It was in 1774 that Mesmer astonished Vienna with his marvels of mystic magnetism. The secret societies of Freemasons and Illuminati, mystic in their ceremonies and chimerical in their hopes, — now in quest of the philosopher's stone, now in quest of the perfectibility of mankind, — a mixture of religious, political, and mystical reveries, flourished in all parts of Germany, and in all circles.

With science in so imperfect a condition, we are sure to find a corresponding poverty in material comfort and luxury. High-roads, for example, were only found in certain parts of Germany; Prussia had no *chaussée* till 1787. Milestones were unknown, although finger-posts existed. Instead of facilitating the transit of travellers, it was thought good political economy to obstruct them, for the longer they remained the more money they spent in the country. A century earlier, stage-coaches were known in England; but in Germany, public conveyances, very rude to this day in places where no railway exists, were few and miserable; nothing but open carts with unstuffed seats. Diligences on springs were unknown before 1800; and what they were, even twenty years ago, many readers doubtless remember. Then as to speed. In 1754 there was "the flying coach" running from Manchester to London, but taking four days and a half on the journey. In 1763 there was a coach between Edinburgh and London, once a month; it passed twelve or fourteen days on the road; though even in our own stage-coach days the distance was performed in forty-eight hours. And as

England was a busy nation, always in a hurry, we may gather from these details some idea of the rapidity of German travel. Germans were not flurried by agitations as to loss of time : if you travelled post, it was said with pride that seldom more than an hour's waiting was necessary before the horses were got ready, — at least on frequented routes. Mail travelling was at the rate of five English miles in an hour and a quarter. Letters took nine days from Berlin to Frankfurt, which in 1854 required only twenty-four hours. So slow was the communication of news that, as we learn from the Stein correspondence, the death of Frederick the Great was only known in Carlsbad as a rumor a week afterwards. " By this time," writes Goethe, "you must know in Weimar if it be true." With these obstacles to locomotion, it was natural that men travelled but rarely, and mostly on horseback. What the inns were may be imagined from the infrequency of travellers, and the general state of domestic comfort.

The absence of comfort and luxury (luxury as distinguished from ornament) may be gathered from the Memoirs of the time, and from such works as Bertuch's *Mode Journal.* Such necessities as good locks, doors that shut, drawers opening easily, tolerable knives, carts on springs, or beds fit for a Christian of any other than " the German persuasion," are still (1854) rarities in Thuringia ; but in those days, when sewers were undreamed of, and a post-office was only a vision, much that we moderns consider as comfort was necessarily wanting. The furniture, even of palaces, was extremely simple. In the houses of wealthy bourgeois, chairs and tables were of common deal ; not until the close of the eighteenth century did mahogany make its appearance. Looking-glasses followed. The chairs were covered with a coarse green cloth; the tables likewise ; and carpets are only now beginning to loom upon the national mind as a possible luxury.

The windows were hung with woollen curtains, when the extravagance of curtains was ventured on. Easy-chairs were unknown ; the only arm-chair allowed was the so-called *grandfather's chair*, which was reserved for the dignity of gray hairs, or the feebleness of ill health.

The *salon de réception,* or drawing-room, into which greatly honored visitors were shown, had of course a kind of Sunday splendor, not dimmed by week-day familiarity.   There hung the curtains ; the walls were adorned with family portraits or some work of native talent ; the tables alluring the eye with china, in guise of cups, vases, impossible shepherds, and very allegorical dogs.   Into this room the honored visitor was ushered ; and there, no matter what the hour, refreshment of some kind was handed.   This custom — a compound product of hospitality and bad inns — lingered until lately in England, and perhaps is still not unknown in provincial towns.

On eating and drinking was spent the surplus now devoted to finery.   No one then, except gentlemen of the first water, boasted of a gold snuff-box ; even a gold-headed cane was an unusual elegance.   The dandy contented himself with a silver watch.   The fine lady blazoned herself with a gold watch and heavy chain ; but it was an heirloom!   To see a modern dinner-service glittering with silver, glass, and china, and to think that even the nobility in those days ate off pewter, is enough to make the lapse of time very vivid to us.   A silver teapot and tea-tray were held as princely magnificence.

The manners were rough and simple.   The journeymen ate at the same table with their masters, and joined in the coarse jokes which then passed for hilarity. Filial obedience was rigidly enforced ; the stick or strap not unfrequently aiding parental authority.   Even the brothers exercised an almost paternal authority over their sisters.   Indeed, the position of women was by no means such as our women can hear of with patience ; not only were they kept under the paternal, marital, and fraternal yoke, but society limited their actions by its prejudices still more than it does now. No woman of the better class of citizens could go out alone ; the servant-girl followed her to church, to a shop, or even to the promenade.

The coarseness of language may be imagined from our own literature of that period. The roughness of manners is shown by such a scene as that in *Wilhelm Meister*, where the *Schöne Seele* in her confessions (speaking of high, well-born society), narrates how, at an evening party, forfeits were introduced ; one of these forfeits is, that a gentleman shall say something gallant to every lady present ; he whispers in the ear of a lady, who boxes his ears, and boxes with such violence that the powder from his hair flies into a lady's eyes ; when she is enabled to see again, it is to see that the husband of the lady has drawn his sword, and stabbed the offender, and that a duel, in the very presence of these women, is only prevented by one of the combatants being dragged from the room.

The foregoing survey would be incomplete without some notice of the prices of things ; the more so as we shall learn hereafter that the pension Karl August gave Schiller was 200 thalers, — about 30 *l.* of our money ; that the salary of Seckendorf as *Kammerherr* was only 600 thalers, or about 100 *l.* ; and that the salary Goethe received, as Councillor of Legation, was only 1,200 thalers, about 200 *l.* per annum. It is necessary I should indicate something like the real relation of these sums to the expense of living. We find, in Schiller's correspondence with Körner, that he hires a riding-horse for sixpence a day (Vol. I. p. 84), and gets a manuscript fairly copied at the rate of three halfpence a sheet of sixteen pages

8

(Vol. I. p. 92) ; with us the charge is twopence for every seventy-two words: the whole of *Don Carlos* cost but three and sixpence for copying.   He hires a furnished apartment, consisting of two rooms and a bedroom, for two pounds twelve and sixpence a quarter (Charlotte von Kalb writing to Jean Paul, November, 1776, says his lodgings will only cost him ten dollars, or thirty shillings, a quarter) ; while his male servant, who in case of need can act as secretary, is to be had for eighteen shillings a quarter (Vol. I. p. 111).   Reckoning up his expenses, he says, "Washing, servants, the barber, and such things, all paid quarterly, and none exceeding six shillings : so that, speaking in round numbers, I shall hardly need more than four hundred and fifty dollars" (Vol. II. p. 94) ; that is, about 70 *l.* a year.   Even when he is married, and sees a family growing round him, he says, "With eight hundred dollars I can live here, in Jena, charmingly, — *recht artig*" (Vol. II. p. 153).

It is evident that in Weimar they led no very sumptuous life.   A small provincial town overshadowed by a Court, its modes of life were the expression of this contrast.   The people, a slow, heavy, ungraceful, ignorant, but good-natured, happy, honest race, feeding on black bread and sausages. Rising higher, there were the cultivated classes of employees, artists, and professors ; and higher still, the aristocracy.   In the theatre, until 1825, the nobility alone were allowed admission to the boxes ; and when the Jena students crowded the pit, elbowing out the Weimar public, that public was forced to return home, or jostle with the students for seats in pit and gallery.   Even when the theatre was rebuilt, and the bourgeoisie was permitted a place in the boxes, its place was on the left side of the house, the right being rigorously reserved for the *Vons.*   This continued until 1848 ; since that year of revolutions the public has had the place it can pay for.

It is quite true, the Weimar court but little corresponded with those conceptions of grandeur, magnificence, and historical or political importance, with which the name of court is usually associated. But just as in gambling the feelings are agitated less by the greatness of the stake than by the variations of fortune, so in the social gambling of court intrigue, there is the same ambition and agitation, whether the green cloth be an empire or a duchy. Within its limits Saxe Weimar displayed all that an imperial court displays in larger proportions : it had its ministers, its army, its chamberlains, pages, and sycophants. Court favor and disgrace elevated and depressed, as if they had been imperial smiles or autocratic frowns. A standing army of six hundred men, with cavalry of fifty hussars, had its War Department, with war minister, secretary, and clerk.*

As the nobles formed the predominating element of Weimar, we see at once how, in spite of the influence of Karl August, and the remarkable men he assembled round him, no real public for Art could be found there. Some of the courtiers played more or less with Art, some had real feeling for it ; but the majority set decided faces against all the *beaux esprits.* When the Duchess Amalia travelled with Merck in 1778, Weimar was loud in anticipatory grumblings : " She will doubtless bring back some *bel esprit* picked up *en route!* " was the common cry. And really when we have learned, as we shall learn in a future chapter, the habits of these *beaux esprits*, and their way of making life " genial," impartiality will force us to confess that this imperfect sympathy on the part of the *Vons* was not without its reason.

Not without profound significance is this fact that in Wei-

* Lest this should appear too ridiculous, I will add that one of the small German princes (the Graf von Limburg Styrum) kept a corps of hussars, which consisted of a colonel, six officers, and two privates !

mar the poet found a Circle, but no Public. To welcome his productions there were friends and admirers; there was no Nation. Germany had no public; nor has it to this day. It was, and is, a collection of cities, not a Nation.* To appreciate by contrast the full significance of such a condition we must look at Greece and Rome. There the history of Art tells the same story as is everywhere told by the history of human effort. It tells us that to reach the height of perfection there must be the co-operation of the Nation with individual Genius. Thus it is necessary for the development of science that science should cease to be the speculation of a few, and become the minister of the many; from the constant pressure of unsatisfied *wants*, Science receives its energetic stimulus; and its highest reward is the satisfaction of those wants. In Art the same law holds. The whole Athenian Nation co-operated with its artists; and this is one cause why Athenian Art rose into unsurpassed splendor. Art was not the occupation of a few, ministering to the luxury of a few; it was the luxury of all. Its triumphs were not hidden in galleries and museums; they blazed in the noonday sun; they were admired and criticised by the whole people; and, as Aristotle expressly says, every free citizen was from youth upwards a critic of Art. Sophocles wrote for all Athens, and by all Athens was applauded. The theatre was open to all free citizens. Phidias and Praxiteles, Scopas and Myron, wrought their marvels in brass and marble, as expressions of a national faith, for the delights of a national mind. Temples and market-places, public groves and public walks, were the galleries wherein these sculptors placed their works. The public treasury was liberal in its rewards; and the rivalry of private munificence was not displayed to secure works for private galleries, but to enrich the public pos-

* The reader must remember this was written in 1854.

sessions.   In this spirit the citizens of Cnidos chose to continue the payment of an onerous tribute rather than suffer
their statue of Venus to quit their city.   And when some
murmurs rose against the expense which Pericles was incur-
ring in the building of the Parthenon, he silenced those murmurs by the threat of furnishing the money from his private
purse, and then placing his name on the majestic work.

Stahr, who has eloquently described the effects of such
national co-operation in Art, compares the similar influence
of publicity during the Middle Ages, when the great painters
and sculptors placed their works in cathedrals, — open all
day long, in council-houses and market-places, whither the
people thronged, — with the fact that in our day Art finds
refuge in the galleries of private persons, or in museums
closed on Sundays and holidays.*

Nor is this all.   The effect of Art upon the Nation is visible in the striking fact that in Greece and Rome the truly
great men were crowned by the public, not neglected for any
artist who pandered to the fashion and the tastes of the few,
or who flattered the *first* impressions of the many.   It was
young Phidias whom the Athenians chose to carve the statue
of Pallas Athene, and to build the Parthenon.   Suppose
Phidias had been an Englishman, would he have been
selected by government to give the nation a statue of Wel-
lington, or to build the Houses of Parliament?   The names
most reverenced by contemporaries, in Greece and in Italy,
are the names which posterity has declared to be the highest.   Necessarily so.   The verdict of the public, when that
public includes the whole intelligence of the nation, *must* be
the correct verdict in Art.

We may now glance at the Court of the reigning Duke
and Duchess, — Karl August and Luise.

* See his *Torso*, pp. 147 - 151.

Of the DUCHESS LUISE no one ever speaks but in terms of veneration.   She was one of those rare beings who, through circumstances the most trying, as well as through the ordinary details of life, manifest a noble character.   The Queen of Prussia and the Duchess of Saxe-Weimar are two of the great figures in modern German history ; they both opposed the chief man of the age, Napoleon, and were both admired by him for that very opposition.   Luise was of a cold temperament, somewhat rigid in her enforcement of etiquette, and wore to the last the old costume which had been the fashion in her youth ; apt in the early years of her marriage to be a little querulous with her husband, but showing throughout their lives a real and noble friendship for him.

And he was worthy of that friendship, much as his strange and in many respects opposite nature may have tried her. KARL AUGUST, whom Frederick the Great pronounced, at fourteen, to be the prince, of all he had seen, who gave the greatest promise, was in truth a very mixed, but very admirable, character.   He can afford to be looked at more closely and familiarly than most princes.   He was a man whose keen appreciation of genius not only drew the most notable men of the day to Weimar, but whose own intrinsically fine qualities *kept* them there.   It is easy for a prince to assemble men of talent.   It is not easy for a prince to make them remain beside him, in the full employment of their faculties, and in reasonable enjoyment of their position.   Karl August was the prince who with the smallest means produced the greatest result in Germany.   He was a man of restless activity.   His eye was on every part of his dominions ; his endeavors to improve the condition of the people were constant.   The recently published correspondence shows how active were his intellectual sympathies.   In his tastes no man in Germany was so simple, except his dearest friend, Goethe,

with whom, indeed, he had many cardinal points in common.
I remember, on first seeing their busts together, being struck
with a sort of faint family resemblance between them. Karl
August might have been a younger brother, considerably "ani-
alized," but still belonging to the family. They had both, on
the paternal side, Thuringian blood in their veins ; and in
many respects Amalia and Frau Aja were akin. But while
Karl August had the active, healthy, sensuous, pleasure-
loving temperament of his friend, he wanted the *tact* which
never allowed Goethe, except in his wildest period, to over-
step limits ; he wanted the tenderness and chivalry which
made the poet so uniformly acceptable to women. He was
witty, but his *bonmots* are mostly of that kind which, repeated
after dinner, are not considered fit for drawing-room publication. Very characteristic is it of him, who had bestowed unusual pains incollecting a *Bibliotheca Erotica*, that when Schiller wrote the *Maid of Orleans* he fancied Schiller was going to
give another version of *La Pucelle*, and abetted his mistress,
the Frau von Heygendorf, in her refusal to play the part of
the rehabilitated Maiden ! He was rough, soldierly, brusque,
and imperious. He was at home when in garrison with
Prussian soldiers, but out of his element when at foreign
Courts, and not always at ease in his own. Goethe describes
him longing for his pipe at the Court of Brunswick in 1774 :
" De son coté notre bon Duc s'ennuie terriblement, il
cherche un interet, il n'y voudrait pas etre pour rien, la
marche très bien mesuree de tout ce qu'on fait ici le gene, il
faut qu'il renonce a sa chere pipe, et une fee ne pourroit lui
rendre un service plus agreable qu'en changeant ce palais
dans une cabane de charbonnier." *

In a letter (unprinted) he writes to Goethe, then at Jena,

* *Briefe an Frau von Stein*, III. p. 85. The French is Goethe's as
also the spelling and accentuation, or rather want of accentuation.

saying he longs to be with him to watch sunrise and sunset,
for he can't see the sunset in Gotha, hidden as it is by the
crowd of courtiers, who are so *comme il faut*, and know their
"fish duty" with such terrible accuracy, that every evening
he feels inclined to give himself to the devil. His delight,
when not with soldiers, was to be with dogs, or with his poet
alone in their simple houses, discussing philosophy, and
"talking of lovely things that conquer death."   He mingled
freely with the people.   At Ilmenau he and Goethe put on
the miners' dress, descended into the mines, and danced all
night with peasant-girls. Riding across country, over rock
and stream, in manifest peril of his neck; teasing the maids
of honor, sometimes carrying this so far as to offend his more
princely wife; wandering alone with his dogs, or with some
joyous companion; seeking excitement in wine, and in making love to pretty women, without much respect of station; of-
fending by his roughness and wilfulness, though never *estrang-
ing* his friends,— Karl August, often grieving his admirers,
was, with all his errors, a genuine and admirable character.
His intellect was active; his judgment, both of men and
things, sound and keen.   Once, when there was a discussion
about appointing Fichte as professor at Jena, one of the opponents placed a work of Fichte's in the Duke's hands, as
sufficient proof that *such* a teacher could not hold a chair.
Karl August read the book,— and appointed Fichte.   He
had great aims; he also had the despotic will which bends
circumstances to its determined issues.   "He was always in
progress," said Goethe to Eckermann; "when anything failed,
he dismissed it at once from his mind.   I often bothered myself how to excuse this or that failure; but he ignored every
shortcoming in the cheerfullest way, and always went forward to something new."
Such was Karl August, as I conceive him from the letters

of the period, and from the reports of those who knew him. Eight years younger than Goethe, he attached himself to him as to a brother. We shall see this attachment and its reciprocal influence in the following pages; clouds sometimes gather, quarrels and dissatisfaction are not absent, (from what long friendship are they absent?) but fifty years of mutual service and mutual love proved the genuineness of both their characters.

HERDER did not come to Weimar till after Goethe, and indeed was drawn thither by Goethe, whose admiration for him, begun at Strasburg, continued unabated. The strange bitterness and love of sarcasm in Herder's nature, which could not repel the young student, did not alter the affection of the man. In one of Goethe's unpublished letters to the Duchess Amalia, there is an urgent appeal on behalf of Herder, whose large family had to be supported on very straitened means; the Duke had promised to provide for one of the children, and Goethe writes to Amalia, begging her to do the same for another. No answer coming to this appeal, or at any rate no prompt notice being taken, he writes again more urgently, adding, that if she does not provide for the child, he (Goethe), out of his small income, will! And this was at a time when Herder was most bitter against Goethe. Well might Merck exclaim, " No one can withstand the disinterestedness of this man ! "

CHAPTER II.

THE FIRST WILD WEEKS AT WEIMAR.

THIS was the Weimar which Goethe entered in all the splendor of youth, beauty, and fame, — Youth, which, accord-

ing to the fine conception of the Greeks, is "the herald of
Venus"; Beauty, which those Greeks adored as the splendor
of Truth; and Fame, which has at all times been a halo daz-
zling to mortal eyes. Thus equipped for conquest, how can
we wonder that he conquered? Even the Duchess Amalia,
angry with him for having ridiculed her darling Wieland,
could not withstand the magic of his presence. Her love of
genius left her no choice. She was fascinated by his wild
ways, and by his splendid talents. One moment he startled
her with a paradox, the next moment he sprang from his seat,
waltzing and whirling round the room with antics which made
her scream with laughter. And Wieland? — he was conquered at once. He shall speak for himself, in a letter written after their first interview : — " How perfectly I felt, at the
first glance, he was a man after my own heart! How I loved
the magnificent youth as I sat beside him at table! All that
I can say (after more than one crisis which I have endured)
is this : since that morning my soul is as full of Goethe as a
dew-drop of the morning sun. . . . . I believe the godlike
creature will remain longer with us than he intended; and if
Weimar *can* do anything, his presence will accomplish it."
This is very honorable to Wieland : Nestor gazes with unen-
vious delight upon the young Achilles. Heroic eyes are always proud to recognize heroic proportions.

After Wieland and the Duchess, the rest were easy to conquer. "He rose like a star in the heavens," says Knebel.
"Everybody worshipped him, especially the women." In the
costume of his own *Werther*, which was instantly adopted by
the Duke, he seemed the ideal of a poet. To moderns there
are no very sentimental suggestions in a costume which was
composed of blue coat and brass buttons, top-boots, and
leather breeches, the whole surmounted by powder and pigtail; but in those days this costume was the suggestion of

everything tender and romantic. Werther had consecrated it.*
The Duke not only adopted it, but made all around him adopt
it also, sometimes paying the tailor's bill himself.   Wieland
alone was excepted ; he was too old for such masqueradings.

Thoroughly to appreciate the effect of Goethe's influence
with women, we must remember the state of feeling and opinion at the time.   Those were the days of gallantry, the days
of

" Puffs, paints, and patches, powders, billets doux."

The laxity of German morals differed from the more audacious licentiousness of France : it had sentimentalism, in lieu
of gayety and luxuriousness, for its basis.   The heart of a
French marquise was lost over a supper-table sparkling with
champagne and *bonmots ;* the heart of a German Gräfin yielded
more readily to moonlight, melancholy, and a copy of verses.
Wit and audacity were the batteries for a Frenchwoman ;
the German was stormed with sonnets, and a threat of suicide.   For the one, Lothario needed sprightliness and *bon
ton ;* for the other, turbulent disgust at all social arrangements,
expressed in interjectional rhetoric, and a deportment outrageous to all conventions.   It is needless to add that marriage
was to a great extent what Sophie Arnould with terrible wit
called it, — "the sacrament of adultery" ; and that on the
subject of the sexes the whole tone of feeling was low.   Poor,
simple, earnest Schiller, whom no one will accuse of laxity,
admired *Les Liaisons Dangereuses,* and saw no reason why
women should not read it; although to our age the infamy of
that book is so great as to stamp a brand upon the society
which produced and applauded it.   Yet even Schiller, who
admired this book, was astounded at the condition of women

---

* It should be remembered, that in Germany, at that time, *boots* were
only worn in very bad weather ; and in the presence of women no one
ever appeared, except in shoes and silk stockings.

at Weimar. "There is hardly one of them," he writes to Körner, "who has not had a *liaison.* They are all coquettes. . . . . One may very easily fall into an 'affair of the heart,' though it will not *last* any time." It was thought, apparently, that since Eros had wings, he must use them — and fly.

With this tone of society we can understand how, as Goethe in after-life confessed to Eckermann, the first years at Weimar were perplexed with love-affairs. A great admirer of women, and greatly admired by them, it was natural he should fall into their snares. Many charmers are named; among them, Fräulein von Kalb, Coroner Schröter, and Kotzebue's sister, Amalia: but I am bound to say, that, after the most diligent inquiry, I can find *no* reliable evidence for believing any one of those named to have been really loved by him. We must content ourselves with the fact of his having flirted considerably: making love to every bright pair of eyes which for a moment could make him believe what he said.

For the first few months he gave himself up to the excitement of this new life. Among other things he introduced skating. Weimar had hitherto seen no gentleman on the ice; but now, Klopstock having made skating famous by his poetry, Goethe made it fashionable by his daring grace. The Duchess soon excelled in the art. Skating on the *Schwansee* became "the rage." Sometimes the banks were illuminated with lamps and torches, and music and fire-works animated the scene. The Duchess and ladies, masked as during carnival, were driven in sledges over the noisy ice. "We are somewhat mad here," Goethe writes to Merck, "and play the devil's own game." Wieland's favorite epithet for him was *wüthig,* — outrageous; and *wüthig* he was. Strange stories are told of him, now dashing across the ice, now loosening his long hair in Bertuch's room, and, with locks flowing over his shoulders, whirling round in mad Bacchante waltz; and finally, standing in the Jena market-place with the Duke, by the hour together, smacking huge sledge-whips for a wager. Imagine a Duke and a Poet thus engaged in a public market-place!

His constant companion, and in all deviltries and dissipation his most jovial associate, was Karl August. All ceremony was laid aside between them. They dined together, often shared the same bedroom, and called each other by the brotherly *thou.* "Goethe will never leave this place again," writes Wieland; "K. A. can no longer swim or wade without him. The court, or rather his liaison with the Duke, wastes his time, which is really a great pity; and yet, with so magnificent and godlike a creature nothing is ever lost!" Weimar was startled in its more respectable circles by the conduct of these two, and their associates: conduct quite in keeping with the period named "the *genial.*" * In their orgies they drank wine out of skulls (as Byron and his friends did in their wild days), and in ordinary intercourse exhibited but a very mitigated respect for *meum* and *tuum*, borrowing handkerchiefs and waistcoats which were never returned. The favorite epithet of that day was "infinite": Genius drank infinitely, loved infinitely, and swallowed infinite sausages.

But the poet's nature soon wearies of such scenes. After some two months of dissipation in masking, skating, hunting, drinking, and dicing, the want to be once more among simple people and lovely scenes drove him away from Weimar to Waldeck. Amid the crowded tumult of life he ever kept his soul sequestered; and from the hot air of society he broke impatiently away to the serenity of solitude. While on this journey along the pine-clad mountains, there came over him a feeling of the past, in which the image of Lili painfully reappeared.

* It is difficult to find an English word to express the German *genial,* which means pertaining to genius. The genial period was the period when every extravagance was excused on the plea of genius.

He was called back to Weimar by the Duke, impatient of his absence; and, while debating in his own mind whether he should accept a place there, or return to Frankfurt, he began to take his seat, as a guest, in the Privy Council. He had tried the Court, and now he was about to try what virtue lay in government. "I am here as if at home," so runs one of his letters, "and the Duke daily becomes dearer to me." Indeed his father's prognostications had failed. The connection between his son and the Duke was of a totally different kind from that between Voltaire and Frederick. In secret Voltaire despised the verses of his patron, and his patron in secret despised the weakness of Voltaire. A few unguarded expressions were enough to snap the link which bound them together; but a lifetime only deepened the friendship of Goethe and Karl August. Nor must it be supposed that their friendship was merely that of boon companions. Both had high aims and strong wills. Prince Hal might recreate himself with Falstaff, Pistol, Bardolph, and the rest; but, while chucking Mrs. Quickly under the chin, he knew he was one day to be England's lord. Karl August and Goethe were not the men to lose themselves in the fleeting hours of dissipation; serious, steady business was transacted almost the moment before some escapade. In their retreat at Ilmenau the poet writes: "My Karl and I here forget the strange mysterious Fate which guides us; and I feel that in these quiet moments we are preparing for new scenes." Yes, they learned "in the happy present to forecast the future."

The Duke knew what he was doing when he overstepped all precedent, and, in June, 1776, elected Goethe to the post of Geheime Legations Rath, with a seat and voice in the Privy Council, and a salary of twelve hundred thalers. In writing to Goethe's father, the Duke intimated that there was

absolute freedom of leaving the service at will, and that indeed the appointment was a mere formality, no measure of
his affection.   "Goethe can have but one position, — that of
my friend.   All others are beneath him."

The post of Geheime Legations Rath at Weimar is not a
very magnificent post ; and the salary of twelve hundred
thalers (about two hundred pounds) seems still less magnificent when we remember that at that period the King of
Prussia gave the Barberini, an Italian dancer, exactly *ten* times the sum.   But, such as it was, the appointment
created great noise.   Weimar was aghast.   The favor shown
to Wieland had not passed without scandal ; but alarming
indeed was this elevation of a Frankfurt bourgeois.   A poet,
who had gone through none of the routine of business, whose
life was anything but "respectable," to be lifted suddenly
over the plodding heads of legitimate aspirants !   If *this* was
to be, what reward could meritorious mediocrity expect ?
what advantage had slowly acquired routiniary knowledge ?

So murmured scandalized officials and their friends.   At
last these murmurs expressed themselves distinctly in the
shape of a protest.   The Duke thought the act worthy of a
deliberate justification, and with his own hand added these
words to the protocol of the acts of his ministry: "Enlightened persons congratulate me on possessing such a man.
His genius and capacity are well known.   To employ a man
of such a stamp in any other functions than those in which
he can render available the extraordinary gifts he possesses,
is to abuse them.   As to the observation that persons of
merit may think themselves unjustly passed over : I observe,
in the first place, that nobody, to my knowledge, in my service
has a right to reckon on an equal degree of favor ; and I
add that I will never consent to be governed by mere length
of service or rotation in my choice of a person whose func-

tions place him in such immediate relation to myself, and are so important to the happiness of my people. In such a case I shall attend to nothing but the degree of confidence I can repose in the person of my choice. The public opinion which perhaps censures the admission of Dr. Goethe to my council without having passed through the previous steps of Amtmann, Professor, Kammerrath, or Regierungsrath, produces no effect on my own judgment. The world forms its opinion on prejudices ; but I watch and work, — as every man must who wishes to do his duty, — not to make a noise, not to attract the applause of the world, but to justify my conduct to God and my conscience."

Assuredly we may echo M. Dumont's sentiment, that " the prince, who, at nineteen, wrote those words, was no ordinary man." He had not only the eye to see greatness, he had also the strong Will to guide his conduct according to his views, untrammelled by routine and formulas. "Say what you will, it is only like can recognize like, and a prince of great capacity will always recognize and cherish greatness in his servants." * People saw that the Duke was resolved. Murmurs were silenced ; or only percolated the gossip of private circles, till other subjects buried them, as all gossip is buried.

The mode of life which the *genial* company led was not only the subject of gossip in Weimar, it grew and grew as scandals grow, *not* losing substance on the way, till it reached the ears of distant friends. Thus, only a month before the appointment, Klopstock wrote to Goethe a letter " which scandal extorted from friendship " : —

" HAMBURG, 8th of May, 1776.

" Here is a proof of my friendship, dearest Goethe ! It is somewhat difficult, I confess, to give it, but it must be given.

* GOETHE in *Eckermann*, III. p. 232.

Do not fancy that I wish to preach to you about your doings, or that I judge harshly of you because you have other views than mine. But, your views and mine quite set aside, what will be the inevitable consequence if your present doings continue? The Duke, if he continues to drink as he does, instead of strengthening, as he says, his constitution, will ruin it, and will not live long. Young men of powerful constitutions — and that the Duke is not — have in this way early perished. The Germans have hitherto, and with justice, complained that their princes would have nothing to do with authors. They now gladly make an exception in favor of the Duke. But what a justification will not the other princes have, if you continue your present tone? If only that should happen which I feel will happen! The Duchess will perhaps still subdue her pain, for she has a strong manly intellect. But that pain will become grief! And can *that* be so suppressed? Louisa's grief, Goethe! . . . . I must add a word about Stolberg. He goes to Weimar out of friendship for the Duke. He must also live well with him. But how? In *his* style? No! unless he, too, becomes altered, he will go away. And then what remains for him? Not in Copenhagen, not in Weimar. I must write to Stolberg; what shall I say to him? You may please yourself about showing this letter to the Duke. I have no objection against it. On the contrary; for he is assuredly not yet arrived at that point when he will not listen to the honest word of a friend.

" KLOPSTOCK."

Goethe's answer, dated the 21st of May, a fortnight later, therefore, runs thus: —

"In future, spare us such letters, dear Klopstock! They do no good, and only breed bad blood. You must feel yourself that I have no answer to make. Either I must, like a

school-boy, begin a *Pater peccavi*, or sophistically excuse, or
as an honest fellow defend, and perhaps a mingling of all
these might express the truth, but to what purpose?   Therefore not a word more between us on this subject.   Believe
me, I should not have a moment's rest if I replied to all such
admonitions.   It pained the Duke a moment to think it was
Klopstock.   He loves and honors you : you know I do the
same.   Good by.   Stolberg must come all the same.   We
are no worse ; and with God's help will be better than what
he has seen us."

To this Klopstock indignantly replied : —

"You have much misunderstood the proof of my friendship, which was great precisely because of my reluctance to
mix myself unasked in the affairs of others.   And as you
include *all* such letters and *all* such admonitions (your expressions are as strong as that) in the same class with the
letter which contained this proof of my friendship, I hereby
declare you unworthy of that friendship.   Stolberg shall not
come, if he listens to me, or rather if he listens to his own
conscience."

The breach thus made was never repaired.   Stolberg did
not come to Weimar, and Klopstock wrote no more.

To return : whatever basis there may have been for the
reports which Gossip magnified, certain it is that the Duke
did not forget the cares of State in these wild orgies.   Both
he and his friend were very active, and very serious.   If
Weimar, according to the historian of Germany,* stands as
an illustrious exception among the German Courts, it was
because Karl August, upheld by his friend, knew how to
carry into earnest practice the axiom of Frederick the Great:
"A king is but the first of subjects."   Goethe's beneficent
activity is seen less in such anecdotes as those often cited

* MENZEL, CCXLI.

of his opening a subscription for Bürger to enable him to complete his translation of *Homer*, and of his relieving Jung Stilling from distress, than in the constant and *democratic* sympathy with which he directed the Duke's endeavors.

It is worth bearing in mind *what* the young Goethe was, that we may the better understand the reason of what he became.   No sooner had he commenced his career as politician, than he began to tone down the extravagance of his demeanor; without foregoing any enjoyments, he tried to accord more with those in whom a staid demeanor was necessitated by their more flagging pulses of lethargic life. One month after his appointment Wieland writes of him : "Goethe did in truth, during the first months of his visit here, scandalize most people (never me); but from the moment that he decided on becoming a man of business, he has conducted himself with blameless σωφροσύνη and all worldly prudence."   Elsewhere he says : "Goethe, with all his real and apparent *sauvagerie*, has, in his little finger, more *conduite* and *savoir faire* than all the court parasites, Boniface sneaks, and political cobweb-spinners have in their whole bodies and souls.   So long as Karl August lives, no power can remove him."

As we familiarize ourselves with the details of this episode, there appears less and less plausibility in the often-iterated declamation against Goethe on the charge of his having "sacrified his genius to the court."   It becomes indeed a singularly foolish display of rhetoric.   Let us for a moment consider the charge.   He had to choose a career.   That of poet was then, as it is still, terribly delusive; verse could create fame, but no money : *fama* and *fames* were then, as now, in dangerous contiguity.   No sooner is the necessity for a career admitted than much objection falls to the ground; for those who reproach him with having wasted his time on court festivities, and the duties of government which others could have done as well, must ask whether he would have *saved* that time had he followed the career of jurisprudence and jostled lawyers through the courts at Frankfurt? or would they prefer seeing him reduced to the condition of poor Schiller, wasting so much of his precious life in literary "hackwork," translating French books for a miserable pittance? *Time*, in any case, would have been claimed; in return for that given to Karl August, he received, as he confesses in the poem addressed to the Duke, "what the great seldom bestow, — affection, leisure, confidence, garden, and house. No one have I to thank but him; and much have I wanted, who, as a poet, ill understood the arts of gain. If Europe praised me, what has Europe done for me? Nothing. Even my works have been an expense to me."

In 1801, writing to his mother on the complaints uttered against him by those who judged falsely of his condition, he says they only saw what he gave up, not what he gained; they could not comprehend how he grew daily richer, though he daily gave up so much. He confesses that the narrow circle of a burgher life would have ill-accorded with his ardent and wide-sweeping spirit. Had he remained at Frankfurt, he would have been ignorant of the world. But here the panorama of life was unrolled before him, and his experience was every way enlarged. Did not Leonardo da Vinci spend much of his time charming the court of Milan with his poetry and lute-playing? Did he not also spend time in mechanical and hydrostatical labors for the State? No reproach is lifted against his august name; no one cries out against *his* being false to his genius; no one rebukes him for having painted so little at one period. The "Last Supper" speaks for him. Will not *Tasso, Iphigenia, Her-*

mann und Dorothea, Faust, Meister, and the long list of Goethe's works, speak for *him?*

I have dwelt mainly on the dissipation of his *time*, because the notion that a court life affected his genius by "corrupting his mind" is preposterous. No reader of this biography, it is to be hoped, will fail to see the true relations in which he stood to the Duke ; how free they were from anything like servility, or suppression of genuine impulse. Indeed, one of the complaints against him, according to the unexceptionable authority of Riemer, was that made by the subalterns, " of his not being sufficiently attentive to court etiquette." To say, as Niebuhr says, that the " court was a Delilah to which he sacrificed his locks," is profoundly to misunderstand his genius, profoundly to misread his life. Had his genius been of that stormy kind which produces great Reformers and great Martyrs, — had it been his mission to agitate mankind by words, reverberating to their inmost recesses, and calling them to lay down their lives in the service of an Idea, — had it been his tendency to meditate upon our far-off destinies, or to sway men by the coercion of grand representative abstractions, — then, indeed, we might say his place was aloof from the motley throng, and not in sailing down the swiftly flowing stream to sounds of mirth and music on the banks. But he was not a Reformer, not a Martyr. He was a Poet, whose religion was Beauty, whose worship was of Nature, whose aim was Culture. His mission was to paint Life, and for that it was requisite he should see it. Happier circumstances might, indeed, have surrounded him, and given him a greater sphere. It would have been very different, as he often felt, if there had been a Nation to appeal to, instead of a heterogeneous mass of small peoples, willing enough to talk of Fatherland, but in no wise prepared to *become* a Nation. They are many other

ifs in which much virtue could be found ; but inasmuch as
he could not create circumstances, we must follow his example, and be content with what the gods provided.   I do
not, I confess, see what other sphere was open to him in
which his genius could have been more sacred ; but I do
see that he built out of circumstances a noble Temple in
which the altar-flame burnt with a steady light.   To hypothetical biographers be left the task of settling what Goethe
might have been ; enough for us to catch some glimpse of
what he was.

"Poetry," says Carlyle, "is the attempt which man makes
to render his existence harmonious."   It is the flower into
which a life expands ; but it is not the life itself, with all
daily needs, daily struggles, daily prosaisms.   The true poet
manfully accepts the condition in which destiny has placed
him, and therein tries to make his existence harmonious ;
the sham poet, like a weak workman, fretful over his tools,
is loud in his assurances of what he *might* be, were it his lot
to live in other circumstances.   Goethe was led by the current of events to a little court, where he was arrested by
friendship, love, leisure, and opportunities of a freer, nobler
life than Frankfurt Law Courts offered him.   After much
deliberation he chose his career : these pages will show how
in it he contrived to be *true* to his genius.

It is scarcely worth while to notice trash about his servility
and court slavery.   He was not required to be servile ; and
his nature was as proud as any prince's.   "They call me a
prince's servant," he said to Eckermann, "and a prince's
slave ; as if there were any meaning in such words !   Whom
do I serve?   A tyrant — a despot?   Do I serve one who
lives for his own pleasures at the people's cost ?   Such
princes and such times are, thank God ! far enough from us.
For more than half a century I have been connected in the

closest relations with the Grand Duke, and for half a century
have striven and toiled with him ; but I should not be speaking truth were I to say that I could name a single day on
which the Duke had not his thoughts busied with something
to be devised and effected for the good of the country :
something calculated to better the condition of each individual in it. As for himself, personally, what has his princely
state given him but a burden and a task ? Is his dwelling,
or his dress, or his table, more sumptuously provided than
that of any private man in easy circumstances? Go into
our maritime cities, and you will find the larder and cellar
of every considerable merchant better filled than his. If,
then, I am a prince's slave, it is at least my consolation that
I am but the slave of one who is himself a slave of the
general good."

And to close this subject, read the following passage from
Merck's letter to Nicolai (the Merck who is said by Falk to
have spoken so bitterly of the waste of Goethe's life at Wiemar) : " I have lately paid Goethe a visit at the Wartburg,
and we have lived together for ten days like children. I am
delighted to have seen with my own eyes what his situation
is. The Duke is the best of all, and has a character firm as
iron : *I would do, for love of him, just what Goethe does.* . . . .
I tell you sincerely, that the Duke is most worthy of respect,
and one of the cleverest men that I have ever seen ; and
consider that he is a prince, and only twenty years of age ! "
The long and friendly correspondence Merck kept up with
the Duke is the best pledge that the foregoing estimate was
sincere.

CHAPTER III.

THE FRAU VON STEIN.

FROM out the many flirtations that amused him, there rises one which grew into predominant importance, swallowing up all the others, and leaping from lambent flame into eager and passionate fire. It was no transitory flash, but a fire which burnt for ten years; and thereby is distinguished from all previous attachments. It is a silver thread woven among the many-colored threads which formed the tapestry of his life. I will here detach it, to consider it by itself.

The Baroness von Stein, "Hofdame," and wife of the Master of the Horse, was, both by family and position, a considerable person. To us she is interesting as having sprung from a Scotch family, named Irving, and as being the sister-in-law to that Baron Imhoff who sold his first wife to Warren Hastings. She was the mother of seven children, and had reached that age which, in fascinating women, is of perilous fascination, — the age of three-and-thirty. We can understand something of her power if we look at her portrait, and imagine those delicate, coquettish features animated with the lures of sensibility, gayety, and experience of the world. She sang well, played well, sketched well, talked well, appreciated poetry, and handled sentiment with the delicate tact of a woman of the world. Her pretty fingers had turned over many a serious book; and she knew how to gather honey from weeds. With moral deficiencies, which this history will betray, she was to all acquaintances a perfectly *charming* woman; and retained her charm even in old age, as many living witnesses testify. Some years after her first acquaintance with Goethe, Schiller thus writes of her to his friend Körner : " She is really a genuine, interesting person, and I quite understand what has attached Goethe to her. Beautiful she can never have been ; but her countenance has a soft earnestness, and a quite peculiar openness. A healthy understanding, truth, and feeling lie in her nature. She has more than a thousand letters from Goethe ; and from Italy he writes to her every week. They say the connection is perfectly pure and blameless."

It was at Pyrmont that Goethe first saw the Frau von Stein's portrait, and was three nights sleepless in consequence of Zimmermann's description of her. In sending her that flattering detail, Zimmermann added, " He will assuredly come to Weimar to see you." Under her portrait Goethe wrote, " What a glorious poem it would be to see how the world mirrors itself in this soul ! She sees the world as it is, and yet withal sees it through the medium of love ; hence sweetness is the dominant expression." In her reply to Zimmermann she begs to hear more about Goethe, and intimates her desire to see him. This calls forth a reply that she " has no idea of the danger of his magical presence." Such dangers pretty women gladly run into, especially when, like Charlotte von Stein, they are perfect mistresses of themselves.

With his heart still trembling from the agitations of victory over its desires, after he had torn himself away from Lili, he saw this charming woman. The earth continues warm long after the sun has glided below the horizon ; and the heart continues warm some time after the departure of its sun. Goethe was therefore prepared to fall desperately in love with one who " viewed all things through the medium of love." And there is considerable interest in noting the *kind* of idol now selected. Hitherto he has been captivated only by very young girls, whose youth, beauty, and girlishness were the

9   M

charms to his wandering fancy; but now he is fascinated by a *woman*, a woman of rank and elegance, a woman of culture and experience, a woman who, instead of abandoning herself to the charm of his affection, knew how, without descending from her pedestal, to keep the flame alive. The others loved him, — showed him their love, — and were forgotten. She contrived to keep him in the pleasant fever of hope; made herself necessary to him; made her love an aim, and kept him in the excitement of one

> " Who never is, but always to be blest."

Considering the state of society and opinion at that period, and considering moreover that, according to her son's narrative, her husband was scarcely seen in his own home more than once a week, and that no pretence of affection existed between them, we can understand how Goethe's notorious passion for her excited sympathy in Weimar. Not a word of blame escaped any one on this subject. They saw a lover whose mistress gave him just enough encouragement to keep him eager in pursuit, and who knew how to check him when that eagerness would press on too far. In his early letters to her there are sudden outbreaks and reserves; sometimes the affectionate *thou* escapes, and the next day, perhaps even in the next sentence, the prescribed *you* returns. The letters follow almost daily.

In a little while the tone grows more subdued. Just as the tone of his behavior in Weimar, after the first wild weeks, became softened to a lower key, so in these letters we see, after a while, fewer passionate outbreaks, fewer interjections, and no more *thous*. But love warms them still. The letters are incessant, and show an incessant preoccupation. Certain sentimental readers will be shocked, perhaps, to find so many details about eating and drinking; but when they remember

Charlotte cutting bread and butter, they may understand the author of *Werther* eloquently begging his beloved to send him a sausage.

The visitor may still read the inscription, at once homage and souvenir, by which Goethe connected the happy hours of love with the happy hours of active solitude passed in his Garden House in the Park. Fitly is the place dedicated to the Frau von Stein. The whole spot speaks of her. Here are the flower-beds from which almost every morning flowers, with the dew still on them, accompanied letters, not less fresh and beautiful, to greet the beloved. Here are the beds from which came the asparagus he was so proud to send her. Here is the orchard in which grew the fruit he so often sent. Here is the room in which he dreamt of her ; here the room in which he worked, while her image hovered round him. The house stands within twenty minutes' walk from the house where she lived, separated from it by clusters of noble trees.

If the reader turns back to the description of the Park, he will ascertain the position of this *Gartenhaus.* Originally it belonged to Bertuch. One day when the Duke was earnestly pressing Goethe to take up his residence at Weimar, the poet (who then lived in the Jägerhaus in the Belvidere Allée), undecided as to whether he should go or remain, let fall, among other excuses, the want of a quiet bit of land, where his taste for gardening could be indulged. " Bertuch, for example, is very comfortable ; if I had but such a piece of ground as that ! " Hereupon the Duke, very characteristically, goes to Bertuch, and without periphrasis, says, " I must have your garden." Bertuch starts : " But, your Highness — " " But me no buts," replies the young prince ; " I can't help you. Goethe wants it, and unless we give it to him we shall never keep him here ; it is the only way to secure him." This reason would probably not have been so

cogent with Bertuch, had not the Duke excused the despotism of his act by giving in exchange more than the value of
the garden. It was at first only lent to Goethe ; but in 1780
it was made a formal gift.

It is charmingly situated, and, although of modest pretensions, is one of the most enviable houses in Weimar. The
Ilm runs through the meadows which front it. The town,
although so near, is completely shut out from view by the
thick-growing trees. The solitude is absolute, broken only
by the occasional sound of the church clock, the music from
the barracks, and the screaming of the peacocks spreading
their superb beauty in the park. So fond was Goethe of
this house, that winter and summer he lived there for seven
years ; and when, in 1782, the Duke made him a present of
the house in the *Frauenplan*, he could not prevail upon himself to sell the Gartenhaus, but continued to make it a favorite retreat. Often when he chose to be alone and undisturbed, he locked all the gates of the bridges which led from
the town to his house, so that, as Wieland complained,
no one could get at him except by aid of picklock and
crow-bar.

It was here, in this little garden, he studied the development of plants, and made many of those experiments and
observations which had given him a high rank among the
discoverers in Science. It was here the poet escaped from
court. It was here the lover was happy in his love. How
modest this Garden House really is ; how far removed from
anything like one's preconceptions of it ! It is true, that the
position is one which many a rich townsman in England
would be glad of, as the site for a handsome villa : a pretty
orchard and garden on a gentle slope ; in front, a good carriage road, running beside a fine meadow, encircled by the
stately trees of the park. But the house a half-pay captain

with us would consider a miserable cottage ; yet it sufficed
for the court favorite and minister.   Here the Duke was constantly with him ; sitting up, till deep in the night, in earnest
discussion ; often sleeping on the sofa instead of going home.
Here both Duke and Duchess would come and dine with
him, in the most simple, unpretending way ; the whole banquet in one instance consisting, as we learn from a casual
phrase in the Stein correspondence, of " a beer soup and a
little cold meat." *

There is something very pleasant in noticing these traits
of the simplicity which was then practised.   The Duke's own
hut — the *Borkenhaus* — has already been described (page
162).   The hut, for it was nothing else, in which Goethe
lived in the Ilmenau Mountains, and the more than
bourgeois simplicity of the Garden House, make us aware of
one thing among others, namely, that if he sacrificed his
genius to a court, it assuredly was not for loaves and fishes,
not for luxury and material splendor of any kind.   Indeed,
such things had no temptation to a man of his simple tastes.
" Rich in money," he writes to his beloved, " I shall never
become ; but, therefore, all the richer in Confidence, Good
Name, and influence over the minds of men."

It was his love of Nature which made him so indifferent
to luxury.   That love gave him simplicity and hardihood.   In
many things he was unlike his nation : notably in his voluntary exposure to two bright, wholesome things, which to his
contemporaries were little less than bugbears, — I mean fresh
air and cold water.   The nation which consented to live in
the atmosphere of iron stoves, tobacco, and bad breath, and
which deemed a pint of water all that man could desire for
his ablutions, must have been greatly perplexed at seeing

* Compare also the *Briefwechsel zwischen Karl August und Goethe,*
I. 27.

Goethe indulge in fresh air and cold water as enjoyingly as if they were vices.

Two anecdotes will bring this contrast into relief. So great was the German reluctance to even a necessary exposure to the inclemencies of open-air exercise, that historians inform us "a great proportion, especially among the learned classes, employed a miserable substitute for exercise in the shape of a machine, by means of which they comfortably took their dose of movement without leaving their rooms."* And Jacobs, in his *Personalien*, records a fact which, while explaining how the above-named absurdity could have gained ground, paints a sad picture of the life of German youth in those days. Describing his boyish days at Gotha, he says: "Our winter pleasures were confined to a not very spacious court-yard, exchanged in summer for a little garden within the walls, which my father hired. *We took no walks. Only once a year, when the harvest was ripe, our parents took us out to spend an evening in the fields.*" † So little had Goethe of this prejudice against fresh air, that when he began the rebuilding of his Gartenhaus, instead of sleeping at an hotel or at the house of a friend, he lived there through all the building period; and we find him writing, "At last I have a window once more, and can make a fire." On the 3d of May he writes, "Good morning: here is asparagus. How were you yesterday? Philip baked me a cake; and thereupon, wrapped up in my blue cloak, I laid myself on a dry corner of the terrace and slept amid thunder, lightning, and rain, so gloriously that my bed was afterwards quite disagreeable." On the 19th he writes, "Thanks for the breakfast. I send you something in return. Last night I slept on the

* BIEDERMANN, *Deutschland's Politische Materielle und Sociale Zustände*, I. p. 343.

† Quoted by Mrs. AUSTIN, *Germany from 1760 to 1814*, p. 85.

terrace, wrapped in my blue cloak, awoke three times, at 12, 2, and 4, and *each time there was a new splendor in the heavens.*" There are other traces of this tendency to bivouac, but these will suffice. He bathed, not only in the morning sunlight, but also in the Ilm. when the moonlight shimmered on it.

One night, while the moon was calmly shining on our poetical bather, a peasant, returning home, was in the act of climbing over the bars of the floating bridge when Goethe espied him, and, moved by that spirit of deviltry which so often startled Weimar, he gave utterance to wild sepulchral tones, raised himself half out of water, ducked under, and reappeared howling, to the horror of the aghast peasant, who, hearing such sounds issue from a figure with long floating hair, fled as if a legion of devils were at hand. To this day there remains an ineradicable belief in the existence of the water-sprite who howls among the waters of the Ilm.

———•———

CHAPTER IV.

PRIVATE THEATRICALS.

"LET my present life," writes Goethe to Lavater, January, 1777, "continue as long as it will, at any rate I have heartily enjoyed a genuine experience of the variegated throng and press of the world, — Sorrow, Hope, Love, Work, Wants, Adventure, Ennui, Impatience, Folly, Joy, the Expected and the Unknown, the Superficial and the Profound, — just as the dice threw — with fêtes, dances, sledgings — adorned in silk and spangles — a marvellous *ménage!* And withal, dear brother, God be praised, in myself and in my real aims in life I am quite happy."

"Goethe plays indeed a high game at Weimar," writes Merck, "but lives at Court after his own fashion. The Duke is an excellent man, let them say what they will, and in Goethe's company will become still more so. What you hear is Court scandal and lies. It is true the intimacy between master and servant is very great, but what harm is there in that? *Were Goethe a nobleman it would be thought quite right.* He is the soul and direction of everything, and all are contented with him, because he serves many and injures no one. Who can withstand the disinterestedness of this man?"

He had begun to make his presence felt in the serious department of affairs ; not only in educating the Duke who had chosen him as his friend, but also in practical ameliorations. He had induced the Duke to call Herder to Weimar, as *Hof Prediger* (Court chaplain) and *General-superintendent ;* whereat Weimar grumbled and gossiped, setting afloat stories of Herder having mounted the pulpit in boots and spurs. Not content with these efforts in a higher circle, Goethe sought to improve the condition of the people ; and among his plans we note one for the opening of the Ilmenau mines, which for many years had been left untouched.

Amusement went hand in hand with business. Among the varied amusements, one, which greatly occupied his time and fancy, deserves a more special notice, because it will give us a glimpse of the Court, and will also show us how the poet turned sport into profit. I allude to the private theatricals which were started shortly after his arrival. It should be premised that the theatre was still in ashes from the fire of 1774.* Seyler had carried his troupe of players elsewhere ; and Weimar was without its stage. Just at this period private

* On the state of the theatre before Goethe's arrival and subsequently, see PASQUE, *Goethe's Theaterleitung in Weimar,* 1863.

theatricals were even more "the rage" than they are in England at present. In Berlin, Dresden, Frankfurt, Augsburg, Nuremberg, and Fulda were celebrated amateur troupes. In Würtzburg, for a long while, a *noble* company put on sock and buskin; in Eisenach, Prince and Court joined in the sport. Even the Universities, which in earlier times had, from religious scruples, denounced the drama, now forgot their antagonism, and in Vienna, Halle, Göttingen, and Jena allowed the students to have private stages.

The Weimar theatre surpassed them all. It had its poets, its composers, its scene-painters, its costumers. Whoever showed any talent for recitation, singing, or dancing, was pressed into service, and had to work as hard as if his bread depended on it. The almost daily rehearsals of drama, opera, or ballet occupied and delighted men and women glad to have something to do. The troupe was distinguished: the Duchess Amalia, Karl August, Prince Constantine, Bode, Knebel, Einsiedel, Musäus, Seckendorf, Bertuch, and Goethe, with Corona Schröter, Kotzebue's sister Amalia, and Fräulein Göchhausen. These formed a curious strolling company, wandering from Weimar to all the palaces in the neighborhood — Ettersburg, Tiefurt, Belvedere, even to Jena, Dornburg, and Ilmenau. Often did Bertuch, as Falk tells us, receive orders to have the sumpter wagon, or travelling kitchen, ready for the early dawn, when the Court would start with its wandering troupe. If only a short expedition was intended, three sumpter asses were sufficient. If it was more distant, over hill and dale, far into the distant country, then indeed the night before was a busy one, and all the ducal pots and pans were in requisition. Such boiling and stewing and roasting! such slaughter of capons, pigeons, and fowls! The ponds of the Ilm were dragged for fish; the woods were robbed of their partridges; the cellars were

9*

lightened of their wines. With early dawn rode forth the merry party, full of anticipation, wild with animal spirits. On they went through solitudes, the grand old trees of which were wont only to see the soaring hawk poised above their tops, or the wild-eyed deer bounding past the hut of the charcoal-burner. On they went: youth, beauty, gladness, and hope, a goodly train, like that which animated the forest of Ardennes, when "under the shade of melancholy boughs" the pensive Duke and his followers forgot awhile their cares and "painted pomps."

Their stage was soon arranged. At Ettersburg the traces are still visible of this forest stage, where, when weather permitted, the performances took place. A wing of the château was also made into a theatre. But the open-air performances were most relished. To rehearsals and performances in Ettersburg the actors, sometimes as many as twenty, were brought in the Duke's equipages ; and in the evening, after a joyous supper often enlivened with songs, they were conducted home by the Duke's body-guard of Hussars bearing torches. It was here they performed Einsiedel's opera, *The Gypsies*, with wonderful illusion. Several scenes of *Götz von Berlichingen* were woven into it. The illuminated trees, the crowd of gypsies in the wood, the dances and songs under the blue starlit heavens, while the sylvan bugle sounded from afar, made up a picture the magic of which was never forgotten. On the Ilm also, at Tiefurt, just where the river makes a beautiful bend round the shore, a regular theatre was constructed. Trees, and other poetical objects, such as fishermen, nixies, water-spirits, moon, and stars, — all were introduced with effect.

I find further that when a travesty of the "Birds" of Aristophanes was performed at Ettersburg, the actors were all dressed in real feathers, their heads completely covered, though free to move. Their wings flapped, their eyes rolled, and ornithology was absurdly parodied. It is right to add that besides these extravagances and *ombres chinoises*, there were very serious dramatic efforts: among them we find Goethe's second dramatic attempt, *Die Mitschuldigen*, which was thus cast : —

Alceste	Goethe.
Söller	Bertuch.
Der Wirth	Musäus.
Sophie	Corona Schröter.

Another play was the *Geschwister*, written in three evenings, it is said, but without evidence, out of love for the sweet eyes of Amalia Kotzebue, sister of the dramatist, then a youth. Kotzebue thus touches the point in his *Memoirs:* "Goethe had at that time just written his charming piece, *Die Geschwister.* It was performed at a private theatre at Weimar, he himself playing William, and my sister, Marianne; while to me — yes, to me — was allotted the important part of Postilion! My readers may imagine with what exultation I trod the stage for the first time before the mighty public itself." Another piece was Cumberland's *West-Indian*, in which the Duke played Major O'Flaherty; Eckhoff (the great actor), the Father; and Goethe, Belcour, dressed in a white coat with silver lace, blue silk vest, and blue silk knee-breeches, in which, it is said, he looked superb.

While mentioning these, I must not pass over the *Iphigenia* (then in prose), which was thus cast : —

Orestes	Goethe.
Pylades	Prince Constantine.
Thoas	Knebel.
Arkas	Seidler.
Iphigenia	Corona Schröter.

" Never shall I forget," exclaims Dr. Hufeland, "the impression Goethe made as Orestes, in his Grecian costume ; one might have fancied him Apollo. Never before had there been seen such union of physical and intellectual beauty in one man ! His acting, as far as I can learn, had the ordinary defects of amateur acting ; it was impetuous and yet stiff, exaggerated and yet cold ; and his fine sonorous voice displayed itself without nice reference to shades of meaning. In comic parts, on the other hand, he seems to have been excellent ; the broader the fun, the more at home he felt ; and one can imagine the rollicking animal spirits with which he animated the Marktschreier in the *Plundersweilern ;* one can picture him in the extravagance of the *Geflickte Braut,** giving vent to his sarcasam on the " sentimental " tone of the age, ridiculing his own *Werther,* and merciless to *Woldemar.* †

I have thus brought together, irrespective of dates, the scattered indications of these theatrical amusements. How much enjoyment was produced by them ! what social pleasure ! and what endless episodes, to which memory recurred in after times, when the actors were seated round the dinner-table ! Nor were these amusements profitless. *Wilhelm Meister* was designed and partly written about this period ; and the reader, who knows Goethe's tendency to make all his works biographical, will not be surprised at the amount of theatrical experience which is mirrored in that work ; nor at the ear nestness which is there made to lurk beneath amusement, so that what to the crowd seems no more than a flattery of their tastes, is to the man himself a process of the highest culture.

Boar-hunting in the light of early dawn, sitting in the middle of the day in grave diplomacy and active council, rehears-

---

* Published under a very mitigated form, as the *Triumph der Empfindsamkeit* See the next chapter for further notice of this piece.

† Jacobi and Wieland were both seriously offended with his parodies of their writings ; but both soon became reconciled to him.

ing during the afternoon, and enlivening the evening with grotesque serenades or torchlight sledgings, — thus passed many of his days ; not to mention flirtations, balls, masquerades, concerts, and verse-writing. The muse was, however, somewhat silent, though *Hans Sachs' poetische Senndung, Lila,* some charming lyrics, and the dramas and operas, written for the occasion, forbid the accusation of idleness. He was storing up materials. *Faust, Egmont, Tasso, Iphigenia,* and *Meister* were germinating.

The muse was silent, but was the soul inactive ? As these strange and variegated scenes passed before his eyes, was he a *mere* actor, and not also a spectator ? Let his works answer. To some indeed it has seemed as if in thus lowering great faculties to the composition of slight operas and festive pieces, Goethe was faithless to his mission, false to his own genius. Herder thought that the Chosen One should devote himself to great works. This is the objection of a man of letters who can conceive no other aim than the writing of books. But Goethe needed to *live* as well as to write. Life is multiplied and rendered infinite by Feeling and Knowledge. He sought both to feel and to know. The great works he has written — works high in conception, austerely grand in execution, the fruits of earnest toil and lonely self-seclusion — ought to shield him *now* from any charge of wasting his time on frivolities. But to Herder and Merck such a point of view was denied.

It was his real artistic nature, and genuine poetic mobility, that made him scatter with a prodigal hand the trifles which distressed his friends. Poetry was a melodious voice breathing from his entire manhood, not a profession, not an act of duty. It was an impulse : the sounding chords of his poetic nature vibrated to every touch, grave and stately, sweet and impassioned, delicate and humorous. He wrote not for

Fame. He wrote not for Money. He wrote poetry because he had *lived* it; and sang as the bird sings on its bough. Open to every impression, touched to ravishment by Beauty, he sang whatever at the moment filled him with delight, — now trilling a careless snatch of melody, now a simple ballad, now a majestic hymn ascending from the depths of the soul on incense-bearing rhythms, and now a grave quiet chant, slow with its rich burden of meanings. Men in whom the productive activity is great cannot be restrained from throwing off trifles, as the plant throws off buds beside the expanded flowers. Michael Angelo carved the Moses, and painted the ceiling of the Sistine Chapel, but did he not also lend his master-hand to the cutting of graceful cameos?

CHAPTER V.

MANY-COLORED THREADS.

HITHERTO our narrative of this Weimar period has moved mainly among generalities, for only by such means could a picture of this episode be painted. Now, as we advance further, it is necessary to separate the threads of his career from those of others with which it was interwoven.

It has already been noted that he began to tire of the follies and extravagances of the first months. In this year, 1777, he was quiet in his Garden House, occupied with drawing, poetry, botany, and the one constant occupation of his heart, — love for the Frau von Stein. Love and ambition were the guides which led him through the labyrinth of the court. Amid those motley scenes, amid those swiftly succeeding pleasures, Voices, sorrowing Voices of the Past, made themselves audible above the din, and recalled the vast hopes which once had given energy to his aims; and these reverberations of an ambition once so cherished, arrested and rebuked him, like the deep murmurs of some solemn bass moving slowly through the showering caprices of a sportive melody. No soul can endure uninterrupted gayety and excitement : weary intervals will occur : the vulgar soul fills these intervals with the long lassitude of its ennui; the noble soul with reproaches at the waste of irrevocable hours.

The quiet influence exercised by the Frau von Stein is visible in every page of his letters. As far as I can divine the state of things in the absence of her letters, I fancy she coquetted with him ; when he showed any disposition to throw off her yoke, when his manner seemed to imply less warmth, she lured him back with tenderness ; and vexed him with unexpected coldness when she had drawn him once more to her feet. "You reproach me," he writes, "with alternations in my love. It is not true ; but it is well that I do not every day feel how utterly I love you." Again : "I cannot conceive why the main ingredients of your feeling have lately been Doubt and want of Belief. But it is certainly true that one who did not hold firm his affection might have that affection doubted away, just as a man may be persuaded that he is pale and ill." That she tormented him with these coquettish doubts is but too evident ; and yet when he is away from her she writes to tell him he is become dearer! "Yes, my treasure!" he replies, "I believe you when you say your love increases for me during absence. When away, you love the idea you have formed of me ; but when present, that idea is often disturbed by my folly and madness. . . . . I love you better when present than when absent : hence, I conclude my love is truer than yours." At times he seems himself to have doubted whether he really loved her, or only loved the delight of her presence.

With these doubts mingles another element, his ambition to do something which will make him worthy of her.   In spite of his popularity, in spite of his genius, he has not subdued her heart, but only agitated it.   He endeavors, by *devotion,* to succeed.   Thus love and ambition play into each other's hands, and keep him in a seclusion which astonishes and pains several of those who could never have enough of his company.

In the June of this year his solitude was visited by one of the agitations he could least withstand, — the death of his only sister, Cornelia.   *Sorrows and dreams* is the significant entry of the following day in his journal.

It was about this time that he undertook the care of Peter Imbaumgarten, a Swiss peasant boy, the *protégé* of his friend Baron Lindau.   The death of the Baron left Peter once more without protection.   Goethe, whose heart was open to all, especially to children, gladly undertook to continue the Baron's care ; and as we have seen him sending home an Italian image-boy to his mother at Frankfurt, and *Wilhelm Meister* undertaking the care of *Mignon* and *Felix,* so does this "cold" Goethe add love to charity, and become a father to the fatherless.

The autumn tints were beginning to mingle their red and yellow with the dark and solemn firs of the Ilmenau Mountains ; Goethe and the Duke could not long keep away from the loved spot, where poetical and practical schemes occupied the day, and many a wild prank startled the night.   There they danced with peasant-girls till early dawn; one result of which was a swelled face, forcing Goethe to lay up.

On his return to Weimar he was distressed by the receipt of one of the many letters which *Werther* drew upon him.   He had made sentimentality poetical ; it soon became a fashion. Many were the melancholy youths who poured forth their sorrows to him, demanding sympathy and consolation. Nothing could be more antipathetic to his clear and healthy nature. It made him ashamed of his *Werther.* It made him merciless to all Wertherism. To relieve himself of the annoyance, he commenced the satirical extravaganza of the *Triumph der Empfindsamkeit.* Very significant, however, of the unalterable kindliness of his disposition is the fact, that although these sentimentalities had to him only a painful or a ludicrous aspect, he did not suffer his repugnance to the malady to destroy his sympathy for the patient. There is a proof of this in the episode he narrates of his Harz journey, made in November and December of this year,* known to most readers through his poem, *Die Harzreise in Winter.* The object of that journey was twofold ; to visit the Ilmenau mines, and to visit an unhappy misanthrope whose Wertherism had distressed him.

The letter of the misanthrope just alluded to was signed Plessing, and dated from Wernigerode. There was something remarkable in the excess of its morbidity, accompanied by indications of real talent. Goethe did not answer it, having already hampered himself in various ways by responding to such extraneous demands upon his sympathy ; another and more passionate letter came imploring an answer, which was still silently avoided. But now the idea of personally ascertaining what manner of man his correspondent was, made him swerve from his path ; and under his assumed title of landscape-painter he called on Plessing.

On hearing that his visitor came from Gotha, Plessing eagerly inquired whether he had not visited Weimar, and whether he knew the celebrated men who lived there? With perfect simplicity Goethe replied that he did, and began

* And *not* in 1776, as he says ; that date is disproved by his letters to the Frau von Stein.

N

talking of Kraus, Bertuch, Musäus, Jagemann, etc., when he was impatiently interrupted with, " But why don't you mention Goethe?" He answered that Goethe also had he seen; upon this he was called upon to give a description of that great poet, which he did in a quiet way, sufficient to have betrayed his incognito to more sagacious eyes.

Plessing then with great agitation informed him that Goethe had not answered a most pressing and passionate letter in which he, Plessing, had described the state of his mind, and had implored direction and assistance. Goethe excused himself as he best could ; but Plessing insisted on reading him the letters, that he might judge whether they deserved such treatment.

He listened, and tried by temperate sympathetic counsel to wean Plessing from his morbid thoughts by fixing them on external objects, especially by some active employment. These were impatiently rejected, and Goethe left him, feeling that the case was almost beyond help.

He was subsequently able to assist Plessing, who, on visiting him at Weimar, discovered his old acquaintance, the landscape-painter.* But the characteristic part of this anecdote — and that which makes me cite it here — is, the practical illustration it gives of his fundamental realism, which looked to nature and earnest activity as the sole cure for megrims, sentimentalisms, and self-torturings. Turn your

---

* In 1788, Plessing was appointed professor of philosophy in the university of Duisburg, where Goethe visited him on his return home from the campaign in France, 1792. The reader may be interested to know, that Plessing entirely outlived his morbid melancholy, and gained a respectable name in German letters His principal works are *Osiris und Socrates*, 1783 ; *Historische und philosophische Untersuchungen über die Denkart, Theologie und Philosophie der ältesten Völker*, 1785 ; and *Memnomium, oder Versuche zur Enthüllung der Geheimnisse des Alterthums*, 1787. He died 1806.

mind to realities, he said, and the self-made phantoms which darken your soul will disappear like night at the approach of dawn

In the January of the following year (1778) Goethe was twice brought face to face with Death. The first was during a boar-hunt : his spear snapped in the onslaught, and he was in imminent peril, but fortunately escaped. On the following day, while he and the Duke were skating (perhaps talking over yesterday's escape), there came a crowd over the ice, bearing the corpse of the unhappy Fräulein von Lassberg, who, in the despair of unrequited love, had drowned herself in the Ilm, close by the very spot where Goethe was wont to take his evening walk. At all times this would have been a shock to him, but the shock was greatly intensified by the fact that in the pocket of the unfortunate girl was found a copy of *Werther !** It is true we never reproach an author in such cases. No reflecting man ever reproached Plato with the suicide of Cleombrotus, or Schiller with the brigandage of highwaymen. Yet when fatal coincidences occur, the author, whom we absolve, cannot so lightly absolve himself. It is in vain to argue that the work does not, rightly considered, lead to suicide ; if it does so, *wrongly* considered, it is the proximate cause ; and the author cannot easily shake off that weight of blame. Goethe, standing upon logic, might have said : "If Plato instigated the suicide of Cleombrotus, certainly he averted that of Olympiodorus ; if I have been one of the many causes which moved this girl towards that fatal act, I have also certainly been the cause of saving others, notably that young Frenchman who wrote to thank me." He might have argued thus ; but Conscience is tenderer than

---

* Riemer, who will never admit anything that may seem to tell against his idol, endeavors to throw a doubt on this fact, saying it was reported only out of malice. But he gives no reasons.

Logic ; and if in firing at a wild beast I kill a brother hunter, my conscience will not leave me altogether in peace.

The body was borne to the house of the Frau von Stein, which stood nearest the spot, and there he remained with it the whole day, exerting himself to console the wretched parents. He himself had need of some consolation. The incident affected him deeply, and led him to speculate on all cognate subjects, especially on melancholy. "This inviting sadness," he beautifully says, "has a dangerous fascination, *like water itself, and we are charmed by the reflex of the stars of heaven which shines through both.*"

He was soon, however, "*forced* into theatrical levity" by the various rehearsals necessary for the piece to be performed on the birthday of the Duchess. This was the *Triumph der Empfindsamkeit.* The adventure with Plessing, and finally the tragedy of the Fräulein von Lassberg, had given increased force to his antagonism against Wertherism and Sentimentality, which he now lashed with unsparing ridicule. The hero of his extravaganza is a Prince, whose soul is only fit for moonlight ecstasies and sentimental rhapsodies. He adores Nature ; not the rude, rough, imperfect Nature whose gigantic energy would alarm the sentimental mind ; but the beautiful rose-pink Nature of books. He likes Nature as one sees it at the Opera. Rocks are picturesque it is true ; but they are often crowned with tiaras of snow, sparkling, but apt to make one "chilly" ; turbulent winds howl through their clefts and crannies, alarming to delicate nerves. The Prince is not fond of the winds. Sunrise and early morn are lovely, but damp ; and the Prince is liable to rheumatism.

To obviate all such inconveniences he has had a mechanical imitation of Nature executed for his use ; and this accompanies him on his travels ; so that at a moment's notice, in secure defiance of rheumatism, he can enjoy a moonlight scene, a sunny landscape, or a sombre grove.

He is in love; but his mistress is as factitious as his land-scapes. Woman is charming but capricious, fond but exacting; and therefore the Prince has a doll dressed in the same style as the woman he once loved. By the side of this doll he passes hours of rapture; for it he sighs; for it he rhapsodizes.

The *real* woman appears, — the original of that much-treasured image. Is he enraptured? Not in the least. His heart does not palpitate in her presence; he does not recognize her; but throws himself once more into the arms of his doll, and thus sensibility triumphs.

There are five acts of this "exquisite fooling." Originally it was much coarser and more personal than we now see it. Böttiger says that there remains scarcely a shadow of its flashing humor and satiric caprice. The whip of Aristophanes was applied with powerful wrist to every fashionable folly, in dress, literature, or morals, and the spectators saw themselves as in a mirror of sarcasm. At the conclusion, the doll was ripped open, and out fell a multitude of books, such as were then the rage, upon which severe and ludicrous judgments were passed, — and the severest upon *Werther.* The whole piece was interspersed with ballets, music, and comical changes of scene; so that what now appears a tiresome farce, was then an irresistible extravaganza.

This extravaganza has the foolery of Aristophanes, and the physical fun of that riotous wit, whom Goethe was then studying. But when critics are in ecstasies with its wit and irony, I confess myself at a loss to conceive clearly what they mean. National wit, however, is perhaps scarcely amenable to criticism. What the German thinks exquisitely ludicrous, is to a Frenchman or an Englishman often of mediocre mirthfulness. Wit requires delicate handling; the Germans generally touch it with gloved hands. Sarcasm is

with them too often a sabre, not a rapier, hacking the victim
where a thrust would suffice.   It is a noticeable fact that
amid all the riches of their Literature they have little that is
comic of a high order.   They have produced no Comedy.
To them may be applied the couplet wherein the great
original of Grotesque Seriousness set forth its verdict, —

> Κωμῳδοδιδασκαλίαν εἶναι χαλεπώτατον ἔργον ἁπάντων.
> Πολλῶν γὰρ δὴ πειρασάντων αὐτὴν ὀλίγοις χαρίσασθαι.*

Which I will venture to turn thus, —

> " Miss Comedy is a sad flirt, as we guess
> From the number who court her, the few she doth bless."

———◆———

CHAPTER VI.

THE REAL PHILANTHROPIST.

A STRANGE phantasmagoria is the life he leads at this
epoch.   His employments are manifold, yet his studies, his
drawing, etching, and rehearsing are carried on as if they
alone were the occupation of the day.   His immense activity,
and power of varied employment, scatter the energies which
might be consecrated to some great work ; but, in return,
they give him the varied store of material of which he stood
so much in need.   At this time he is writing *Wilhelm Meister,*
and *Egmont; Iphigenia* is also taking shape in his mind.

This man, whose diplomatic coldness and aristocratic
haughtiness have formed the theme of so many long tirades,
was of all Germans the most sincerely democratic, until the
Reign of Terror in France frightened him, as it did others,
into more modified opinions.   Not only was he always de-

---

* ARISTOPHANES, *Equites,* V. 516.

lighted to be with the people, and to share their homely ways, which were consonant with his own simple tastes, but we find him in the confidence of intimacy expressing his sympathy with the people in the heartiest terms. When among the miners he writes to his beloved, "How strong my love has returned upon me for these lower classes! which one calls the lower, but which in God's eyes are assuredly the highest! Here you meet all the virtues combined: Contentedness, Moderation, Truth, Straightforwardness, Joy in the slightest good, Harmlessness, Patience . . . Patience . . . Constancy in . . . in . . . I will not lose myself in panegyric!" Again, he is writing *Iphigenia*, but the news of the misery and famine among the stocking-weavers of Apolda paralyzes him. "The drama will not advance a step: it is cursed; the King of Tauris must speak as if no stocking-weaver in Apolda felt the pangs of hunger!"

In striking contrast stands the expression of his contempt for what was called the great world, as he watched it in his visits to the neighboring courts. If affection bound him to Karl August, whom he was forming, and to Luise, for whom he had a chivalrous regard, his eyes were not blind to the nullity of other princes and their followers. "Good society have I seen," runs one of his epigrams, "they call it the 'good' whenever there is not in it the material for the smallest of poems."

> "Gute Gesellschaft hab' ich gesehen ; man nennt sie die gute
> Wenn sie zum kleinsten Gedicht keine Gelegenheit giebt."

Notably was this the case in his journey with the Duke to Berlin, May, 1778. He only remained a few days there; *saw* much, and not without contempt. "I have got quite close to old Fritz, having seen his way of life, his gold, his silver, his statues, his apes, his parrots, and heard his own curs twaddle about the great man." Potsdam and Berlin

were noisy with preparations for war.   The great King was
absent ; but Prince Henry received the poet in a friendly
manner, and invited him and Karl August to dinner.   At
table there were several generals ; but Goethe, who kept his
eyes open, sternly kept his mouth closed.   He seems to have
felt no little contempt for the Prussian Court, and its great
men, who appeared very small men in his eyes.   "I have
spoken no word in the Prussian dominions which might not
be made public.   Therefore I am called haughty, and so
forth."   Varnhagen intimates that the ill-will he excited by
not visiting the literati, and by his reserve, was so great as to
make him averse to hearing of his visit in after years.*
What, indeed, as Varnhagen asks, had Goethe in common
with Nicolai, Ramler, Engel, Zellner, and the rest ?   He did
visit the poetess Karschin and the artist Chodowiecki ; but
from the rest he kept aloof.   Berlin was not a city in which
he could feel himself at home ; and he doubtless was fully
aware of the small account in which he was held by Frederick, whose admiration lay in quite other directions.

On returning to Weimar, Goethe occupied himself with
various architectural studies, *apropos* of the rebuilding of the
palace ; and commenced those alterations in the park, which
resulted in the beautiful distribution formerly described.   But
I pass over many details of his activity, to narrate an episode
which must win the heart of every reader.   In these pages it
has been evident, I hope, that no compromise with the truth
has led me to gloss over faults, or to conceal shortcomings.
All that testimony warrants I have reproduced : good and
evil, as in the mingled yarn of life.   Faults and deficiencies,
even grievous errors, do not estrange a friend from our
hearts ; why should they lower a hero ?   Why should the
biographer fear to trust the tolerance of human sympathy ?

* *Vermischte Schriften*, III. p 62.

Why labor to prove a hero faultless?   The reader is no *valet de chambre* incapable of crediting greatness in a *robe de chambre.*   Never should we forget the profound saying of Hegel in answer to the vulgar aphorism (" No man is a hero to his *valet de chambre* ") namely, " This is not because the Hero is no Hero, but because the Valet is a Valet." *   Having trusted to the effect which the true man would produce, in spite of all drawbacks, and certain that the true man was *lovable* as well as admirable, I have made no direct appeal to the reader's sympathy, nor tried to make out a case in favor of extraordinary virtue.

But the tribute of affectionate applause is claimed now we have arrived at a passage in his life so *characteristic* of the delicacy, generosity, and nobility of his nature, that I cannot understand how it is possible for any one not to love him, after reading it.   Of generosity, in the more ordinary sense, there are abundant examples in his history.   Riemer has instanced several,† but these are acts of kindness, thoughtfulness, and courtesy, such as one expects to find in a prosperous poet.   That he was kind, gave freely, sympathized freely, acted disinterestedly, and that his kindness showed itself in trifles quite as much as in important actions (a most significant trait),‡ is known to all persons moderately ac-

---

* " Nicht aber darum weil dieser kein Held ist, sondern weil jener der Kammerdiener ist." — *Philosophie der Geschichte,* p. 40.   Goethe repeated this as an epigram ; and Carlyle has wrought it into the minds of hundreds ; but Hegel is the originator.

† *Mittheilungen,* Vol. I. 102 – 105.

‡ There is lamentable confusion in our estimate of character on this point of generosity.   We often mistake a spasm of sensibility for the strength of lovingness, — making an *occasional* act of kindness the sign of a kind nature.   Benj. Constant says of himself: " *Je puis faire de bonnes et fortes actions : je ne puis avoir de bons procédés.*" There are hundreds like him.   On the other hand, there are hundreds who willingly

quainted with German literature. But the disposition exhibited in the story I am about to tell is such as few persons would have imagined to be lying underneath the stately prudence and calm self-mastery of the man so often styled " heartless."

This is the story : A man (his name still remains a secret) of a strange, morbid, suspicious disposition had fallen into destitution, partly from unfortunate circumstances, partly from his own fault. He applied to Goethe for assistance, as so many others did'; and he painted his condition with all the eloquence of despair.

" According to the idea I form of you from your letters," writes Goethe, " I fancy I am not deceived, and this to me is very painful, in believing that I cannot give help or hope to one who needs so much. But I am not the man to say, ' Arise, and go farther.' Accept the little that I can give, as a plank thrown towards you for momentary succor. If you remain longer where you are, I will gladly see that in future you receive some slight assistance. In acknowledging the receipt of this money, pray inform me how far you can make it go. If you are in want of a dress, great-coat, boots, or warm stockings, tell me so ; I have some that I can spare.

" Accept this drop of balsam from the compendious medicine-chest of the Samaritan, in the same spirit as it is offered."

This was on the 2d of November, 1778. On the 11th he writes again, and from the letter we see that he had resolved to do *more* than throw out a momentary plank to the shipwrecked man, — in fact he had undertaken to support him.

" In this parcel you will receive a great-coat, boots, stock-

perform many little acts of kindness and courtesy, but who never rise to the dignity of generosity; these are *poor* natures, ignorant of the grander throbbings.

ings, and some money. My plan for you this winter is this : —

"In Jena living is cheap. I will arrange for board and lodging, etc., on the strictest economy, and will say it is for some one who, with a small pension, desires to live in retirement. When that is secured I will write to you ; you can then go there, establish yourself in your quarters, and I will send you cloth and lining, with the necessary money, for a coat, which you can get made, and I will inform the rector that you were recommended to me, and that you wish to live in retirement at the University.

"You must then invent some plausible story, have your name entered on the books of the University, and no soul will ever inquire more about you, neither Burgomaster nor Amtmann. *I have not sent you one of my coats, because it might be recognized in Jena.* Write to me and let me know what you think of this plan, and at all events in what character you propose to present yourself."

The passage in italics indicates great thoughtfulness. Indeed the whole of this correspondence shows the most tender consideration for the feelings of his *protégé*. In the postscript he says : "And now step boldly forth again upon the path of life ! We live but once. . . . . Yes, I know perfectly what it is to take the fate of another upon one's own shoulders, but you shall not perish!" On the 23d he writes : —

"I received to-day your two letters of the 17th and 18th, and have so far anticipated their contents as to have caused inquiry to be made in Jena for the fullest details, as for one who wished to live there under the quiet protection of the University. Till the answer arrives keep you quiet at Gera, and the day after to-morrow I will send you a parcel and say more.

" Believe me you are not a burden on me ; on the contrary, it teaches me economy; *I fritter away much of my income which I might spare for those in want.* And do you think that your tears and blessings go for nothing ? *He who has, must give, not bless ; and if the Great and the Rich have divided between them the goods of this world, Fate has counterbalanced these by giving to the wretched the powers of blessing, powers to which the fortunate know not how to aspire.*"

Noble words ! In the mouth of a pharisaical philanthropist *declaiming* instead of *giving*, there would be something revolting in such language ; but when we know that the hand which wrote these words was " open as day to melting charity," when we know that (in spite of all other claims) he gave up for some years the sixth part of his very moderate income to rescue this stranger from want, when we know by the irrefragable arguments of deeds, that this language was no hollow phrase, but the deep and solemn utterance of a thoroughly human heart, then indeed those words awaken reverberations within our hearts, calling up feelings of loving reverence for him who uttered them.

How wise and kind is this also : " Perhaps there will soon turn up occasions for you to be useful to me where you are, for it is not the Project-maker and Promiser, but he who in trifles affords real service, that is welcome to one who would so willingly do something good and enduring.

" Hate not the poor philanthropists with their precautions and conditions, for one need diligently pray to retain, amid such bitter experience, the good-will, courage, and levity of youth, which are the main ingredients of benevolence. And it is more than a benefit which God bestows when he calls us, who can so seldom do anything to lighten the burden of one truly wretched."

The next letter, dated December 11, explains itself : —

"Your letter of the 7th I received early this morning. And first, to calm your mind : you shall be forced to nothing ; the hundred dollars you shall have, live where you may : but now listen to me.

"I know that to a man his ideas are realities ; and although the image you have of Jena is false, still I know that nothing is less easily reasoned away than such hypochondriacal anxieties. I think Jena the best place for your residence, and for many reasons. The University has long lost its ancient wildness and aristocratic prejudices ; the students are not worse than in other places, and among them there are some charming people. In Jena they are so accustomed to the flux and reflux of men, that no individual is remarked. And there are too many living in excessively straitened means, for poverty to be either a stigma or a noticeable peculiarity. Moreover it is a city where you can more easily procure all necessities. In the country during the winter, ill, and without medical advice, would not that be miserable ?

"Further, the people to whom I referred you are good domestic people, who, on my account, would treat you well. Whatever might occur to you, I should be in a condition, one way or another, to assist you. I could aid you in establishing yourself : need only for the present guarantee your board and lodging, and pay for it later on. I could give you a little on New Year's day, and procure what was necessary on credit. You would be nearer to me. Every market day I could send you something, — wine, victuals, utensils that would cost me little, and would make your existence more tolerable ; and I could thus make you more a part of my household expenses. The objection to Gera is, that communication with it is so difficult ; things do not arrive at proper times, and cost money which benefits no one. You would probably remain six months in Jena before any one remarked your presence. This is the reason why I preferred Jena to every other place, and you would do the same if you could but see things with untroubled vision. How, if you were to make a trial? However, I know a fly can distract a man with sensitive nerves, and that, in such cases, reasoning is power-less.

" Consider it: it will make all things easier. I promise you, you will be comfortable in Jena. But if you cannot overcome your objections, then remain in Gera. At New Year you shall have twenty-five dollars, and the same regularly every quarter. I cannot arrange it otherwise. I must look to my own house-hold demands ; that which I have given you already, because I was quite unprepared for it, has made a hole, which I must stop up as I can. If you were in Jena, I could give you some little commissions to execute for me, and perhaps some occupation ; I could also make your personal acquaint-ance, and so on. But act just as your feelings dictate ; if my reasons do not convince you, remain in your present solitude. Commence the writing of your life, as you talk of doing, and send it me piecemeal, and be persuaded that I am only anx-ious for your quiet and comfort, and choose Jena simply be-cause I could there do more for you."

The hypochondriacal fancies of the poor man were invinci-ble ; and instead of going to Jena he went to Ilmenau, where Goethe secured him a home, and sent him books and money. Having thus seen to his material comforts, he besought him to occupy his mind by writing out the experience of his life, and what he had observed on his travels. In the following letter he refers to his other *protégé*, Peter Imbaumgarten :—

" I am very glad the contract is settled. Your mainte-nance thus demands a hundred dollars yearly, and I will guar-antee the twenty-five dollars quarterly, and contrive also that by the end of this month you shall receive a regular allowance for pocket-money.   I will also send what I can *in natura*, such as paper, pens, sealing-wax, etc.   Meanwhile here are some books.

"Thanks for your news ; continue them.   The wish to do good is a bold, proud wish ; we must be thankful when we can secure even a little bit.   I have now a proposition to make.   When you are in your new quarters I wish you would pay some attention to a boy, whose education I have undertaken, and who learns the huntsman's craft in Ilmenau.   He has begun French; could you not assist him in it ?   He draws nicely; could you not keep him to it ?   I would fix the hours when he should come to you.   You would lighten my anxiety about him if you could by friendly intercourse ascertain the condition of his mind, and inform me of it ; and if you could keep an eye upon his progress.   But of course this depends on your feeling disposed to undertake such a task.   Judging from myself,—*intercourse with children always makes me feel young and happy*.   On hearing your answer, I will write more particulars.   *You will do me a real service, and I shall be able to add monthly the trifle which I have set aside for the boy's education.*   I trust I shall still be able to lighten your sad condition, so that you may recover your cheerfulness."

Let me call attention to the delicacy with which he here intimates that he does not mean to occupy Kraft's* time without remunerating it.   If that passage be thoroughly considered, it will speak as much for the exquisite kindness of Goethe's nature as any greater act of liberality.   Few persons would have considered themselves unentitled to *ask* such a service from one whose existence they had secured.   To pay for it would scarcely have entered their thoughts.   But Goethe felt that to demand a service, which might be irksome, would, in a certain way, be selling benevolence ; if he

* Herr Kraft was the *assumed* name of this still anonymous *protégé*.

employed Kraft's time, it was right that he should pay what he would have paid another master.   On the other hand, he instinctively shrank from the indelicacy of making a decided *bargain.*   It was necessary to intimate that the lessons would be paid for ; but with that intimation he also conveyed the idea that in undertaking such a task Kraft would be conferring an *obligation* upon him ; so that Kraft might show his gratitude, might benefit his benefactor, and nevertheless be benefited.   After reading such a sentence, I could, to use Wieland's expression, " have eaten Goethe for love ! "

Kraft accepted the charge ; and Goethe having sent him some linen for shirts, some cloth for a coat, and begged him to write without the least misgiving, now sends this letter : —

" Many thanks for your care of Peter ; the boy greatly interests me, for he is a legacy of the unfortunate *Lindau.*   Do him all the good you can quietly.   How you may advance him !   I care not whether he reads, draws, or learns French, so that he does occupy his time, and I hear your opinion of him.   For the present, let him consider his first object is to acquire the huntsman's craft, and try to learn from him how he likes it, and how he gets on with it.   For, believe me, man must have a trade which will support him.   The artist is never paid ; it is the artisan.   Chodowiecki, the artist whom we admire, would eat but scanty mouthfuls ; but Chodowiecki, the artisan, who with his woodcuts illumines the most miserable daubs, he is paid."

In a subsequent letter he says : "Many thanks.   By your attention to these things, and your care of Peter, you have performed true service for me, and richly repaid all that I may have been able to do for you.   Be under no anxiety about the future, there will certainly occur opportunities wherein you can be useful to me ; meanwhile, continue as heretofore."   This was written on the *very day* of his return to Weimar from the Swiss journey! If this tells us of his attention to his *protégé* the next letter tells us of his anticipating even the casualty of death, for he had put Kraft on the list of those whom he left as legacies of benevolence to his friends. It should be remarked that Goethe seems to have preserved profound secrecy with respect to the good he was then doing; not even in his confidential letters to Frau von Stein is there one hint of Kraft's existence. In short, *nothing* is wanting to complete the circle of genuine benevolence.

The year 1781 began with an increase of Kraft's pension; or rather, instead of paying a hundred dollars for his board and lodging, and allowing him pocket-money, he made the sum two hundred dollars. "I can spare as much as that; and you need not be anxious about every trifle, but can lay out your money as you please. Adieu; and let me soon hear that all your sorrows have left you." This advance seems to have elicited a demand for *more* money, which produced the following characteristic answer:—

"You have done well to disclose the whole condition of your mind to me: I can make all allowances, little as I may be able to completely calm you. My own affairs will not permit me to promise you a farthing more than the two hundred dollars, unless I were to get into debt, which in my place would be very unseemly. This sum you shall receive regularly. Try to make it do.

"I certainly do not suppose that you will change your place of residence without my knowledge and consent. Every man has his duty: make a duty of your love to me and you will find it light.

"It would be very disagreeable to me if you were to *borrow* from any one. It is precisely this miserable unrest now troubling you which has been the misfortune of your whole life, and you have never been more contented with a thousand dollars than you now are with two hundred; because you always still desired something which you had not, and have never accustomed your soul to accept the limits of necessity. I do not reproach you with it; I know, unhappily too well, how it pertains to you, and feel how painful must be the contrast between your present and your past. But enough! One word for a thousand: at the end of every quarter you shall receive fifty dollars; for the present an advance shall be made. Limit your wants: the *Must* is hard, and yet solely by this *Must* can we show how it is with us in our inner man. To live according to caprice requires no peculiar powers." *

The following explains itself:—

" If you once more read over my last letter, you will see plainly that you have misinterpreted it. You are neither *fallen in my esteem*, nor have I a *bad opinion* of you, neither have I suffered my *good opinion* to be led astray, nor has your mode of thinking become *damaged* in my eyes; all these are exaggerated expressions, such as a rational man should not permit himself. Because I also speak out my thoughts with *freedom*, because I wish certain traits in your conduct and views somewhat different, does that mean that I look on you as a *bad man*, and that I wish to discontinue our relations?

" It is these hypochondriacal, weak, and exaggerated notions, such as your last letter contains, which I blame and regret. Is it proper that you should say to me, *I am to prescribe the tone in which all your future letters must be written?* Does one command an honorable, rational man such things as that? Is it ingenuous in you on such an occasion to *underline* the words that you eat *my bread?* Is it becoming in

---

* I will give the original of this fine saying, as I have rendered it but clumsily: Das *Muss* ist hart, aber deim *Muss* kann der Mensch allein zeigen wie's inwendig mit ihm steht. Willkürlich leben kann jeder.

a moral being, when one gently blames him, or names something in him as a malady, to fly out as if one had pulled the
house about his ears ?   Do not misconstrue me, therefore, if
I wish to see you contented and satisfied with the little I can do
for you.   So, if you will, things shall remain just as they were ;
at all events I shall not change my behavior towards you."

The unhappy man seems to have been brought to a sense
of his unjustice by this, for although there is but one more
letter, bearing the date 1783, that is, two years subsequent to
the one just given, the connection lasted for seven years.
When Goethe undertook to write the life of Duke Bernhard,
he employed Kraft to make extracts for him from the
Archives ; which extracts, Luden, when he came to look over
them with a biographical purpose, found utterly worthless.*
The last words we find of Goethe's addressed to Kraft are :
"You have already been of service to me, and other opportunities will offer.   I have no grace to dispense, and my favor is not so fickle.   Farewell, and enjoy your little in peace."
It was terminated only by the death of the poor creature
in 1785.   Goethe buried him at his own expense, but even
to the Jena officials he did not disclose Kraft's real name.†

To my apprehension these letters reveal a nature so exquisite in far-thoughted tenderness, so true and human in its
sympathies with suffering, and so ready to alleviate suffering
by sacrifices rarely made to friends, much less to strangers,
that, after reading them, the epithets of "cold" and "heartless," often applied to Goethe, sound like blasphemies against
the noblest feelings of humanity.   Observe, this Kraft was
no romantic object appealing to the sensibility ; he had no
thrilling story to stimulate sympathy ; there was no subscrip-

* See LUDEN's *Rückblicke in Mein Leben.*

† I learn this from a letter to the Judge at Jena, which was exhibited
at the *Goethe Ausstellung* in Berlin, 1861.

tion list opened for him ; there were no coteries weeping over
his misfortunes.   Unknown, unfriended, ill at ease with himself and with the world, he revealed his wretchedness in
secret to the great poet, and in secret that poet pressed his
hand, dried his eyes, and ministered to his wants.   And he
did this not as *one* act, not as one passing impulse, but as
the sustained sympathy of seven years.

Pitiful and pathetic is the thought that such a man can, for
so many years, both in his own country and in ours, have
been reproached, nay, even vituperated, as cold and heartless !   A certain reserve and stiffness of manner, a certain
soberness of old age, a want of political enthusiasm, and
some sentences wrenched from their true meaning, are the
evidences whereon men build the strange hypothesis that he
was an Olympian Jove sitting *above* Humanity, *seeing* life but
not *feeling* it, his heart dead to all noble impulses, his career
a calculated egotism.   And in this world in which there are
so few voices and so many echoes, a phrase easily becomes
a tradition.   Hundreds now repeat like parrots the phrase
which describes Goethe as calmly contemplating life after
the manner of the Gods.   How it was that one so heartless
became the greatest poet of modern times, — how it was that
he whose works contained the widest compass of human life,
should himself be a bloodless, pulseless diplomatist, — no one
thought of explaining till Menzel arose, and with unparal-
leled effrontery maintained that Goethe had no genius, but
only talent, and that the miracle of his works lies in their
style,—a certain adroitness in representation.   Menzel is a
man so completely rejected by England, the translation of
his work met with such hopeless want of encouragement, that
I am perhaps wrong to waste a line upon it ; but the bold style
in which his trenchant accusations are made, and the assumption of a certain manliness as the momentum to his sar-

casms, have given his attacks on Goethe a circulation independent of his book.   To me he appears radically incompe-
tent to appreciate a poet.   I should as soon think of asking
the first stalwart Kentish farmer for his opinion on the Parthenon.   The farmer would doubtless utter some energetic
sentences expressing his sense of its triviality ; but the coarse
energy of his language would not supply the place of knowledge, feeling, and taste ; nor does the coarse energy of Menzel's style supply those deficiencies of nature and education
which incapacitate him for the perception of Art.

The paradox still remains, then, in spite of Menzel : a
great poet destitute of the feelings which poetry incarnates,
— a man destitute of soul giving expression to all the emotions he has not, — a man who wrote *Werther, Egmont, Faust,
Hermann und Dorothea,* and *Meister,* yet knew not the joys
and sorrows of his kind ; will any one defend that paradox ?*
Not only that paradox, but this still more inexplicable one,
that all who knew Goethe, whether they were his peers or his
servants, loved him only as lovable natures can be loved.
Children, women, clerks, professors, poets, princes, — all
loved him.   Even Herder, bitter against every one, spoke of
him with a reverence which astonished Schiller, who writes :
" He is by many besides Herder named with a species of
devotion, and *still more loved as a man* than admired as an
author.   Herder says he has a clear, universal mind, the
truest and deepest feeling, and the greatest purity of heart." †
Men might learn so much from his works, had not the notion
of his coldness and indifference disturbed their judgment.

* I remember once, as we were walking along Piccadilly, talking about
the infamous *Büchlein von Goethe,* Carlyle stopped suddenly, and with
his peculiar look and emphasis said : " Yes, it is the wild cry of amaze-
ment on the part of all spooneys that the Titan was not a spooney too !
Here is a godlike intellect, and yet you see he is not an idiot !   Not in
the least a spooney ! "

† *Briefw. mit Körner,* I. p. 136.

"In no line," says Carlyle, "does he speak with asperity of any man, scarcely of anything. He knows the good and loves it ; he knows the bad and hateful and rejects it ; but in neither case with violence. His love is calm and active ; his rejection implied rather than pronounced."

And Schiller, when he came to appreciate by daily inter- course the qualities of his great friend, thus wrote of him : "It is not the greatness of his intellect which binds me to him. If he were not as a man more admirable than any I have ever known, I should only marvel at his genius from the distance. But I can truly say that in the six years I have lived with him, I have never for one moment been deceived in his character. He has a high truth and integrity, and is thoroughly in earnest for the Right and the Good ; hence all hypocrites and phrase-makers are uncomfortable in his pres- ence." And the man of whom Schiller could think thus is believed by many to have been a selfish egotist, "wanting in the higher moral feelings ! "

But so it is in life : a rumor, originating perhaps in thought- less ignorance, and circulated by malice, gains credence in spite of its improbability, and then no amount of evidence suffices to dissipate it. There is an atmosphere round certain names, a halo of glory or a halo of infamy, and men are aware of the halo without seeking to ascertain its origin. Every public man is in some respects mythical ; and fables are believed in spite of all the contradictions of evidence. It is useless to hope that men will pause to inquire into the truth of what they hear said of another, before accepting and re- peating it ; but with respect to Goethe, who has now been nearly half a century in his grave, one may hope that evi- dence so strong as these pages furnish may be held more worthy of credence than anything which gossip or ignorance, misconception or partisanship, has put forth without proof.

BOOK THE FIFTH.

1779 TO 1793.

CHAPTER I.

NEW BIRTH.

THE changes slowly determining the evolution of character, when from the lawlessness of Youth it passes into the
clear stability of Manhood, resemble the evolution of harmony in the tuning of an orchestra, when from stormy dis-
cords wandering in pursuit of concord, all the instruments
gradually subside into the true key : round a small centre the
hurrying sounds revolve, one by one falling into that centre,
and increasing its circle, at first slowly, and afterwards with
ever-accelerated velocity, till victorious concord emerges
from the tumult. Or they may be likened to the gathering
splendor of the dawn, as at first slowly, and afterwards with
silent velocity, it drives the sullen darkness to the rear, and
with a tidal sweep of light takes tranquil possession of the
sky. Images such as these represent the dawn of a new
epoch in Goethe's life, — an epoch when the wanderings of
an excitable nature are gradually falling more and more
within the circle of law ; when aims, before vague, now
become clear ; when in the recesses of his mind much that
was fluent becomes crystallized by the earnestness which gives
a definite purpose to his life. All men of genius go through
this process of crystallization. Their youths are disturbed
by the turbulence of errors and of passions ; if they outlive
these errors they convert them into advantages. Just as the

sides of great mountain ridges are rent by fissures filled with molten rock, which fissures, when the lava cools, act like vast supporting ribs strengthening the mountain mass, so, in men of genius, passions first rend, and afterwards buttress life. The diamond, it is said, can only be polished by its own dust ; is not this symbolical of the truth that only by its own fallings-off can genius properly be taught? And is not our very walk, as Goethe says, a series of falls?

He was now (1779) entering his thirtieth year. Life slowly emerged from the visionary mists through which hitherto it had been seen ; the solemn earnestness of manhood took the place of the vanishing thoughtlessness of youth, and gave a more commanding unity to his existence. He had "resolved to deal with Life no longer by halves, but to work it out in its totality, beauty, and goodness, — *vom Halbem zu entwöhnen, und im Ganzen, Guten, Schönen resolut zu leben."* It is usually said that the residence in Italy was the cause of this change ; but the development of his genius was the real cause. The slightest acquaintance with the period we are now considering suffices to prove that long before he went to Italy the change had taken place. An entry in his Diary at this date is very significant. " Put my things in order, looked through my papers, and burnt all the old chips. Other times, other cares ! Calm retrospect of Life, and the extravagances, impulses, and eager desires of youth ; how they seek satisfaction in all directions. How I have found delight, especially in mysteries, in dark imaginative connections ; how I only half seized hold of Science, and then let it slip ; how a sort of modest self-complacency runs through all I wrote ; how short-sighted I was in divine and human things ; how many days wasted in sentiments and shadowy passions ; how little good I have drawn from them, and now the half of life is over, I find myself advanced no step on my way, but stand here as one who, escaped from the waves, begins to dry himself in the sun! The period in which I have mingled with the world since October, 1775, I dare not yet trust myself to look at. God help me further, and give me light, that I may not so much stand in my own way, but see to do from morning till evening the work which lies before me, and obtain a clear conception of the order of things, that I be not as those are who spend the day in complaining of headache, and the night in drinking the wine which gives the headache!"

There is something quite solemn in those words. The same thought is expressed in a letter to Lavater: "The desire to raise the pyramid of my existence, the basis of which is already laid, as high as practicable in the air, absorbs every other desire, and scarcely ever quits me. I dare not longer delay; I am already advanced in life, and perhaps Death will break in at the middle of my work, and leave the Babelonic tower incomplete. At least men shall say it was boldly schemed, and if I live my powers shall, with God's aid, reach the completion." And in a recently published letter to the Duke, he says: "I let people say what they will, and then I retire into my old fortress of Poetry and work at my *Iphigenia.* By this I am made sensible that I have been treating this heavenly gift somewhat too cavalierly, and there is still time and need for me to become more economical if ever I am to bring forth anything." *

No better index of the change can be named than his *Iphigenia auf Tauris*, written at this period. The reader will learn with some surprise that this wonderful poem was originally written in prose. It was the fashion of the day. *Götz, Egmont, Tasso,* and *Iphigenia,* no less than Schiller's *Robbers, Fiesco, Kabale und Liebe,* were written in prose; and when

* *Briefwechsel zwischen Karl August und Goethe,* I. ii.

Iphigenia assumed a poetic form, the Weimar friends were disappointed, — they *preferred* the prose.

This was part of the mania for returning to Nature. Verse was pronounced unnatural : a fallacy : verse is not more unnatural than song. Song is to speech what poetry is to prose ; it expresses a different mental condition. Impassioned prose *approaches* poetry in the rhythmic impulse of its movements ; as impassioned speech in its various cadences also approaches the intonations of music. Under great emotional excitement, the Arabs give their language a recognizable metre, and almost talk poetry. But prose never *is* poetry, or is so only for a moment ; nor is speech song. Schiller learned to see this, and we find him writing to Goethe : " I have never before been so palpably convinced as in my present occupation how closely in poetry Substance and Form are connected. Since I have begun to transform my prosaic language into a poetic rhythmical one, I find myself *under a totally different jurisdiction;* even many motives which in the prosaic execution seemed to me to be perfectly in place, I can no longer use : they were merely *good for the common domestic understanding, whose organ prose seems to be;* but verse absolutely demands reference to the imagination, and thus I was obliged to become poetical in many of my motives."

That Goethe should have fallen into the fallacy which asserted prose to be more natural than verse is surprising. His mind was full of song. To the last he retained the faculty of singing melodiously, when his prose had degenerated into comparative feebleness. And this prose *Iphigenia* is saturated with verses ; which is also the case with *Egmont.* He *meant* to write prose, but his thoughts instinctively expressed themselves in verse. The critical reader will do well to compare the prose with the poetic version.* He

* See Vol. XXXIV. of the edition of 1840.

will not only see how frequent the verses are, but how few were the alterations necessary to be made to transform the prose drama into a poem.   They are just the sort of touches which elevate poetry above prose.   Thus, to give an example, in the prose he says : *unnütz seyn, ist todt seyn* (to be useless is to be dead), which thus grows into a verse, —

"Ein unnütz Leben ist ein früher Tod.*

Again, in the speech of Orestes (Act II. Sec. I.), there is a fine and terrible allusion to Clytemnestra, — " Better die here before the altar than in an obscure nook where the nets of murderous near *relatives* are placed."   In the prose this allusion is not clear : Orestes simply says, the " nets of assassins." †

In the begining of 1779 we find Goethe very active in his new official duties.   He has accepted the direction of the War Department, which suddenly assumes new importance, owing to the preparations for a war.   He is constantly riding about the country, and doing his utmost to alleviate the condition of the people.   " Misery," he says, " becomes as prosaic and familiar to me as my own hearth, but nevertheless I do not let go my idea, and will wrestle with the unknown Angel, even should I halt upon my thigh.   No man knows what I do, and with how many foes I fight to bring forth a little."

Among his undertakings may be noted an organization of Firemen, then greatly wanted.   Fires were not only numerous, but were rendered terrible by the want of any systematic service to subdue them.   Goethe, who in Frankfurt had rushed into the bewildered crowd, and astonished spec-

---

* A life not useful is an early death.

† Neither Taylor nor Miss Swanwick appears to have seized the allusion.   One translates it, "by the *knives of avenging kindred*" ; the other, " where *near hands* have spread *assassination's wily net.*"

tators by his rapid peremptory disposition of their efforts into a system, — who in Apolda and Ettersburg lent aid and command, till his eyebrows were singed and his feet were burned,—naturally took it much to heart that no regular service was supplied; and he persuaded the Duke to institute one.

On this (his thirtieth) birthday the Duke, recognizing his official services, raised him to the place of *Geheimerath.* " It is strange and dreamlike," writes the Frankfurt burgher in his new-made honor, " that I in my thirtieth year enter the highest place which a German citizen can reach. *On ne va jamais plus loin que quand on ne sait où l'on va,* said a great climber of this world." If he thought it strange, Weimar thought it scandalous. " The hatred of people here," writes Wieland, " against our Goethe, who has done no one any harm, has grown to such a pitch since he has been made Geheimerath, that it borders on fury." But the Duke, if he heard these howls, paid no attention to them. He was more than ever with his friend. They started on the 12th of September on a little journey into Switzerland, in the strictest incognito, and with the lightest of travelling-trunks. They touched at Frankfurt, and stayed in the old house in the *Hirschgraben,* where Rath Goethe had the pride of receiving not only his son as Geheimerath, but the Prince, his friend and master. Goethe's mother was, as may be imagined, in high spirits, — motherly pride and housewifely pride being equally stimulated by the presence of such guests.

From Frankfurt they went to Strasburg. There the recollection of Frederika irresistibly drew him to Sesenheim. In his letter to the Frau von Stein he says : " On the 25th I rode towards Sesenheim, and there found the family as I had left it eight years ago. I was welcomed in the most friendly manner. The second daughter loved me in those days bet-

ter than I deserved, and more than others to whom I have
given so much passion and faith. I was forced to leave her
at a moment when it nearly cost her her life ; she passed
lightly over that episode to tell me what traces still remained
of the old illness, and behaved with such exquisite delicacy
and generosity from the moment that I stood before her unexpected on the threshold, that I felt quite relieved. I must
do her the justice to say that she made not the slightest attempt to rekindle in my bosom the cinders of love. She led
me into the arbor, and there we sat down. It was a lovely
moonlight, and I inquired after every one and everything.
Neighbors had spoken of me not a week ago. I found old
songs which I had composed, and a carriage I had painted.
We recalled many a pastime of those happy days, and I found
myself as vividly conscious of all, as if I had been away only
six months. The old people were frank and hearty, and
thought me looking younger. I stayed the night there, and
departed at dawn, leaving behind me friendly faces ; so that
I can now think once more of this corner of the world with
comfort, and know that they are at peace with me."

There is something very touching in this interview, and in
his narrative of it, forwarded to the woman he *now* loves, and
who does not repay him with a love like that which he believes he has inspired in Frederika. He finds this charming
girl still unmarried, and probably is not a little flattered at
the thought that she still cherishes his image to the exclusion
of every other. She tells him of Lenz having fallen in love
with her, and is silent respecting her own share in that little
episode ; a silence which all can understand and few will
judge harshly ; the more so as her feelings towards Lenz were
at that time doubtless far from tender. Besides, apart from
the romance of meeting with an old lover, there was the
pride and charm of thinking what a world-renowned name

her lover had achieved. It was no slight thing even to have
been jilted by such a man ; and she must have felt that he
had not behaved to her otherwise than was to have been expected under the circumstances.

On the 26th, Goethe rejoined his party, and " in the afternoon I called on Lili, and found the lovely *Grasaffen** with a
baby of seven weeks old, her mother standing by. There
also I was received with admiration and pleasure. I made
many inquiries, and to my great delight found the good creature happily married. Her husband, from what I could
learn, seems a worthy, sensible fellow, rich, well placed in the
world ; in short, she has everything she needs. He was absent. I stayed dinner. After dinner went with the Duke
to see the Cathedral, and in the evening saw Paesiello's
beautiful opera, *L'Infante di Zamora.* Supped with Lili, and
went away in the moonlight. The sweet emotions which accompanied me I cannot describe."

We may read in these two descriptions the difference of
the two women, and the difference of his feeling for them.
From Strasburg he went to Emmendingen, and there visited
his sister's grave. Accompanied by such thoughts as these
three visits must have called up, he entered Switzerland.
His *Briefe aus der Schweitz*, mainly composed from the letters to the Frau von Stein, will inform the curious reader of
the effect these scenes produced on him ; we cannot pause here
in the narrative to quote from them. Enough if we mention that
in Zurich he spent happy hours with Lavater, in communication
of ideas and feelings ; and that on his way home he composed the little opera of *Jery und Bätely*, full of Swiss inspiration. In Stuttgart the Duke took it into his head to visit the
Court, and as no presentable costume was ready, tailors had

* *Grasaffen*, that is, "green monkey," is Frankfurt slang for "bud-
ding miss," and alludes to the old days when he knew Lili.

to be set in activity to furnish the tourists with the necessary clothes. They assisted at the New Year festivities of the Military Academy, and here for the first time Schiller, then twenty years of age, with the *Robbers* in his head, saw the author of *Götz* and *Werther*.

It is probable that among all the figures thronging in the hall and galleries on that imposing occasion, none excited in the young ambitious student so thrilling an effect as that of the great poet, then in all the splendor of manhood, in all the lustre of an immense renown. Why has no artist chosen this for an historical picture? The pale, sickly young Schiller, in the stiff military costume of that day, with pigtail and papillotes, with a sword by his side, and a three-cornered hat under his arm, stepping forward to kiss the coat of his sovereign Duke, in grateful acknowledgment of the three prizes awarded to him for Medicine, Surgery, and Clinical science ; conscious that Goethe was looking on, and could know nothing of the genius which had gained, indeed, trivial medical prizes, but had failed to gain a prize for German composition. This pale youth and this splendid man were in a few years to become noble rivals and immortal friends ; to strive with generous emulation, and feel the most genuine delight in each other's prowess ; presenting such an exemplar of literary friendship as the world has seldom seen. At this moment, although Schiller's eyes were intensely curious about Goethe, he was to the older poet nothing beyond a rather promising medical student.

Karl August on their return to Frankfurt again took up his abode in the Goethe family, paying liberal attention to Frau Aja's good old Rhine wine, and privately sending her a sum of money to compensate for the unusual expenses of his visit. By the 13th January he was in Weimar once more, having spent nearly nine thousand dollars on the journey, including purchases of works of art.

Both were considerably altered to their advantage. In his Diary Goethe writes : " I feel daily that I gain more and more the confidence of people ; and God grant that I may deserve it, not in the easy way, but in the way I wish. What I endure from myself and others no one sees. The best is the deep stillness in which I live *vis-à-vis* to the world, and thus win what fire and sword cannot rob me of." He was crystallizing slowly ; slowly gaining the complete command over himself. " I will be lord over myself. No one who cannot master himself is worthy to rule, and only he *can* rule." But with such a temperament this mastery was not easy ; wine and woman's tears, he felt, were among his weaknesses : —

> " Ich könnte viel glücklicher seyn,
> Gäb's nur keinen Wein
> Und keine Weiberthränen."

He could not entirely free himself from either. He was a Rhinelander, accustomed from boyhood upwards to the stimulus of wine ; he was a poet, never aloof from the fascinations of woman. But just as he was never known to lose his head with wine, so also did he never lose himself entirely to a woman ; the stimulus never grew into intoxication.

One sees that his passion for the Frau von Stein continues ; but it is cooling. It was necessary for him to love some one, but he was loving here in vain, and he begins to settle into a calmer affection. He is also at this time thrown more and more with Corona Schröter ; and his participation in the private theatricals is not only an agreeable relaxation from the heavy pressure of official duties, but is giving him materials for *Wilhelm Meister*, now in progress. " Theatricals," he says, "remain among the few things in which I still have the pleasure of a child and an artist." Herder, who had hitherto held somewhat aloof, now draws closer and closer to him, probably on account of the change which is coming over his way of life. And this intimacy with Herder awakens in him the desire to see Lessing; the projected journey to Wolfenbüttel is arrested, however, by the sad news which now arrives : Lessing is dead ; the great gladiator is at peace.

Not without significance is the fact that, coincident with this change in Goethe's life, comes the passionate study of Science ; a study often before taken up in desultory impatience, but now commencing with that seriousness which is to project it as an active tendency through the remainder of his life. In an unpublished " Essay on Granite," written about this period, he says : "No one acquainted with the charm which the secrets of Nature have for man, will wonder that I have quitted the circle of observations in which I have hitherto been confined, and have thrown myself with passionate delight into this new circle. I stand in no fear of the reproach that it must be a spirit of contradiction which has drawn me from the contemplation and portraiture of the human heart to that of Nature. For it will be allowed that all things are intimately connected, and that the inquiring mind is unwilling to be excluded from anything attainable. And I who have known and suffered from the perpetual agitation of feelings and opinions in myself and in others, delight in the sublime repose which is produced by contact with the great and eloquent silence of Nature." He was trying to find a secure basis for his aims ; it was natural he should seek a secure basis for his mind ; and with such a mind that basis could only be found in the study of Nature. If it is true, as men of science sometimes declare with a sneer, that Goethe was a poet in science (which does not in the least disprove the fact that he was great in science, and made great discoveries), it is equally true that he was a scientific poet. In a future chapter we shall have to consider what his position in science truly is ; for the present we merely indicate the course of his studies.

Buffon's wonderful book, *Les Époques de la Nature*,—rendered antiquated now by the progress of geology, but still attractive in its style and noble thoughts,—produced a profound impression on him.   In Buffon, as in Spinoza, and later on, in Geoffroy St. Hilaire, he found a mode of looking at Nature which thoroughly coincided with his own, gathering many details into a poetic synthesis.   Saussure, whom he had seen at Geneva, led him to study mineralogy; and as his official duties gave him many occasions to mingle with the miners, this study acquired a practical interest, which soon grew into a passion,— much to the disgust of Herder, who, with the impatience of one who thought books the chief objects of interest, was constantly mocking him for "bothering himself about stones and cabbages."   To these studies must be added anatomy, and in particular osteology, which in early years had also attracted him, when he attained knowledge enough to draw the heads of animals for Lavater's *Physiognomy*.   He now goes to Jena to study under Loder, professor of anatomy.[*]   For these studies his talent, or want of talent, as a draughtsman, had further to be cultivated.   To improve himself he lectures to the young men every week on the skeleton.   And thus, amid serious duties and many distractions in the shape of court festivities, balls, masquerades, and theatricals, he found time for the prosecution of many and various studies.   He was, like Napoleon, a giant-worker, and never so happy as when at work.

Tasso was conceived and commenced (in prose) at this time, and *Wilhelm Meister* grew under his hands, besides smaller works.   But nothing was published.   He lived for himself, and the small circle of friends.   The public was never thought of.   Indeed the public was then jubilant in beer-houses, and scandalized in salons, at the appearance of the

[*] Comp. *Briefw. zwischen Karl August und Goethe*, I. 25, 26.

Robbers; and a certain Küttner, in publishing his *Characters of German Poets and Prose Writers* (1781), could complacently declare that the shouts of praise which intoxicated admirers had once raised for Goethe were now no longer heard. Meanwhile *Egmont* was in progress, and assuming a far different tone from that in which it was originated.

It is unnecessary to follow closely all the details, which letters abundantly furnish, of his life at this period. They will not help us to a nearer understanding of the man, and they would occupy much space. What we observe in them all is, a slow advance to a more serious and decisive plan of existence. On the 27th of May his father dies. On the 1st of June he comes to live in the town of Weimar, as more consonant with his position and avocations. The Duchess Amalia has promised to give him a part of the necessary furniture. He quits his *Gartenhaus* with regret, but makes it still his retreat for happy hours. Shortly afterwards the Duchess Amalia demonstrates to him at great length the necessity of his being ennobled; the Duke, according to Düntzer, not having dared to break the subject to him. In fact, since he had been for six years at court without a patent of nobility, he may perhaps have felt the "necessity" as somewhat insulting. Nevertheless, I cannot but think that the Frankfurt citizen soon became reconciled to the *von* before his name; the more so as he was never remarkable for a contempt of worldly rank. Immediately afterwards the President of the Chamber, von Kalb, was suddenly dismissed from his post, and Goethe was the substitute, at first merely occupying the post *ad interim ;* but not relinquishing his place in the Privy Council.

More important to us is the relation in which he stands to Karl August, and to the Frau von Stein. Whoever reads with proper attention the letters published in the Stein correspondence will become aware of a notable change in their relation about this time (1781–2). The tone, which had grown calmer, now rises again into passionate fervor, and every note reveals the happy lover.

While he was thus happy, thus settling down into clearness, the young Duke, not yet having worked through the turbulence of youth, was often in discord with him. In the published correspondence may be read confirmation of what I have elsewhere learned, namely, that although during their first years of intimacy the poet stood on no etiquette in private with his sovereign, and although to the last Karl August continued the brotherly *thou*, and the most affectionate familiarity of address, yet Goethe soon began to perceive that another tone was called for on his part. His letters become singularly formal as he grows older; at times almost unpleasantly so. The Duke writes to him as to a friend, and he replies as to a sovereign.

Not that his affection diminished; but as he grew more serious, he grew more attentive to decorum. For the Duchess he seems to have had a tender admiration, something of which may be read in *Tasso*. Her dignified, though rather inexpressive nature, the greatness of her heart, and delicacy of her mind, would all the more have touched him, because he knew and could sympathize with what was not perfectly happy in her life. He was often the pained witness of little domestic disagreements, and had to remonstrate with the Duke on his occasional roughness.

From the letters to the Frau von Stein we gather that Goethe was gradually becoming impatient with Karl August, whose excellent qualities he cherished while deploring his extravagances. "Enthusiastic as he is for what is good and right, he has, notwithstanding, less pleasure in it than in what is improper; it is wonderful how reasonable he can be, what insight he has, how much he knows; and yet when he sets about anything good, he must needs begin with something foolish. Unhappily, one sees it lies deep in his nature, and that the frog is made for the water even when he has lived some time on land." In the following we see that the " servile courtier " not only remonstrates with the Duke, but refuses to accompany him on his journey, having on a previous journey been irritated by his manners. " Here is an epistle. If you think right, send it to the Duke, speak to him and do not spare him. I only want quiet for myself, and for him to know with whom he has to do. *You can tell him also that I have declared to you I will never travel with him again.* Do this in your own prudent, gentle way." Accordingly he lets the Duke go away alone ; but they seem to have come to some understanding subsequently, and the threat was not fulfilled. Two months after, this sentence informs us of the reconciliation : " I have had a long and serious conversation with the Duke. In this world, my best one, the dramatic writer has a rich harvest ; and the wise say, Judge no man until you have stood in his place." Later on we find him complaining of the Duke going wrong in his endeavors to do right. " God knows if he will ever learn that fireworks at midday produce no effect. I don't like always playing the pedagogue and bugbear, and from the others he asks no advice, nor does he ever tell them of his plans." Here is another glimpse : "The Duchess is as amiable as possible ; the Duke is a good creature, and one could heartily love him if he did not trouble the intercourse of life by his manners, and did not make his friends indifferent as to what befalls him by his break-neck recklessness. It is a curious feeling, that of daily contemplating the possibility of our nearest friends breaking their necks, arms, or legs, and yet I have grown quite callous to the idea !" Again : " The Duke goes to Dresden. He has begged me to go with him, or at least to follow him, but I shall stay here. . . . . The preparations for the Dresden journey are quite against my taste. The Duke arranges them in his way, i. e., not always the best, and disgusts one after the other. I am quite calm, for it is not alterable, and I only rejoice that there is no kingdom for which such cards could be played often."

These are little discordant tones which must have arisen as Goethe grew more serious. The real regard he had for the Duke is not injured by these occasional outbreaks. "The Duke," he writes, "is guilty of many follies which I willingly forgive, remembering my own." He knows that he can at any moment put his horses to the carriage and drive away from Weimar, and this consciousness of freedom makes him contented; although he now makes up his mind that he is destined by nature to be an author and nothing else. "I have a purer delight than ever, when I have written something which well expresses what I meant. . . . . I am truly born to be a private man, and do not understand how fate has contrived to throw me into a ministry and into a princely family." As he grows clearer on the true mission of his life, he also grows happier. One can imagine the strange feelings with which he would now take up *Werther*, and for the first time during ten years read this product of his youth. He made some alterations in it, especially in the relation of Albert to Lotte ; and introduced the episode of the peasant who commits suicide from jealousy. Schöll, in his notes to the *Stein Correspondence*,* has called attention to a point worthy of notice, namely, that Herder, who helped Goethe in the revision of this work, had pointed out to him the very same fault in its composition which Napoleon two-and-twenty years later laid his finger on ; the fault, namely, of making Werther's suicide partly the consequence of frustrated ambition and

* Vol. III. p. 268.

partly of unrequited love, — a fault which, in spite of Herder and Napoleon, in spite also of Goethe's aquiescence, I venture to think no fault at all, as will be seen when the interview with Napoleon is narrated.

———◆———

CHAPTER II.

PREPARATIONS FOR ITALY.

WITH the year 1783 we see him more and more seriously occupied. He has ceased to be "the Grand Master of all the Apes," and is deep in old books and archives. The birth of a crown prince came to fill Weimar with joy, and give the Duke a sudden seriousness. The baptism, which took place on the 5th of February, was a great event in Weimar. Herder preached "like a God," said Wieland, whose cantata was sung on the occasion. Processions by torchlight, festivities of all kinds, poems from every poet, *except* Goethe, testified the people's joy. There is something very generous in this silence. It could not be attributed to want of affection. But he who had been ever ready with ballet, opera, or poem, to honor the birthday of the two Duchesses, must have felt that now, when all the other Weimar writers were pouring in their offerings, he ought not to throw the weight of his position in the scale against them. Had his poem been the worst of the offerings, it would have been prized the highest because it was his.

The Duke, proud in his paternity, writes to Merck : " You have reason to rejoice with me ; for if there be any good dispositions in me they have hitherto wanted a fixed point, but now there is a firm hook upon which I can hang my pictures.

With the help of Goethe and good luck I will so paint that, if possible the next generation shall say, He too was a painter!" And from this time forward there seems to have been a decisive change in him; though he does complain of the "taciturnity of his *Herr Kammerpräsident*" (Goethe), who is only to be drawn out by the present of an engraving. In truth this *Kammerpräsident* is very much oppressed with work, and lives in great seclusion, happy in love, active in study. The official duties, which formerly he undertook so gayly, are obviously becoming burdens to him, the more so now his mission rises into greater distinctness. The old desire for Italy begins to torment him. "The happiest thing is, that I can now say I am on the right path, and from this time forward nothing will be lost."

He had many unpleasant hours as Controller of the Finances, striving in vain to make the Duke keep within a prescribed definite sum for expenses, — a thing always found next to impossible with Princes (not often possible with private men), and by no means accordant with our Duke's temperament. "Goethe contrives to make the most sensible representations," Wieland writes to Merck, "and is indeed *l'honnête homme à la cour;* but suffers terribly in body and soul from the burdens which for our good he has taken on himself. It sometimes pains me to the heart to see how good a face he puts on while sorrow like an inward worm is silently gnawing him. He takes care of his health as well as he can, and indeed he has need of it." Reports of this seem to have reached the ears of his mother, and thus he endeavors to reassure her: "You have never known me strong in stomach and head; and that one must be serious with serious matters is in the nature of things, especially when one is thoughtful and desires the good and true. . . . . I am, after my manner, tolerably well, am able to do all my work, to enjoy the intercourse of good friends, and still find time enough for all my favorite pursuits. I could not wish myself in a better place, now that I know the world and know how it looks behind the mountains. And you, on your side, content yourself with my existence, and should I quit the world before you, I have not lived to your shame ; I leave behind me a good name and good friends, and thus you will have the consolation of knowing that I *am not entirely dead.* Meanwhile live in peace ; fate may yet give us a pleasant old age, which we will also live through gratefully."

It is impossible not to read, beneath these assurances, a tone of sadness, such as corresponds with Wieland's intimation. Indeed, the Duke, anxious about his health, had urged him in the September of this year to make a little journey in the Harz. He went, accompanied by Fritz von Stein, the eldest son of his beloved, a boy of ten years of age, whom he loved and treated as a son. "Infinite was the love and care he showed me," said Stein, when recording those happy days. He had him for months living under the same roof, taught him, played with him, formed him. His native delight in children was sharpened by his love for this child's mother. A pretty episode in the many-colored Weimar life is this, of the care-worn minister and occupied student snatching some of the joys of paternity from circumstances which had denied him wife and children.

The Harz journey restored his health and spirits : especially agreeable to him was his intercourse with Sömmering, the great anatomist, and other men of science. He returned to Weimar to continue *Wilhelm Meister,* which was now in its fourth book ; to continue his official duties ; to see more and more of Herder, then writing his *Ideen ;* and to sun himself in the smiles of his beloved.

His osteological studies brought him this year the discov-

11 *

ery of an intermaxillary bone in man, as well as in animals.*
In a future chapter † this discovery will be placed in its historical and anatomical light ; what we have at present to do
with it, is to recognize its biographical significance. Until
this discovery was made, the position of man had always
been separated from that of even the highest animals, by the
fact (assumed) that he had *no* intermaxillary bone. Goethe,
who everywhere sought unity in Nature, believed that such a
difference did not exist; his researches proved him to be
right. Herder was at that time engaged in proving that no
structural difference could be found between men and animals ; and Goethe, in sending Knebel his discovery, says
that it will support this view. "Indeed, man is most intimately allied to animals. The co-ordination of the Whole
makes every creature to be that which it is, and man is as
much man through the form of his upper jaw, as through the
form and nature of the last joint of his little toe. And thus
is every creature but *a note of the great harmony*, which must
be studied in the Whole, or else it is nothing but a dead letter.
From this point of view I have written the little essay, and
that is, properly speaking, the interest which lies hidden
in it."

The discovery is significant, therefore, as an indication of
his tendency to regard Nature in her unity. It was the prel-
ude to his discoveries of the metamorphosis of plants, and
of the vertebral theory of the skull : all three resting on the
same mode of conceiving Nature. His botanical studies re-

---

* He thus announces it to Herder, 27th March, 1784 : "I hasten to
tell you of the fortune that has befallen me. I have found neither gold
nor silver, but that which gives me inexpressible joy, the *os intermaxil-
lare* in Man ! I compared the skulls of men and beasts, in company
with Loder, came on the trace of it, and lo ! there it is." — *Aus Herder's
Nachlass*, I. 75.

† See, further on, the chapter on *The Poet as a Man of Science.*

ceived fresh impulse at this period.   The work of Linnæus was a constant companion on his journeys, and we see him with eagerness availing himself of all that the observations and collections of botanists could offer him in aid of his own. " My geological speculations," he writes to the Frau von Stein, " make progress.   I see much more than the others who accompany me, because I have discovered certain funda-mental laws of formation, which I keep secret, and can from them better observe and judge the phenomena before me. . . . . Every one exclaims about my solitude, which is a riddle, because no one knows with what glorious unseen beings I hold communion."   It is interesting to observe his delight at seeing a zebra, — which was a novelty in Germany, — and his inexhaustible pleasure in the elephant's skull, which he has procured for study.   Men confined to their libraries, whose thoughts scarcely venture beyond the circle of Literature, have spoken with sarcasm and with pity of this waste of time.   But — dead bones for dead bones — there is as much poetry in the study of an elephant's skull, as in the study of those skeletons of the past, — History and Classics. All depends upon the mind of the student ; to one man a few old bones will awaken thoughts of the great organic pro-cesses of Nature, thoughts as far-reaching and sublime as those which the fragments of the past awaken in the histori-cal mind.   But there are minds, and these form the majority, to whom dry bones are dry bones, and nothing more.   " How legible the book of Nature becomes to me," Goethe writes, " I cannot express to thee ; my long lessons in spelling have helped me, and now my quiet joy is inexpressible.   Much as I find that is new, I find nothing unexpected ; everything fits in, because I have no system, and desire nothing but the pure truth."   To help him in his spelling he begins algebra ; but the nature of his talent was too unmathematical for him to pursue that study long.

The Duke increased his salary by 200 thalers, and this, with the 1,800 thalers received from the paternal property, made his income now 3,200 thalers (less than £500). He had need of money, both for his purposes and his numerous charities. We have seen, in the case of Kraft, how large was his generosity; and in one of his letters to his beloved, he exclaims, "God grant that I may daily become more economical, that I may be able to do more for others." The reader knows this is not a mere phrase thrown in the air. All his letters speak of the suffering he endured from the sight of so much want in the people. "The world is narrow," he writes, "and not every spot of earth bears every tree; mankind suffers, and *one is ashamed to see one's self so favored above so many thousands.* We hear constantly how poor the land is, and daily becomes poorer; but we partly think this is not true, and partly hurry it away from our minds when once we see the truth with open eyes, see the irremediableness, and see how matters are always bungled and botched!" That he did his utmost to ameliorate the condition of the people in general, and to ameliorate particular sorrows as far as lay in his power, is strikingly evident in the concurrent testimony of all who knew anything of his doings. If he did not write dithyrambs of Freedom, and was not profoundly enthusiastic for Fatherland, let us attribute it to any cause but want of heart.

The stillness and earnestness of his life seem to have somewhat toned down the society of Weimar. He went very rarely to Court; and he not being there to animate it with his inventions, the Duchess Amalia complained that they were all asleep; the Duke also found society insipid : "the men have lived through their youth, and the women mostly married." The Duke altered with the rest. The influence of his dear friend was daily turning him into more resolute paths; it had even led him to the study of science, as we learn from his letters. And Herder, also, now occupied with his great work, shared these ideas, and enriched himself with Goethe's friendship.

His scientific studies became enlarged by the addition of a microscope, with which he followed the investigations of Gleichen, and gained some insight into the marvels of the world of Infusoria. His drawings of the animalcules seen by him were sent to the Frau von Stein; and to Jacobi he wrote: "Botany and the microscope are now the chief enemies I have to contend against. But I live in perfect solitude apart from all the world, as dumb as a fish." Amid these multiform studies, — mineralogy, osteology, botany, and constant "dipping" into Spinoza, — his poetic studies might seem to have fallen into the background, did we not know that *Wilhelm Meister* has reached the fifth book, the opera of *Scherz List und Rache* is written, the great religious-scientific poem *Die Geheimnisse* is planned, *Elpenor* has two acts completed, and many of the minor poems are written. Among these poems, be it noted, are the two songs in *Wilhelm Meister, Kennst Du das Land?* and *Nur wer die Sehnsucht kennt?* which speak feelingly of his longing for Italy. The preparations for that journey are made in silence. He is studying Italian, and undertakes the revision of his works for a new edition, in which Wieland and Herder are to help him.

Seeing him thus happy in love, in friendship, in work, with young Fritz living with him, to give him, as it were, a home, and every year bringing fresh clearness in his purposes, one may be tempted to ask what was the strong impulse which could make him break away from such a circle, and send him lonely over the Alps? Nothing but the impulse of genius. Italy had been the dream of his youth. It was the land where self-culture was to gain rich material and firm basis. That he was born to be a Poet, he now deliberately acknowledged; and nothing but solitude in the Land of Song seemed wanting to him. Thither he yearned to go; thither he would go.

He accompanied the Duke, Herder, and the Frau von Stein to Carlsbad in July, 1786, taking with him his works to be revised for Göschen's new edition. The very sight of these works must have strengthened his resolution. And when Herder and the Frau von Stein returned to Weimar, leaving him alone with the Duke, the final preparations were made. He had studiously concealed this project from every one except the Duke, whose permission was necessary; but even from him the project was partially concealed. "Forgive me," he wrote to the Duke, "if at parting I spoke vaguely about my journey and its duration. I do not yet know myself what is to become of me. You are happy in a chosen path. Your affairs are in good order, and you will excuse me if I now look after my own; nay, you have often urged me to do so. I am at this moment certainly able to be spared; things are so arranged as to go on smoothly in my absence. In this state of things all I ask is an indefinite furlough." He says that he feels it necessary for his intellectual health that he should "lose himself in a world where he is unknown"; and begs that no one may be informed of his intended absence. "God bless you, is my hearty wish, and keep me your affection. Believe me that if I desire to make my existence more complete, it is that I may enjoy it better with you and yours."

This was on the 2d September, 1786. On the 3d he quitted Carlsbad incognito. His next letter to the Duke begins thus: "One more friendly word out of the distance, without date or place. Soon will I open my mouth and say how I get on.   How it will rejoice me once more to see your handwriting!"   And it ends thus : "Of course you let people believe that you know where I am."   In the next letter he says, "I must still keep the secret of my whereabouts a little longer."

------◆------

CHAPTER III.

ITALY.

THE long yearning of his life was at last fulfilled : he was in Italy.   Alone, and shrouded by an assumed name from all the interruptions with which the curiosity of admirers would have perplexed the author of *Werther*, but which never troubled the supposed merchant Herr Möller, he passed amid orange-trees and vineyards, cities, statues, pictures, and buildings, feeling himself "at home in the wide world, no longer an exile."   The passionate yearnings of Mignon had grown with his growth and strengthened with his strength, through the early associations of childhood, and all the ambitions of manhood, till at last they made him sick at heart. For some time previous to his journey he had been unable to look at engravings of Italian scenery, unable even to open a Latin book, because of the overpowering suggestions of the language ; so that Herder could say of him that the only Latin author ever seen in his hand was Spinoza.   The feeling grew and grew, a mental home-sickness which nothing but Italian skies could cure.   We have only to read Mignon's song, *Kennst Du das Land?* which was written before this journey, to perceive how dream-like were his conceptions of Italy, and how restless was his desire to journey there.

And now this deep unrest was stilled.   Italian voices were

loud around him, Italian skies were above him, Italian art
was before him.   He felt this journey as a new birth.   His
whole being was filled with warmth and light.   Life stretched
itself before him calm, radiant, and strong.   He saw the
greatness of his aims, and felt within him powers adequate
to those aims.

Curious it is to notice his open-eyed interest in all the
geological and meteorological phenomena which present
themselves; an interest which has excited the sneers of some
who think a poet has nothing better to do than to rhapsodize.
They tolerate his enthusiasm for Palladio, because Architecture is one of the Arts; and forgive the enthusiasm which
seized him in Vicenza, and made him study Palladio's works
as if he were about to train himself for an architect; but
they are distressed to find him, in Padua, once more occupied with "cabbages," and tormented with the vague conception of a Typical Plant, which will not leave him.   Let
me confess, however, that some cause for disappointment
exists.   The poet's yearning is fulfilled; and yet how little
literary enthusiasm escapes him!   Italy is the land of History, Literature, Painting, and Music; its highways are
sacred with associations of the Past; its by-ways are centres of biographic and artistic interest.   Yet Goethe, in
raptures with the climate, and the beauties of Nature, is
almost silent about Literature, has no sense of Music, and
no feeling for History.   He passes through Verona without
a thought of Romeo and Juliet; through Ferrara without a
word of Ariosto, and scarcely a word of Tasso.   In this
land of the Past, it is the Present only which allures him.
He turns aside in disgust from the pictures of crucifixions,
martyrdoms, emaciated monks, and all the hospital pathos
which makes galleries hideous; only in Raphael's healthier
beauty, and more human conceptions, can he take delight.

He has no historic sense enabling him to qualify his hatred of superstition by recognition of the painful religious struggles which, in their evolutions, assumed these superstitious forms. He considers the pictures as things of the present, and because their motives are hideous he is disgusted. But a man of more historic feeling would, while marking his dislike of such conceptions, have known how to place them in their serial position in the historic development of mankind.

From Venice he passed rapidly through Ferrara, Bologna, Florence, Arezzo, Perugia, Foligno, and Spoleto, reaching Rome on the 28th October.

In Rome, where he stayed four months, enjoyment and education went hand in hand. " All the dreams of my youth I now see living before me. Everywhere I go I find an old familiar face; everything is just what I thought it, and yet everything is new. It is the same with ideas. I have gained no new idea, but the old ones have become so definite, living, and connected one with another, that they may pass as new." The riches of Rome are at first bewildering; a long residence is necessary for each object to make its due impression. Goethe lived there among some German artists : Angelica Kaufmann, for whom he had great regard, Tischbein, Moritz, and others. They respected his incognito as well as they could, although the fact of his being in Rome could not long be entirely concealed. He gained, however, the main object of his incognito, and avoided being lionized. He had not come to Italy to have his vanity tickled by the approbation of society; he came for self-culture, and resolutely pursued his purpose.

Art was enough to occupy him; and for Painting he had a passion which renders his want of talent still more noticeable. He visited Churches and Galleries with steady earnestness; studied Winckelmann, and discussed critical points

Q

with the German artists.   Unhappily he also wasted precious time in fruitless efforts to attain facility in drawing.   These occupations, however, did not prevent his completing the versification of *Iphigenia*, which he read to the German circle, but found only Angelica who appreciated it ; the others having expected something *genialisch*, something in the style of *Götz with the Iron Hand*.   Nor was he much more fortunate with the Weimar circle, who, as we have already seen, preferred the prose version.

Art thus with many-sided influence allured him, but did not completely fill up his many-sided activity.   Philosophic speculations gave new and wondrous meanings to Nature ; and the ever-pressing desire to discover the secret of vegetable forms sent him meditative through the gardens about Rome.   He felt he was on the track of a law which, if discovered, would reduce to unity the manifold variety of forms.   Men who have never felt the passion of discovery may rail at him for thus, in Rome, forgetting, among plants, the quarrels of the Senate and the eloquence of Cicero ; but all who have been haunted by a great idea will sympathize with him, and understand how insignificant is the existence of a thousand Ciceros in comparison with a law of Nature.

On the 22d of February Goethe quitted Rome for Naples, where he spent five weeks of hearty enjoyment.   Throwing aside his incognito, he mixed freely with society, and still more freely with the people, whose happy, careless *far niente* delighted him.

"If in Rome one must *study*," he writes, "here in Naples one can only *live*."   And he lived a manifold life : on the sea-shore, among the fishermen, among the people, among the nobles, under Vesuvius, on the moonlit waters, on the causeway of Pompeii, in Pausilippo, — everywhere drinking in fresh delight, everywhere feeding his fancy and experience with new pictures. Thrice did he ascend Vesuvius; and as we shall see him during the campaign in France pursuing his scientific observations undisturbed by the cannon, so here also we observe him deterred by no perils from making the most of his opportunity.

Pompeii, Herculaneum, and Capua interested him less than might have been anticipated. "The book of Nature," he says, "is after all the only one which has in every page important meanings." Wandering thus lonely, his thoughts hurried by the music of the waves, the long-baffling, long-soliciting mystery of vegetable forms grew into clearness before him, and the typical plant was no more a vanishing conception, but a principle clearly grasped.

On the 2d of April he reached Palermo. He stayed a fortnight among its orange-trees and oleanders, given up to the exquisite sensations which, lotus-like, lulled him into forgetfulness of everything, save the present. Homer here first became a living poet to him. He bought a copy of the *Odyssey*, read it with unutterable delight, and translated as he went, for the benefit of his friend Kniep. Inspired by it, he sketched the plan of the *Nausikaa*, a drama in which the *Odyssey* was to be concentrated. Like so many other plans, this was never completed. The garden of Alcinous had to yield to the *Metamorphoses of Plants*, which tyrannously usurped his thoughts.

Palermo was the native city of Count Cagliostro, the audacious adventurer who, three years before, had made so conspicuous a figure in the affair of the Diamond Necklace. Goethe's curiosity to see the parents of this reprobate led him to visit them, under the guise of an Englishman bringing them news of their son. He has narrated the adventure at some length; but as nothing of biographical interest lies therein, I pass on with this brief indication, adding that his

sympathy, always active, was excited in favor of the poor
people, and he twice sent them pecuniary assistance, confessing the deceit he had practised.

He returned to Naples on the 14th of May, not without a
narrow escape from shipwreck. He had taken with him the
two first acts of *Tasso* (then in prose), to remodel them in
verse. He found on reading them over, that they were soft
and vague in expression, but otherwise needing no material
alteration. After a fortnight at Naples he once more arrived in Rome. This was on the 6th of June, 1787, and he
remained till the 22d of April, 1788 : ten months of labor,
which only an activity so unusual as his own could have
made so fruitful. Much of his time was wasted in the dabbling of an amateur, striving to make himself what Nature
had refused to make him. Yet it is perhaps perilous to say
that with such a mind any effort was fruitless. If he did not
become a painter by his studies, the studies were doubtless
useful to him in other ways. Art and antiquities he studied
in company with artistic friends. Rome is itself an education ; and he was eager to learn. Practice of the art
sharpened his perceptions. He learned perspective, drew
from the model, was passionate in endeavors to succeed
with landscape, and even began to model a little in clay.
Angelica Kaufmann told him, that in art he *saw* better than
any one else ; and the others believed perhaps that with
study he would be able to do more than see. But all his
study and all his practice were vain ; he never attained even
the excellence of an amateur. To think of a Goethe thus
obstinately cultivating a branch of art for which he had no
talent, makes us look with kinder appreciation on the spectacle, so frequently presented, of really able men obstinately
devoting themselves to produce poetry which no cultivated
mind can read ; men whose culture and insight are insuffi-

cient to make them perceive in themselves the difference between aspiration and inspiration.

If some time was wasted upon efforts to become a painter, the rest was well employed. Not to mention his scientific investigations, there was abundance of work executed. *Egmont* was rewritten. The rough draft of the first two acts had been written at Frankfurt, in the year 1775 ; and a rough cast of the whole was made at Weimar, in 1782. He now took it up again, because the outbreak of troubles in the Netherlands once more brought the patriots into collision with the house of Orange. The task of rewriting was laborious, but very agreeable, and he looked with pride on the completed drama, hoping it would gratify his friends. These hopes were somewhat dashed by Herder, who — never much given to praise — would not accept Clärchen, a character which the poet thought, and truly thought, he had felicitously drawn. Besides *Egmont*, he prepared for the new edition of his works, new versions of *Claudine von Villa Bella* and *Erwin unt Elmire*, two comic operas. Some scenes of *Faust* were written ; also these poems : *Amor als Landschaftsmaler ; Amor als Gast ; Künstler's Erdenwallen ;* and *Künstler's Apotheose.* He thus completed the last four volumes of his collected works which Göschen had undertaken to publish, and which we have seen him take to Carlsbad and to Italy as his literary task.

The effect of his residence in Italy, especially in Rome, was manifold and deep. Foreign travel, even to unintelligent, uninquiring minds, is always of great influence, not merely by the presentation of new objects, but also, and mainly, by the withdrawal of the mind from all the intricate connections of habit and familiarity which mask the real relations of life. This withdrawal is important, because it gives a new standing-point from which we can judge ourselves and others, and it shows how much that we have been wont to regard as essential is, in reality, little more than routine. Goethe certainly acquired clearer views with respect to himself and his career : severed from all those links of habit and routine which had bound him in Weimar, he learned in Italy to take another and a wider survey of his position. He returned home, to all appearance, a changed man. The crystallizing process which commenced in Weimar was completed in Rome. As a decisive example, we note that he there finally relinquishes his attempt to become a painter. He feels that he is born only for poetry, and during the next ten years resolves to devote himself to literature.

On the 22d April, 1788, he turned homewards, quitting Rome with unspeakable regret, yet feeling himself equipped anew for the struggle of life. "The chief objects of my journey," he writes to the Duke, "were these : to free myself from the physical and moral uneasiness which rendered me almost useless, and to still the feverish thirst I felt for true art. The first of these is tolerably, the second quite achieved." Taking *Tasso* with him to finish on his journey, he returned through Florence, Milan, Chiavenna, Lake Constance, Stuttgard, and Nürnberg, reaching Weimar on the 18th June, at ten o'clock in the evening.

CHAPTER IV.

RETURN HOME.

GOETHE came back from Italy greatly enriched, but by no means satisfied. The very wealth he had accumulated embarrassed him, by the new problems it presented, and the

new horizons it revealed.   He had in Rome become aware
that a whole life of study would scarcely suffice to still the
craving hunger for knowledge ; and he left Italy with deep
regret.   The return home was thus, in itself, a grief; the
arrival was still more painful.   Every one will understand
this, who has lived for many months away from the circle of
old habits and old acquaintances, feeling in the new world
a larger existence more consonant with his nature and his
aims, and has then returned once more to the old circle, to
find it unchanged, — pursuing its old paths, moved by the
old impulses, guided by the old lights, — so that he feels
himself a *stranger*.   To return to a great capital, after such
an absence, is to feel ill at ease ; but to return from Italy to
Weimar !   If we, on entering London, after a residence
abroad, find the same interests occupying our friends which
occupied them when we left, the same family gossip, the
same books talked about, the same placards loud upon the
walls of the unchanging streets, the world seeming to have
stood still while we have lived through so much : what must
Goethe have felt coming from Italy, with his soul filled with
new experience and new ideas, on observing the quiet, unchanged Weimar ?   No one seemed to understand him ; no
one sympathized in his enthusiasm, or in his regrets.   They
found him changed.   He found them moving in the same
dull round, like blind horses in a mill.

First, let us note that he came back resolved to dedicate
his life to Art and Science, and no more to waste efforts in
the laborious duties of office.

The wise Duke released his friend from the Presidency of
the Chamber, and from the direction of the War Department,
but kept a distinct place for him in the Council, " whenever
his other affairs allowed him to attend."   The poet remained
the adviser of his Prince, but was relieved from the more

onerous duties of office. The direction of the Mines, and of all Scientific and Artistic Institutions, he retained; among them that of the Theatre.

It was generally found that he had grown colder in his manners since his Italian journey. Indeed, the process of crystallization had rapidly advanced; and beyond this effect of development, which would have taken place had he never left Weimar, there was the further addition of his feeling himself at a different standing-point from those around him. The less they understood him, the more he drew within himself. Those who understood him, Moritz, Meyer, the Duke, and Herder, found no cause of complaint.

During the first few weeks he was of course constantly at Court. His official release made the bond of friendship stronger. Besides, every one was naturally anxious to hear about his travels, and he was delighted to talk of them.

But if Weimar complained of the change, to which it soon grew accustomed, there was one who had deeper cause of complaint, and whose nature was not strong enough to bear it, — the Frau von Stein. Absence had cooled the ardor of his passion. In Rome, to the negative influence of absence was added the positive influence of a new love. He had returned to Weimar, still grateful to her for the happiness she had given him, still feeling for her the affection which no conduct of hers could destroy, and which warmed his heart towards her to the last; but he returned also with little of the passion she had for ten years inspired; he returned with a full conviction that he had outlived it. Nor did her presence serve to rekindle the smouldering embers. Charlotte von Stein was now five-and-forty. It is easy to imagine how much he must have been struck with the change in her. Had he never left her side, this change would have approached with gradual steps, stealthily escaping observation;

but the many months' absence removed a veil from his eyes.
She was five-and-forty to him as to others. In this perilous
position she adopted the very worst course. She found him
changed, and told him so, in a way which made him feel
more sharply the change in her. She thought him cold, and
her resource was — reproaches. The resource was more
feminine than felicitous. Instead of sympathizing with him
in his sorrow at leaving Italy, she felt the regret as an offence ; and perhaps it was ; but a truer, nobler nature would
surely have known how to merge its own pain in sympathy
with the pain of one beloved. He regretted Italy ; she was
not a compensation to him ; she saw this, and her self-love
suffered. The coquette who had so long held him captive,
now saw the captive freed from her chains. It was a trying
moment. But even in the worst aspect of the position, there
was that which a worthy nature would have regarded as no
small consolation : she might still be his dearest friend ; and
the friendship of such a man was worth more than the love of
another. But this was not to be.

Before the final rupture he went with her to Rudolstadt,
and there for the first time spoke with Schiller, who thus
writes to Körner, 12th September, 1788 : " At last I can tell
you about Goethe, and satisfy your curiosity. The first sight
of him was by no means what I had been led to expect. He
is of middle stature, holds himself stiffly, and walks stiffly;
his countenance is not open, but his eye very full of expression, lively, and one hangs with delight on his glances. With
much seriousness, his mien has nevertheless much goodness
and benevolence. He is brown-complexioned, and seemed
to me older in appearance than his years. His voice is very
agreeable, his narrations are flowing, animated, and full of
spirit ; one listens with pleasure ; and when he is in good-
humor, as was the case this time, he talks willingly and

12

with great interest. We soon made acquaintance, and without the slightest effort ; the circle, indeed, was too large, and
every one too jealous of him, for me to speak much with him
alone, or on any but general topics. . . . . On the whole, I
must say that my great idea of him is not lessened by this
personal acquaintance ; but I doubt whether we shall ever
become intimate. Much that to me is now of great interest,
he has already lived through ; he is, less in years than in
experience and self-culture, so far beyond me that we can
never meet on the way ; and his whole being is originally
different from mine, his world is not my world, our conceptions are radically different. Time will show."

Could he have looked into Goethe's soul he would have
seen there was a wider gulf between them than he imagined.
In scarcely any other instance was so great a friendship ever
formed between men who at first seemed more opposed to
each other. At this moment Goethe was peculiarly ill-dis-
posed towards any friendship with Schiller, for he saw in him
the powerful writer who had corrupted and misled the nation.
He has told us how pained he was on his return from Italy
to find Germany jubilant over Heinse's *Ardinghello,* and
Schiller's *Robbers* and *Fiesco.* He had pushed far from him,
and forever, the whole *Sturm und Drang* creed ; he had out-
grown that tendency, and learned to hate his own works which
sprang from it ; in Italy he had taken a new direction, hoping to make the nation follow him in this higher region, as it
had followed him before. But while he advanced, the nation
stood still ; he " passed it like a ship at sea." Instead of following him, the public followed his most extravagant imita-
tors. He hoped to enchant men with the calm ideal beauty
of an *Iphigenia,* and the sunny heroism of an *Egmont ;* and
found every one enraptured with *Ardinghello* and *Karl Moor.*
In this frame of mind it is natural that he should keep aloof

from Schiller, and withstand the various efforts made to bring about an intimacy. "To be much with Goethe," Schiller writes in the February following, "would make me unhappy: with his nearest friends he has no moments of overflowingness: I believe, indeed, he is an egoist, in an unusual degree. He has the talent of conquering men, and of binding them by small as well as great attentions: but he always knows how to hold himself free. He makes his existence benevolently felt, but only like a god, without giving himself: this seems to me a consequent and well-planned conduct, which is calculated to insure the highest enjoyment of self-love. . . . . Thereby is he hateful to me, although I love his genius from my heart, and think greatly of him. . . . . It is quite a peculiar mixture of love and hatred he has awakened in me, a feeling akin to that which Brutus and Cassius must have had for Cæsar. I could kill his spirit, and then love him again from my heart." These sentences read very strangely now we know how Schiller came to love and reverence the man whom he here so profoundly misunderstands, and whom he judges thus from the surface. But they are interesting sentences in many respects; in none more so than in showing that if he, on nearer acquaintance, came to love the noble nature of his great rival, it is a proof that he had seen how superficial had been his first judgment. Let the reader who has been led to think harshly of Goethe, from one cause or another, take this into consideration, and ask himself whether he too, on better knowledge, might not alter his opinion.

"With Goethe," so runs another letter, "I will not compare myself, when he puts forth his whole strength. He has far more genius than I have, and greater wealth of knowledge, a more accurate sensuous perception (*eine sichere Sinnlichkeit*), and to all these he adds an artistic taste, cultivated and sharpened

by knowledge of all works of Art." But with this acknowledgment of superiority there was coupled an unpleasant feeling
of *envy* at Goethe's happier lot, a feeling which his own unhappy position renders very explicable. " I will let you see
into my heart," he writes to Körner. " *Once for all, this man,
this Goethe, stands in my way*, and recalls to me so often that
fate has dealt hardly with me. How lightly is *his* genius
borne by his fate; and how must *I* even to this moment
struggle ! "

Fate had indeed treated them very differently. Throughout Schiller's correspondence we are pained by the sight of
sordid cares, and anxious struggles for existence. He is in
bad health, in difficult circumstances. We see him forced to
make literature a trade; and it is a bad one. We see him
anxious to do hack-work, and translations, for a few dollars,
quite cheered by the prospect of getting such work; nay, glad
to farm it out to other writers, who will do it for less than he
receives. We see him animated with high aspirations, and
depressed by cares. He too is struggling through the rebellious epoch of youth, but has not yet attained the clearness
of manhood; and no external aids come to help him through
the struggle. Goethe, on the contrary, never knew such
cares. All his life he had been shielded from the depressing
influence of poverty; and now he has leisure, affluence, renown, social position, — little from *without* to make him unhappy. When Schiller therefore thought of all this, he must
have felt that fate had been a niggard step-mother to him, as
she had been a lavish mother to his rival.

Yet Goethe had his sorrows, too, though not of the same
kind. He bore within him the flame of genius, a flame which
consumes while it irradiates. His struggles were with himself, and not with circumstances. He felt himself a stranger
in the land. Few understood his language; none understood
his aims. He withdrew into himself.

There is one point which must be noticed in this position
of the two poets, namely, that however great Schiller may be
now esteemed, and was esteemed by Goethe after a while, he
was not at this moment regarded with anything beyond the
feeling usually felt for a rising young author. His early works
had indeed a wide popularity ; but so had the works of Klinger, Maler Müller, Lenz, Kotzebue, and others, who never
conquered the great critics; and Schiller was so unrecognized
at this time that, on coming to Weimar, he complains, with
surprise as much as with offended self-love, that Herder
seemed to know nothing of him beyond his name, not having
apparently read one of his works. And Goethe, in the official paper which he drew up recommending Schiller to the
Jena professorship, speaks of him as "a Herr Friedrich Schiller, author of an historical work on the Netherlands." So
that not only was Schiller's tendency antipathetic to all
Goethe then prized, he was not even in that position which
commands the respect of antagonists; and Goethe considered
Art too profoundly important in the development of mankind,
for differences of tendency to be overlooked as unimportant.

CHAPTER V.

CHRISTIANE VULPIUS.

ONE day early in July, 1788, Goethe, walking in the much-
loved park, was accosted by a fresh, young, bright-looking
girl, who, with many reverences, handed him a petition.
He looked into the bright eyes of the petitioner, and then, in
a conciliated mood, looked at the petition, which entreated
the great poet to exert his influence to procure a post for a

young author, then living at Jena by the translation of French and Italian stories. This young author was Vulpius, whose *Rinaldo Rinaldini* has doubtless made some of my readers shudder in their youth. His robber romances were at one time very popular; but his name is now only rescued from oblivion, because he was the brother of that Christiane who handed the petition to Goethe, and who thus took the first step on the path which led to their marriage. Christiane is on many accounts an interesting figure to those who are interested in the biography of Goethe; and the love she excited, no less than the devotedness with which for eight-and-twenty years she served him, deserve a more tender memory than has befallen her.

Her father was one of those wretched beings whose drunkenness slowly but surely brings a whole family to want. He would sometimes sell the coat off his back for drink. When his children grew up, they contrived to get away from him, and to support themselves: the son by literature, the daughters by making artificial flowers,* woollen work, etc. It is usually said that Christiane was utterly uneducated, and the epigrammatic pen glibly records that "Goethe married his servant." She never was his servant. Nor was she uneducated. Her social position indeed was very humble, as the foregoing indications suggest; but that she was not uneducated is plainly seen in the facts of which there can be no doubt, namely, that for her were written the *Roman Elegies*, and the *Metamorphoses of Plants;* and that in her company Goethe pursued his optical and botanical researches. How much she understood of these researches we cannot know; but it is certain that unless she had shown a lively comprehension he would never have persisted in talk-

* This detail will give the reader a clew to the poem *Der neue Pausias.*

ing of them to her.   Their time, he says, was not spent only in caresses, but also in rational talk : —

"Wird doch nicht immer geküsst, es wird vernünftig gesprochen."

This is decisive.   Throughout his varied correspondence we always see him presenting different subjects to different minds, treating of topics in which his correspondents are interested, not dragging forward topics which merely interest *him;* and among the wide range of subjects he had mastered, there were many upon which he might have conversed with Christiane, in preference to science, had she shown any want of comprehension of scientific phenomena.   There is one of the *Elegies*, the eighth, which in six lines gives us a distinct idea of the sort of cleverness and the sort of beauty which she possessed ; a cleverness not of the kind recognized by schoolmasters, because it does not display itself in aptitude for book-learning ; a beauty not of the kind recognized by conventional taste, because it wants the conventional regularity of feature.*   Surely the poet's word is to be taken in such a case !

While, however, rectifying a general error, let me not fall into the opposite extreme.   Christiane had her charm ; but she was not a highly gifted woman.   She was not a Frau von Stein, capable of being the companion and the sharer of his highest aspirations.   Quick mother-wit, a lively spirit, a loving heart, and great aptitude for domestic duties, she undoubtedly possessed : she was gay, enjoying, fond of pleasure even to excess, and — as may be read in the poems which she inspired — was less the mistress of his Mind than

* "When you tell me, dearest, that as a child you were not admired, and even your mother scorned you, till you grew up and silently developed yourself, I can quite believe it.   I can readily imagine you as a peculiar child.   If the blossoms of the vine are wanting in color and form, the grapes once ripe are the delight of gods and men."

of his Affections.   Her golden-brown locks, laughing eyes, ruddy cheeks, kiss-provoking lips, small and gracefully rounded figure, gave her " the appearance of a young Dionysos." *
Her *naïveté*, gayety, and enjoying temperament completely fascinated Goethe, who recognized in her one of those free, healthy specimens of Nature which education had not distorted with artifice.   She was like a child of the sensuous Italy he had just quitted with so much regret ; and there are few poems in any language which approach the passionate gratitude of those in which he recalls the happiness she gave him.

Why did he not marry her at once?   His dread of marriage has already been shown ; and to this abstract dread there must be added the great disparity of station, — a disparity so great that not only did it make the *liaison* scandalous, it made Christiane herself reject the offer of marriage.   Stahr reports that persons now living have heard her declare that it was her own fault her marriage was so long delayed ; and certain it is that when — Christmas, 1789 — she bore him a child (August von Goethe, to whom the Duke stood godfather), he took her with her mother and sister to live in his house, and always regarded the connection as a marriage.   But however he may have regarded it, Public Opinion has not forgiven this defiance of social laws. The world blamed him loudly ; even his admirers cannot think of the connection without pain.   " The Nation," says Schäfer, " has never forgiven its greatest poet for this rupture with Law and Custom ; nothing has stood so much in the way of a right appreciation of his moral character, nothing has created more false judgments on the tendency of his writings, than his half-marriage."

But let us be just.   While no one can refrain from deplor-

* So says Madame Schopenhauer, *not* a prejudiced witness.

ing that Goethe, so eminently needing a pure domestic life, should not have found a wife whom he could avow, — one who would in all senses have been a wife to him, the mistress of his house, the companion of his life ; on the other hand, no one who knows the whole circumstances can refrain from confessing that there was also a bright side to this dark episode.   Having indicated the dark side, and especially its social effect, we have to consider what happiness it brought him at a time when he was most lonely, most unhappy.   It gave him the joys of paternity, for which his heart yearned. It gave him a faithful and devoted affection.   It gave him one to look after his domestic existence, and it gave him a peace in that existence which hitherto he had sought in vain.

There is a letter still extant (unpublished) written ten years after their first acquaintance, in which, like a passionate lover, he regrets not having taken something of hers on his journey, — even her slipper, — that he might feel less lonely. To have excited such love, Christiane must have been a very different woman from that which it is the fashion in Germany to describe her as being.   In conclusion, let it be added that his mother not only expressed herself perfectly satisfied with his choice, received Christiane as a daughter, and wrote affectionately to her, but refused to listen to the officious meddlers who tried to convince her of the scandal which the connection occasioned.

Had Goethe written nothing but the *Roman Elegies*, he would hold a first place among German poets.   These elegies are, moreover, scarcely less interesting in their biographical significance.   They speak plainly of the effect of Italy upon his mind ; they speak eloquently of his love for Christiane. There are other tributes to her charms, and to the happiness she gave him ; but were there no other tributes, these would suffice to show the injustice of the opinion which the malicious

tongues of Weimar have thrown into currency respecting
her, — opinions, indeed, which received some countenance
from her subsequent life, when she had lost youth and beauty,
and when the faults of her nature had acquired painful
prominence.   It is Goethe's misfortune with posterity that he
is mostly present to our minds as the calm old man, seldom
as the glorious youth.   The majority of busts, portraits, and
biographic details are of the late period of his career.   In
like manner, it is the misfortune of his wife that testimonies
about her come mostly from those who only saw her when
the grace and charm of youth had given place to a coarse
and corpulent age.   But the biographer's task is to ascertain
by diligent inquiry what is the truth at the various epochs of
a career, not limiting himself to one epoch; and as I have
taken great pains to represent the young Goethe, so also
have I tried to rescue the young Christiane from the falsifica-
tions of gossip, and the misrepresentations derived from
judging her youth by her old age.

It has already been intimated that Weimar was loud in dis-
approbation of this new *liaison*, although it had uttered no
word against the *liaison* with the Frau von Stein.   The great
offence seems to have been his choosing one beneath him in
rank.   A chorus of indignation rose.   It produced the final
rupture between him and the Frau von Stein.

He offered friendship in vain; he had wounded the self-
love of a vain woman; there is a relentless venom when the
self-love is wounded, which poisons friendship and destroys
all gratitude.   It was not enough for the Frau von Stein that
he had loved her so many years with a rare devotion; it was
not enough that he had been more to her child than its own
father was; it was not enough that now the inevitable change
had come, he still felt tenderness and affection for her, grateful for what she *had* been to him; the one fact, that he had

ceased to love her, expunged the whole past.   A nature with
any nobleness never forgets that once it loved, and once was
happy in that love; the generous heart is grateful in its
memories.   The heart of the Frau von Stein had no memory
but for its wounds.   She spoke with petty malice of the "low
person" who had usurped her place; rejected Goethe's
friendship; affected to pity him; and circulated gossip about
his beloved.   They were forced to meet; but they met no
longer as before.   To the last he thought and spoke of her
tenderly; and I know on unexceptionable authority that when
there was anything appetizing brought to table, which he
thought would please her, he often said, "Send some of this
to the Frau von Stein."

CHAPTER VI.

THE POET AS A MAN OF SCIENCE.

To the immense variety of his studies in Art and Science
must now be added a fragmentary acquaintance with the philosophy of Kant.   He had neither the patience nor the delight in metaphysical abstractions requisite to enable him to
master the Critique of Pure Reason; but he read here and
there in it, as he read in Spinoza; and was especially interested in the æsthetical portions of the *Kritik der Urtheilskraft*.
This was a means of bringing him nearer to Schiller, who still
felt the difference between them to be profound; as we see in
what he wrote to Körner: "His philosophy draws too much
of its material from the world of the senses, where I only draw
from the soul.   His mode of presentation is altogether too
sensuous for me.   But his spirit works and seeks in every di-

rection, striving to create a whole, and that makes him in my eyes a great man."

Remarkable indeed is the variety of his strivings. After completing *Tasso*, we find him writing on the Roman Carnival, and on Imitation of Nature, and studying with strange ardor the mysteries of Botany and Optics. In poetry it is only necessary to name the *Roman Elegies*, to show what productivity in that direction he was capable of; although, in truth, his poetical activity was then in subordination to his activity in science. He was, socially, in an unpleasant condition; and, as he subsequently confessed, would never have been able to hold out, had it not been for his studies in Art and Nature. In all times these were his refuge and consolation.

On Art, the world listened to him attentively. On Science, the world would not listen, but turned away in silence, sometimes in derision. In both he was only an amateur. He had no executive ability in Painting or Sculpture to give authority to his opinions, yet his word was listened to with respect, often with enthusiasm.* But while artists and the public admitted that a man of genius might speak with some authority, although an amateur, men of science were not willing that a man of genius should speak on *their* topics until he had passed College Examinations and received his diploma. The veriest blockhead who had received a diploma considered himself entitled to sneer at the poet who " dabbled in comparative anatomy." Nevertheless, that poet made discoveries and enunciated laws, the importance of which the professional sneerer could not even appreciate, so far did they transcend his knowledge.

Professional men have a right to be suspicious of the ama-

---

* RAUCH, the sculptor, told me that among the influences of his life, he reckons the enthusiasm which Goethe's remarks on Art excited in him. Many others would doubtless say the same.

teur, for they know how arduous a training is required by Science.   But while it is just that they should be *suspicious*, it is absurd for them to shut their eyes.   When the amateur brings forward crudities, which he announces to be discoveries, their scorn may be legitimate enough ; but when he happens to bring forward a discovery, and they treat it as a crudity, their scorn becomes self-stultification.   If their professional training gives them superiority, that superiority should give them greater readiness of apprehension.   The truth is, however, that ordinary professional training gives them nothing of the sort.   The mass of men, simply because they are a mass of men, receive with difficulty every new idea, unless it lies in the track of their own knowledge ; and this opposition, which every new idea must vanquish, becomes tenfold greater when the idea is promulgated from a source not in itself authoritative.

But whence comes this authority ?   From the respect paid to genius and labor.   The man of genius who is known to have devoted much time to the consideration of any subject is justly supposed to be more competent to speak on that subject than one who has paid little attention to it.   No amount of genius, no amount of study, can secure a man from his native fallibility ; but, after adequate study, there is a presumption in his favor ; and it is this presumption which constitutes authority.   In the case of a poet who claims to be heard on a question of science, we hastily assume that he has not given the requisite labor ; and on such topics genius without labor carries no authority.   But if his researches show that the labor *has* been given, we must then cease to regard him as a poet, and admit him to the citizenship of science.   No one disputes the immense glory of a Haller or a Redi, on the ground of their being poets.   They were poets and scientific workers ; and so was Goethe.   This would perhaps have been more readily acknowledged if he had walked in the well-beaten tracks of scientific thought ; but he opened new tracks, and those who might perhaps have accepted him as a colleague, were called upon to accept him as a guide.   Human nature could not stand this.   The presumption against a poet was added to the presumption against novelty; singly each of these would have been an obstacle to a ready acceptance; united they were insuperable.

When Goethe wrote his exquisite little treatise on the *Metamorphoses of Plants,** he had to contend against the two-fold obstacle of resistance to novelty, and his own reputation. Had an obscure professor published this work, its novelty would alone have sufficed to render it unacceptable ; but the obscurest name in Germany would have had a *prestige* greater than the name of the great poet.   All novelty is *prima facie* suspicious ; none but the young welcome it ; for is not every new discovery a kind of slur on the sagacity of those who overlooked it?   And can novelty in science, promulgated by a poet, be worth the trouble of refutation?   The professional authorities decided that it could not.   The publisher of Goethe's works, having consulted a botanist, declined to undertake the printing of the *Metamorphoses of Plants.*   The work was only printed at last because an enterprising book-seller hoped thereby to gain the publication of the other works.   When it appeared, the public saw in it a pretty piece of fancy, nothing more.   Botanists shrugged their shoulders, and regretted the author had not reserved his imagination for his poems.   No one believed in the theory, not even his attached friends.   He had to wait many years before seeing it generally accepted, and it was then only accepted because great botanists had made it acceptable.   A considerable authority on this matter has told us how long the theory was

* He has also a poem on this subject, but it is scarcely more poetical.

neglected, and how "depuis dix ans (written in 1838) il n'a peut-être pas été publié un seul livre d'organographie, ou de botanique descriptive, qui ne porte l'empreinte des idées de cet écrivain illustre."* It was the fact of the theory being announced by the author of *Werther* which mainly retarded its acceptance; but the fact also that the theory was leagues in advance of the state of science in that day, must not be overlooked. For it is curious that the leading idea had been briefly yet explicitly announced as early as 1759, by Caspar Friedrich Wolff, in his now deservedly celebrated *Theoria Generationis*, and again, in 1764, in his *Theorie von der Generation*.† I shall have to recur to Wolff; at present it need only be noted that even *his* professional authority and remarkable power could not secure the slightest attention from botanists for the morphological theory, — a proof that the age was not ripe for its acceptance.

A few of the eminent botanists began, after the lapse of some years, to recognize the discovery. Thus Kieser declared it to be "certainly the vastest conception which vegetable physiology had for a long time known." Voigt expressed his irritation at the blindness of the botanists in refusing to accept it. Nees von Esenbeck, one of the greatest names in the science, wrote, in 1818, "Theophrastus is the creator of modern botany. Goethe is its tender father, to whom it will raise looks full of love and gratitude, as soon as it grows out of its infancy, and acquires the sentiment which it owes to him who has raised it to so high a position." And Sprengel, in his *History of Botany*, frequently mentions the theory. In one

---

* AUGUSTE ST. HILAIRE, *Comptes Rendus des Séances de l'Acad.*, VII. 437. See also his work *Morphologie Végétale*, Vol I p. 15.

† I have only been able to procure this latter work, which is a more popular and excursive exposition of the principles maintained in the Inaugural Dissertation of 1759.

place he says, "The *Metamorphoses* had a meaning so profound, joined to such great simplicity, and was so fertile in consequences, that we must not be surprised if it stood in need of multiplied commentaries, and if many botanists failed to see its importance." It is now, and has been for some years, the custom to insert a chapter on Metamorphosis in every work which pretends to a high scientific character.

He was not *much* hurt at the reception of his work. He knew how unwilling men are to accord praise to any one who aims at success in different spheres, and found it perfectly natural they should be so unwilling; adding, however, that "an energetic nature feels itself brought into the world for *its own development, and not for the approbation of the public.*"

Side by side with botanical and anatomical studies must be placed his optical studies. A more illustrative contrast can scarcely be found than is afforded by the history of his efforts in these two directions. They throw light upon scientific Method, and they throw light on his scientific qualities and defects. If we have hitherto followed him with sympathy and admiration, we must now be prepared to follow him with that feeling of pain which rises at the sight of a great intellect struggling in a false direction. His botanical and anatomical studies were of that high character which makes one angry at their cold reception; his optical studies were of a kind to puzzle and to irritate the professional public.

He has written the history of these studies also. From youth upwards he had been prone to theorize on painting, led thereto, as he profoundly remarks, by the very absence of a talent for painting. It was not necessary for him to theorize on poetry; he had within him the creative power. It *was* necessary for him to theorize on painting, because he wanted "by reason and insight to fill up the deficiencies of nature." In Italy these theories found abundant stimulus.

With his painter friends he discussed color and coloring, trying by various paradoxes to strike out a truth. The friends were all deplorably vague in their notions of color. The critical treatises were equally vague. Nowhere could he find firm ground. He began to think of the matter from the opposite side, — instead of trying to solve the artists' problem, he strove to solve the scientific problem. He asked himself, What is color? Men of science referred him to Newton; but Newton gave him little help. Professor Büttner lent him some prisms and optical instruments, to try the prescribed experiments. He kept the prisms a long while, but made no use of them. Büttner wrote to him for his instruments; Goethe neither sent them back, nor set to work with them. He delayed from day to day, occupied with other things. At last Büttner became uneasy, and sent for the prisms, saying they should be lent again at a future period, but that at any rate he must have them returned. Forced thus to part with them, yet unwilling to send them back without making one effort, he told the messenger to wait, and taking up a prism, looked through it at the white wall of his room, expecting to see the whole wall colored in various tints, according to the Newtonian statement. To his astonishment, he saw nothing of the kind. He saw that the wall remained as white as before, and that only there, where an opaque interfered, could a more or less decisive color be observed; that the window-frames were most colored, while the light gray heaven without showed no trace of color. "It needed very little meditation to discover that to produce color a *limit* was necessary, and instinctively I exclaimed, 'Newton's theory is false!'" There could be no thought of sending back the prisms at such a juncture; so he wrote to Büttner begging for a longer loan, and set to work in real earnest.

This was an unhappy commencement. He began with a false conception of Newton's theory, and thought he was overthrowing Newton when, in fact, he was combating his own error. The Newtonian theory does *not* say that a white surface seen through a prism appears colored, but that it appears white, its edges only colored. The fancied discovery of Newton's error stung him like a gadfly. He multiplied experiments, turned the subject incessantly over in his mind, and instead of going the simple way to work, and learning the a, b, c, of the science, tried the very longest of all short cuts, namely, experiment on insufficient knowledge. He made a white disk on a black ground, and this, seen through the prism, gave him the spectrum, as in the Newtonian theory; but he found that a black disk on a white ground also produced the same effect. " ' If Light,' said I to myself, ' resolves itself into various colors in the first case, then must Darkness also resolve itself into various colors in this second case.' " And thus he came to the conclusion that Color is not contained in Light, but is the product of an intermingling of Light and Darkness.

" Having no experience in such matters, and not knowing the direction I ought to take, I addressed myself to a Physicist of repute, begging him to verify the results I had arrived at. I had already told him my doubts of the Newtonian hypothesis, and hoped to see him at once share my conviction. But how great was my surprise when he assured me that the phenomenon I spoke of was already known, and perfectly explained by the Newtonian theory. In vain I protested and combated his arguments; he held stolidly to the *credo*, and told me to repeat my experiments in a *camera obscura*."

Instead of quieting him, this rebuff only turned him away from all Physicists, that is, from all men who had special

1788.]   THE POET AS A MAN OF SCIENCE.   283

knowledge on the subject, and made him pursue in silence his own path. Friends were amused and interested by his experiments; their ignorance made them ready adepts. The Duchess Luise showed especial interest; and to her he afterwards dedicated his *Farbenlehre.* The Duke also shared the enthusiasm. The Duke of Gotha placed at his disposal a magnificent laboratory. Prince August sent him splendid prisms from England. Princes and poetasters believed he was going to dethrone Newton; men of science only laughed at his pretension, and would not pay his theory the honor of a refutation. One fact he records as very noticeable, namely, that he could count Anatomists, Chemists, Littérateurs, and Philosophers, such as Loder, Sömmering, Göttling, Wolff, Forster, Schelling (and, subsequently, Hegel), among his adherents; but not one Physicist. Nor does he, in recording this fact, see that it is destructive of his pretensions.

What claim had Anatomists, Littérateurs, and Philosphers to be heard in such a controversy? Who would listen to a mathematician appealing to the testimony of zoölogists against the whole body of mathematicians past and present? There is this much, however, to be said for Goethe : he had already experienced neglect from professional authorities when he discovered the intermaxillary bone, and when, in the *Metamorphoses of Plants,* he laid before them a real discovery, the truth of which he profoundly felt. He was prepared therefore for a similar disregard of his claims when he not only produced a new theory, but attacked the highest scientific authority. He considered that Newtonians looked on him as a natural enemy. He thought them steadfastly bent on maintaining established prejudice. He thought they were a guild united against all innovation by common interest and common ignorance. Their opposition never made him pause; their arguments never made him swerve. He thought them profoundly in error when they imagined optics to be a part of mathematics; and as he did not understand mathematics, he could not appreciate their arguments.

His *Beiträge zur Optik*, which appeared in 1791, was a sort of feeler thrown out to the great public. The public was utterly unsympathizing. The ignorant had no interest in such matters, and certainly would not address themselves to a poet for instruction; the physicists saw that he was wrong. "Everywhere," he says, "I found incredulity as to my competence in such a matter; everywhere a sort of repulsion at my efforts; and the more learned and well informed the men were, the more decided was their opposition."

For years and years he continued his researches with a patience worthy of admiration. Opposition moved him not; it rather helped to increase his obstinacy. It extorted from him expressions of irritability and polemical bad taste, which astound us in one elsewhere so calm and tolerant. Perhaps, as Canon Kingsley once suggested to me, he had a vague feeling that his conclusions were not sound, and felt the jealousy incident to imperfect conviction. Where his conviction was perfect, he was calm. The neglect of his Metamorphoses, the denial of his discovery of the intermaxillary bone, the indifference with which his essays on Comparative Anatomy were treated, — all this he bore with philosophic serenity. But on the *Farbenlehre* he was always sensitive, and in old age ludicrously so. Eckermann records a curious conversation, wherein he brings forward a fact he has observed, which contradicts the theory of colors; and Goethe not only grows angry, but refuses to admit the fact. In this matter of Color he showed himself morally weak, as well as intellectually weak. "As for what I have done as a poet," said the old man once, "I take no pride in it whatever. Excellent poets have lived at the same time with myself; more excellent poets have lived before me, and will come after me. But that in my century I am the only person who knows the truth in the difficult science of colors — of that, I say, I am not a little proud."

The reader will doubtless be curious to know something of this Theory of Colors ; and although it must necessarily appear greatly to its disadvantage in the brief abstract for which alone I can find space, an abstract without the numerous illustrations and experiments which give the theory a plausible aspect, yet the kernel of the matter will appear.

The Newtonian theory is that white light is composed of the seven prismatic colors, i. e. rays having different degrees of refrangibility. Goethe says it is not composed at all, but is the simplest and most homogeneous thing we know.* It is absurd to call it composed of *colors*, for every light which has taken a color is darker than colorless light. Brightness cannot therefore be a compound of darkness. There are but two pure colors, *blue* and *yellow*, both of which have a tendency to become *red*, through *violet* and *orange ;* there are also two mixtures, *green* and *purple.* Every other color is a degree of one of these, or is impure. Colors originate in the modification of Light by outward circumstances. They are not developed *out* of Light, but *by* it. For the phenomenon of Color, there is demanded Light and Darkness. Nearest the Light appears a color we name *yellow ;* nearest the Darkness, a color we name *blue.* Mix these two and you have *green.*

Starting from the fundamental error of the simplicity of

---

* "Let us thank the gods," exclaims SCHELLING, "that they have emancipated us from the Newtonian spectrum (*spectrum truly !*) of composed light. We owe this to the genius to whom our debt is already so large." — *Zeitschrift für spekul. Philos.*, II. p. 60. To the same effect HEGEL in his *Encyklopädie der philos. Wissenschaften.*

Light, Goethe undertakes to explain all the phenomena of Color, by means of what he calls the *Opaques*, — the media. He maintains that on the one hand there is Light, and on the other Darkness; if a semi-transparent medium be brought between the two, from these contrasts and this medium, Colors are developed, contrasted in like manner, but soon through a reciprocal relation tending to a point of reunion.

The highest degree of Light seen through a medium very slightly thickened appears *yellow*. If the density of the medium be increased, or if its volume become greater, the light will gradually assume a *yellow-red*, which deepens at last to a *ruby*.

The highest degree of Darkness seen through a semi-transparent medium, which is itself illuminated by a light striking on it, gives a *blue* color; which becomes paler as the density of the medium is increased; but on the contrary becomes darker and deeper as the medium becomes more transparent. In the least degree of dimness short of absolute transparency, the deep *blue* becomes the most beautiful *violet*.

There are many interesting facts adduced in illustration. Thus smoke appears yellow or red before a light ground, blue before a dark ground; the blue color, at the under part of a candle-flame, is also a case of blue seen opposite a dark ground. Light transmitted through the air is yellow, orange, or red, according to the density of the air; Darkness transmitted through the air is blue, as is the case of the sky, or distant mountains.

He tells a curious anecdote in illustration of this blueness of darkness. A painter had an old portrait of a theologian to clean; the wet sponge passing over the black velvet dress, suddenly changed it to a *light blue plush*. Puzzled at this truly remarkable phenomenon, and not understanding how light blue could be the ground of deep black, he was in great grief at the thought of having thus ruined the picture. The next morning, to his joy, he found the black velvet had resumed its pristine splendor. To satisfy his curiosity, he could not refrain from wetting a corner once more, and again he saw the *blue* appear. Goethe was informed of the phenomenon, which was once more produced, in his presence. " I explained it," he says, " by my doctrine of the semi-opaque medium. The original painter, in order to give additional depth to his black, may have passed some particular varnish over it ; on being washed, this varnish imbibed some moisture, and hence became semi-opaque, in consequence of which the *black* beneath immediately appeared *blue*." The explanation is very ingenious ; nor does the Edinburgh reviewer's answer seem to meet the question, when he says :* " As there is no gum or resin, or varnish of any kind that possesses the property of yielding blue or any other color by being wetted, we have no doubt the varnish had been worn off, or else the picture never had been varnished." It is not a question of wetted varnish yielding blue, but of wetted varnish furnishing the medium through which black appears blue. The reviewer's explanation, however, is probably correct. He assumes that there was no varnish, and that the particles of bodies which produce blackness, on the usual theory, are smaller than those which produce blue or any other color ; and if we increase the size of the particles which produce blackness by the smallest quantity, they yield the *blue* color described by Goethe. The action of the water swelled them a little, and thus gave them the size which fitted them to reflect *blue* rays.

The theory loses much of its seductive plausibility when thus reduced to its simplest expression. Let us, however, do the same for the Newtonian theory, and then estimate their comparative value. Newton assumes that white Light is a

* Edin. Rev., October, 1840, p. 117.

compound ; and he proves this assumption by decomposing a beam of light into its elements.   These elements are rays, having different degrees of refrangibility, separable from each other by different media.   Each ray produces its individual color.   Not only will the beam of white Light in passing through a prism be separated into its constituent rays, or colors, but these rays may be again collected by a large lens, and, in being thus brought together, again reappear as white Light.   There are few theories in science which present a more satisfactory union of logic and experiment.

It cannot be denied that Goethe's theory is also extremely plausible ; and he has supported it with so many accurate experiments and admirable observations, that to this day it has not only found ardent advocates, even among men of science, though these are few, but has very sorely perplexed many Newtonians, who, relying on the mathematical accuracy of their own theory, have contemptuously dismissed Goethe's speculation instead of victoriously refuting it.   His obstinacy was excusable, since believing himself to be in the right he challenged refutation, and no one picked up his gauntlet. They declined in contempt, which he interpreted as bigotry. He tried to get the French Academy to make a report on his work.   This honor was withheld : Cuvier disdainfully declaring that such work was not one to occupy an Academy ; Delambre answering all solicitations with this phrase : " Des observations, des expériences, et surtout ne commençons pas par attaquer Newton."   As if the *Farbenlehre* were not founded on observations and experiments ! as if the glory of Newton were to stand inviolate before all things ! Goethe might well resent such treatment.   If he was wrong in his theory, if his experiments were incomplete, why were these errors not pointed out?   To contradict Newton might offer a presumption against the theory ; but Newtonians were called upon not to explain the contradiction between Goethe and Newton, which was vociferously announced, but the contradiction between Goethe and Truth, which they contemptuously asserted.

As this is a branch of science in which I can pretend to no competence, and as I have met with no decisive refutation of Goethe which can be quoted here, I should consider it sufficient to say that the fact of the vast majority of physicists in Europe refusing to pay any attention to the *Farbenlehre*, although not in itself more than a presumption against that theory, is nevertheless a presumption so very strong as only to be set aside by stringently coercive evidence. Looking at the *Farbenlehre* from the impartial, if imperfect, point of view of an outsider, I should say that not only has Goethe manifestly misunderstood Newton, but has presented a theory which is based on a radical mistake. The mistake is that of treating Darkness as a positive quality, rather than as a simple negation of Light. By means of this Darkness, as a *co-operating agent* with Light, colors are said to arise. Stripped of all the ambiguities of language, the theory affirms that Light is itself perfectly colorless until mingled with various degrees of Nothing, or, in other words, until it suffers various diminutions; and with each diminution the colors become of a deeper hue. This may seem too preposterous for belief; yet what is Darkness but the negation of Light? It is true that Goethe has in one place named Darkness, in the abstract, a pure negation ; but it is not less true that in the construction of his theory, Darkness plays the part of a positive, and necessarily so; for if we once conceive it as a simple negative, the theory falls to the ground. Light being assumed as colorless, no diminution of the colorless can give colors. Unless Darkness be positive, — co-operative, — we are left to seek the elements of color *in* Light ; and this is precisely where the Newtonian theory finds it.

It was an old idea that the different confines of shadow variously modify light, producing various colors. This Newton has elaborately refuted (*Optics*, Part II. Book I.), proving by simple experiments that all colors show themselves indifferently in the confines of shadow; and that when rays which differ in refrangibility are separated from one another, and any one is considered apart, "the color of the light which it composes cannot be changed by any refraction or reflection whatever, as it ought to be were colors nothing else than modifications of light caused by refractions, reflections, and shadows."

It should be emphatically stated that the highest physical authorities have borne testimony to the accuracy of Goethe's facts ; and as these facts are exceedingly numerous, and often highly important, the value of his optical studies must be estimated as considerable. He was a man of genius, and he labored with the passionate patience of genius. But in awarding our admiration to the man, we may withhold assent from his theory. That which has exasperated men of science, and caused them to speak slightingly of his labors, is the bitterly polemical tone of contempt with which he announced a discovery which they could not recognize as true. He was aggressive and weak. He vociferated that Newton was in error ; and a casual glance at his supposed detection of the error discovered a fundamental misconception. If we stand aloof from these heats of personal conflict, and regard the subject with a calmer eye, we shall see that the question simply reduces itself to this : which of the two theories offers the fullest and clearest explanation of the facts?

Light and Colors are, like Sound and Tones, to be viewed as objective phenomena, related to certain external conditions ; or as subjective phenomena, related to certain sensations. Before asking, What is Light or Sound? we must consider whether we seek the objective fact, or the subjective sensation. Every one admits that, apart from a sensitive organism, the objective phenomena of Light and Sound exist, although *not* as the Light and Sound known in our sensations. But as we can only know them through our sensations, it seems eminently philosophical to begin our study with these. And this Goethe has done. He first unfolds the laws of physiological colors, i. e. the modifications of the retina ; and his immense services in this direction have been cordially recognized by Physiologists. Since, however, we can never learn thus what are the external *conditions* of the phenomena, we have to seek in objective facts such an explanation as will best guide us. The assumption of rays having different degrees of refrangibility may one day turn out to be erroneous ; but it is an assumption which colligates the facts better than any other hitherto propounded, and therefore it is accepted. By regarding both Sound and Light as produced from waves of an elastic medium, acoustic and optic phenomena are reducible to *calculation.* It is true they thus incur Goethe's reproach of ceasing to be concrete objects to the mind, and becoming mathematical symbols ; but this is the very ambition of scientific research : a point to which I shall presently return. Let us compare the objective and subjective facts.

If an elastic rod be made to vibrate, the ear perceives nothing until the vibrations reach sixteen in a second, at which point the lowest tone becomes audible ; if the rapidity of the vibrations be now constantly accelerated, tones higher and higher in the scale become audible, till the vibrations reach thirty-two thousand in a second, at which point the ear again fails to detect any sound. In like manner, it is calculated that when vibrations reach four hundred and eighty-three billions in a second, Light, or rather the red ray, begins to manifest itself to the retina ; with increasing rapidity of vibration, the colors pass into orange, yellow, green, blue, and violet, till seven hundred and twenty-seven billions are reached, at which point no *light* is perceptible. Here chemical action begins; and the rays are called chemical rays; as at the other end of the spectrum they are called heat rays. These are objective *conditions* which have been rigorously ascertained; and most important results have been arrived at through them.

The subjective facts according to Goethe lead to the belief that Tones are the product of Sound and Silence, as Colors are of Light and Darkness. Sound is made various (in tones) by various intermixtures with Silence. Descending from the highest audible note there is a gradual retardation of the vibrations, caused by the gradual encroachments of Silence, until at length Silence predominates and no Sound is heard. Suppose this hypothesis granted, we shall still have to ask what are the *conditions* of this Silence? If these are retardations of vibration, we may dispense with the hypothetical Silence. By similar reasoning we dispense with the hypothetical Darkness.

The assumption of different rays of unequal refrangibility is not only supported by the prismatic decomposition and recomposition of light, but also finds confirmation in the law of Refraction discovered by Snellius. And the consequence drawn from it, namely, that the relation of the sine of incidence, though constant for each color, *varies* in the different colors of the spectrum, brings the whole question within the domain of mathematical calculation. The phenomena cease to be *qualitative* only, and become *quantitative:* they are measureable, and are measured. On Goethe's theory, granting its truth, the phenomena are not measurable; and whoever glances into a modern work on Optics will see that the precision and extent to which calculation has been carried, are in themselves sufficient grounds for assigning the preference to the theory which admits such calculation.

Goethe's want of acquaintance with Mathematics and with the Methods of Physical Science prevented his understanding the defect in his own theory, and the manifest superiority of the theory which he attacked. He opposed every mathematical treatment of the subject as mischievous ; and Hegel, who has shown himself still more opposed to the Methods of science, applauds him on this very point.

" I raised the whole school of Mathematicians against me," says Goethe, "and people were greatly amazed that one who had no insight into Mathematics could venture to contradict Newton. *For that Physics could exist independently of Mathematics no one seemed to have the slightest suspicion.*" Nor has that suspicion gained yet any ground with men in the least conversant with Physics, however necessary it may sometimes have been to protest against too exclusive an employment of Mathematics. But the misconception which lies at the bottom of Goethe's polemics was a very natural one to a poet never trained in Mathematical or Experimental science, and unaware of the peculiar position occupied by Mathematics as the great Instrument of research. In his essay *Ueber Mathematik und deren Missbrauch,** he compares the philosopher employing such an instrument to a man who should invent a machine for drawing a cork, an operation which two arms and hands very easily effect.

To make his error intelligible, let us suppose a man of great intellectual acuteness and energy suddenly to light upon the idea that our chemical theories were vitiated by a false basis, —that the atomic theory was not only an hypothesis, but an hypothesis which misrepresented the order of Nature ; there being, in truth, none of the quantitative relations presupposed

* *Werke*, XL. p. 468.

in that theory.   Imagine the reformer setting to work, multi-
plying experiments, inventing explanations, disregarding all
that the accumulated experience of ages had stored up on this
very matter, and above all despising, as useless or worse, the
very Instrument which rescues Chemistry from rough guess-
work, and elevates it into the possibility of a science, — the
Instrument known as the Balance.   It is probable that our
reformer would make many curious observations, some of them
quite new.   It is probable that he would in many directions
stimulate research.   But it is certain that he would be hope-
lessly wrong in his theories, for he would necessarily be imperfect in his data.   Without the delicate control of the Balance, chemical experiment can never become *quantitative;*
and without quantitative knowledge there can be no chemical
science strictly so called, but only *qualitative,* i. e. approximative knowledge.   No amount of observation will render
observation precise, unless it can be measured.   No force of
intellect will supply the place of an Instrument.   You may
watch falling bodies for an eternity, but without Mathematics
mere watching will yield no law of gravitation.   You may mix
acids and alkalis together with prodigality, but no amount of
experiment will yield the secret of their composition, if you
have flung away the Balance.

Goethe flung away the Balance.   Hegel boldly says this
is Goethe's merit.   He praises the " pure sense of Nature,"
which in the poet rebelled against Newton's " barbarism of
Reflection."   To the same effect Schelling, who does not
hesitate to choose it as the very ground for proclaiming
Goethe's superiority over the Newtonians, that " instead of the
artificially confused and disfiguring experiments of the Newtonians, he places the purest, simplest verdicts of Nature herself before us " ; he adds, " it is not surprising that the blind
and slavish followers of Newton should oppose researches

which prove that precisely the very section of Physics, in which up to this time they have imagined the most positive, nay almost geometric evidence, to be on their side, is based on a fundamental error." *

This point of Method, if properly examined, will help to elucidate the whole question of Goethe's aptitude for dealing with physical science. The native direction of his mind is visible in his optical studies as decisively as in his poetry ; that direction was towards the *concrete* phenomenon, not towards abstractions. He desired to explain the phenomena of color, and in Mathematics these phenomena disappear ; that is to say, the very *thing* to be studied is hurried out of sight and masked by abstractions. This was utterly repugnant to his mode of conceiving Nature. The marvellous phenomena of polarized light in the hands of Mathematicians excited his boundless scorn. " One knows not," he says, " whether a body or a mere ruin lies buried under those formulas." † The name of Biot threw him into a rage ; and he was continually laughing at the Newtonians about their prisms and Spectra, as if Newtonians were pedants who preferred their dusky rooms to the free breath of heaven. He always spoke of observations made in his garden, or with a simple prism in the sunlight, as if the natural and simple Method were much more certain than the artificial Method of Science. In this he betrayed his misapprehension of Method. He thought that Nature revealed herself to the patient observer —

" Und was sie deinem Geist nicht offenbaren mag,
    Das zwingst du ihr nicht ab mit Hebeln und mit Schrauben."

" And what she does not reveal to the Mind will not be extorted from her by Levers and Screws." Hence his fail-

* SCHELLING, *Zeitschrift für spekulative Philos.*, II. p. 60.
† *Werke*, XL. 473.

ure ; hence also his success : for we must not forget that if as
a contribution to Optics his *Farbenlehre* be questionable, as a
contribution to the knowledge of color demanded by Artists
it is very valuable.   Painters have repeatedly acknowledged
the advantage they have derived from it ; and I remember
hearing Riedel, at Rome, express the most unbounded
enthusiasm for it ; averring that, as a colorist, he had learned
more from the *Farbenlehre* than from all the other teachers
and books he had ever known.   To artists and physiologists — i. e. to those who are mainly concerned with the
phenomena of color as perceptions, and who demand qualitative rather than quantitative knowledge — his labors have
a high value ; and even physicists must admit, that however
erroneous the theory and imperfect the method he has adopted, still the immense accumulation and systematization of
facts, and the ingenuity with which he explains them, deserve
serious respect.   As Bacon felicitously says, a tortoise on
the right path will beat a racer on the wrong path ; and if it
be true that Goethe was on the wrong path, it is not less
true that he shows the thews and sinews of a racer.

It is with other feelings that we contemplate him laboring
in the organic sciences.   There the native tendencies of his
mind and the acquired tendencies of education better fitted
him for success.   Biology has peculiar fascinations for the
poetical mind, and has seduced several poets to become
physiologists.   Mathematics are not required.   Concrete
observations furnish the materials for a keen and comprehensive comparison.

Let it be distinctly understood, and that not on the testimony of the admiring biographer, but on some of the highest
scientific testimonies in Europe,* that in the organic sciences

* In the first edition of this work several passages were quoted in support of the assertion in the text ; but one effect of this chapter has been

Goethe holds an eminent place, — eminent not because of his rank as a poet, but in spite of it.   Let it be understood that in these sciences he is not to be treated as a poet, a facile amateur, but as a *thinker*, who, having mastered sufficient knowledge to render his path secure, gave an impulse to the minds of contemporaries and successors, which is not even yet arrested.

We will glance at his achievements in this field.   The intermaxillary bone * was long a bone of contention among anatomists.   Vesalius — one of the grandest and boldest of the early pioneers who wrote against Galen, as the philosophers wrote against Aristotle — declared, and with justice, that Galen's anatomy was not founded on the dissection of the *human* body, but on that of animals.   A proof, said he, is that " Galen indicates a separate bone connected with the maxillary by sutures ; a bone which, as every anatomist can satisfy himself, exists only in animals."   The Galenists were in arms.   They could bring no fact in evidence, but *that* was of very little consequence ; if facts were deficient, was not hypothesis always ready ?   Sylvius, for example,

to render such evidence superfluous, Goethe's position in science becoming daily more widely recognized.   The following references are therefore all that need now be given : AUGUSTE ST. HILAIRE, *Morphologie Végétale*, I. p. 15 ; OSCAR SCHMIDT, *Goethe's Verhältniss zu den organischen Wissenschaften*, p. 10 ; JOHANNES MUELLER, *Ueber phantastische Gesichtserscheinungen*, p. 104 ; CUVIER, *Histoire des Sciences Naturelles*, IV. p. 316 ; ISIDORE GEOFFROY ST. HILAIRE, *Essais de Zoologie générale*, p. 139 ; OWEN, *Archetype and Homologies of the Skeleton*, p. 3 ; HELMHOLTZ, *Allgemeine Monatsschrift*, May, 1853 ; VIRCHOW, *Goethe als Naturforscher*.   The profound reach of Goethe's biological conceptions has been well displayed by MR. DARWIN's brilliant disciple, HAECKEL, in his two works, *Generelle Morphologie* and *Natürliche Schöpfungsgeschichte.*

* It is the centre bone of the upper jaw, — that which contains the incisor teeth.

13 *

boldly said that man *had formerly* an intermaxillary bone. If
he has it no longer, he *ought* to have it.   It is luxury, it is
sensuality which has gradually deprived man of this bone.*
(What has not luxury been made to answer for!)   The dispute was carried down through centuries, no one attempting
to demonstrate anatomically the existence of the bone.
Camper actually raised this presumed absence of the bone
into the one distinguishing mark separating man from the
ape ; which is doubly unfortunate, for in the first place the
bone is not absent in man, and secondly, in as far as it can
be considered absent in man, it is equally absent in the
chimpanzee, the highest of the apes.†   Thus was anatomy a
treacherous ally in this question, although Camper knew
not how treacherous.

This slight historical sketch will serve to show that the discovery, if unimportant, was at least far from easy ; indeed so
little did it lie in the track of general knowledge, that it was
at first received with contemptuous disbelief, even by men so
eminent as Blumenbach,‡ and it was forty years gaining
general acceptance, although Loder, Spix, and Sömmering at
once recognized it. Camper, to whom Goethe sent the
manuscript, found that it was *très élégant, admirablement bien
écrit, c'est à dire d'une main admirable,* but thought a better

* This same Sylvius it was who replied to Vesalius that Galen was not
wrong when he described man as having seven bones in his sternum
(there are only three).   "For," said he, "in ancient times the robust
chests of heroes might very well have had more bones than our degen-
erate day can boast."   It is impossible to decide upon what might have
been ; but the mummies are ancient enough, and they have no more
bones than we.

† Blumenbach had already noted that in some young apes and baboons
no trace was discoverable of the bone.

‡ See his *Comparative Anatomy,* translated by Lawrence ; and the
translator's note, p. 60.

Latin style desirable. Goethe began to despise the pedantry
of professional men who would deny the testimony of their
five senses in favor of an old doctrine ; and he admirably
says, " The phrases men are accustomed to repeat incessantly
end by becoming convictions, *and ossify the organs of intelligence."* *

The most remarkable point in this discovery is less the
discovery than the Method which led to it. The intermaxillary bone in animals contains the incisor teeth. Man has
incisor teeth ; and Goethe, fully impressed with the conviction
that there was Unity in Nature, boldly said, if man has the
teeth in common. with animals, he must have the bone in
common with animals. Anatomists, lost in details, and
wanting that fundamental conception which. now underlies all
philosophical anatomy, saw no abstract necessity for such
identity of composition ; the more so, because *evidence* seemed
wholly against it. But Goethe was not only guided by the
true philosophic conception, he was also instinctively led to
the true Method of demonstration, namely, Comparison of
the various modifications which this bone underwent in the
animal series. This Method has now become *the* Method ;

---

* Since the first edition of this work was published, I have met with
a piquant illustration of the not very honorable tendency in men to
plume themselves on the knowledge of a discovery which they had formerly rejected. VICQ D'AZYR, *Discours sur l'Anatomie* (*Œuvres*, IV.
159), mentioning his discovery of the intermaxillary, adds, " J'ai appris
de M. Camper, dans son dernier voyage à Paris, *que cet os lui est connu
depuis très long temps."* Now this same Camper, on receiving the anonymous dissertation in which Goethe propounded the discovery, said,
" Je dois ré-examiner tout cela " ; but on learning that Goethe was the
author, he wrote to Merck that he had " convinced himself that the bone
did not exist" (see VIRCHOW, *Goethe als Naturforscher*, p 79) ; yet no
sooner does a great anatomist tell him that the bone exists than he complacently declares, " I have known it a long while."

and we require to throw ourselves into the historical position to appreciate its novelty, at the time he employed it. He found on comparison that the bone varied with the nutrition of the animal, and the size of its teeth. He found, moreover, that in some animals the bone was not separated from the jaw ; and that in children the sutures were traceable. He admitted that, seen from the front, no trace of the sutures was visible, but on the interior there were unmistakable traces. Examination of the fœtal skull has since set the point beyond dispute. I have seen one where the bone was distinctly separated ; and I possess a skull, the ossification of which is far advanced at the parietal sutures, yet internally faint traces of the intermaxillary are visible.*

Goethe made his discovery in 1784, and communicated it to several anatomists. Loder mentions it in his *Compendium* in 1787.

Respecting Goethe's claim to the honor of this discovery, I have recently ascertained a fact which is of great or small significance according to the views we hold respecting such claims ; namely, whether the clear enunciation of an idea, though never carried out in detail, suffices to give priority ; or whether, in the words of Owen,† "he becomes the true discoverer who establishes the truth, and the sign of the proof is the general acceptance. Whoever, therefore, resumes the investigation of a neglected or repudiated doctrine, elicits its true demonstration, and discovers and explains the nature of the errors which have led to its tacit or declared rejection, may

---

* These might be considered abnormal cases. But M. J. Weber has devised a method of treating the skull with dilute nitric acid, which makes the separation of the bones perfect. — *Froriep's Notizen*, 1828, bd. 19, 282. VIRCHOW, l. c., p. 80.

† OWEN, *Homologies of the Skeleton*, p. 76. Comp. also MALPIGHI, *Opera Posthuma*, 1697, p. 5.

calmly and confidently await the acknowledgments of his rights in its discovery." If we hold the former view, we must assign the discovery of the intermaxillary in man to Vicq d'Azyr ; if we hold the latter, to Goethe. In the *Traité d'Anatomie et de Physiologie,* which the brilliant anatomist published in 1786, we not only find him insisting on the then novel idea of an uniform plan in the structure of organic beings, according to which nature " semble opérer toujours d'après un modèle primitif et général, dont elle ne s'écarte qu'à regret et dont on recontre partout des traces " ;* but we find this explicit illustration given among others : " Peut-on s'y refuser enfin " (i. e. to admit the traces of a general plan) " en comparant les os maxillaires antérieurs que j'appelle *incisifs* dans les quadrupèdes, avec cette pièce osseuse qui soutient les dents incisives supérieures dans l'homme, où elle est séparée de l'os maxillaire par une petite fêlure très remarquable dans les fœtus, à peine visible dans les adultes, et dont personne n'avoit connu l'usage ? " In a subsequent passage of the second *Discours* he says : " Toutes ces dents sont soutenues dans la mâchoire antérieure par un os que j'ai décrit sous le nom d'incisif ou labial, que quelques-uns appellent intermaxillaire, que l'on à découvert depuis peu dans les morses, et *dont j'ai reconnu les traces dans les os maxillaires supérieurs du fœtus humain.*" †

The reader will remark that this is not simply the announcement of the fact, but is adduced in illustration of the very same doctrine which Goethe invoked. The *Traité d'Anatomie,* as we have seen, was published in 1786 ; that is to say, two years after Goethe had made his discovery ; and Sömmering, in writing to Merck, ‡ says : " I have expressed my opin-

* Vicq d'Azyr, *Œuvres,* IV. p. 26. The work is there called *Discours sur l'Anatomie.*

† *Ibid*, p. 159.

‡ *Briefe an Merck,* p. 493.

ion on Vicq d'Azyr's work the *Götting. Gelehrt. Anzeig.* It is the best we have. But as far as the work has yet gone, Goethe is not mentioned in it." From which it may be inferred that Sömmering supposed Vicq d'Azyr to have been acquainted with Goethe's contemporary labors ; but against such a supposition we must remember that, if Germany took note of what was passing in France, discoveries made in Germany travelled with great slowness across the Rhine ; and in illustration of this slowness we may note that Geoffroy St. Hilaire, who was several years afterwards nobly working out conceptions of Philosophical Anatomy in a spirit identical with that of Goethe, was utterly unconscious of the existence of a predecessor, and noticing the monograph of G. Fischer, said, " *Gœthes* aurait le premier découvert l'interpariétal dans quelques rongeurs, et se serait contenté d'en faire mention par une note manuscrite sur un exemplaire d'un traité d'anatomie comparée." *

But the conclusive point is this : although the *Traité d'Anatomie* did not appear till 1786, the discovery of the intermaxillary was published by Vicq d'Azyr in the Académie des Sciences for 1779,† five years before Goethe announced his discovery to Herder. The question of priority is therefore settled. The Frenchman had no need of any acquaintance with what the German poet had worked out ; and Merck's astonishment at finding Goethe's " so-called discovery accepted by Vicq d'Azyr " was wholly misplaced ; but can we

---

* *Philosophie Anatomique*, II. p. 55. GEOFFROY was afterwards very proud to have the suffrage of *Gœthes ;* and Geoffroy's son has spoken most honorably of the coincidence between the speculations of his father and those of the poet.

† In the first edition I stated that " from a note to BLUMENBACH's *Comparative Anatomy* (p. 19), it seems as if Vicq d'Azyr had made this observation as early as 1780." The date in the text is given by Vicq d'Azyr himself. — *Œuvres*, IV. 159.

be equally sure that Goethe was altogether ignorant of his predecessor? I think he was. The sudden enthusiasm, the laborious investigation, the jubilate of triumph, are evidences that if ever his predecessor's discovery had come under his notice (which is highly improbable), it was completely forgotten ; and we may judge how completely Vicq d'Azyr's announcement had been without echo in the scientific world, from the fact that the three most illustrious men of the day, Camper, Blumenbach, and Sömmering knew nothing of it, and denied the existence of the bone Goethe claimed to have discovered. Thus, in assigning priority to Vicq d'Azyr, we by no means diminish Goethe's merit. He it was who thoroughly worked out the discovery ; he it was who gave it a fixed and definite place in science ; he it is who is always named as the discoverer.

The only importance of this discovery is the philosophic Method which it illustrates ; the firm belief it implies that all organisms are constructed on an uniform plan, and that Comparative Anatomy is only valid because such a plan is traceable. In our day it seems an easy conception. We are so accustomed to consider all the variations in organic struct ures as modifications of a type, that we can hardly realize to ourselves any other conception. That it was by no means an obvious idea, nor one easy to apply, may be seen in two brilliant applications — the metamorphosis of plants, and the vertebral theory of the skull.

Place a flower in the hands of the cleverest man of your acquaintance, providing always he has not read modern works of science, and assure him that leaf, calyx, corolla, bud, pistil, and stamen, differing as they do in color and in form, are nevertheless all modified leaves ; assure him that flower and fruit are but modifications of one typical form, which is the leaf ; and if he has any confidence in your knowledge he may accept the statement, but assuredly it will seem to him a most incomprehensible paradox. Place him before a human skeleton, and, calling his attention to its manifold forms, assure him that every bone is either a vertebra, or the appendage to a vertebra, and that the skull is a congeries of vertebræ under various modifications; he will, as before, accept your statement, perhaps; but he will, as before, think it one of the refinements of transcendental speculation to be arrived at only by philosophers. Yet both of these astounding propositions are first principles in Morphology; and in the History of Science both of these propositions are to be traced to Goethe. Botanists and anatomists have, of course, greatly modified the views he promulgated, and have substituted views nearer and nearer the truth, without yet being quite at one. But he gave the impulse to their efforts.

While botanists and anatomists were occupied in analysis, striving to distinguish separate parts, and give them distinct names, his poetical and philosophic mind urged him to seek the supreme synthesis, and reduce all diversities to a higher unity. In his poem addressed to Christiane he says :—

"Thou, my love, art perplexed with the endless seeming confusion
  Of the luxuriant wealth which in the garden is spread ;
  Name upon name thou hearest, and in thy dissatisfied hearing,
  With a barbarian noise one drives another along.
  All the forms resemble, yet none is the same as another ;
  Thus the whole of the throng points at a deep-hidden law." *

To prove this identity was no easy task. He imagined an ideal typical plant (*Urpflanze*), of which all actual plants were the manifold realizations ; and this I cannot but agree with Schleiden in considering a conception at once misleading and infelicitous. He was happier in the conception of all the various organs of the plant as modifications of one

* Whewell's translation, *Hist. Inductive Sciences*, III. 360.

fundamental type ; this type he names the *Leaf.* Not that we are to understand the metamorphosis of plants to be anal- ogous to the metamorphosis of animals (an error into which I fell in my first edition, as Ferdinand Cohn properly points out), nor indeed is it such a metamorphosis at all. The pistil and petal are not first developed into leaves, and from these leaves changed into petal and pistil ; as a caterpillar develops into a grub, and the grub into a butterfly. This would be metamorphosis. Instead of this we must conceive the whole plant as a succession of repetitions of the original type variously modified ; in some of these repetitions the modification has been slight, in others considerable. The two typical forms are stem and leaf. From the seed there is an ascending and a descending axis, formed of a succession of stems : the ascending axis is called the aërial stem ; the descending axis is the root. From both of these stems lat- eral stems or branches are given off ; and from these again others. The Leaf is the second type : it forms all the other organs by various modifications. Widely as a pistil differs from a petal, and both from an ordinary leaf, they are dis- closed as identical by the history of their development.

It is impossible to be even superficially acquainted with biological speculations, and not to recognize the immense importance of the recognition of a Type. As Helmholtz truly observes, " The labors of botanists and zoölogists did little more than collect materials, nntil they learned to dis- pose them in such a series that the laws of dependence and a generalized type could be elicited. Here the great mind of our poet found a field suited to it ; and the time was favorable. Enough material had been collected in botany and comparative anatomy for a clear survey to be taken ; and although his contemporaries all wandered without a com- pass, or contented themselves with a dry registration of facts,

T

he was able to introduce into science two leading ideas of infinite fruitfulness."

And here the question presents itself: Is Goethe rightfully entitled to the honor universally awarded to him of having founded the Morphology of Plants? We must again evoke the distinction previously stated (p. 300). No one denies that the doctrine was so entirely novel that most botanists at first rejected it with contempt, and only consented to accept it when some eminent botanists had shown it to be true. No one denies that Goethe worked it out; if any predecessor had conceived the idea, no one had carried the idea into its manifold applications. But he has himself named Linnæus and Wolff as his precursors; and it is of some interest to ascertain in what degree these percursors have claim to the honor of the discovery.

It has been remarked by the eminent botanist Ferdinand Cohn,* that the great Linnæus mingled with his observation much fantastic error, which the poet Goethe was the first to eliminate. But Dr. Hooker, while admitting the metaphysical and speculative matter which Linnæus has mixed up with his statements, is disposed to value them highly.

The *aperçu* was in Linnæus: a spark awaiting the presence of some inflammable imagination; and when we remember how fond Goethe was of Linnæus, we can hardly suppose that this *aperçu* had not more than once flashed across his mind as a gleam of the truth. With regard to Caspar Friedrich Wolff, the evidence is far from satisfactory. It is certain that Wolff in his immortal work on "Generation" had clearly grasped the morphological principles, and had left Goethe very little to add to them. But it is very uncertain whether Goethe had ever read Wolff. Some years

* *Goethe und die Metamorphosen der Pflanzen*, in the *Deutsches Museum* of PRUTZ, IV. Jan., 1862.

after the publication of his work he mentions with pride the fact of Wolff having been his " admirable precursor," and says that his attention to the work had been drawn by a namesake of the great embryologist. It was with no little surprise, therefore, that I read in Düntzer * the unhesitating assertion that in 1785 Herder had made Goethe a present of Wolff's *Theoria Generationis*, which contained a rough outline of several of Goethe's favorite ideas. If this statement were correct, Goethe would be under serious suspicion ; but it is not correct. On referring to the passage in Herder's letter to Knebel, which Düntzer pretends is the authority for this statement, I find, in the first place, that Herder does not specify the *Theoria Generationis*, nor, indeed, can we be sure he refers to C. F. Wolff at all ; he merely says, " Wolff," which is a common name among German authors ; in the second place he does not say that he has *given* the book to Goethe, but that he *intends* doing so when he can get a copy ; meanwhile Knebel is not to mention the book to Goethe. And out of such a sentence as this, Düntzer has constructed a " fact," which, while it gives his pedantry the small delight of correcting in a foot-note Goethe's assertion that F. A. Wolff directed his attention to the *Theoria Generationis*, lays Goethe open to the charges of having borrowed his morphology from Wolff, of having concealed the fact, and of having pretended never to have seen his predecessor's work until his attention was directed to it some years afterwards. Against such charges the following arguments may be urged. First, there is Goethe's own explicit statement ; and his veracity is not lightly to be questioned. Secondly, if the work referred to by Herder was the *Theoria Generationis* (which is probable, but not certain), and if it was given as intended (also probable, but not certain),we

* *Goethe und Karl August*, 1861, p. 212.

have no evidence that Goethe read it. Thirdly, and conclu-
sively, the date of the very letter in which Herder mentions
his intention is ten years *later* (1795) than Düntzer would
have us suppose ; and is thus five years *after* the publication
of Goethe's views (1790).*

The *Metamorphosen* was published in 1790. In 1817
Goethe says that he had requested his scientific friends to
make notes of any passages they might meet in earlier writers
relative to the topic he had treated, because he was convinced
that in science there was nothing absolutely new. His friend
F. A. Wolff directed him to Caspar Friedrich. In expressing
his admiration for his great predecessor, he is proud to acknowledge how much he has learned from him during five-and-
twenty years. Now, five-and-twenty years from 1817 brings
us back to 1792, — that is to say, two years after the publication of the *Metamorphosen*, and three years before the letter
written by Herder.† So that if we assume the work in ques-
ion to have been the *Theoria Generationis*, Goethe was perfectly correct in mentioning F. A. Wolff, and not Herder, as
the friend to whom he was first indebted for a knowledge of
its existence.

The tone in which Goethe speaks of Caspar Friedrich
Wolff is assuredly not that of a man who had any obligations
to conceal ; but, of a man who, recognizing a precursor
with pleasure, speaks of the two theories as two independent
modes of conceiving the phenomena, the theory of his precursor being pre-eminently physiological, while his own was
pre-eminently morphological.

* See Knebel, *Nachlass*, II. 268.

† It should be added that Knebel's editors place a (?) after the date 1795.
But we have no reason to suppose they could err by *ten* years in assigning
this letter its place ; Düntzer professes no doubt as to the accuracy of the
date ; and internal evidence, taken with what is said above, renders it
highly probable that 1795 is very little removed from the correct date.

With regard both to Linnæus and Wolff, it may be said that they anticipated the morphology of plants, but that to Goethe belongs the credit of establishing it. We do not take from the credit of Columbus by showing that, five centuries before he discovered the New World, Scandinavian voyagers had repeatedly touched on those shores ; nor do we diminish the value of Goethe's contribution to Science, by showing that before him Wolff had perceived the identity of the various organs of the plant. It was not the purpose of the Scandinavians to discover the New World. They did not make their discovery a possession for mankind. Neither was it Wolff's purpose to create a new theory in Botany. He discovered a process of nature while he was seeking the laws of Epigenesis, and he only used his discovery as one of several illustrations. Columbus set out with the distinct purpose of discovery, and made his discovery a possession for all time. So also Goethe set out with the distinct purpose, and Botanists justly declare that to his work they owe the idea of plant metamorphosis.

Whatever may be the final decision upon the Metamorphoses of Plants, there must ever remain the great and unique glory of a poet having created a new branch of science, and by means as legitimately scientific as those of any other creation. Morphology now counts among its students illustrious names, and crowds of workers. And this science we owe to the author of *Faust*. Nor is this all. He has priority in some of the most luminous and comprehensive ideas which are now guiding philosophic speculation on the science of life.

Let me repeat, as a matter of justice, and not to allow the high praise bestowed on Goethe's efforts to mislead the reader's expectation, that the merit is that of a *thinker in science*, not the merit of an industrious discoverer and collector of details.

His great effort was to create a Method, to establish principles upon which the science could be founded.

As a thinker in Science Goethe was truly remarkable, and as a worker not contemptible. To prove how far he was in advance of his age we have only to cite a single passage, which, in its aphoristic, pregnant style, contains the clear announcement of biological laws, which have since been named among the glories of Geoffroy St. Hilaire, Von Baer, Milne-Edwards, Cuvier, and Lamarck : —

" Every living being is not a unity but a plurality. Even when it appears as an individual, it is the reunion of beings living and existing in themselves, identical in origin, but which may appear identical or similar, different or dissimilar.

" The *more imperfect* a being is the more do its individual parts *resemble each other*, and the more do these parts *resemble the whole*. The *more perfect* the being is the more *dissimilar are its parts*. In the former case the parts are more or less a repetition of the whole : in the latter case they are totally unlike the whole.

" The more the parts resemble each other, the less subordination is there of one to the other. *Subordination of parts indicates high grade of organization.*" *

To illustrate by familiar examples. Take a polyp and cut it into several pieces ; each piece will live and manifest all those phenomena of nutrition and sensibility which the whole polyp manifested. Turn it inside out like a glove, the internal part becomes its skin, the external part becomes its stomach. The reason is, that in the simple structure of the polyp, the parts resemble each other and resemble the whole. There is no individual organ, or apparatus of organs, performing one function, such as nutrition, and nothing else. Every function is performed by every part ; just as in savage

* *Zur Morphologie,* 1807 (written in 1795), *Werke,* XXXVI. p. 7.

societies, every man is his own tailor, his own armorer, his own cook, and his own policeman. But take an animal higher in the scale, and there you find the structure composed of dissimilar parts, and each part having a different office. That animal cannot be hewn in pieces and each piece continue to live as before. That animal cannot have its skin suddenly turned into a stomach. That animal, in the social body, cannot make his own clothes or his own musket ; the division of labor which has accompanied his higher condition has robbed him of his universal dexterity.

The law invoked by Goethe is now to be met with in every philosophic work on zoölogy. One form of it is known in England as Von Baer's law, viz. that Development proceeds from the Like to the Unlike, from the General to the Particular, from the Homogeneous to the Heterogeneous. I have too profound an admiration for Von Baer to wish in any way to diminish his splendid claims, but I cannot help remarking that when writers attribute to him the merit of having discovered this law, they are in direct contradiction with Von Baer himself, who not only makes no such claim, but in giving the formula adds, " this law of development has indeed never been overlooked."* His merit is the splendid application and demonstration of the law, not the first perception of it.

It is generally known that the law of " division of labor in the animal organism " is claimed by Milne-Edwards, the great French zoölogist, as a discovery of his own. Yet we see how

---

* " Dieses Gesetz der Ausbildung ist wohl nie verkannt worden." — *Zur Entwickelungsgeschichte.* Erster Theil, p. 153. Among others, WOLFF has clearly stated it. *Theorie von der Generation*, § 28, p. 163. See also MECKEL, *Traité d'Anatomie Comparée*, French trans. I. 297. BUFFON also says : " Un corps organisé, dont toutes les parties seraient semblables à lui-même, est la plus simple, car ce n'est que la répétition de la même forme." — *Hist Nat.*, 1749, II. 47.

clearly it is expressed in Goethe's formula. And with even
more clearness do we see expressed Cuvier's principle of
classification, viz. the *subordination of parts.* I do not wish
to press this point further, nor do I wish that these great men
should be robbed of any merit in order to glorify Goethe with
their trophies.   The student of history knows how discoveries
are, properly speaking, made by the Age, and not by men.
He knows that all discoveries have had their anticipations ;
and that the world justly credits the man who makes the
discovery *available*, not the man who simply perceived that it
was possible.   I am not here writing the history of science,
but the biography of Goethe ; and the purpose of these citations is to show that he placed himself at the highest point of
view possible to his age, and that as a thinker he thought the
thoughts which the greatest men have subsequently made
popular.

Observe, moreover, that Goethe's anticipation is not of
that slight and fallacious order which, like so many other
anticipations, rests upon a vague or incidental phrase.   He
did not simply attain an *aperçu* of the truth.   He mastered
the law, and his mastery of that law sprang from his mastery
of the whole series of conceptions in which it finds its place.
Thus in his " Introduction to Comparative Anatomy," written
in 1795, he pointed out the essentially sterile nature of the
comparisons then made, not only in respect of comparing
animals with men and with each other, not only in the abuse
of final causes, but also in taking man as the standard, instead
of commencing with the simplest organisms and rising gradually upwards.   One year after this, Geoffroy St. Hilaire
ignorant of what was passing in the study at Weimar and in
the Museum at Jena, published his *Dissertation sur les Makis,*
wherein he began his renovation of the science.   He, too,
like Goethe, was bent on the creation of a Type according to

which all organized structures could be explained.   This conception of a Type (*Allgemeines Bild*), according to which the
whole animal kingdom may be said to be constructed, was a
truly scientific conception, and has borne noble fruit.   It must
not, however, be confounded with a Platonic Idea.   It was
not metaphysical entity, it was simply a scientific artifice.
Goethe expressly says that we are not for an instant to
believe in the *existence* of this Type as an objective reality,
although it is the generalized expression of that which really
exists.   This caution has not been sufficiently present to the
minds of several speculators; and the idea of a Type has
engendered not a few extravagances.   Nevertheless, the net
result of these speculations has been good.

Fifteen years after Goethe had passed away from this
world, and when therefore there was no power of reply, Oken
in the *Isis* (1847, *Heft* VII.,) made an accusation against
Goethe's claim to the origination of the vertebral theory of the
skull.   His statement completely staggered me, suggesting
very painful feelings as to Goethe's conduct.   Indeed, the
similarity in the stories of both suggests suspicion.   Goethe,
during one of his rambles in the Jewish cemetery near Venice, noticed the skull of a ram, which had been cut longitu-
dinally, and on examining it, the idea occurred to him that the
face was composed of three vertebræ : " the transition from
the anterior sphenoid to the ethmoid was evident at once."
Now, compare Oken's story.   He narrates how in 1802, in a
work on the Senses, he had represented these organs as repetitions of lower organs, although he had not then grasped
the idea, which lay so close at hand, respecting the skull as a
repetition of the spinal column.   In 1806 he identified the
jaws of insects as limbs of the head ; and in 1806, while
rambling in the Harz Mountains, he picked up the skull of a
deer : on examining it, he exclaimed, " That is a vertebral

14

column!" Virchow admits that the coincidence in the stories is singular, but adds that the discovery is just as probable in the one case as in the other; all that is proved by the
coincidence being that both minds were on the verge of the
discovery. Goethe by long physiognomical and osteological
studies was prepared for the idea; and was naturally led
from the Metamorphoses of Plants to those of Insects; and
if Oken reversed this order, passing from insects to mam-
mals, he was, nevertheless, many years later than Goethe, as
dates unequivocally prove. It is important to bear in mind
that the vertebral theory is only another application of those
morphological doctrines which Goethe had developed and
applied to plants; and although it is quite *possible* that he
might have held these views without making the special
application to the skull, yet we know as a fact that he at
once saw how the morphological laws must necessarily apply
to animals, since he expressly states this in announcing his
discovery to Herder.* Nay, he shortly afterwards wrote,
"In Natural History I shall bring you what you little expect.
I believe myself to be very near the law of organization."
Still it may be objected, This is no proof; it only shows that
Goethe applied his doctrines to the animal organization, not
that he made a special application to the skull. Even this
doubt, however, has been finally settled by the recently published correspondence, which gives us a letter from Goethe
to Herder's wife, dated 4th May, 1790, from Venice.
"Through a singular and lucky accident I have been enabled to take a step forwards in my explanation of the animal
development (*Thierbildung*). My servant, in jest, took up the
fragment of an animal's skull from the Jewish cemetery, pre-
tending to offer it me as a Jewish skull." Now when we
remember that Goethe in after years affirmed that it was in

* *Italiänische Reise*, II. p. 5.

r790, and in the Jewish cemetery of Venice, that the idea of the vertebral structure of the skull flashed upon him, the evidence of this letter is conclusive.

Oken declares he made his discovery in 1806, and that in 1807 he wrote his Academic Programme. He was then a *Privat Docent* in Göttingen, "at a time, therefore, when Goethe certainly knew nothing of my existence." He sent his dissertation to Jena, where he had just been appointed professor. Of that university Goethe was curator. Oken considers this fact decisive : namely, that Goethe would assuredly have remonstrated against Oken's claim to the discovery had he not recognized its justice. The fact, however, is by no means decisive : we shall see presently that Goethe had his own reasons for silence. " I naturally sent Goethe a copy of my programme. This discovery pleased him so much that he invited me, at Easter, 1808, to spend a week with him at Weimar, which I did. As long as the discovery was ridiculed by men of science, Goethe was silent, but no sooner did it attain renown through the works of Meckel, Spix, and others, than there grew up a murmur among Goethe's servile admirers that this idea originated with him. About this time Bojanus went to Weimar, and hearing of Goethe's discovery, half believed it, and sent the rumor to me, which I thoughtlessly printed in the *Isis* (1818, p. 509) ; whereupon I announced that I made my discovery in the autumn of 1806." This is equivocal. He did *not* throw any doubt on Goethe's claim to priority, he only asserted his own originality. " Now that Bojanus had brought the subject forward," he adds, " Goethe's vanity was piqued, and he came afterwards, thirteen years subsequent to my discovery, and said he had held the opinion for thirty years."

Why was Goethe silent when Oken first announced his discovery? and why did not Oken make the charge of plagiarism during Goethe's lifetime? The first question may be answered from Goethe's own works. In a note entitled *Das Schädelgerüst aus sechs Wirbelknochen auferbaut*, after alluding to his recognition first of three and subsequently of six vertebræ in the skull, which he spoke of among his friends, who set to work to demonstrate it if possible, he says : " In the year 1807 this theory appeared tumultuously and imperfectly before the public, and naturally awakened great disputes and some applause. How seriously it was damaged by the incomplete and fantastic method of exposition, History must relate. This criticism of the exposition will be understood by every one who has read Oken, and who knows Goethe's antipathy to metaphysics.* With all his prepossession in favor of a Type, he could not patiently have accepted an exposition which " tumultuously " announced that " the whole man is but a vertebra." Accordingly he took no notice of the tumultuous metaphysician ; and in his *Tag und Jahres Hefte* he mentions that while he was working out his theory with two friends, Riemer and Voigt, they brought him, with some surprise, the news that this idea had just been laid before the public in an academic programme, " a fact," he adds, " *which they, being still alive, can testify.*" Why did he not claim priority? " I told my friends to keep quiet, for the idea was not properly worked out in the programme ; and that it was not elaborated from original observations would be plain to all scientific men. I was frequently besought to speak plainly on the subject ; but I was firm in my silence."

When I first discussed this question, and knew nothing of the decisive evidence which lay unpublished in the letter to Herder's wife, I said that this statement carried complete

---

* So also CUVIER's antipathy to this exposition made him blind to the truth which it contained.

conviction to my mind. It was published many years before
Oken made his charge, and it accused him in the most
explicit terms of having prematurely disclosed an idea Goethe
was then elaborating with the assistance of his friends.
Nor was this all. It appealed to two honorable and respected men, then living, as witnesses of the truth. Oken said
nothing when the question could have been peremptorily settled by calling upon Voigt and Riemer. He waited till
death rendered an appeal impossible. He says, indeed, that
he made no answer to the first passage I have cited, because
he was not *named* in it, and he "did not wish to involve himself in a host of disagreeables." But this is no answer to the
second passage. There he is indicated as plainly as if the
name of Oken were printed in full; and not only is he indicated, but Goethe's friends speak of Oken's coming forward
with Goethe's idea as a matter which "surprised" them.
Those to whom this reasoning was not conclusive are now
referred to the confirmation it receives from the letter to
Herder's wife.

Having vindicated Goethe's character, and shown that *biographically* we are fully justified in assigning to him the honor
of having first conceived this theory, it now remains to be
added that *historically* the priority of Oken's claim must be
admitted. In writing the poet's biography, it is of some importance to show that he was not indebted to Oken for the
discovery. In writing the history of science, it would be to
Oken that priority would be assigned, simply because, according to the judicious principles of historical appreciation, priority of publication carries off the prize. No man's claim to
priority is acknowledged unless he can bring forward the evidence of publication; otherwise every discovery might be
claimed by those who have no right to it. Moreover, Oken
has another claim: to him undeniably belongs the merit of

having introduced the idea into the scientific world, accompanied with sufficient amount of detail to make it acceptable to scientific minds, and to set them to work in verifying the idea. On these grounds I think it indisputable that the vertebral theory must be attributed to Oken, and not to Goethe ; although it is not less indisputable that Goethe did anticipate the discovery by sixteen years, and would have earned the right to claim it of History, had he made his discovery public, instead of privately discussing it with his friends. Virchow thinks otherwise ; he assigns priority to Goethe ; but he would, I am sure, admit the generally received principle that priority of publication is the test upon which alone History can rely.

To conclude this somewhat lengthy chapter on the scientific studies, it must be stated that, for the sake of bringing together his various efforts into a manageable whole, I have not attended strictly to chronology. Nor have I specified the various separate essays he has written. They are all to be found collected in his works. My main object has been to show what were the directions of his mind, what were his achievements and failures in Science, what place Science filled in his life, and how false the supposition is that he was a mere dabbler. What Buffon says of Pliny may truly be said of Goethe, that he had *cette facilité de penser en grand qui multiple la science;* and it is only as a thinker in this great department that I claim a high place for him.

CHAPTER VII.

THE CAMPAIGN IN FRANCE.

In 1790 Goethe undertook the government of all the Institutions for Science and Art, and busied himself with the arrangement of the Museums and Botanical Gardens at Jena. In March of the same year he went once more to Italy to meet the Duchess Amalia and Herder in Venice. There he tried in Science to find refuge from troubled thoughts. Italy on a second visit seemed, however, quite another place to him. He began to suspect that there had been considerable illusion in the charm of his first visit. The *Venetian Epigrams*, if compared with the *Roman Elegies*, will indicate the difference of his mood. The yearning regret, the fulness of delight, the newness of wonder which give their accents to the Elegies, are replaced by sarcasms and the bitterness of disappointment. It is true that many of these epigrams were written subsequently, as their contents prove, but the mass of them are products of the Venetian visit. Something of this dissatisfaction must be attributed to his position. He was ill at ease with the world. The troubles of the time, and the troubles of his own domestic affairs, aggravated the dangers which then threatened his aims of self-culture, and increased his difficulty in finding that path in Science and Art whereon the culture of the world might be pursued.

In June he returned to Weimar. In July the Duke sent for him at the Prussian Camp in Silesia, "where, instead of stones and flowers, he would see the field sown with troops." He went unwillingly, but compensated himself by active researches into "stones and flowers," leaving to the Duke and others such interest as was to be found in soldiers. He lived like a hermit in the camp, and began to write an essay on the development of animals, and a comic opera.

In August he returned to Weimar. The Duchess Amalia and Herder, impatient at "such waste of time over old bones," plagued him into relinquishing osteology, and urged him to complete *Wilhelm Meister.* He did not, however, proceed far with it. The creative impulse was past ; and to disprove Newton was a more imperious desire. In 1791, which was a year of quiet study and domestic happiness for him, the Court Theatre was established. He undertook the direction with delight.

And now he was to be torn from his quiet studies to follow the fortunes of an unquiet camp. The King of Prussia and the Duke of Brunswick at the head of a large army invaded France, to restore Louis XVI. to his throne, and save legitimacy from the sacrilegious hands of Sansculottism. France, it was said, groaned under the tyranny of factions, and yearned for deliverance. The emigrants made it clear as day that the Allies would be welcomed by the whole nation ; and the German rulers willingly lent their arms to the support of legitimacy. Karl August, passionately fond of the army, received the command of a Prussian regiment. And Goethe, passionately fond of Karl August, followed him into the field. But he followed the Duke, — he had no sympathy with the cause. Indeed, he had no strong feeling either way. Legitimacy was no passion with him ; still less was Republicanism. Without interest in passing politics, profoundly convinced that all salvation could only come through inward culture, and dreading disturbances mainly because they rendered culture impossible, he was emphatically the " Child of Peace," and could at no period of his life be brought to sympathize with great struggles. He disliked the Revolution as he disliked the Reformation, because they both thwarted the peaceful progress of development.

It was not in Goethe's nature to be much moved by events, to be deeply interested in the passing troubles of external life. A meditative mind like his naturally sought in the eternal principles of Nature the stimulus and the food which other minds sought in passing phenomena of the day. A poet and a philosopher is bound to be interested in the great questions of poetry and philosophy ; but to rail at him for not also taking part in politics, is as irrational as to rail at a prime minister because he cares not two pins for Greek Art, and has no views on the transmutation of species. It is said, and very foolishly said, that Goethe turned from politics to art and science, because politics disturbed him, and because he was too *selfish* to interest himself in the affairs of others. But this accusation is on a par with those ungenerous accusations which declare heterodoxy to be the shield of profligacy : as if doubts proceeded only from dissolute habits. How unselfish Goethe was, those best know who know him best ; it would be well if we could say so much of many who devote themselves to patriotic schemes. Patriotism may be quite as selfish as Science or Art, even when it is a devout conviction ; nor is it likely to be less selfish when, as so often happens, patriotism is only an uneasy pauperism.

That Goethe sincerely desired the good of mankind, and that he labored for it in his way with a perseverance few have equalled, is surely enough to absolve him from the charge of selfishness, because his labors did not take the special direction of politics. What his opinions were is one thing, another thing his conduct. Jean Paul says, " He was more far-sighted than the rest of the world, for in the beginning of the French Revolution he despised the patriots as much as he did at the end." I do not detect any feeling so deep as contempt, either late or early; but it is certain that while Klopstock and others were madly enthusiastic at the opening of this terrible drama, they were as madly fanatical against it before its close; whereas Goethe seems to have held pretty much the same opinion throughout.

The Allies entered France, believing the campaign would be a mere promenade. Longwy they were assured would soon surrender, and the people receive them with open arms. Longwy did surrender; but the people, so far from showing any disposition to welcome them, everywhere manifested the most determined resistance.

The defeat at Valmy, slight as it was, discouraged the Prussians and exhilarated the French. The Prussians startled at the cry of *Vive la Nation !* with which the republicans charged, and finding themselves on foreign ground, without magazines, stores, or any proper preparations for a long conflict, perceived the mistake they had made, and began to retreat. It was doubtless a relief to Goethe to hear that he had not much longer to endure the hardships of campaigning. He had no interest in the cause, and he had not gained by actual contact with its leaders a higher opinion of them. Although his return home was slow, and French arms were everywhere victorious in his rear, he finally reached Weimar in safety, and was able to resume the old tenor of his life.

BOOK THE SIXTH.

1794 TO 1805.

———◆———

CHAPTER I.

GOETHE AND SCHILLER.

THERE are few nobler spectacles than the friendship of two great men ; and the History of Literature presents nothing comparable to the friendship of Goethe and Schiller. The friendship of Montaigne and Etienne de la Boëtie was, perhaps, more passionate and entire ; but it was the union of two kindred natures, which from the first moment discovered their affinity, not the union of two rivals incessantly contrasted by partisans, and originally disposed to hold aloof from each other. Rivals Goethe and Schiller were and are ; natures in many respects directly antagonistic ; chiefs of opposing camps, and brought into brotherly union only by what was highest in their natures and their aims.

To look on these great rivals was to see at once their profound dissimilarity. Goethe's beautiful head had the calm victorious grandeur of the Greek ideal ; Schiller's the earnest beauty of a Christian looking towards the Future. The massive brow, and large-pupilled eyes, — like those given by Raphael to the infant Christ, in the matchless Madonna di San Sisto, — the strong and well-proportioned features, lined indeed by thought and suffering, yet showing that thought and suffering have troubled, but not vanquished, the strong man, — a certain healthy vigor in the brown skin, make Goethe a striking contrast to Schiller, with his eager eyes, narrow brow, — tense and intense, — his irregular features worn by thought and suffering, and weakened by sickness. The one *looks*, the other *looks out.* Both are majestic ; but one has the majesty of repose, the other of conflict. Goethe's frame is massive, imposing ; he seems much taller than he is. Schiller's frame is disproportioned, he seems less than he is. Goethe holds himself stiffly erect ; the long-necked Schiller " walks like a camel." * Goethe's chest is like the torso of the Theseus ; Schiller's is bent, and has lost a lung.

A similar difference is traceable in details. " An air that was beneficial to Schiller acted on me like poison," Goethe said to Eckermann. " I called on him one day, and as I did not find him at home, I seated myself at his writing-table to note down various matters. I had not been seated long, before I felt a strange indisposition steal over me, which gradually increased, until at last I nearly fainted. At first I did not know to what cause I should ascribe this wretched and to me unusual state, until I discovered that a dreadful odor issued from a drawer near me. When I opened it, I found to my astonishment that it was full of rotten apples. I immediately went to the window and inhaled the fresh air, by which I was instantly restored. Meanwhile, his wife came in, and told me that the drawer was always filled with rotten apples, because the scent was beneficial to Schiller, and he could not live or work without it."

As another and not unimportant detail, characterizing the healthy and unhealthy practice of literature, it may be added that Goethe wrote in the freshness of morning, entirely free

* This picturesque phrase was uttered by Tieck, the sculptor, to Rauch, from whom I heard it. Let me add that Schiller's brow is called in the text "narrow," in defiance of Dannecker's bust, with which I compared Schiller's skull, and found that the sculptor, as usual, had grossly departed from truth in his desire to idealize.

from stimulus ; Schiller worked in the feverish hours of night, stimulating his languid brain with coffee and champagne.

. In comparing one to a Greek ideal, the other to a Christian ideal, it has already been implied that one was the representative of Realism, the other of Idealism. Goethe has himself indicated the capital distinction between them : Schiller was animated with the idea of Freedom ; Goethe, on the contary, was animated with the idea of Nature. This distinction runs through their works: Schiller always pining for something greater than Nature, wishing to make men Demigods ; Goethe always striving to let Nature have free development, and produce the highest forms of Humanity. The Fall of Man was to Schiller the happiest of all events, because thereby men fell away from pure *instinct* into conscious *freedom ;* with this sense of freedom came the possibility of Morality. To Goethe this seemed paying a price for Morality which was higher than Morality was worth ; he preferred the ideal of a condition wherein Morality was unnecessary. Much as he might prize a good police, he prized still more a society in which a police would never be needed.

Goethe and Schiller were certainly different natures ; but had they been so fundamentally opposed as it is the fashion to consider them, they could never have become so intimately united. They were opposite and allied, with somewhat of the same differences and resemblances as are traceable in the Greek and Roman Mars. In the Greek Mythology the God of War had not the prominent place he attained in Rome ; and the Greek sculptors, when they represented him, represented him as the victor returning, after conflict, to repose, holding in his hand the olive branch, while at his feet sat Eros. The Roman sculptors, or those who worked for Rome, represented Mars as the God of War in all his terrors, in the

very act of leading on to victory. But, different as these
two conceptions were, they were both conceptions of the God
of War ; Goethe may be likened to the one, and Schiller to
the other: both were kindred spirits united by a common
purpose.

Having touched upon the points of contrast, it will now be
needful to say a word on those points of resemblance which
served as the basis of their union.   It will be unnecessary to
instance the obvious points which two such poets must have
had in common ; the mention of some less obvious will suffice
for our present purpose. They were both profoundly convinced that Art was no luxury of leisure, no mere amusement
to charm the idle, or relax the careworn ; but a mighty influence, serious in its aims although pleasurable in its means ;
a sister of Religion, by whose aid the great world-scheme was
wrought into reality.   This was with them no mere sonorous
phrase. They were thoroughly in earnest. They believed
that Culture would raise Humanity to its full powers ; and
they, as artists, knew no Culture equal to that of Art.   It was
probably a perception of this belief that made Karl Grun say,
" Goethe was the most ideal Idealist the earth has ever borne ;
an *æsthetic* Idealist." And hence the origin of the wide-
spread error that Goethe " only looked at life as an artist,"
i. e. cared only for human nature inasmuch as it afforded him
materials for Art ; a point which will be more fully examined
hereafter. The phases of their development had been very
similar, and had brought them to a similar standing-point,
They both began rebelliously ; they both emerged from titanic
lawlessness in emerging from youth to manhood.   In Italy
the sight of ancient masterpieces completed Goethe's metamorphosis. Schiller had to work through his in the gloomy
North, and under the constant pressure of anxieties. He,
too, pined for Italy, and thought the climate of Greece would

make him a poet. But his intense and historical mind found neither stimulus nor enjoyment in plastic Art. Noble men and noble deeds were the food which nourished his great soul. " His poetic purification came from moral ideals ; whereas in Goethe the moral ideal came from the artistic."* Plutarch was Schiller's Bible. The ancient masterpieces of poetry came to him in this period of his development, to lead him gently by the hand onwards to the very point where Goethe stood. He read the Greek tragedians in wretched French translations, and with such aid laboriously translated the *Iphigenia* of Euripides. Homer, in Voss's faithful version, became to him what Homer long was to Goethe. And how thoroughly he threw himself into the ancient world may be seen in his poem, *The Gods of Greece.* Like Goethe, he had found his religious opinions gradually separating him more and more from the orthodox Christians ; and, like Goethe, he had woven for himself a system out of Spinoza, Kant, and the Grecian sages.

At the time, then, that these two men seemed most opposed to each other, and *were* opposed in feeling, they were gradually drawing closer and closer in the very lines of their development, and a firm basis was prepared for solid and enduring union. Goethe was five-and-forty, Schiller five-and-thirty. Goethe had much to give, which Schiller gratefully accepted ; and if he could not in return influence the developed mind of his great friend, nor add to the vast stores of its knowledge and experience, he could give him that which was even more valuable, *sympathy* and *impulse.* He excited Goethe to work. He withdrew him from the engrossing pursuit of science, and restored him once more to poetry. He urged him to finish what was already commenced, and not to leave his works all fragments. They worked together with the same

* *Gervinus,* V. p. 152.

purpose and with the same earnestness, and their union is the most glorious episode in the lives of both, and remains as an eternal exemplar of a noble friendship.

Of all the tributes to Schiller's greatness which an enthusiastic people has pronounced, there is perhaps nothing which carries a greater weight of tenderness and authority than Goethe's noble praise. It is a very curious fact in the history of Shakespeare, that he is not known to have written a single line in praise of any contemporary poet. The fashion of those days was for each poet to write verses in eulogy of his friends ; and the eulogies written by Shakespeare's friends are such as to satisfy even the idolatry of admirers in our day ; but there exists no eulogy, no single verse, from him whose eulogy was more worth having than that of all the rest put together.* Had literary gossip, pregnant with literary malice, produced the absurd impression that Shakespeare was cold, selfish, and self-idolatrous, this curious fact would have been made a damning proof. I have so often in these pages used Shakespeare as a contrast to Goethe, that it would be wrong not to contrast him also on this point. Of all the failings usually attributed to literary men, Goethe had the least of what could be called jealousy ; of all the qualities which sit gracefully on greatness, he had the most of magnanimity. The stream of time will carry down to after ages the memory of several whose names will live only in his praise ; and the future students of Literary History will have no fact to note of Goethe similar to that noted of Shakespeare : they will see

* There is, indeed, a couplet in the *Passionate Pilgrim* which names Spenser with high praise ; but it is doubtful whether the *Passionate Pilgrim* is anything but the attempt of a bookseller to palm off on the public a work which Shakespeare never wrote ; and it is certain that Shakespeare is not the author of the sonnet in which Spenser is mentioned, that sonnet having been previously published by a Richard Barnfield.

how enthusiastic was his admiration of his rivals, Schiller, Voss, and Herder, and how quick he was to perceive the genius of Scott, Byron, Béranger, and Manzoni.

But I must quit this attempt to characterize the two rivals, and proceed to narrate their active co-operation in the common work.

While the great world was agitated to its depths by the rapid march of the Revolution, the little world of Weimar pursued the even tenor of its way, very much as if nothing concerning the destinies of mankind were then in action. Because Goethe is the greatest figure in Germany, the eyes of all Germans are turned towards him, anxious to see how he bore himself in those days. They see him — not moving with the current of ideas, not actively sympathizing with events ; and some of them find no better explanation of what they see than the brief formula that " he was an egotist." If they look, however, at his companions and rivals, they will find a similar indifference. Wieland, the avowed enemy of all despotism, was frightened by the Reign of Terror into demanding a dictatorship. Nor — strange as it may appear — was Schiller, the poet of Freedom, the creator of Posa, more favorable to the French than Goethe himself. The Republic had honored him in a singular way. It had forwarded him the diploma of citizenship ; a dignity conferred at the same time on Washington, Franklin, Tom Paine, Pestalozzi, Campe, and Anacharsis Clootz ! The diploma signed by Danton and Roland, dated 6th September, 1792, is now preserved in the Library at Weimar, where visitors will notice the characteristic accuracy of the French in the spelling of Schiller's name, — *à Monsieur Gille, publiciste allemand.* This honor Schiller owed to his *Robbers*, or, as his admirers called it, *Robert, chef de Brigands.* From the very first he had looked with no favorable eye on the Revolution, and the trial of Louis XVI. produced so deep an impression on him, that he commenced an address to the National Convention, which was, however, outrun by rapid events. Like Wieland, he saw no hope but in a dictatorship.

Such being the position of the leading minds, we are not to wonder if we find them pursuing their avocations just as if nothing were going on in France or elsewhere. Weimar could play no part in European politics. The men of Weimar had their part to play in Literature, through which they saw a possible regeneration. Believing in the potent efficacy of culture, they devoted themselves with patriotism to that. A glance at the condition of German Literature will show how patriotism had noble work to do in such a cause.

The Leipsic Fair was a rival to our Minerva Press ; Chivalry-romances, Robber-stories and Spectre-romances, old German superstitions, Augustus Lafontaine's sentimental family-pictures, and Plays of the *Sturm und Drang* style, swarmed into the sacred places of Art, like another invasion of the Goths. On the stage Kotzebue was king. The *Stranger* was filling every theatre, and moving the sensibilities of a too readily moved pit. Klopstock was becoming more and more oracular, less and less poetical. Jean Paul indeed gave signs of power and originality ; but except Goethe and Schiller, Voss, who had written his *Luise* and translated *Homer*, alone seemed likely to form the chief of a school of which the nation might be proud.

It was in this state of things that Schiller conceived the plan of a periodical, — *Die Horen*, — memorable in many ways to all students of German Literature. Goethe, Herder, Kant, Fichte, the Humboldts, Klopstock, Jacobi, Engel, Meyer, Garve, Matthisson, and others, were to form a phalanx whose irresistible might should speedily give them possession of the land.

Such was the undertaking which formed the first link in the friendship of Goethe and Schiller. How they stood towards each other has been seen in the preceding Book. One day, in May, 1794, they met, coming from a lecture given by Batsch at the Natural History Society in Jena ; in talking over the matter, Goethe, with pleased surprise, heard Schiller criticise the fragmentary Method which teachers of Science uniformly adopted. When they arrived at Schiller's house, Goethe went in with him, expounding the Theory of Metamorphoses with great warmth. Taking up a pen, he made a rapid sketch of the typical plant. Schiller listened with great attention, seizing each point clearly and rapidly, but shaking his head at last, and saying, "This is not an observation, it is an Idea." Goethe adds : " My surprise was painful, for these words clearly indicated the point which separated us. The opinions he had expressed in his essay on *Anmuth und Würde* recurred to me, and my old repulsion was nearly revived. But I mastered myself, and answered that I was delighted to find I had Ideas without knowing it, and to be able to contemplate them with my own eyes." There can be little question of Schiller having been in the right, though perhaps both he and Goethe assigned an exclusively subjective meaning to the phrase. The typical plant, Goethe knew very well, was not to be found in nature ; but he thought it was *revealed* in plants.* Because he arrived at the belief in a type through direct observation and comparison, and not through *à priori* deduction, he maintained that this type was an intuition (*Anschauung*), not an idea. Probably Schiller was more impressed with the metaphysical nature of the conception than with the physical evi-

* Goethe, speaking of his labors in another department, says, " I endeavored to find the Primitive Animal (Urthier), in other words, the Conception, the Idea of an Animal." — *Werke*, XXXVI. p. 14.

dence on which it had been formed. The chasm between them was indeed both broad and deep ; and Goethe truly says : " It was in a conflict between the Object and the Subject, the greatest and most interminable of all conflicts, that began our friendship, which was eternal." A beginning had been made. Schiller's wife, for whom Goethe had a strong regard, managed to bring them together ; and the proposed journal, *Die Horen*, brought their activities and sympathies into friendly union. Rapid was the growth of this friendship, and on both sides beneficial. Schiller paid a fortnight's visit at Weimar ; Goethe was frequently in Jena. They found that they agreed not only on subjects, but also on the mode of looking at them. " It will cost me a long time to unravel all the ideas you have awakened in me," writes Schiller ; "but I hope none will be lost."

Regretting that he could not give the novel *Wilhelm Meister* for the *Horen*, having already promised it to a publisher, Goethe nevertheless sends Schiller the manuscript from the third book onwards, and gratefully profits by the friendly criticism with which he reads it. He gave him, however, the two *Epistles*, the *Unterhaltungen deutscher Ausgewanderten*, the *Roman Elegies*, and the essay on *Literary Sansculottism*.

The mention of *Wilhelm Meister* leads us to retrace our steps a few months, when the active interest he took in the direction of the Weimar Theatre revived his interest in this novel, over which he had dawdled so many years. He finished it ; but he finished it in quite a different spirit from that in which it was commenced, and I do not at all feel that Schiller's criticisms really were of advantage to it.

Towards the end of July he went to Dessau, and from thence to Dresden, where he strove with Meyer to forget the troubles of the time in contemplation of the treasures of Art.

"All Germany," he writes to Fritz von Stein, "is divided into anxious, croaking, or indifferent men. For myself I find nothing better than to play the part of Diogenes, and roll my tub." He returned, and daily grew more and more intimate with Schiller. They began the friendly interchange of letters, which have since been published in six volumes, known to every student. In Goethe's letters to other friends at this time, 1795, is noticed an inward contentment, which he rightly attributes to this new influence. "It was a new spring to me," he says, "in which all seeds shot up, and gayly blossomed in my nature." Contact with Schiller's earnest mind and eager ambition gave him the stimulus he so long had wanted. The ordinary spurs to an author's activity — the need of money or the need of fame — pricked him not. He had no need of money ; of fame he had enough ; and there was no nation to be appealed to. But Schiller's restless striving, and the emulation it excited, acted like magic upon him ; and the years of their friendship were for both the most productive. In an unpublished letter from Frau von Stein to Charlotte von Lengefeld, dated 1795, there is this noticeable sentence : "I also feel that Goethe is drawing nearer to Schiller, for he has appeared to be now a little more aware of my existence. He seems to me like one who has been shipwrecked for some years on one of the South Sea Islands, and is now beginning to think of returning home." By the shipwreck is of course meant Christiane Vulpius ; and by home, the salon of the Frau von Stein. It is possible, however, to reverse these positions.

On the 1st of November another son is born to Goethe. He bids Schiller to bring his contribution in the shape of a daughter, that the poetic family may be united and increased by a marriage. But this child only lives a few days. On the 20th, Schiller writes : "We have deeply grieved for your loss. You can console yourself with the thought that it has come so early, and thus more affects your *hopes* than your love." Goethe replies : "One knows not whether in such cases it is better to let sorrow take its natural course, or to repress it by the various aids which culture offers us. If one decides upon the latter method, *as I always do*, one is only strengthened for a moment ; and I have observed that Nature always asserts her right through some other crisis."

No other crisis seems to have come in this case. He was active in all directions. Göttling, in Jena, had just come forward with the discovery that phosphorus burns in nitrogen ; and this drew Goethe's thoughts to Chemistry, which for a time was his recreation. Anatomy never lost its attraction : and through the snow on bitter mornings he was seen trudging to Loder's lectures, with a diligence young students might have envied. The Humboldts, especially Alexander, with whom he was in active correspondence, kept alive his scientific ardor ; and it is to their energetic advice that we owe the essays on Comparative Anatomy. He was constantly talking to them on these subjects, eloquently expounding his ideas, which would probably never have been put to paper had they not urged him to it. True it is, that he did not finish the Essays ; and only in 1820 did he print what he had written.* These conversations with the Humboldts embraced a wide field. "It is not, perhaps, presumptuous to suppose," he says, "that many ideas have thence, through *tradition*, become the common property of science, and have blossomed successfully, although the gardener who scattered the seeds is never named."

* This detail is important, as indeed every question of date must be in science. When the Essays were published, the principal ideas had already been brought before the world ; when the Essays were written, the ideas were extraordinary novelties.

Poetical plans were numerous ; some of them were carried into execution. A tragedy on the subject of " Prometheus Unbound" was begun, but never continued. The *Hymn to Apollo* was translated. *Alexis und Dora*, the *Vier Jahres Zeiten*, and several of the smaller poems, were written and given to Schiller for the *Horen* or the *Musen Almanach ;* not to mention translations from Madame de Staël, and the *Autobiography of Benvenuto Cellini.* But the product of this time which made the greatest sensation was the *Xenien.*

It has already been indicated that the state of German Literature was anything but brilliant, and that public taste was very low. The *Horen* was started to raise that degraded taste by an illustrious union of " All the Talents." It came — was seen — and made *no* conquest. Mediocrity in arms assailed it in numerous journals. Stupidity, against which, as Schiller says, " the gods themselves are powerless," was not in the least moved. The *Horen* was a double failure, for it failed to pay its expenses, and it failed to excite any great admiration in the few who purchased it. Articles by the poorest writers were attributed to the greatest. Even Frederick Schlegel attributed a story by Caroline von Wolzogen to Goethe. The public was puzzled — and somewhat *bored.* " All the Talents " have never yet succeeded in producing a successful periodical, and there are some good reasons for supposing that they never will. The *Horen* met with the fate of *The Liberal,* in which Byron, Shelley, Leigh Hunt, Moore, Hazlitt, and Peacock were engaged. But the two great poets who had taken the greatest interest in it were not to be ignored with impunity. They resolved on a literary vengeance, and their vengeance was the *Xenien.*

A small library might be collected of the works called forth by these epigrams ; but for the English reader the topic necessarily has but slender interest. He is not likely to exclaim with Boas: "On the 31st of October, 1517, was commenced the Reformation of the Church in Germany; in October, 1796, commenced the Reformation of Literature. As Luther published his Theses in Wittenberg, so Goethe and Schiller published their *Xenien*. No one before had the courage so to confront sacred Dulness, so to lash all Hypocrisy." One sees that some such castigation was needed, by the loud howling which was set up from all quarters; but that any important purification of Literature was thereby effected is not so clear.

The idea was Goethe's. It occurred to him while reading the *Xenia* of Martial; and having thrown off a dozen epigrams, he sent them to Schiller for the *Musen Almanach*. Schiller was delighted, but said there must be a hundred of them, chiefly directed against the journals which had attacked the *Horen;* the hundred was soon thought too small a number, and was enlarged to a thousand. They were written in the most thorough spirit of collaboration, the idea being sometimes given by one, and the form by another; one writing the first verse, and leaving the second to the other. There is no accurate separation of their epigrams, giving each to each, although critics have made an approximative selection; and Maltzahn has recently aided this by collation of the original manuscripts; from this it appears that Goethe wrote about one sixth of the whole, and those the least personal and offensive epigrams.

The sensation was tremendous. All the bad writers in the kingdom, and they were an army, felt themselves personally aggrieved. The pietists and sentimentalists were ridiculed; the pedants and pedagogues were lashed. So many persons and so many opinions were scarified, that no wonder if the public ear was startled at the shrieks of pain. Counterblasts were soon heard, and the *Xenien-Sturm* will remain as a curious episode of the war of the "many foolish heads against the two wise ones." "It is amusing," writes Goethe to Schiller, "to see what has really irritated these fellows, what they believe will irritate us, how empty and low is their conception of others, how they aim their arrows merely at the outworks, and how little they dream of the inaccessible citadel inhabited by men who are in earnest." The sensation produced by the *Dunciad* and by the *English Bards and Scotch Reviewers* was mild compared with the sensation produced by the *Xenien;* although the wit and sarcasm of the *Xenien* is as milk and water compared with the vitriol of the *Dunciad* and the *English Bards.*

Read by no stronger light than that which the appreciation of wit *as* wit throws on these epigrams, and not by the strong light of personal indignity or personal malice, the *Xenien* will appear very weak productions, and the sensation they excited must appear somewhat absurd. But a similar disappointment meets the modern reader of the *Anti-Jacobin.* We know that its pages were the terror of enemies, the malicious joy of friends. We know that it was long held as a repertory of English wit, and the "Days of the *Anti-Jacobin*" are mentioned by Englishmen as the days of the *Xenien* are by Germans. Yet now that the *personal* spice is removed, we read both of them with a feeling of wonder at their enormous influence. In the *Xenien* there are a few epigrams which still titillate the palate, for they have the salt of wit in their lines. There are many also which have no pretension to wit, but are admirable expressions of critical canons and philosophic ideas. If good taste could not be created by attacks on bad taste, there was at any rate some hope that such a castigation would make certain places sore; and in this sense the *Xenien* did good service.

CHAPTER II.

THE ROMANTIC SCHOOL.

" AFTER the mad challenge of the *Xenien*," writes Goethe
to Schiller, "we must busy ourselves only with great and
worthy works of Art, and shame our opponents by the manifestation of our poetical natures in forms of the Good and
Noble." This trumpet-sound found Schiller alert. The two
earnest men went earnestly to work, and produced their
matchless ballads, and their great poems, *Hermann und
Dorothea* and *Wallenstein.* The influence of these men on
each other was very peculiar. It made Goethe, in contradiction to his native tendency, speculative and theoretical. It
made Schiller, in contradiction to his native tendency, realis-
tic. Had it not urged Goethe to rapid production, we might
have called the influence wholly noxious ; but seeing what
was produced, we pause ere we condemn. "You have created a new youth for me," writes Goethe, "and once more
restored me to Poetry, which I had almost entirely given up."
They were both much troubled with Philosophy at this epoch.
Kant and Spinoza occupied Schiller ; Kant and scientific
theories occupied Goethe. They were both, moreover, becoming more and more imbued with the spirit of ancient Art, and
were bent on restoring its principles. They were men of
genius, and therefore these two false tendencies — the tendency to Reflection and the tendency to Imitation — were less
hurtful to *their* works than to the national culture. Their
genius saved them, in spite of their errors ; but their errors
misled the nation. It is remarked by Gervinus, that Philosophy was restored in the year 1781, and profoundly affected
all Germany. Let any one draw up a statistical table of our

literary productions, and he will be amazed at the decadence of Poetry during the last fifty years, in which Philosophy has been supreme." Philosophy has distorted Poetry, and been the curse of Criticism. It has vitiated German Literature; and it produced, in combination with the tendency to Imitation, that brilliant error known as the Romantic School.

A few words on this much-talked-of school may not be unacceptable. Like its offspring, *L'École Romantique* in France, it had a critical purpose which was good, and a retrograde purpose which was bad. Both were insurgent against narrow critical canons; both proclaimed the superiority of Mediæval Art; both sought in Catholicism and in national Legends meanings profounder than those current in the literature of the day. The desire to get deeper than Life itself led to a disdain of reality and the present. Hence the selection of the Middle Ages and the East as regions for the ideal; they were not present, and they were not classical; the classical had already been tried, and against it the young Romantic School was everywhere in arms.

In their crusade against the French, in their naturalization of Shakespeare, and their furtherance of Herder's efforts towards the restoration of a Ballad Literature and the taste for Gothic Architecture, these Romanticists were with the stream. They also flattered the national tendencies when they proclaimed "Mythology and Poetry, symbolical Legend and Art, to be one and indivisible,"* whereby it became clear that a new Religion, or at any rate a new Mythology, was needed, for "the deepest want and deficiency of all modern Art lies in the fact that the artists have no Mythology." †

While Fichte, Schelling, and Schleiermacher were tormented with the desire to create a new philosophy and a new

---

* F. SCHLEGEL, *Gespräche über Poesie*, p. 263.
† Ibid., p. 274.

religion, it soon became evident that a Mythology was not to be created by programme ; and as a Mythology was indispensable, the Romanticists betook themselves to Catholicism, with its saintly Legends and saintly Heroes ; some of them, as Tieck and A. W. Schlegel, out of little more than poetic enthusiasm and dilettantism : others, as F. Schlegel and Werner, with thorough conviction, accepting Catholicism and all its consequences.

Solger had called Irony the daughter of Mysticism ; and how highly these Romanticists prized Mysticism is known to all readers of Novalis.   To be mystical was to be poetical as well as profound ; and critics glorified mediæval monstrosities because of the deep spiritualism which stood in contrast with the pagan materialism of Goethe and Schiller.   Once commenced, this movement carried what was true in it rapidly onwards to the confines of nonsense.   Art became the hand-maid of Religion.   The canon was laid down that only in the service of Religion had Art ever flourished, — only in that service *could* it flourish : a truth from which strange conclusions were drawn.   Art became a propaganda.   Fra Angelico and Calderon suddenly became idols.   Werner was proclaimed a Colossus by Wackenroder, who wrote his *Herzensergiessungeneines Kunstliebenden Klosterbruders*, with Tieck's aid, to prove, said Goethe, that because some monks were artists, all artists should turn monks.   Then it was that men looked to Faith for miracles in Art.   Devout study of the Bible was thought to be the readiest means of rivalling Fra Angelico and Van Eyck ; inspiration was sought in a hair-shirt. Catholicism had a Mythology, and painters went over in crowds to the Roman Church.   Cornelius and Overbeck lent real genius to the attempt to revive the dead forms of early Christian Art, as Goethe and Schiller did to revive the dead forms of Grecian Art.   Overbeck, who painted in a cloister,

was so thoroughly penetrated by the ascetic spirit, that he refused to draw from the living model, lest it should make his
works too *naturalistic;* for to be true to Nature was tanta-
mount to being false to the higher tendencies of Spiritualism.
Some had too much of the artistic instinct to carry their
principles into these exaggerations ; but others less gifted, and
more bigoted, carried the principles into every excess.   A
band of these reformers established themselves in Rome,
and astonished the Catholics quite as much as the Protes-
tants.   Cesar Masini, in his work, *Dei Puristi in Pittura,*
thus describes them: " Several young men came to Rome
from Northern Germany in 1809.   They abjured Protestantism, adopted the costume of the Middle Ages, and began
to preach the doctrine that painting had died out with
Giotto, and, to revive it, a recurrence to the old style was
necessary.   Under such a mask of piety they concealed
their nullity.   Servile admirers of the rudest periods in Art,
they declared the pygmies were giants, and wanted to bring
us back to the dry hard style and barbarous imperfection of a
Buffalmacco, Calandrino, Paolo Uccello, when we had a
Raphael, a Titian, and a Correggio."   In spite of their exaggerated admiration of the Trecentisti, in spite of a doctrine
which was fundamentally vicious, the Romanticists made a
decided revolution, not only in Literature but in Painting, and
above all in our general estimate of painters.   If we now learn
to look at the exquisite works of Fra Angelico, Ghirlandajo,
and Masaccio with intense pleasure, and can even so far
divest ourselves of the small prejudices of criticism, as to be
deeply interested in Giotto, Gozzoli, or Guido da Arezzo,
feeling in them the divine artistic faculty which had not yet
mastered artistic expression, it is to the preaching of the Romanticists that we owe this source of noble enjoyment.   In
poetry the Romanticists were failures, but in painting they

achieved marked success. Whatever may be thought of the German School, it must be confessed that before Overbeck, Cornelius, Schadow, Hess, Lessing, Hübner, Sohn, and Kaulbach, the Germans had no modern painters at all ; and they have in these men painters of very remarkable power.

To return to Goethe. He was led by Schiller into endless theoretical discussions. They philosophized on the limits of epic and dramatic poetry ; read and discussed Aristotle's Poetics : discussions which resulted in Goethe's essay, *Ueber epische und dramatische Poesie;* and, as we gather from their correspondence, scarcely ventured to take a step until they had seen how Theory justified it. Goethe read with enthusiasm Wolf's *Prolegomena* to Homer, and at once espoused its principles. The train of thought thus excited led him from the origin of epic songs to the origin of the Hebrew songs, and Eichhorn's *Introduction to the Old Testament* led him to attempt a new explanation of the wanderings of the people of Israel, which he subsequently inserted in the notes to the *Westöstliche Divan.*

Nor was he only busy with epical theories ; he also gave himself to the production of epics. *Hermann und Dorothea,* the most perfect of his poems, was written at this time. *Achilleis* was planned and partly executed ; *Die Jagd* was also planned, but left unwritten, and subsequently became the prose tale known as *Die Novelle.* This year of 1797 is moreover memorable as the year of ballads, in which he and Schiller, in friendly rivalry, gave Germany lyrical masterpieces. His share may be estimated, when we learn that in this year were written the *Bride of Corinth,* the *Zauberlehrling, der Gott und die Bajadere,* and the *Schatzgräber.*

In the same year *Faust* was once more taken up. The *Dedication,* the *Prologue in Heaven,* and the Intermezzo of *Oberon and Titania's Marriage* were written. But while he was in this mood, Hirt came to Weimar, and in the lively reminiscences of Italy, and the eager discussions of Art which his arrival awakened, all the northern phantoms were exorcised by southern magic. He gave up *Faust*, and wrote an essay on the *Laokoon*. He began once more to pine for Italy. This is characteristic of his insatiable hunger for knowledge; he never seemed to have mastered *material* enough. Whereas Schiller, so much poorer in material, and so much more inclined to production, thought this Italian journey would only embarrass him with fresh objects; and urged Meyer to dissuade him from it. He did not go; and I think Schiller's opinion was correct : at the point now reached he had nothing to do but to give a form to the materials he had accumulated.

In the July of this year he, for the third time, made a journey into Switzerland. In Frankfort he introduced Christiane and her boy to his Mother, who received them very heartily, and made the few days' stay there very agreeable. It is unnecessary for us to follow him on his journey, which is biographically interesting only in respect to the plan of an epic on *William Tell* which he conceived, and for which he studied the localities. The plan was never executed. He handed it over to Schiller for his drama on that subject, giving him at the same time the idea of the character of Tell, and the studies of localities, which Schiller managed to employ with a mastery quite astonishing to his friend. The same brotherly co-operation is seen in the composition of *Wallenstein.* It is not true, as was currently supposed in Germany, that Goethe wrote any portions of that work. He has told us himself he only wrote two unimportant lines. But his counsel aided Schiller through every scene; and the bringing it on the stage was to him like a triumph of his own.

In the spring of 1798 Schelling's Philosophy of Nature, and his own plans for a History of the Theory of Colors, lured

him from poetry ; but Schiller again brought him back to it.
Faust was resumed, and the last tragic scenes of the First
Part were written.   In the summer he was much at Jena with
Schiller, consequently with poetry.   Achilles and Tell, the
ancient and the modern world, as Schäfer remarks, struggled
for priority, but neither obtained it, because he was still perplexed in his epic theories.   The studies of the *Iliad* had
" hunted him through the circle of enthusiasm, hope, insight,
and despair."   No sooner did he leave Jena than, as he confessed, he was drawn by another polarity.   Accordingly, we
see him busy with an art-journal, the *Propyläen*.   He was
also busy with the alteration of the Theatre, the boards of
which, on the 12th of October, 1798, were made forever
memorable by the production of *Wallenstein's Camp* and
Prologue.   On the 30th January, 1799, the birthday of the
Duchess Luise, the *Piccolomini* was produced ; and, on the
20th of April, *Wallenstein's Tod.*

It was in this year that a young advocate, in Edinburgh,
put forth a translation of *Götz von Berlichingen*, and preluded
to a fame as great as Goethe's own ; and it was in the December of this year that Karl August's generosity enabled Schiller
to quit Jena, and come to Weimar for the rest of his life,
there in uninterrupted intercourse with Goethe to pursue the
plans so dear to both, especially in the formation of a national
stage.

CHAPTER III.

SCHILLER'S LAST YEARS.

IN the year 1800 Schiller settled at Weimar, there to end
his days in noble work with his great friend.   It may interest

the reader to have a glimpse of Goethe's daily routine ; the more so, as such a glimpse is not to be had from any published works.

He rose at seven, sometimes earlier, after a sound and prolonged sleep ; for, like Thorwaldsen, he had a " talent for sleeping," only surpassed by his talent for continuous work. Till eleven he worked without interruption. A cup of chocolate was then brought, and he resumed work till one. At two he dined. This meal was the important meal of the day. His appetite was immense. Even on the days when he complained of not being hungry, he ate much more than most men. Puddings, sweets, and cakes were always welcome. He sat a long while over his wine, chatting gayly to some friend or other (for he never dined alone), or to one of the actors, whom he often had with him, after dinner, to read over their parts, and to take his instructions. He was fond of wine, and drank daily his two or three bottles.

Lest this statement should convey a false impression, I hasten to recall to the reader's recollection the habits of our fathers in respect of drinking. It was no unusual thing to be a " three-bottle man " in those days in England, when the three bottles were of Port or Burgundy ; and Goethe, a Rhinelander, accustomed from boyhood to wine, drank a wine which his English contemporaries would have called water. The amount he drank never did more than exhilarate him ; never made him unfit for work or for society.

Over his wine he sat some hours : no such thing as dessert was seen upon his table in those days : not even the customary coffee after dinner. His mode of living was extremely simple ; and even when persons of very modest circumstances burned wax, two poor tallow candles were all that could be seen in his rooms. In the evening he went often to the theatre, and there his customary glass of punch

15*

was brought at six o'clock. When he was not at the theatre, he received friends at home. Between eight and nine a frugal supper was laid, but he never ate anything except a little salad or preserves. By ten o'clock he was usually in bed.

Many visitors came to him. From the letters of Christiane to Meyer we gather that he must have exercised hospitality on a large scale, since about every month 50 pounds of butter are ordered from Bremen, and the cases of wine have frequently to be renewed. It was the pleasure and the penalty of his fame, that all persons who came near Weimar made an effort to see him. Sometimes these visitors were persons of great interest ; oftener they were fatiguing bores, or men with pretensions more offensive than dulness. To those who pleased him he was inexpressibly charming : to the others he was stately, even to stiffness. While, therefore, we hear some speak of him with an enthusiasm such as genius alone can excite, we hear others giving vent to the feelings of disappointment, and even of offence, created by his manners. The stately minister exasperated those who went to see the impassioned poet. As these visitors were frequently authors, it was natural they should avenge their wounded self-love in criticisms and epigrams. To cite but one example among many : Bürger, whom Goethe had assisted in a pecuniary way, came to Weimar, and announced himself in this preposterous style, "You are Goethe, — I am Bürger," evidently believing he was thereby maintaining his own greatness, and offering a brotherly alliance. Goethe received him with the most diplomatic politeness and the most diplomatic formality ; instead of plunging into discussions of poetry, he would be brought to talk of nothing but the condition of the Göttingen University, and the number of its students. Bürger went away furious, avenged this reception in an epigram, and related to all comers the experience he had had of the proud, cold, diplomatic Geheimerath. Others had the like experience to recount; and a public, ever greedy of scandal, ever willing to believe a great man is a small man, echoed these voices in swelling chorus. Something of offence lay in the very nature of Goethe's bearing, which was stiff, even to haughtiness. His appearance was so imposing, that Heine humorously relates how, on the occasion of his first interview with him, an elaborately prepared speech was entirely driven from his memory by the Jupiter-like presence, and he could only stammer forth "a remark on the excellence of the plums which grew on the road from Jena to Weimar." An imposing presence is irritating to mean natures. Goethe might have gained universal applause, if, like Jean Paul, he had worn no cravat, and had let his hair hang loose upon his shoulders.

The mention of Jean Paul leads me to quote *his* impression of Goethe. "I went timidly to meet him. Every one had described him as cold to everything upon earth. Frau von Kalb said he no longer admires anything, not even himself. Every word is ice. Nothing but curiosities warm the fibres of his heart; so I asked Knebel if he could petrify me, or incrust me in some mineral spring, that I might present myself as a statue or a fossil." How one hears the accents of village gossip in these sentences! To Weimarian ignorance Goethe's enthusiasm for statues and natural products seemed monstrous. "His house," Jean Paul continues, "or rather his palace, pleased me; it is the only one in Weimar in the Italian style; with such a staircase! A Pantheon full of pictures and statues. Fresh anxiety oppressed me. At last the god entered, cold, monosyllabic. 'The French are drawing towards Paris,' said Knebel. 'H'm!' said the god. His face is massive and animated; his eye a ball of light !

At last, as conversation turned on art, he warmed, and was himself. His conversation was not so rich and flowing as Herder's, but penetrating, acute, and calm. Finally, he read, or rather performed, an unpublished poem, in which the flames of his heart burst through the external crust of ice ; so that he greeted my enthusiasm with a pressure of the hand. He did it again as I took leave, and urged me to call. By heaven ! we shall love each other ! He considers his poetic career closed. There is nothing comparable to his reading. It is like deep-toned thunder blended with whispering rain-drops."

Now let us hear what Jean Paul says of Schiller. " I went yesterday to see the stony Schiller, from whom all strangers spring back as from a precipice. His form is wasted, yet severely powerful, and very angular. He is full of acumen, but without love. His conversation is as excellent as his writings." He never repeated this visit to Schiller, who doubtless quite subscribed to what Goethe wrote : " I am glad you have seen Richter. His love of truth, and his wish for self-improvement, have prepossessed me in his favor ; but the social man is a sort of theoretical man, and I doubt if he will approach us in a practical way."

If to pretenders and to *strangers* Goethe was cold and re-pellent, he was warm and attractive enough to all with whom he could sympathize. Brotherly to Schiller and Herder, he was fatherly in his loving discernment and protection to such men as Hegel, then an unknown teacher, and Voss, the son of the translator of Homer.* He excited passionate attach-ments in all who lived in his intimacy; and passionate hatred in many whom he would not admit to intimacy.

The opening of this century found Schiller active and

* Note Voss's enthusiastic gratitude in his *Mittheilungen über Goethe und Schiller.*

anxious to stimulate the activity of his friend. But theories hampered the genius of Goethe; and various occupations disturbed it. He was not, like Schiller, a reflective, critical poet, but a spontaneous, instinctive poet. The consequence was, that Reflection not only retarded, but misled him into Symbolism, — the dark corner of that otherwise sunny palace of Art which he has reared. He took up *Faust,* and wrote the classic intermezzo of *Helena.* He was very busy with the Theatre, and with Science; and at the close of the year fell into a dangerous illness, which created much anxiety in the Weimar circle. He recovered in a few weeks, and busied himself with the translation of *Theophrastus on Colors,* with *Faust,* and the *Natürliche Tochter.*

While the two chiefs of Literature were in noble emulation and brotherly love, working together, each anxious for the success of the other, the nation divided itself into two parties, disputing which was the greater poet of the two; as in Rome the artists dispute about Raphael and Michael Angelo. "It is difficult to appreciate one such genius," says Goethe of the two painters, "still more difficult to appreciate both. Hence people lighten the task by partisanship." The partisanship in the present case was fierce, and has continued. Instead of following Goethe's advice, and rejoicing that it had two such poets to boast of, the public has gone on crying up one at the expense of the other. Schiller himself, with charming modesty, confessed his inferiority; and in one of his letters to Körner he says: "Compared with Goethe I am but a poetical bungler, — *gegen Goethe bin und bleib' ich ein poetischer Lump.*" But the majority have placed him higher than his rival, at least higher in their hearts. Gervinus has remarked a cu- rious contradiction in the fate of their works. Schiller, who wrote for men, is the favorite of women and youths; Goethe, who remained in perpetual youth, is only relished by men.

The secret of this is, that Schiller had those passions and en-
thusiasms which captivate youth. Goethe told Eckermann
that his works never could be popular; and, except the
minor poems and *Faust*, there are none of his productions
which equal the popularity of Schiller's.

While discussing Physical Science with Ritter, Comparative Anatomy with Loder, Optics with Himly, and making
observations on the Moon, the plan of a great poem, *De Natura Rerum*, rose in Goethe's mind, and like so many other
plans, remained a plan.   Intercourse with the great philologist Wolff led him a willing student into Antiquity ; and from
Voss he tried to master the principles of Metre with the zeal
of a philologist.   There is something very piquant in the
idea of the greatest poet of his nation, the most musical master of verse in all possible forms, trying to acquire a theoretic
knowledge of that which on instinct he did to perfection.   It
is characteristic of his new tendency to theorize on poetry.

In December, 1803, Weimar had a visitor whose rank is
high among its illustrious guests, — Madame de Staël.   Napoleon would not suffer her to remain in France ; she was
brought by Benjamin Constant to the German Athens, that
she might see and know something of the men her work *De
l'Allemagne* was to reveal to her countrymen.   It is easy to
ridicule Madame de Staël ; to call her, as Heine does, "a
whirlwind in petticoats," and a "Sultana of mind."   But
Germans should be grateful to her for that book, which still
remains one of the best books written about Germany ; and
the lover of letters will not forget that her genius has, in
various departments of literature, rendered illustrious the
power of the womanly intellect.   Goethe and Schiller, whom
she stormed with cannonades of talk, spoke of her intellect
with great admiration.   Of all living creatures he had seen,
Schiller said, she was "the most talkative, the most comba-

tive, the most gesticulative"; but she was "also the most cultivated, and the most gifted." The contrast between her French culture and his German culture, and the difficulty he had in expressing himself in French, did not prevent his being much interested. In the sketch of her he sent to Goethe it is well said, "She insists on explaining everything, understanding everything, measuring everything. She admits of no Darkness, nothing Incommensurable; and where her torch throws no light, there nothing can exist. Hence her horror for the Ideal Philosophy, which she thinks leads to mysticism and superstition. For what we call poetry she has no sense; she can only appreciate what is passionate, rhetorical, universal. She does not prize what is false, but does not always perceive what is true."

The Duchess Amalia was enchanted with her, and the Duke wrote to Goethe, who was at Jena, begging him to come over, and be seen by her, which Goethe very positively declined. He said, if she wished very much to see him, and would come to Jena, she should be very heartily welcomed; a comfortable lodging and a bourgeoise table would be offered her, and every day they could have some hours together when his business was over; but he could not undertake to go to court and into society; he did not feel himself strong enough. In the beginning of 1804, however, he came to Weimar, and there he made her acquaintance; that is to say, he received her in his own house, at first tête-à-tête, and afterwards in small circles of friends.

Except when she managed to animate him by her paradoxes or wit, he was cold and formal to her, even more so than to other remarkable people; and he has told us the reason. Rousseau had been drawn into a correspondence with two women, who addressed themselves to him as admirers; he had shown himself in this correspondence by no means to his advantage, now (1803) that the letters appeared in print.* Goethe had heard or read of this correspondence ; and Madame de Staël had frankly told him she intended to print his conversation.† This was enough to make him ill at ease in her society; and although she said he was "un homme d'un esprit prodigieux en conversation .... quand on le sait faire parler il est admirable," she never saw the real, but a factitious Goethe. By dint of provocation — and champagne — she managed to make him talk brilliantly ; she never got him to talk to her seriously. On the 29th of February she left Weimar, to the great relief both of Goethe and Schiller.

Nothing calls for notice during the rest of this year, except the translation of an unpublished work by Diderot, *Rameau's Nephew*, and the commencement of the admirable work on *Winckelmann and his Age.* The beginning of 1805 found him troubled with a presentiment that either he or Schiller would die in this year. Both were dangerously ill. Christiane, writing to her friend Nicolaus Meyer, says, that for the last three months the Geheimerath has scarcely had a day's health, and at times it seemed as if he must die. It was a touching scene when Schiller, a little recovered from his last attack, entered the sick-room of his friend. They walked up to each other, and, without speaking a word, expressed their joy at meeting in a long and manly kiss. Both hoped with the return of spring for return of health and

* The correspondence alluded to can be no other than that of Rousseau with Madame de la Tour-Franqueville and her friend, whose name is still unknown ; it is one of the most interesting among the many interesting correspondences of women with celebrated men. A charming notice of it may be found in St. Beuve's *Causeries du Lundi*, Vol. II.

† In the *Tag und Jahres Hefte*, 1804 (*Werke*, XXVII. p. 143), the reader will find Goethe's account of Madame de Staël and her relation to him.

power. Schiller meanwhile was translating the *Phèdre* of Racine ; Goethe was translating the *Rameau's Nephew*, and writing the history of the *Farbenlehre*.

The spring was coming, but on its blossoms Schiller's eyes were not to rest. On the 30th of April the friends parted for the last time. Schiller was going to the theatre. Goethe, too unwell to accompany him, said good by at the door of Schiller's house. During Schiller's illness Goethe was much depressed. Voss found him once pacing up and down his garden, crying by himself. He mastered his emotion as Voss told him of Schiller's state, and only said, " Fate is pitiless, and man but little."

It really seemed as if the two friends were to be united in the grave as they had been in life. Goethe grew worse. From Schiller life was fast ebbing. On the 8th of May he was given over. "His sleep that night was disturbed ; his mind again wandered ; with the morning he had lost all consciousness. He spoke incoherently and chiefly in Latin. His last drink was champagne. Towards three in the afternoon came on the last exhaustion ; the breath began to fail. Towards four he would have called for naphtha, but the last syllable died upon his lips ; finding himself speechless, he motioned that he wished to write something ; but his hand could only trace three letters, in which was yet recognizable the distinct character of his writing. His wife knelt by his side : he pressed her hand. His sister-in-law stood with the physician at the foot of the bed, applying warm cushions to the cold feet. Suddenly a sort of electric shock came over his countenance ; the head fell back ; the deepest calm settled on his face. His features were as those of one in a soft sleep.

"The news of Schiller's death soon spread through Weimar. The theatre was closed ; men gathered into groups.

w

Each felt as if he had lost his dearest friend. To Goethe, enfeebled himself by long illness, and again stricken by some relapse, no one had the courage to mention the death of his beloved rival. When the tidings came to Henry Meyer, who was with him, Meyer left the house abruptly lest his grief might escape him. No one else had courage to break the intelligence. Goethe perceived that the members of his household seemed embarrassed and anxious to avoid him. He divined something of the fact, and said at last, 'I see — Schiller must be very ill.' That night they overheard him, — the serene man who seemed almost above human affection, who disdained to reveal to others whatever grief he felt when his son died, — they overheard Goethe weep! In the morning he said to a friend, 'Is it not true that Schiller was very ill yesterday?' The friend (it was a woman) sobbed. 'He is dead,' said Goethe faintly. 'You have said it,' was the answer. 'He is dead,' repeated Goethe, and covered his face with his hands." *

"The half of my existence is gone from me," he wrote to Zelter. His first thoughts were to continue the *Demetrius* in the spirit in which Schiller had planned it, so that Schiller's mind might still be with him, still working at his side. But the effort was vain. He could do nothing. "My diary," he says, "is a blank at this period; the white pages intimate the blank in my existence. In those days I took no interest in anything."

* BULWER's *Life of Schiller.*

BOOK THE SEVENTH.

1805 TO 1832.

———◆———

CHAPTER I.

THE BATTLE OF JENA.

THE death of Schiller left Goethe very lonely. It was more than the loss of a friend ; it was the loss also of an energetic stimulus which had urged him to production ; and in the activity of production he lived an intenser life. During the long laborious years which followed, — years of accumulation, of study, of fresh experience, and of varied plans, — we shall see him produce works of which many might be proud ; but the noonday splendor of his life has passed, and the light which we admire is the calm effulgence of the setting sun. During the following month, Gall visited Jena, in the first successful eagerness of propagating his system of phrenology, which was then a startling novelty. All who acknowledge the very large debt which physiology and psychology owe to Gall's labors (which acknowledgment by no means implies an acceptance of the premature, and, in many respects, imperfect, system founded on those labors) will be glad to observe that Goethe not only attended Gall's lectures, but in private conversations showed so much sympathy, and such ready appreciation, that Gall visited him in his sick-room, and dissected the brain in his presence, communicating all the new views to which he had been led. Instead of meeting this theory with ridicule, contempt, and the opposition of ancient prejudices, — as men of science, no less than men of

the world, were and are still wont to meet it, — Goethe saw
at once the importance of Gall's mode of dissection (since
generally adopted), and of his leading views ; * although he
also saw that science was not sufficiently advanced for a
correct verdict to be delivered.   Gall's doctrine pleased him
because it determined the true position of psychology in the
study of man.   It pleased him because it connected man
with Nature more intimately than was done in the old
schools, showing the identity of all mental manifestation in
the animal kingdom.†

But these profound and delicate investigations were in the
following year interrupted by the roar of cannon.   On the
14th of October, at seven o'clock in the morning, the thunder
of distant artillery alarmed the inhabitants of Weimar.   The
battle of Jena had begun.   Goethe heard the cannon with
terrible distinctness ; but as it slackened towards noon, he sat
down to dinner as usual.   Scarcely had he sat down, when
the cannon burst over their heads.   Immediately the table
was cleared.   Riemer found him walking up and down the
garden.   The balls whirled over the house ; the bayonets of
the Prussians in flight gleamed over the garden wall.   The
French had planted a few guns on the heights above Weimar,
from which they could fire on the town.   It was a calm bright
day.   In the streets everything appeared dead.   Every one
had retreated under cover.   Now and then the boom of a
cannon broke silence ; the balls, hissing through the air,
occsionally struck a house.   The birds were singing sweetly
on the esplanade ; and the deep repose of nature formed an
awful contrast to the violence of war.

* Compare *Freundschaftliche Briefe von Goethe und seine Frau an N.
Meyer*, p. 19.

† Gall's assertion that Goethe was born for political Oratory more
than for Poetry has much amused those who know Goethe's dislike of
politics ; and does not, indeed, seem a very happy hit.

In the midst of this awful stillness a few French hussars
rode into the city, to ascertain if the enemy were there.
Presently a whole troop galloped in.   A young officer came
to Goethe to assure him that his house would be secure from
pillage ; it had been selected as the quarters of Marshal
Augereau.   The young hussar who brought this message was
Lili's son !   He accompanied Goethe to the palace.   Meanwhile several of the troopers had made themselves at home in
Goethe's house.   Many houses were in flames.   Cellars were
broken open.   The pillage began.

Goethe returned from the palace, but without the Marshal,
who had not yet arrived.   They waited for him till deep in
the night.   The doors were bolted and the family retired to
rest.   About midnight two tirailleurs knocked at the door and
insisted on admittance.   In vain they were told the house
was full, and the Marshal expected.   They threatened to
break in the windows, if the door were not opened.   They
were admitted.   Wine was set before them, which they drank
like troopers, and then they insisted on seeing their host.
They were told he was in bed.   No matter ; he must get up ;
they had a fancy to see him.   In such cases, resistance is
futile.   Riemer went up and told Goethe, who, putting on his
dressing-gown, came majestically down stairs, and by his
presence considerably awed his drunken guests, who were as
polite as French soldiers can be when they please.   They
talked to him ; made him drink with them, with friendly clink
of glasses ; and suffered him to retire once more to his room.
In a little while, however, heated with wine, they insisted on
a bed.   The other troopers were glad of the floor ; but these
two would have nothing less than a bed.   They stumbled up
stairs ; broke into Goethe's room, and there a struggle ensued,
which had a very serious aspect.   Christiane, who throughout
displayed great courage and presence of mind, procured a

rescue, and the intruders were finally dragged from the room. They then threw themselves on the bed kept for the Marshal; and no threats would move them. In the morning the Marshal arrived, and sentinels protected the house. But even under this protection, the disquiet may be imagined when we read that twelve casks of wine were drunk in three days; that eight-and-twenty beds were made up for officers and soldiers, and that the other costs of this billeting amounted to more than 2,000 dollars.

The sun shining with continuous autumnal splendor in these days looked down on terrible scenes in Weimar. The pillage was prolonged, so that even the palace was almost stripped of the necessaries of life. In this extremity, while houses were in flames close to the palace, the Duchess Luise manifested that dauntless courage which produced a profound impression on Napoleon, as he entered Weimar, surrounded by all the terrors of conquest, and was received at the top of the palace stairs by her, — calm, dignified, unmoved. " *Voilà une femme à laquelle même nos deux cent canons n'ont pu faire peur !*" he said to Rapp. She pleaded for her people; vindicated her husband; and by her constancy and courage prevailed over the conquerer, who was deeply incensed with the Duke, and repeatedly taunted him with the fact that he spared him solely out of respect for the Duchess.

The rage of Napoleon against the Duke was as unwise as it was intemperate; but I do not allude to it for the purpose of showing how petty the great conqueror could be; I allude to it for the purpose of quoting the characteristic outburst which it drew from Goethe. " Formed by nature to be a calm and impartial spectator of events, even I am exasperated," said Goethe to Falk, "when I see men required to perform the impossible. That the Duke assists wounded Prussian officers robbed of their pay; that he lent the lion-hearted Blücher four thousand dollars after the battle of Lübeck, — that is what you call a conspiracy! — that seems to you a fit subject for reproach and accusation! Let us suppose that to-day misfortune befalls the grand army; what would a general or a field-marshal be worth in the Emperor's eyes, who would act precisely as our Duke has acted under these circumstances? I tell you the Duke *shall* act as he acts! He *must* act so! He would do great injustice if he ever acted otherwise! Yes; and even were he thus to lose country and subjects, crown and sceptre, like his ancestor, the unfortunate John; yet must he not deviate one hand's breadth from his noble manner of thinking, and from that which the duty of a man and a prince prescribes in the emergency. Misfortune! What is misfortune? This is a misfortune, — that a prince should be compelled to endure such things from foreigners. And if it came to the same pass with him as with his ancestor, Duke John, — if his ruin were certain and irretrievable, let not that dismay us: we will take our staff in our hands, and accompany our master in adversity, as old Lucas Kranach did: we will never forsake him. The women and children, when they meet us in the villages, will cast down their eyes and weep, and say to one another, 'That is old Goethe, and the former Duke of Weimar, whom the French Emperor drove from his throne, because he was so true to his friends in misfortune; because he visited his uncle on his death-bed; because he would not let his old comrades and brothers in arms starve!'"

"At this," adds Falk, "the tears rolled in streams down his cheeks. After a pause, having recovered himself a little, he continued: 'I will sing for bread! I will turn strolling ballad-singer, and put our misfortunes into verse! I will wander into every village and into every school wherever the name of Goethe is known; I will chant the dishonor of Germany, and the children shall learn the song of our shame till they are men ; and thus they shall sing my master upon his throne again, and yours off his ! ' "

I shall have to recur to this outburst on a future occasion, and will now hasten to the important event which is generally supposed to have been directly occasioned by the perils of the battle of Jena. I mean his marriage.

———◆———

CHAPTER II.

GOETHE'S WIFE.

THE judgments of men are curious. No action in Aristotle's life subjected him to more calumny than his generous marriage with the friendless Phythia ; no action in Goethe's life has excited more scandal than his marriage with Christiane. It was thought disgraceful enough in him to have taken her into his house (a *liaison* out of the house seeming, in the eyes of the world, a venial error, which becomes serious directly it approaches nearer to the condition of marriage) ; but for the great poet actually to complete such an enormity as to crown his connection with Christiane by a legal sanction, *this* was indeed more than society could tolerate.

I have already expressed my opinion of this unfortunate connection, a *mésalliance* in every sense ; but I must emphatically declare my belief that the redeeming point in it is precisely that which has created the scandal. Better far had there been no connection at all ; but if it was to be, the nearer it approached a real marriage, and the further it was removed from a fugitive indulgence, the more moral and healthy it became. The fact of the *mésalliance* was not to be got over. Had he married her at first, this would always have existed.

But many other and darker influences would have been averted. There would have been no such " skeleton in the closet of his life " as, unfortunately, we know to have existed. Let us for a moment look into that closet.

Since we last caught a glimpse of Christiane Vulpius, some fifteen years have elapsed, in the course of which an unhappy change has taken place. She was then a bright, lively, pleasure-loving girl. Years and self-indulgence have now made havoc with her charms. The evil tendency, which youth and animal spirits kept within excess, has asserted itself with a distinctness which her birth and circumstances may explain, if not excuse, but which can only be contemplated in sadness. Her father, we know, ruined himself by intemperance; her brother impaired fine talents by similar excess; and Christiane, who inherited the fatal disposition, was not saved from it by the checks which refined society imposes, for in Weimar she was shut out from society by her relation to Goethe. Elsewhere, as we learn from her letters to Meyer, she was not quite excluded from female society. Professor Wolff and Kapellmeister Reichardt presented her to their daughters; and she danced at public balls. But in Weimar this was impossible. There she lived secluded, shunned, and had to devote herself wholly to her domestic duties, which for one so lively and so eager for society must have had a depressing influence. Fond of gayety, and especially of dancing, she was often seen at the students' balls at Jena; and she accustomed herself to an indulgence in wine, which rapidly destroyed her beauty, and which was sometimes the cause of serious domestic troubles. I would fain have passed over this episode in silence: but it is too generally known to be ignored; and it suggests a tragedy in Goethe's life little suspected by those who saw how calmly he bore himself in public. The mere mention of such a fact at once suggests the conflict of feelings

16

hidden from public gaze; the struggle of indignation with pity, of resolution with weakness.   I have discovered but one printed indication of this domestic grief, and that is in a letter from Schiller to Körner, dated 21st October, 1800.   "On the whole he produces very little now, rich as he still is in invention and execution.   His spirit is not sufficiently at ease; his wretched domestic circumstances, which he is too weak to alter, make him so unhappy."

Too weak to alter!   Yes, there lies the tragedy, and there the explanation.   Tender, and always shrinking from inflicting pain, he had not the sternness necessary to put an end to such a condition.   He suffered so much because he could not inflict suffering.   To the bystander such endurance seems inexplicable; for the bystander knows not how the insidious first steps are passed over, and how endurance strengthens with repeated trials; he knows nothing of those hopes of a change which check violent resolutions; nor how affection prompts and cherishes such hopes against all evidence.   The bystander sees certain broad facts, which are inexplicable to him only because he does not see the many subtle links which bind those facts together; he does not see the mind of the sufferer struggling against a growing evil, and finally resigning itself, and trying to put a calm face on the matter.   It is easy for us to say, Why did not Goethe part from her at once?   But parting was not easy.   She was the mother of his child; she had been the mistress of his heart, and still was dear to him.   To part from her would not have arrested the fatal tendency; it would only have accelerated it. He was too weak to alter his position.   He was strong enough to bear it.   Schiller divined this by his own moral instincts.   "I wish," he writes in a recently discovered letter, "that I could justify Goethe in respect to his domestic relations as I can confidently in all points respecting literature and social life. But unfortunately, by some false notions of domestic happiness, and an unlucky aversion to marriage, he has entered upon an engagement which weighs upon him in his domestic circle, and makes him unhappy, yet to shake off which, I am sorry to say, he is too weak and soft-hearted. This is the only shortcoming in him ; but even this is closely connected with a very noble part of his character, and he hurts no one but himself."

And thus the years rolled on. Her many good qualities absolved her few bad qualities. He was sincerely attached to her, and she was devoted to him ; and now, in his fifty-eighth year, when the troubles following the battle of Jena made him " feel the necessity of drawing all friends closer," who, among those friends, deserved a nearer place than Christiane ? He resolved on marrying her.

It is not known whether this thought of marriage had for some time previous been in contemplation, and was now put in execution when Weimar was too agitated to trouble itself with his doings ; or whether the desire of legitimizing his son in these troublous days suggested the idea. Riemer thinks the motive was gratitude for her courageous and prudent conduct during the troubles ; but I do not think that explanation acceptable, the more so as, according to her own statement, marriage was proposed in the early years of their acquaintance. In the absence of positive testimony, I am disposed to rely on psychological evidence ; and, assuming that the idea of marriage *had* been previously entertained, the delay in execution is explicable when we are made aware of one peculiarity in his nature, namely, a singular hesitation in adopting any decisive course of action, — singular in a man so resolute and imperious when once his decision had been made. This is the weakness of imaginative men. However strong the volition, when once it is set going, there is in men of active intellects, and especially in men of imaginative, apprehensive intellects, a fluctuation of motives keeping the volition in abeyance, which practically amounts to weakness, and is only distinguished from weakness by the strength of the volition when let loose. Goethe, who was aware of this peculiarity, used to attribute it to his never having been placed in circumstances which required prompt resolutions, and to his not having educated his will ; but I believe the cause lay much deeper, lying in the nature of psychological actions, not in the accidents of education.

But be the cause of the delay this or any other, it is certain that on the 19th of October, i. e. five days after the battle of Jena, and *not*, as writers constantly report, " during the cannonade," he was united to Christiane, in the presence of his son, and of his secretary, Riemer.

The scandal which this act of justice excited was immense, as may readily be guessed by those who know the world. His friends, however, loudly applauded his emergence from a false position. From that time forward, no one who did not treat her with proper respect could hope to be well received by him. She bore her new-made honors unobtrusively, and with a quiet good sense, which managed to secure the hearty good-will of most of those who knew her.

CHAPTER III.

BETTINA AND NAPOLEON.

It is very characteristic that during the terror and the pillage of Weimar, Goethe's greatest anxiety on his own account was lest his scientific manuscripts should be destroyed. Wine, plate, furniture, could be replaced ; but to lose his manuscripts was to lose what was irreparable. Herder's posthumous manuscripts *were* destroyed ; Meyer lost everything, even his sketches : but Goethe lost nothing, except wine and money.*

The Duke, commanded by Prussia to submit to Napoleon, laid down his arms and returned to Weimar, there to be received with the enthusiastic love of his people, as some compensation for the indignities he had endured. Peace was restored. Weimar breathed again. Goethe availed himself of the quiet to print his *Farbenlehre* and *Faust*, that they might be rescued from any future peril. He also began to meditate once more an epic on William Tell ; but the death of the Duchess Amalia on the 10th April drove the subject from his mind.

On the 23d of April Bettina came to Weimar. We must pause awhile to consider this strange figure, who fills a larger space in the literary history of the nineteenth century than any other German woman. Every one knows " the Child " Bettina Brentano, — daughter of the Maximiliane Brentano with whom Goethe flirted at Frankfurt in the Werther days, — wife of Achim von Arnim, the fantastic Romanticist, — the worshipper of Goethe and Beethoven, — for some time the privileged favorite of the King of Prussia, — and writer of that wild, but unveracious book, *Goethe's Correspondence with a Child*. She is one of those phantasts to whom everything seems permitted. More elf than woman, yet with flashes of genius which light up in splendor whole chapters of nonsense, she defies criticism, and puts every verdict at

---

* It is at once ludicrous and sad to mention that even *this* has been the subject of malevolent sneers against him. His antagonists cannot forgive him the good fortune which saved *his* house from pillage, when the houses of others were ransacked. They seem to think it a mysterious result of his selfish calculations !

fault. If you are grave with her, people shrug their shoulders, and saying, "She is a Brentano," consider all settled. "At the point where the folly of others ceases, the folly of the Brentanos begins," runs the proverb in Germany.

I do not wish to be graver with Bettina than the occasion demands; but while granting fantasy its widest license, while grateful to her for the many picturesque anecdotes she has preserved from the conversation of Goethe's mother, I must consider the history of her relation to Goethe seriously, because out of it has arisen a charge against his memory which is very false and injurious. Many unsuspecting readers of her book, whatever they may think of the passionate expressions of her love for Goethe, whatever they may think of her demeanor towards him, on first coming into his presence, feel greatly hurt at his coldness; while others are still more indignant with him for keeping alive this mad passion, feeding it with poems and compliments, and doing this out of a selfish calculation, in order that *he might gather from her letters materials for his poems!* In both these views there is complete misconception of the actual case. True it is, that the *Correspondence* furnishes ample evidence for both opinions; and against that evidence there is but one fact to be opposed, but the fact is decisive: the *Correspondence* is a romance.

A harsher phrase would be applied were the offender a man, or not a Brentano; for the romance is put forward as biographical fact, not as fiction playing around and among fact. How much is true, how much exaggeration, and how much pure invention, I am in no position to explain. But Riemer, the old and trusted friend of Goethe, living in the house with him at the time of Bettina's arrival, has shown the *Correspondence* to be a "romance which has only borrowed from reality the time, place, and circumstances"; and from other sources I have learned enough to see both Goethe's conduct and her own in quite a different light from that presented in her work.

A young, ardent, elfin creature worships the great poet at a distance, writes to tell him so, is attentive to his mother, who gladly hears praises of her son, and is glad to talk of him. He is struck with her extraordinary mind, is grateful to her for the attentions to his mother, and writes as kindly as he can without compromising himself. She comes to Weimar. She falls into his arms, and, according to her not very credible account, goes to sleep in his lap on their first interview ; and ever afterwards is ostentatious of her adoration and her jealousy. If the story is true, the position was very embarrassing for Goethe : a man aged fifty-eight worshipped by a girl who, though a woman in years, looked like a child, and worshipped with the extravagance, partly mad, and partly wilful, of a Brentano, — *what* could he do ? He could take a base advantage of her passion ; he could sternly repress it ; or he could smile at it, and pat her head as one pats a whimsical, amusing child. These three courses were open to him, and only these. He adopted the last, until she forced him to adopt the second ; forced him by the very impetuosity of her adoration. At first the child's coquettish, capricious ways amused him ; her bright-glancing intellect interested him ; but when her demonstrations became obtrusive and fatiguing, she had to be " called to order " so often, that at last his patience was fairly worn out. The continuation of such a relation was obviously impossible. She gave herself the license of a child, and would not be treated as a child. She fatigued him.

Riemer relates that during this very visit she complained to him of Goethe's coldness. This coldness, he rightly says, was simply patience ; a patience which held out with diffi-

culty against such assaults.   Bettina quitted Weimar, to return in 1811, when by her own conduct she gave him a
reasonable pretext for breaking off the connection ; a pretext, I am assured, he gladly availed himself of.   It was this.
She went one day with Goethe's wife to the Exhibition of
Art, in which Goethe took great interest ; and there her satirical remarks, especially on Meyer, offended Christiane, who
spoke sharply to her.   High words rose, gross insult followed.   Goethe took the side of his insulted wife, and
forbade Bettina the house.   It was in vain that on a subsequent visit to Weimar she begged Goethe to receive
her.   He was resolute.   He had put an end to a relation which
could not be a friendship, and was only an embarrassment.*

Such being the real story, as far as I can disentangle it, we
have now to examine the authenticity of the *Correspondence*, in
as far as it gives support to the two charges : first, of Goethe's
alternate coldness and tenderness ; second, of his using her
letters as material for his poems.   That he was ever tender to
her, is denied by Riemer, who pertinently asks how we are to
believe that the coldness of which she complained during her
visit to Weimar grew in her absence to the lover-like warmth
glowing in the sonnets addressed to her?   This is not credible ; but the mystery is explained by Riemer's distinct denial
that the sonnets were addressed to her.   They were *sent* to
her, as to other friends ; but the poems, which she says were
inspired by her, were in truth written for another.   The
proof is very simple.   These sonnets were written before she

* I give this story as it was told me, by an authority quite unexceptionable ; nevertheless, in all such narratives there is generally some
inaccuracy, even when relating to contemporary events, and the details
above given may not be absolutely precise, although the net result certainly is there expressed.

came to Weimar, and had already passed through Riemer's hands, like other works, for his supervision.   Riemer, moreover, knew to *whom* these passionate sonnets were addressed, although he did not choose to name her.   I have no such cause for concealment, and declare the sonnets to have been addressed to Minna Herzlieb, of whom we shall hear more presently ; as indeed the charade on her name, which closes the series (*Herz-Lieb*), plainly indicates.   Not only has Bettina appropriated the sonnets which were composed at Jena while Riemer was with Goethe, and inspired by one living at Jena, but she has also appropriated poems known by Riemer to have been written in 1813–1819, she then being the wife of Achim von Arnim, and having since 1811 been resolutely excluded from Goethe's house.   To shut your door against a woman, and yet write love-verses to her, — to respond so coldly to her demonstrations that she complains of it, and yet pour forth sonnets throbbing with passion, — is a course of conduct certainly not credible on evidence such as the *Correspondence with a Child.*   Hence we are the less surprised to find Riemer declaring that some of her letters are " little more than meta- and para- phrases of Goethe's poems, *in which both rhythm and rhyme are still traceable.*"   So that instead of Goethe turning her letters into poems, Riemer accuses her of turning Goethe's poems into her letters.   An accusation so public and so explicit — an accusation which ruined the whole authenticity of the *Correspondence* — should at once have been answered.   The production of the originals with their postmarks might have silenced accusers.   But the accusation has been many years before the world, and no answer attempted.

Although the main facts had already been published, a loud uproar followed the first appearance of this chapter in Germany.   Some ardent friend of Bettina's opened fire upon me

in a pamphlet,* which called forth several replies in news-
papers and journals ; † and I believe there are few Germans
who now hesitate to acknowledge that the whole correspondence has been so tampered with as to have become,
from first to last, a romance.   For the sake of any still
unconvinced partisans in England, a few evidences of the
manipulation which the correspondence has undergone may
not be without interest.   .

   In the letter bearing date 1st March, 1807, we read of the
King of Westphalia's court, when, unless History be a liar,
the kingdom of Westphalia was not even in existence.   Goethe's
mother, in another letter, speaks of her delight at Napoleon's
appearance, — four months before she is known to have set
eyes upon him.   The letters of Goethe, from November to
September, all imply that he was at Weimar ; nay, he invites
her to Weimar on the 16th July ; she arrives there at the
end of the month ; visits him, and on the 16th August he
writes to her from thence.   Düntzer truly says, that these
letters *must* be spurious, since Goethe left for Karlsbad on
the 25th May, and did not return till September.   Not only
does Bettina visit Goethe at Weimar at a time when he is
known to have been in Bohemia, but she actually receives
letters from his mother dated the 21st September and 7th
October, 1808, although the old lady died on the 13th September.   One may overlook Bettina's intimating that she was
only thirteen, when the parish register proves her to have
been two-and-twenty ; but it is impossible to place the
slightest reliance on the veracity of a book which exhibits
flagrant and careless disregard of facts ; and if I have been

* *An G. H. Lewes, Eine Epistel von Heinrich Siegfried.*   Berlin,
1858.
   † See in particular the article by DUENTZER, *Allgemeine Zeitung,*
April 20, 1858.

somewhat merciless in the exposure of this fabrication, it is because it has greatly helped to desseminate very false views respecting a very noble nature.

In conclusion, it is but necessary to add, that Bettina's work thus deprived of its authenticity, all those hypotheses which have been built on it respecting Goethe's conduct fall to the ground. Indeed, when one comes to think of it, the hypothesis of his using her letters as poetic materials does seem the wildest of all figments; for not only was he prodigal in invention and inexhaustible in material, but he was especially remarkable for always expressing his own feelings, his own experience, not the feelings and experience of others.

We part here from Bettina; another and very different figure enters on the scene: Napoleon at the Congress of Erfurt. It was in September, 1808, that the meeting of the Emperors of France and Russia, with all the minor potentates, took place at the little town of Erfurt, a few miles from Weimar. It was a wonderful sight. The theatre was opened, with Talma and the Parisian troupe performing the finest tragedies of France before a parterre of kings. "Exactly in front of the pit sat the two Emperors, in arm-chairs, in familiar conversation; a little in their rear the kings; and then the reigning princes and hereditary princes. Nothing was seen in the whole pit but uniforms, stars, and orders. The lower boxes were filled with staff-officers and the most distinguished persons of the imperial bureaux; the upper front with princesses; and at their sides foreign ladies. A strong guard of grenadiers of the imperial guard was posted at the entrance. On the arrival of either emperor the drum beat thrice; on that of any king, twice. On one occasion the sentinel, deceived by the outside of the King of Würtemberg's carriage, ordered the triple salute to be given, on which the officer in command cried out, in an angry tone, 'Taisez-vous, — ce n'est qu'un roi !'"*

Napoleon, on this occasion, gave a friendly reception to the Duke of Weimar, and to Goethe and Wieland, with whom he talked about literature and history. Goethe went to Erfurt on the 29th of September, and that evening saw *Andromaque* performed. On the 30th, there was a grand dinner given by the Duke, and in the evening *Britannicus* was performed. In the *Moniteur* of the 8th of October he is mentioned among the illustrious guests : "Il paraît apprécier parfaitement nos acteurs, et admirer surtout les chefs-d'œuvre qu'ils représentent." On the 2d of October he was summoned to an audience with the Emperor, and found him at breakfast, Talleyrand and Daru standing by his side, Berthier and Savary behind. Napoleon, after a fixed look, exclaimed, "Vous êtes un homme !" a phrase which produced a profound impression on the flattered poet. "How old are you?" asked the Emperor. "Sixty." "You are very well preserved." After a pause, "You have written tragedies?" Here Daru interposed, and spoke with warmth of Goethe's works, adding that he had translated Voltaire's *Mahomet.* "It is not a good piece," said Napoleon, and commenced a critique on *Mahomet*, especially on the unworthy portrait given of that conqueror of a world. He then turned the conversation to *Werther*, which he had read seven times, and which accompanied him to Egypt. "After various remarks, all very just," says Goethe, "he pointed out a passage, and asked me why I had written so : it was contrary to nature. This opinion he developed with great clearness. I listened calmly, and smilingly replied that I did not know whether the objection had ever been made before, but that I found it

* Kanzler von Müller in Mrs. AUSTIN'S *Germany from* 1760 *to* 1814, p. 307.

perfectly just. The passage was unnatural; but perhaps the poet might be pardoned for the artifice which enabled him to reach his end in an easier, simpler way. The Emperor seemed satisfied and returned to the drama, and criticised it like a man who had studied the tragic stage with the attention of a criminal judge, and who was keenly alive to the fault of the French in departing from nature. He disapproved of all pieces in which fate played a part. 'Ces pièces appartiennent à une époque obscure. Au reste, que veulent-ils dire avec leur fatalité? La politique est la fatalité.'"

The interview lasted nearly an hour. Napoleon inquired after his children and family; was very gracious; and wound up almost every sentence with, "Qu'en dit M. Goet?" As Goethe left the room, Napoleon repeated to Berthier and Daru, "Voilà un homme!"

A few days after, Napoleon was in Weimar, and great festivities were set on foot to honor him; among them a *chasse* on the battle-field of Jena; a grand ball at court; and *La Mort de César* at the theatre, with Talma as Brutus. During the ball, Napoleon talked at great length with Goethe and Wieland. Speaking of ancient and modern literature, Napoleon touched on Shakespeare, whom he was too French to comprehend, and said to Goethe: "Je suis étonné qu'un grand esprit comme vous n'aime pas les genres tranchés." Goethe might have replied that *les grands esprits* have almost universally been the very reverse of *tranchés* in their tastes; but of course it was not for him to controvert the Emperor. As Johnson said on a similar occasion, "Sir, it was not for me to bandy words with my sovereign." After speaking magniloquently of tragedy, Napoleon told him he ought to write a *Death of Cæsar*, but in a grander style than the tragedy of Voltaire. "Ce travail pourrait devenir la principale tâche de votre vie. Dans cette tragédie il faudrait montrer au monde comment César aurait pu faire le bonheur de l'humanité si on lui avait laissé le temps d'exécuter ses vastes plans." One cannot help thinking of Goethe's early scheme to write *Julius Cæsar*, and how entirely opposed it would have been to the *genre tranché* so admired by Napoleon.

A proposition more acceptable than that of writing tragedies at his age was that of accompanying Napoleon to Paris. " Venez à Paris, je l'exige de vous ; là vous trouverez un cercle plus vaste pour votre esprit d'observation ; là vous trouverez des matières immenses pour vos créations poétiques." He had never seen a great capital like Paris or London, and there was something very tempting in this invitation. F. von Müller says he often spoke with him on the probable expense of the journey, and of the Parisian usages ; but the inconvenience of so long a journey (in those days), and his sixty years, seem to have checked his desire.

On the 14th of October he and Wieland received the cross of the Legion of Honor, — then an honor ; and the two Emperors quitted Erfurt. Goethe preserved complete silence on all that had passed between him and Napoleon. Indeed, when he recorded the interviews, many years later, in the annals of his life, he did so in the most skeleton-like manner.

To the oft-repeated question, What was the passage in *Werther* indicated by Napoleon as contrary to Nature, he always returned a playful answer, referring the questioner to the book, on which to exercise his own ingenuity in discovery. He would not even tell Eckermann. He was fond, in this later period of life, of playing hide-and-seek with readers, and enjoyed their efforts to unravel mysteries. The present mystery has been cleared up by the Chancellor von Müller, to whom we owe most of the details respecting this interview with Napoleon. The objection raised by Napoleon was none other than the objection raised by Herder when *Werther* was revised by him in 1782, — viz., that Werther's melancholy which leads him to suicide, instead of proceeding solely from frustrated love, is complicated by his frustrated ambition. Herder thought this a fault in art, Napoleon thought it contrary to nature ; and, strange to say, Goethe agreed with both, and had altered his work in obedience to Herder's criticism, though he forgot all about it when Napoleon once more brought the objection forward. Against Herder, Napoleon, and Goethe himself, it is enough to oppose the simple fact : Werther (i. e. Jerusalem) *was* suffering from frustrated ambition, as well as from frustrated love ; and what Goethe found him, that he made him. We have only to turn to Kestner's letter, describing Jerusalem and his unhappy story, to see that Goethe, in *Werther*, followed with the utmost fidelity the narrative which was given him. This anecdote affords a piquant commentary on the value of criticism : three men so illustrious as Napoleon, Goethe, and Herder, pointing to a particular treatment of a subject as contrary to Art *and* contrary to Nature ; the treatment being all the while strictly in accordance with Nature.

That he was extremely flattered by the attentions of Napoleon has been the occasion of a loud outcry from those who, having never been subjected to any flattery of this nature, find it very contemptible. But the attentions of a Napoleon were enough to soften in their flattery even the sternness of a republican ; and Goethe, no republican, was all his life very susceptible to the gratification which a Frankfurt citizen must feel in receiving the attention of crowned heads. There is infinite insincerity uttered on this subject ; and generally the outcry is loudest from men who would themselves be most dazzled by court favor of any kind. To hear them talk of Goethe's servility, and worship of rank, one might fancy that they stood on a moral elevation, looking down upon him with a superior pity which in some sort compensated their inferiority of intellect.

It is true that Goethe was not only far removed from republican austerity, but placed more value on his star and title of Excellency than his thorough-going partisans are willing to admit. If that be a weakness, let him be credited with it ; but if he were as vain of such puerilities as an English Duke is of the Garter, I do not see any cause for serious reproach in it. So few poets have been Excellencies, so few have worn stars on their breast, that we have no means of judging whether Goethe's vanity was greater or less than we have a right to expect. Meanwhile it does seem to me that sneers at his title, and epigrams on his stars, come with a very bad grace from a nation which is laughed at for nothing more frequently than for its inordinate love of titles. Nor are Englishmen so remarkable for their indifference to rank, as to make them the fittest censors of this weakness in a Goethe.

CHAPTER IV.

POLITICS AND RELIGION.

AMONG the Jena friends whom Goethe saw with constant pleasure was Frommann, the bookseller, in whose family there was an adopted child, by name Minna Herzlieb, strangely interesting to us as the original of Ottilie in the *Wahlverwandt-schaften.* As a child she had been a great pet of Goethe's ; growing into womanhood, she exercised a fascination over him which his reason in vain resisted. The disparity of years was great ; but how frequently are young girls found bestowing the bloom of their affections on men old enough to be their fathers! and how frequently are men at an advanced age found trembling with the passion of youth! In the Sonnets addressed to her, and in the novel of *Elective Affinities*, may be read the fervor of his passion, and the strength with which he resisted it. Speaking of this novel, he says : "No one can fail to recognize in it a deep passionate wound which shrinks from being closed by healing, a heart which dreads to be cured. . . . . In it, as in a burial-urn, I have deposited with deep emotion many a sad experience. The 3d of October, 1809 (when the publication was completed), set me free from the work ; but the feelings it embodies can never quite depart from me." If we knew as much of the circumstances out of which grew the *Elective Affinities* as we do of those out of which grew *Werther*, we should find his experience as clearly embodied in this novel as it is in *Werther;* but conjecture in such cases being perilous, I will not venture beyond the facts which have been placed at my disposal ; and may only add therefore that the growing attachment was seen by all with pain and dismay. At length it was resolved to send Minna to school,* and this absolute separation saved them both.

Minna Herzlieb, to whom we owe the *Wahlverwandtschaften*, subsequently married unhappily.† Goethe long carried the arrow in his heart. In 1810, he once more gave poetic expression to his experience in an erotic poem, setting forth the conflict of Love and Duty. The nature of this poem, however, prevented its publication, and it still exists only as a manuscript. In this year also he commenced his *Autobiography*, the first part of which appeared in 1811. The public, anxious for autobiography, received it with a disappointment

* In the novel, Ottilie also is sent back to school.

† Read the story as narrated by STAHR, *Goethe's Frauengestalten*, 1870, II. 261.

which is perfectly intelligible ; charming as the book is in every other respect, it is tantalizing to a reader curious to see the great poet in his youth.

Before writing this *Autobiography* he had to outlive the sorrow for his mother's death.   She died on the 13th of September, 1808, in her 78th year.   To the last, her love for her son, and his for her, had been the glory and sustainment of her happy old age.   He had wished her to come and live with him at Weimar ; but the circle of old Frankfurt friends, and the influence of old habits, kept her in her native city, where she was venerated by all.

A volume would be required to record with anything like fulness the details of the remaining years.   There is no deficiency of material : in his letters, and the letters of friends and acquaintances, will be found an ample gleaning ; but, unhappily, the materials are abundant precisely at the point where the interest of the story begins to fade.   From sixty to eighty-two is a long period ; but it is not a period in which persons and events influence a man ; his character, already developed, can receive no new direction.   At this period biography is at an end, and necrology begins.   For Germans, the details to which I allude have interest ; but the English reader would receive with mediocre gratitude a circumstantial narrative of all Goethe did and studied ; all the excursions he made ; every cold and toothache which afflicted him ; every person he conversed with.

The year 1813, which began the War of Independence, was to Goethe a year of troubles.   It began with an affliction, — the death of his old friend Wieland, — which shook him more than those who knew him best were prepared for.   Herder, Schiller, the Duchess Amalia, his mother, and now Wieland, one by one had fallen away, and left him lonely, advancing in years.

Nor was this the only source of unhappiness. Political troubles came to disturb his plans. Germany was rising against the tyranny of Napoleon ; rising, as Goethe thought, in vain. "You will not shake off your chains," he said to Körner; "the man is too powerful ; you will only press them deeper into your flesh." His doubts were shared by many; but happily the nation shared them not. While patriots were rousing the wrath of the nation into the resistance of despair, he tried to "escape from the present, because it is impossible to live in such circumstances and not go mad"; he took refuge, as he always did, in Art. He wrote the ballads *Der Todtentanz, Der getreue Eckart,* and *Die wandelude Glocke;* wrote the essay *Shakspeare und kein Ende,* and finished the third volume of his *Autobiography.* He buried himself in the study of Chinese history. Nay, on the very day of the battle of Leipsic, he wrote the epilogue to the tragedy of *Essex,* for the favorite actress, Madame Wolf.*

Patriotic writers are unsparing in sarcasms on a man who could thus seek refuge in Poetry from the bewildering troubles of politics, and they find no other explanation than that he was an Egoist. Other patriotic writers, among them some of ultra-republicanism, such as Karl Grün, have eloquently defended him. I do not think it necessary to add arguments to those already suggested respecting his relation to politics. Those who are impatient with him for being what he was, and not what they are, will listen to no arguments. It is needless to point out how, at sixty-four, he was not likely to become a politician, having up to that age sedulously avoided politics. It is needless to show that he was not in a position which called upon him to *do* anything. The grievance seems to be

---

* Curiously enough, on that very day of Napoleon's first great defeat, his medallion, which was hung on the wall of Goethe's study, fell from its nail on to the ground.

that he wrote no war-songs, issued no manifestoes, but strove
to keep himself as much as possible out of the hearing of
contemporary history.   If this was a crime, the motive was
not criminal.   Judge the act as you will, but do not misjudge
the motive.   To attribute such an act to cowardice, or fear of
compromising himself, is unwarrantable, in the face of all the
evidence we have of his character.

When the mighty Napoleon threatened the Grand Duke, we
have seen how Goethe was roused.   That was an individual
injustice, which he could clearly understand, and was prepared
to combat.   For the Duke he would turn ballad-singer ; for
the Nation he had no voice ; and why ?   Because there was
no Nation.   He saw clearly then, what is now seen clearly by
others, that Germany had no existence as a Nation : it was a
geographical fiction ; and such it remained till our day.
And he failed to see what is now clearly seen, that the German Peoples were, for the time, united by national enthusiasm,
united by a common feeling of hatred against France ; failing
to see this, he thought that a collection of disunited Germans
was certain to be destroyed in a struggle with Napoleon.   He
was wrong ; the event has proved his error ; but his error of
opinion must not be made an accusation against his sincerity.
When Luden the historian, whose testimony is the weightier
because it is that of a patriot, had that interview with him,
after the battle of Leipsic, which he has recorded with so
much feeling,* the impression left was, he says, " that I was
deeply convinced they are in grievous error who blaim Goethe
for a want of love of country, a want of German feeling, a
want of faith in the German people, or of sympathy with its
honor and shame, its fortune or misery.   His silence about
great events was simply a painful resignation, to which he was
necessarily led by his position and his knowledge of mankind."

* LUDEN'S *Rückblicke in mein Leben*, p. 113, *seq.*

He was not likely to be found among the enthusiasts of that day, had he been at the age of enthusiasm. But, as he said to Eckermann, who alluded to the reproaches against him for not having written war-songs, " How could I take up arms without hatred, and how could I hate without youth? If such an emergency had befallen me when twenty years old, I should certainly not have been the last; but it found me past sixty. Besides, we cannot all serve our country in the same way, but each does his best according as God has endowed him. I have toiled hard enough during half a century. I can say, that in those things which nature has appointed for my daily work, I have permitted myself no relaxation or repose, but have always striven, investigated, and done as much, and as well, as I could. If every one can say the same of himself, it will prove well with all. To write military songs, and sit in a room! That forsooth was my duty! To have written them in the bivouac, when the horses at the evening's outposts are heard neighing at night, would have been well enough : that was not my way of life nor my business, but that of Theodore Körner. His war-songs suit him perfectly. But to me, who am not of a warlike nature, and who have no warlike sense, war-songs would have been a mask which would have fitted my face very badly. I have never affected anything in my poetry. I have never uttered anything which I have not experienced, and which has not urged me to production. I have only composed love-songs when I have loved; and how could I write songs of hatred without hating ? "

Connected with this political indifference, and mainly the cause of it, was his earnestness in Art ; an earnestness which has been made the evidence of this most extraordinary charge against him, namely, that he " looked on life only as an artist." The shallow phrase has become stereotyped.

Every one has heard it who has heard anything of him. It is uttered with the confidence of conviction, and is meant to convey a volume of implicit reprobation. When a man devotes himself to a special science, gives to it the greater part of his time, his thoughts and sympathies, we marvel at his energy, and laud his passionate devotion; we do not make his earnestness a crime; we do not say of a Liebig that he "looks at life only as a chemist"; of a Darwin, "that he looks at life only as a zoölogist." It is understood that any great pursuit must necessarily draw away the thoughts and activities from other pursuits. Why then is Art to be excluded from the same serious privilege? Why is the artist, who is in earnest, excluded from the toleration spontaneously awarded to the philosopher? I know but of one reason, and that is the indisposition in men to accept Art as serious. Because Art ministers directly to our pleasures, it is looked on as the child of luxury, the product of idleness; and those who cannot rise to the height of the conception which animated a Goethe and a Schiller are apt to treat it as mere rhetoric and self-importance in men who speak of Art as the noblest form of culture. Indeed those who regard painting and sculpture as means of supplying their dining-rooms and galleries with costly ornaments; music, as furnishing the excuse for a box at the opera; and poetry as an agreeable pastime, may be justified in thinking lightly of painters, sculptors, musicians, and poets. But I will not suppose the reader to be one of this class; and may therefore appeal to his truer appreciation for a verdict in favor of the claims made by Art to serious recognition, as one among the many forms of national culture. This granted, it follows that the more earnestly the artist accepts and follows his career, the more honor does he claim from us.

Now Goethe was a man of too profoundly serious a nature

not to be in earnest with whatever he undertook ; he led an earnest and laborious life, when he might have led one of pleasure and luxurious idleness. "To scorn delights and live laborious days," with no other reward than the reward of activity, the delight of development, was one of the necessities of his nature. He worked at Science with the patient labor of one who had to earn his bread ; and he worked in the face of dire discouragement, with no reward in the shape of pence or praise. In Art, which was the main region of his intellectual strivings, he naturally strove after completeness. If the philosopher is observed drawing materials for his generalizations out of even the frivolities of the passing hour, learning in the theatre, the ball-room, or in the incoherent talk of railway passengers, to detect illustrations of the laws he is silently elaborating, we do not accuse him of looking on life only as a philosopher, thereby implying that he is deficient in the feelings of his kind ; yet something like this is done by those who make a crime of Goethe's constant endeavor to collect from life material for Art.

If when it is said "he looked on life only as an artist," the meaning is that he, as an artist, necessarily made Art the principal occupation of his life, — the phrase is a truism; and if the meaning is that he isolated himself from the labors and pursuits of his fellow-men, to play with life, and arrange it as an agreeable drama, — the phrase is a calumny. It is only through deep sympathy that a man can become a great artist; those who play with life can only play with art. The great are serious. That Goethe was a great artist all admit. Has the life we have narrated shown him to be deficient in benevolence, in lovingness, in sympathy with others and their pursuits? has it shown any evidence of a nature so wrapped in self-indulgence, and so coldly calculating, that life *could* become a mere playing to it? If the answer be No, then let us hear no more about Goethe's looking on life only as an artist. The vulgar may blame a devotion which they cannot understand; do not let us imitate the vulgar.

While one party has assailed him for his political indifference, another, and still more ungenerous, party has assailed him for what they call his want of religion. The man who can read Goethe's works and not perceive in them a spirit deeply religious must limit the word "religion" to the designation of his own doctrines; and the man who, reading them, discovers that Goethe was not orthodox, is discovering the sun at mid-day. Orthodox he never pretended to be. His religious experiences had begun early, and his doubts began with them. There are those who regard Doubt as criminal in itself; but no human soul that has once struggled, that has once been perplexed with baffling thoughts which it has been too sincere to huddle away and stifle in precipitate conclusions, dreading to face the consequences of doubt, will speak thus harshly and unworthily of it.

The course of his opinions, as we have seen, was often altered. At times he approached the strictness of strict sects; at times he went great lengths in scepticism. The Fräulein von Klettenberg taught him to sympathize with the Moravians; but Lavater's unconscious hypocrisy, and the moral degradation of the Italian priesthood, gradually changed his respect for the Christian churches into open and sometimes sarcastic contempt of priests and priesthoods. In various epochs of his long life he expressed himself so variously that a pietist may claim him, or a Voltairian may claim him: both with equal show of justice. The secret of this contradiction lies in the fact that he had deep religious sentiments, with complete scepticism on most religious doctrines. Thus, whenever the Encyclopedists attacked Christianity he was ready to defend it ;* but when he was brought in contact with dogmatic Christians, who wanted to force their creed upon him, he resented the attempt, and answered in the spirit of his scepticism.   To the Encyclopedists he would say, " Whatever frees the intellect, without at the same time giving us command over ourselves, is pernicious " ; or he would utter one of his profound and pregnant aphorisms, such as

" Nur das Gesetz kann uns die Freiheit geben,"

i. e. only within the circle of law can there be true freedom. We are not free when we acknowledge to higher power, but when we acknowledge it, and in reverence raise ourselves by proving that a Higher lives in us.

But against dogmatic teachings he opposed the fundamental rule, that all conceptions of the Deity must necessarily be *our* individual conceptions, vàlid for us, but not to the same extent for others.   Each soul has its own religion ; must have it as an individual possession ; let each see that he be true to it, which is far more efficacious than trying to accommodate himself to another's !

" Im Innern ist ein Universum auch ;
Daher der Völker löblicher Gebrauch
Dass Jeglicher das Beste was er kennt,
Er Gott, ja seinen Gott benennt."

---

* ABEKEN was told by a lady that she once heard Goethe soundly rate a respected friend, because she spoke of sacred persons in the tone of vulgar rationalism.

17   Y

CHAPTER V.

THE ACTIVITY OF AGE.

WHATEVER else he has been accused of, Goethe has never been accused of not having striven incessantly to reach a full development of his own being, and to aid the culture of his nation.   There is something truly grand in the picture of his later years, so calm, and yet so active.   His sympathy, instead of growing cold with age, seems every year to become more active.   Every discovery in Science, every new appearance in Literature, every promise in Art, finds him eager as a child to be instructed, and ready with aid or applause to further it.

Old age, indeed, is a relative term.   Goethe at seventy was younger than many men at fifty ; and at eighty-two he wrote a scientific review of the great discussion between Cuvier and Geoffroy St. Hilaire on Philosophic Zoölogy, a review which few men in their prime could write.   Sophocles, who is said to have written his masterpiece at eighty, is an example of great poetic capacity thus prolonged.   The reflective powers often retain their capacity, and by increase of material seem to *increase* it ; but not so the productive powers.   Yet in Goethe we see extraordinary fertility, even in the latest years : the Second Part of *Faust* was completed in his eighty-first year, and the *west-ostliche Divan* was written in his sixty-fifth. Although we cannot by any means consider these works as equal to the works of his earlier days, we must still consider them as marvellous productions to issue under the sunset of a poet.

The *west-ostliche Divan* was a refuge from the troubles of

the time.　Instead of making himself unhappy with the politics of Europe, he made himself happy studying the history and poetry of the East.　He even began to study the Oriental languages, and was delighted to be able to copy the Arabic manuscripts in their peculiar characters.　Von Hammer, De Sacy, and other Orientalists had given him abundant material; his poetic activity soon gave that material shape.*　But while donning the Turban, and throwing the Caftan over his shoulders, he remained a true German.　He smoked opium, and drank *Foukah :* but his dreams were German, and his songs were German.　This forms the peculiarity of the *Divan,* — it is West-Eastern : the images are Eastern ; the feeling is Western.　Precisely as in the Roman Elegies he had thrown himself into the classical past, reproducing its forms with unsurpassed ease and witchery, yet never for a moment ceasing to be original, never ceasing to be German, so also in this Eastern world we recognize the Western Poet.　He follows the Caravan slowly across the desert ; he hears the melancholy chant of the Bulbul singing on the borders of sparkling fountains ; he listens devoutly to the precepts of Mohammed, and rejoices in the strains of Hafis.　The combination is most felicitous.　It produced an epoch in German Literature.　The Lyrists, according to Gervinus, suddenly following this example, at once relinquished their warlike and contemporary tone to sing the songs of the East.

In the year 1816 he began to publish an Art Journal,

---

* I do not think it necessary to make more than a passing allusion to the preposterous idea of Goethe's having been assisted in these poems by the Frau von Willemer, who in her seventieth year first revealed the secret to Hermann Grimm that she was the inspirer of many and the author of some of these exquisite lyrics !　It is the story of Bettina over again.

Kunst und Alterthum, which continued till 1828, a curious
monument of the old man's studies and activity. It is
curious, morever, as indicating a change in the direction of
his ideas. We have seen what his relation was to the
Romantic School, and how the tendencies of his nature and
education led him to oppose to the characteristics of that
school the characteristics of Greek Art. The *Propyläen*
represents the Greek tendency : *Kunst und Alterthum* represents a certain leaning towards the Romantic. Gothic
Art, the old German and Netherlandish painters, no longer
seemed to him objectionable ; but the discovery of the Elgin
marbles once more awakened his enthusiasm for that perfection of form which was the ideal of Greek Art ;* and I have
heard Rauch, the sculptor, humorously narrate Goethe's
whimsical outbreaks when the young sculptor Rietschl seemed
in danger of perverting his talent by executing designs in the
spirit of the Romantic School.

Strong, however, as the opposition was which he felt to the
vagaries of the so-called Christian Art, he had too mnch of
the spirit which inspired the *Faust* to keep entirely aloof
from the Romanticists. In his old age the tendency to substitute Reflection for Inspiration naturally assumed greater
force ; and his love of mystification was now wearing a serious
aspect, duping himself perhaps as much as it duped others.
The German nation had persisted in discovering profound
meanings in passages which he had written without any
recondite meaning at all ; finding himself a prophet when he
meant only to be a poet, he gradually fell into the snare, and
tried to be all the more a prophet now he could no longer be
so great a poet as before. Every incident was to be typical.
Every phrase was of importance. Whether the lion should
roar at a particular time (in the *Novelle*), or whether he

* See his letter to Haydon in the *Life of Haydon*, Vol. II. p. 295.

should be silent, were subjects of long deliberation. The *Wanderjahre* was one great arsenal of symbols, the Second Part of *Faust* another. He delighted in seeing the philosophic critics outdoing each other in far-fetched ingenuity, "explaining" his *Faust* and *Meister;* and very astutely he refused to come to their aid. He saw libraries filled with discussions as to what he had intended ; but no one ever seduced him into an explanation which would have silenced these discussions. Instead of doing so, he seemed disposed to furnish the world with more riddles. In a word, he mystified the public ; but he did so in a grave, unconscious way, with a certain belief in his own mystification.

In the year 1816, Saxe Weimar was made a Grand Duchy ; and he received the Falcon Order, together with an increase of salary, which now became three thousand thalers, with extra allowance for his equipage. Two other events made this year memorable. Lotte, — Werther's Lotte, — now a widow in her sixtieth year, and mother of twelve children, pays him a visit at Weimar. They had not met since her marriage, and what a meeting this must have been for both ! how strange a mingling of feelings recurrent to a pleasantly agitated past, and of feelings perplexed by the surprise at finding each other so much changed !

The second and far more serious event of the year is the death of his wife. Many affected to consider this " a happy release." People are fond of arranging the lives of others according to their own conceptions, interpreting afflictions like these without regard to the feelings of the afflicted. The blow was heavy to bear. She who for eight-and-twenty years had loved and aided him, who — whatever her faults — had been to him what no other woman was, could not be taken from him without his deeply feeling the loss. His self-mastery was utterly shaken. He kneeled at her bedside, seizing her

cold hands, and exclaiming, " Thou wilt not forsake me !
No, no; thou must not forsake me ! "   He has expressed his
feelings in two passages only ; in the exquisite lines he wrote
on the day of her death, and in a letter to Zelter.   These are
the lines : —

> " Du versuchst, O Sonne, vergebens
>   Durch die düstern Wolken zu scheinen !
>   Der ganze Gewinn meines Lebens
>   Ist, ihren Verlust zu beweinen." *

And to Zelter the words were these : " When I tell thee, thou
rough and sorely tried son of earth, that my dear little wife
has left me, thou wilt know what that means."

In Science he strove to find forgetfulness ; and the loneliness of his house was next year changed into an unaccustomed
liveliness by the marriage of his son with Ottilie von Pog-
wisch, one of the gayest and most brilliant of the Weimar
circle.   She was always a great favorite with her father-in-law,
and during the remainder of his life not only kept his house
for him, and received his numerous guests, but became a
privileged favorite, to whom everything was permitted.   In
the year following he sang a cradle song over his first grand-
child.

With Döbereiner, he followed all the new phenomena
which Chemistry was then bringing before the astonished
world.   He also prepared his own writings on Morphology
for the press ; and studied Greek mythology, English literature, and Gothic Art.   Byron's *Manfred* he reviewed in the
Kunst und Alterthum, and enthusiastically welcomed our
great poet as the greatest product of modern times.   Scott
also he read with ever-increasing admiration.   Homer,

---

* " In vain, O Sun, you struggle to shine through the dark clouds;
the whole gain of my life is to bewail her loss."

always studied with delight, now reassumed to him that individuality which Wolff had for a time destroyed; Schubarth's *Ideen über Homer* having brought him round once more to the belief in the existence of "the blind old man of Scio's rocky isle."* Painting, sculpture, architecture, geology, meteorology, anatomy, optics, Oriental literature, English literature, Calderon, and the romantic school in France, — these were the subjects which by turns occupied his inexhaustible activity. "Life," he says, "resembles the Sibylline Books; it becomes dearer the less there remains of it." To one who could so worthily occupy the last remaining years of a long life, they must indeed have been precious. As he grew older, he worked harder. He went less into society. To court he very seldom went. "I would n't send the picture," writes the Duke to him, "because I hoped it might lure thee out, now Candlemas is over, a day when every bear and badger leaves his lair." But in lieu of his going to court, the court went to him. Once every week the Grand Duchess paid him a visit, sometimes bringing with her a princely visitor, such as the late Emperor of Russia, then Grand Duke, or the King of Würtemberg. He had always something new and interesting set aside for this visit, which was doubly dear to him, because he had a tender regard for the Grand Duchess, and it pleased him to be able to show her a new engraving, medallion, book, poem, or some scientific novelty. Karl August came often, but not on particular days. He used to walk up into the simple study, and chat there as with a brother. One day Goethe had a Jena student paying him a visit; the student saw an elderly gentleman walk unannounced into the room, and quietly seat himself on a chair; the student continued his harangue, and when it was concluded, Goethe quietly said, "But I must in-

* See the little poem *Homer wider Homer.*

troduce the gentleman : his Royal Highness the Grand Duke
of Saxe Weimar, Herr ——, student from Jena." Never did
the student forget the embarrassment of that moment.

While a strong feeling of opposition against him was growing up in his own nation, a feeling which such works as the
Wanderjahre were not likely to mitigate, his fame began to
extend to Italy, England, and France. His active interest
in the important productions of foreign literature was recip-
rocated in the admiration expressed for him by men like
Manzoni, Scott, Byron, Carlyle, Stapfer, Ampère, Soret, and
others. He had written of Manzoni's *Carmagnola*, defending
it against adverse criticism, with a fervor which, according
to Manzoni, secured his reputation in Europe. " It is certain that I owe to Goethe's admiration all the praise I have
received. I was very ill-treated until he so nobly defended
me, and since then I have not only seen public opinion
change, but I myself have learned to look at my productions
in a new light." How profound was his admiration for Byron,
and how flattered Byron was by it, is well known. The poem
he sent to Byron, in answer to the dedication of *Werner*,
reached him just as he was setting out on the expedition to
Greece.

Nor was his activity confined to reading. Oersted's magnificent discovery of electro-magnetism awakened his keenest
interest. He made Döbereiner exhibit the phenomena,
and shortly afterwards had Oersted to visit him. D'Alton's
anatomical work on the Sloth and Megatherium found him as
ready as a young reviewer to proclaim its importance to the
world. He wrote also the account of his *Campaign in
France;* the *Annals* of his Life ; Essays on Art ; smaller
poems ; the epigrams, *Zahme Xenien ;* translated modern
Greek songs ; and sketched a restoration of the lost drama
Phaëton, by Euripides.

It is evident then that there was abundant life in the old Jupiter, whose frame was still massive and erect; whose brow had scarcely a wrinkle of old age ; whose head was still as free from baldness as ever ; and whose large brown eyes had still that flashing splendor which distinguished them.   Hufeland, the physician, who had made a special study of the human organization with reference to its powers of vitality, says, that never did he meet with a man in whom bodily and mental organization were so perfect as in Goethe.

Not only life, but the life of life, the power of loving, was still preserved to him.   *Quisquis amat, nulla est conditione senex,* says old Pontanus ; and the Marquis de Lassay prettily makes the loss of love-dreams a sign of the last sleep : " Hélas, quand on commence à ne plus rêver, ou plutôt à rêver moins, on est près de s'endormir pour toujours."   In the seventy-fourth year of his age, Goethe had still youth enough to love.   At Marienbad he met with a Fräulein von Lewezow.   A passion grew up between them, which, returned on her side with almost equal vehemence, brought back to him once more the exaltation of the *Werther* period. It was thought he would marry her, and indeed he wished to do so ; but the representations of his friends, and perhaps the fear of ridicule, withheld him.   He tore himself away ; and the Marienbad Elegy, which he wrote in the carriage as it whirled him away, remains as a token of the passion and his suffering.

Nor does the Fräulein von Lewezow appear to have been the only one captivated by the " old man eloquent."   Madame Szymanowska, according to Zelter, was " madly in love " with him ; and however figurative such a phrase may be, it indicates, coming from so grave a man as Zelter, a warmth of enthusiasm one does not expect to see excited by a man of seventy-four.

In the following year Germany showed her gratitude to him by a privilege which in itself was the severest sarcasm on German nationality, — the privilege, namely, of a protection of his copyright.   He announced a complete editon of his works, and the *Bundestag* undertook to secure him from piracy in German cities.   Until that time his works had enriched booksellers ; but this tardy privilege secured an inheritance for his children.

In the way of honors, he was greatly flattered by the letter which Walter Scott sent to him, in expression of an old admiration ; and on the 28th of August, 1827, Karl August came into his study, accompanied by the King of Bavaria, who brought with him the Order of the Grand Cross as a homage.   In strict etiquette a subject was not allowed to accept such an Order without his own sovereign's permission, and Goethe, ever punctilious, turned to the Grand Duke, saying, " If my gracious sovereign permits."   Upon which the Duke called out, " *Du alter Kerl! mache doch kein dummes Zeug !*   Come, old fellow, no nonsense."

On the 6th of January, 1827, the Frau von Stein died, in her eighty-fifth year.   And now the good old Duke, whom he affectionately styled his *Waffenbruder*, — his brother in arms, — was to be taken from him.   On the 14th of June, 1828, he was no more.

Knowing Goethe's love for the Duke, his friends entertained great fears that the shock of this event would be terrible.   He was seated at dinner when the news arrived.   It was whispered from one to the other.   At length it was gently broken to him.   They were breathless with suspense.   But his face remained quite calm, — a calmness which betrayed him.   "Ah! this is very sad," he sighed ; "let us change the subject." He might banish the subject from conversation, he could not banish it from his thoughts.   It affected him deeply ; all the more so, because he did not give expression to his grief. "*Nun ist alles vorbei!* Nothing now remains," he said. When Eckermann came in the evening, he found him utterly prostrate.*

Retiring to the pleasant scenes of Dornburg, the old man strove in work and in contemplation of nature to call away his thoughts from his painful loss. The next year — 1829 — he finished the *Wanderjahre* in the form it now assumes, worked at the Second Part of *Faust,* and in conjunction with a young Frenchman, Soret, who was occupied in translating the *Metamorphoses of Plants,* revised his scientific papers.

In February, 1830, the death of the Grand Duchess once more overshadowed the evening of his life. These clouds gathering so fast are significant warnings of the Night which hurries on for him, — "the night in which no man can work"!

CHAPTER VI.

THE CLOSING SCENES.

THE spring of 1830 found Goethe in his eighty-first year, busy with *Faust,* writing the preface to Carlyle's *Life of*

* The calmness with which he received the announcement recalls those grand scenes in Marston's *Malcontent* and Ford's *Broken Heart,* where the subordination of emotion to the continuance of offices of politeness rises into sublimity. Herodotus has touched the same chord in his narrative of the terrific story of Thyestes (*Clio,* 119). Harpagus, on discovering that he has feasted on his own children in the banquet set before him by Thyestes, remains quite calm. Shakespeare has expressed the true philosophy of the matter in his usual pregnant language : —

    "Give sorrow words : the grief that does not speak
    Whispers the o'erfraught heart, and bids it break."

Schiller, and deeply interested in the great philosophical contest which was raging in Paris, between Cuvier and Geoffroy
St. Hilaire, on the question of Unity of Composition in the
Animal Kingdom.   This question, one of the many important
and profound questions which are now agitated in Biology,
which lies, indeed, at the bottom of almost all speculations
on Development, had for very many years been answered by
Goethe in the spirit which he recognized in Geoffroy St.
Hilaire ; and it was to him a matter of keen delight to
observe the world of science earnestly bent on a solution of
the question.   The anecdote which M. Soret narrates in the
supplemental volume to Eckermann's conversations is very
characteristic.

" Monday, 1st August, 1830.   The news of the Revolution
of July reached Weimar to-day, and set every one in commotion.   I went in the course of the afternoon to Goethe.
' Now,' exclaimed he, as I entered, ' what do you think of this
great event ?   The volcano has come to an eruption ; everything is in flames.'   ' A frightful story,' I answered ; ' but
what could be expected otherwise under such notoriously bad
circumstances and with such a ministry, than that the whole
would end in the expulsion of the royal family ? '   'We do not
appear to understand each other, my good friend,' said
Goethe ; ' I am not speaking of those people, but of something quite different.   I am speaking of the contest so important for science between Cuvier and Geoffroy St. Hilaire,
which has come to an open rupture in the Academy.'   This
expression of Goethe's was so unexpected that I did not
know what to say, and for some minutes was perfectly at a
standstill.   'The matter is of the highest importance,' he
continued ; 'and you can form no conception of what I felt
at the intelligence of the *séance* of the 19th July.   We have
now in Geoffroy a powerful and permanent ally.   I see how

great must be the interest of the French scientific world in this affair; because, notwithstanding the terrible political commotion, the *séance* of the 19th July was very fully attended. However, the best of it is that the synthetic manner of looking at Nature, introduced by Geoffroy into France, cannot be kept back any longer. From the present time Mind will rule over Matter in the scientific investigations of the French. There will be glances of the great maxims of creation, — of the mysterious workshop of God! Besides, what is all intercourse with Nature, if we merely occupy ourselves with individual material parts, and do not feel the breath of the spirit which prescribes to every part its direction, and orders or sanctions every deviation by means of an inherent law! I have exerted myself in this great question for fifty years. At first I was alone, then I found support, and now at last to my great joy I am surpassed by congenial minds.'"

Instead of exclaiming against the coldness of the man who at such a moment could turn from politics to science, let us glance at a somewhat parallel case. Englishmen will be slow in throwing stones at the immortal Harvey; let them hear what Dr. Ent reports. Soon after the most agitating event in English history, — the execution of Charles I., — Dr. Ent called on Harvey, and found him seeking solace in anatomical researches. "Did I not," said the great philosopher, "find a balm for my spirit in the memory of my observations of former years, I should feel little desire for life. But so it has been that this life of obscurity, this vacation from public business, which causes tedium and disgust to so many, has proved a sovereign remedy to me."

Goethe was not a politician, and he was a biologist. His view of the superior importance of such an event as the discussion between Geoffroy and Cuvier, to the more noisy but intrinsically less remarkable event, the Revolution of July, is a view which will be accepted by some philosophers, and rejected by all politicians. Goethe was not content with expressing in conversation his sense of the importance of this discussion ; he also commenced the writing of his celebrated review of it, and finished the first part in September.

In November another great affliction smote him; it was the last he had to bear : the news arrived that his only son, who had a little while before gone to Italy in failing health, had died in Rome on the 28th of October. The sorrowing father strove, as usual, to master all expression of emotion, and to banish it by restless work. But vain was the effort to live down this climbing sorrow. The trial nearly cost him his life. A violent hemorrhage in the lungs was the result. He was at one time given over ; but he rallied again, and set once more to work, completing the *Autobiography* and continuing *Faust.*

Ottilie von Goethe, the widow of his son, and his great favorite, devoted herself to cheer his solitude. She read Plutarch aloud to him ; and this, with Niebuhr's Roman History, carried him amid the great pageantries of the past, where his antique spirit could wander as among friends. Nor was the present disregarded. He read with the eagerness of youth whatever was produced by remarkable writers, such as Béranger, Victor Hugo, Delavigne, Scott, or Carlyle. He received the homage of Europe ; his rooms were constantly brightened by the presence of illustrious visitors, among whom the English were always welcome.

Among the English who lived at Weimar during those days was a youth whose name is now carried in triumph wherever English Literature is cherished, — I allude to William Makepeace Thackeray ; and Weimar albums still display with pride the caricatures which the young satirist sketched at that period. He has kindly enabled me to enrich these pages with a brief account of his reminiscences, gracefully sketched in the following letter : —

"LONDON, 28th April, 1855.

"DEAR LEWES, — I wish I had more to tell you regarding Weimar and Goethe. Five-and-twenty years ago, at least a score of young English lads used to live at Weimar for study, or sport, or society ; all of which were to be had in the friendly little Saxon capital. The Grand Duke and Duchess received us with the kindliest hospitality. The court was splendid, but yet most pleasant and homely. We were invited in our turns to dinners, balls, and assemblies there. Such young men as had a right, appeared in uniforms, diplomatic and military. Some, I remember, invented gorgeous clothing: the kind old Hof Marschall of those days, M. de Spiegel (who had two of the most lovely daughters eyes ever looked on), being in nowise difficult as to the admission of these young Englanders. Of the winter nights we used to charter sedan chairs, in which we were carried through the snow to those pleasant court entertainments. I for my part had the good luck to purchase Schiller's sword, which formed a part of my court costume, and still hangs in my study, and puts me in mind of days of youth, the most kindly and delightful.

"We knew the whole society of the little city, and but that the young ladies, one and all, spoke admirable English, we surely might have learned the very best German. The society met constantly. The ladies of the court had their evenings. The theatre was open twice or thrice in the week, where we assembled, a large family party. Goethe had retired from the direction, but the great traditions remained still. The theatre was admirably conducted; and besides the excellent Weimar company, famous actors and singers from various parts of Germany performed *Gastrolle** through the winter. In that winter I remember we had Ludwig Devrient in Shylock, Hamlet, Falstaff, and the *Robbers ;* and the beautiful Schröder in *Fidelio.*

"After three-and-twenty years' absence, I passed a couple of summer days in the well-remembered place, and was fortunate

* What in England are called "starring engagements."

enough to find some of the friends of my youth. Madame de Goethe was there, and received me and my daughters with the kindness of old days. We drank tea in the open air, at the famous cottage in the park,* which still belongs to the family, and had been so often inhabited by her illustrious father.

"In 1831, though he had retired from the world, Goethe would nevertheless very kindly receive strangers. His daughter-in-law's tea-table was always spread for us. We passed hours after hours there, and night after night with the pleasantest talk and music. We read over endless novels and poems in French, English, and German. My delight in those days was to make caricatures for children. I was touched to find that they were remembered, and some even kept until the present time; and very proud to be told, as a lad, that the great Goethe had looked at some of them.

" He remained in his private apartments, where only a very few privileged persons were admitted; but he liked to know all that was happening, and interested himself about all strangers. Whenever a countenance struck his fancy, there was an artist settled in Weimar who made a portrait of it. Goethe had quite a gallery of heads, in black and white, taken by this painter. His house was all over pictures, drawings, casts, statues, and medals.

"Of course I remember very well the perturbation of spirit with which, as a lad of nineteen, I received the long-expected intimation that the Herr Geheimerath would see me on such a morning. This notable audience took place in a little antechamber of his private apartments, covered all round with antique casts and bas-reliefs. He was habited in a long gray or drab redingot, with a white neckcloth and a red ribbon in his buttonhole. He kept his hands behind his back, just as in Rauch's statuette. His complexion was very bright, clear, and rosy. His eyes extraordinarily dark,† piercing, and brilliant. I felt quite afraid before them, and recollect comparing them to the eyes of the

* The *Gartenhaus.*

† This must have been the effect of the position in which he sat with regard to the light. Goethe's eyes were dark brown, but not very dark.

hero of a certain romance called *Melmoth the Wanderer*, which used to alarm us boys thirty years ago ; eyes of an individual who had made a bargain with a Certain Person, and at an extreme old age retained these eyes in all their awful splendor. I fancied Goethe must have been still more handsome as an old man than even in the days of his youth. His voice was very rich and sweet. He asked me questions about myself, which I answered as best I could. I recollect I was at first astonished, and then somewhat relieved, when I found he spoke French with not a good accent.

" *Vidi tantum.* I saw him but three times. Once walking in the garden of his house in the *Frauenplan;* once going to step into his chariot on a sunshiny day, wearing a cap and a cloak with a red collar. He was caressing at the time a beautiful little golden-haired granddaughter, over whose sweet fair face the earth has long since closed too.

" Any of us who had books or magazines from England sent them to him, and he examined them eagerly. *Fraser's Magazine* had lately come out, and I remember he was interested in those admirable outline portraits which appeared for a while in its pages. But there was one, a very ghastly caricature of Mr. Rogers, which, as Madame de Goethe told me, he shut up and put away from him angrily. 'They would make me look like that,' he said ; though in truth I can fancy nothing more serene, majestic, and *healthy* looking than the grand old Goethe.

" Though his sun was setting, the sky round about was calm and bright, and that little Weimar illumined by it. In every one of those kind salons the talk was still of art and letters. The theatre, though possessing no very extraordinary actors, was still conducted with a noble intelligence and order. The actors read books, and were men of letters and gentlemen, holding a not unkindly relationship with the *Adel.* At court the conversation was exceedingly friendly, simple, and polished. The Grand Duchess [the present Grand Duchess Dowager], a lady of very remarkable endowments, would kindly borrow our books from us, lend us her own, and graciously talk to us young men about our

z

literary tastes and pursuits.   In the respect paid by this court to the Patriarch of letters, there was something ennobling, I think, alike to the subject and sovereign.   With a five-and-twenty years' experience since those happy days of which I write, and an acquaintance with an immense variety of human kind, I think I have never seen a society more simple, charitable, courteous, gentlemanlike than that of the dear little Saxon city, where the good Schiller and the great Goethe lived and lie buried.

"Very sincerely yours,

"W. M. THACKERAY."

His last secretary, Kräuter, who never speaks of him but with idolatry, describes his activity even at this advanced age as something prodigious.   It was moreover systematic.   A certain time of the day was devoted to his correspondence ; then came the arrangement of his papers, or the completion of works long commenced.   One fine spring morning, Kräuter tells me, Goethe said to him, "Come, we will cease dictation; it is a pity such fine weather should not be enjoyed : let us go into the park and do a bit of work there."   Kräuter took the necessary books and papers, and followed his master, who, in his long blue overcoat, a blue cap on his head, and his hands in the customary attitude behind his back, marched on, upright and imposing.   Those who remember Rauch s statuette will picture to themselves the figure of the old man in his ordinary attitude; but perhaps they cannot fully picture to themselves the imposing effect of that Jupiter-head which, on this occasion, arrested an old peasant, and so absorbed him, that leaning his hands upon his rake, and resting his chin upon his hands, he gazed on the spectacle in forgetfulness so complete that he did not move out of the way, but stood gazing immovable, while Kräuter had to step aside to pass.

It is usually said, indeed, that Goethe showed no signs of age ; but this is one of the exaggerations which the laxity of ordinary speech permits itself. His intellect preserved a wonderful clearness and activity, as we know ; and, indeed, the man who wrote the essay on Cuvier and Geoffroy's discussion, and who completed the *Faust* in his eighty-second year, may fairly claim a place among the Nestors for whom remains

> " Some work of noble note,
> Not unbecoming men who strove with gods."

But the biographer is bound to record that in his intellect, as in his body, the old man showed unmistakably that he was old. His hearing became noticeably impaired ; his memory of recent occurrences was extremely treacherous ; but his eyesight remained strong, and his appetite good. In the later years of his life he presented a striking contrast to the earlier years in his preference for close rooms. The heated and impure atmosphere of an unventilated room was to him so agreeable that it was difficult to persuade him to have a window open for the purpose of ventilation. Always disliking the cold, and longing for warmth like a child of the South, he sat in rooms so heated that he was constantly taking cold. This did not prevent his enjoyment of the fresh air when he was in the country. The mountain air of Ilmenau, especially, seemed to give him health and enjoyment. It was to Ilmenau he went to escape from the festivities preparing for his last birthday. He ascended the lovely heights of the Gickelhahn, and went into the wood hut where so many happy days had been spent with Karl August. There he saw on the wall those lines he had years before written in pencil, —

> " Ueber allen Gipfeln
> Ist Ruh,
> In allen Wipfeln
> Spürest du
> Kaum einen Hauch ;

> Die Vögelein schweigen im Walde.
> Warte nur, balde
> Ruhest du auch."

And wiping the tears from his eyes, — tears which rose at the memory of Karl August, Charlotte von Stein, and his own happy youth, — he repeated the last line, " *Ja, warte nur, balde ruhest du auch.* — Yes, wait but a little, soon wilt thou too be at rest."

That rest was nearer than any one expected. On the 16th of March following, his grandson, Wolfgang, coming into his room as usual to breakfast with him, found him still in bed. The day before, in passing from his heated room across the garden, he had taken cold. The physician, on arriving, found him very feverish, with what is known in Weimar as the "nervous fever," which acts almost like a pestilence. With the aid of remedies, however, he rallied towards evening, and became talkative and jocose. On the 17th he was so much better that he dictated a long letter to W. von Humboldt. All thought of danger ceased. But during the night of the 19th, having gone off into a soft sleep, he awoke about midnight, with hands and feet icy cold, and fierce pain and oppression of the chest. He would not have the physician disturbed, however, for he said there was no danger, only pain. But when the physician came in the morning, he found that a fearful change had taken place. His teeth chattered with the cold. The pain in his chest made him groan, and sometimes call out aloud. He could not rest in one place, but tossed about in bed, seeking in vain a more endurable position. His face was ashen gray; the eyes, deep sunk in the sockets, were dull, and the glance was that of one conscious of the presence of death. After a time these fearful symptoms were allayed, and he was removed from his bed into the easy-chair, which stood at his bedside. There, towards evening, he was once more restored to perfect calmness, and spoke with clearness and interest of ordinary matters; especially pleased he was to hear that his appeal for a young artist, a *protégé*, had been successful; and with a trembling hand he signed an official paper which secured a pension to another artist, a young Weimar lady, for whom he had interested himself.

On the following day, the approach of death was evident. The painful symptoms were gone. But his senses began to fail him, and he had moments of unconsciousness. He sat quiet in the chair, spoke kindly to those around him, and made his servant bring Salvandy's *Seize Mois, ou la Révolution et les Révolutionnaires,* which he had been reading when he fell ill; but after turning over the leaves, he laid it down, feeling himself too ill to read. He bade them bring him the list of all the persons who had called to inquire after his health, and remarked that such evidence of sympathy was not to be forgotten when he recovered. He sent every one to bed that night, except his copyist. He would not even allow his old servant to sit up with him, but insisted on his lying down to get the rest he so much needed.

The following morning — it was the 22d March, 1832 — he tried to walk a little up and down the room, but, after a turn, he found himself too feeble to continue. Reseating himself in the easy-chair, he chatted cheerfully with Ottilie on the approaching spring, which would be sure to restore him. He had no idea of his end being so near.

The name of Ottilie was frequently on his lips. She sat beside him, holding his hand in both of hers. It was now observed that his thoughts began to wander incoherently. "See," he exclaimed, "the lovely woman's head — with black curls — in splendid colors — a dark background!" Presently, he saw a piece of paper on the floor, and asked them how they could leave Schiller's letters so carelessly lying about.   Then he slept softly, and, on awakening, asked for the sketches he had just seen.   These were the sketches seen in a dream.   In silent anguish the close now so surely approaching was awaited.   His speech was becoming less and less distinct.   The last words audible were, "*More light!*"   The final Darkness grew apace, and he whose eternal longings had been for more Light gave a parting cry for it, as he was passing under the shadow of Death.

He continued to express himself by signs, drawing letters with his forefinger in the air, while he had strength, and finally, as life ebbed, drawing figures slowly on the shawl which covered his legs.   At half past twelve he composed himself in the corner of the chair.   The watcher placed a finger on her lip to intimate that he was asleep.   If sleep it was, it was a sleep in which a great life glided from the world.

THE END.

Italy

www.ingramcontent.com/pod-product-compliance
Lightning Source LLC
Chambersburg PA
CBHW030826110726
47900CB00006B/1759